He leaned nea was on her. On her eyes. Her lips. He was going to kiss her.

The realization rocketed through Lucy's head. It made her breath catch in her throat. Her heart hammered. He was going to kiss her, and she wasn't at all sure what she was going to do about it.

She knew there were a hundred reasons he shouldn't. A thousand. But she couldn't think of one. And she wasn't sure she wanted to try.

His eyes held hers. They were heavy with emotion, dark with a secret she didn't understand. His look invited her to tip her head back. To close her eyes.

Lucy did. She held her breath, waiting for the warm press of his lips against hers. She felt him move closer. His breath was warm against her cheek. It brushed her ear. His voice was low and soft.

"We're being followed," he whispered.

# Devil's Diamond

by

## Constance Laux

A TOPAZ BOOK

TOPAZ
Published by the Penguin Group
Penguin Putnam Inc., 375 Hudson Street,
New York, New York 10014, U.S.A.
Penguin Books Ltd, 27 Wrights Lane,
London W8 5TZ, England
Penguin Books Australia Ltd, Ringwood,
Victoria, Australia
Penguin Books Canada Ltd, 10 Alcorn Avenue,
Toronto, Ontario, Canada M4V 3B2
Penguin Books (N.Z.) Ltd, 182–190 Wairau Road,
Auckland 10, New Zealand

Penguin Books Ltd, Registered Offices:
Harmondsworth, Middlesex, England

First published by Topaz, an imprint of Dutton Signet,
a member of Penguin Putnam Inc.

First Printing, April, 1998
10  9  8  7  6  5  4  3  2  1

*For Carole Tanyer Cohen.*
*Welcome Home!*

# Chapter 1

*London*
*June 1897*

"**B**ut he thinks he's Sherlock Holmes!" Lucy Barnstable drew in a long, shaky breath. She steadied herself, her hands flat against the rosewood table, and fought to control the tremor of emotion that vibrated inside her and threatened to spill into her voice. She refused to let that happen.

She had to be logical, she reminded herself. She had to remain unemotional. She couldn't afford to lose her advantage now.

If she did, she was sure the two constables who sat in her small but immaculate parlor would see her as nothing more than another in a long line of hysterical young women.

And she knew exactly how members of the London Metropolitan Police Force treated women they thought to be hysterical.

The women were ignored or, worse yet, patronized. They were told to go home and have a nice hot cup of tea. They were told not to worry.

She knew that well enough. It was exactly what they'd been telling her for the last six weeks.

Holding as tight to her emotions as she was to her opinion of what, exactly, she thought the police could do with their nice hot cups of tea, Lucy smoothed her next-to-best black skirt. She swept an errant strand of dark hair out of her eyes, and looking from Constable George Mullen to his companion, Constable Robert Crookston, she waited for them to recognize the merits of her argument.

"Well . . ." Mullen was the eldest of the two policemen and such a fixture in the London neighborhood where Lucy had spent all her life that she thought of him as a friend. In fact, Lucy was convinced it was the only reason he was here at all tonight. It was obvious from the moment he and Crookston walked in that they weren't here to help. They were here to say they'd tried.

Mullen was a bulky man with long legs and powerful arms, and he shifted awkwardly in the chair closest to the fireplace. Stalling for time, he stirred the cup of tea Lucy had poured for him. With all the delicacy of a dowager, he tapped the spoon against the rim of the cup and took a careful sip. Sure the tea was neither too hot nor too cold, he drank it down.

"It ain't that we don't sympathize, Miss Lucy," Mullen said. He deposited his cup back on the tea tray and reached for one of the scones Lucy had brought from the kitchen.

"It's just that . . . well, let me be honest with you. I've known your father as long as I've been patrollin' this street." Mullen jabbed the scone in the direction of the front of the house where rain beat against the windows. "And as near as I can figure, that's well on to twenty-five years, right when you"—he stabbed the scone at Lucy—"was just a little babe. You've got to realize, Miss Lucy, we all know what Alfie's like. Ain't that right, Crookston?"

Constable Crookston had neither Mullen's years nor his friendly manner. Though Lucy had never met him before, she decided on first glance that he was as conscientious as he was both tall and lean. Every sandy-colored hair on his head was in place. Every brass button on his blue uniform gleamed. From the moment Crookston had walked in, his keen gaze had taken in everything, from the chemistry paraphernalia Alfie had arranged in one corner of the room to the basket of mending Lucy had in the other.

He seemed sensible enough, and that in itself appealed to Lucy. He was not at all as gregarious as Mullen, but then, Lucy did not expect him to be. He was diligent. She hoped that would be enough.

Engrossed in scribbling everything they said into a small, leather-bound notebook, Crookston's face flooded with color. He lifted his pencil, but he firmly refused to meet Lucy's eyes.

"I believe what Constable Mullen means . . . that is, I . . . er . . ." Crookston's face went two shades darker. He cleared his throat. "I mean . . ."

"What Crookston means to say is that 'e knows I'm right. Alfie Barnstable is maggoty. That's what he means." As if emphasizing his point, Mullen chomped into the scone. "Beggin' your pardon, Miss Lucy, on account of 'cause you're as nice and as normal a young lady as whatever lived, but even you have to admit the truth. This ain't no new revelation like Moses comin' down off the mountain with the tablets. Your father is daft. He's as odd a fellow as ever walked the streets of London. Think about it." Mullen finished the scone and reached for another.

"I've seen ol' Alfie have a go at spiritualism," he said, his mouth full. "I've come around to call when 'e's been tinkerin' in the back garden, inventin' all kinds of peculiar things. Remember when 'e thought 'e could make a machine what could fly?" Mullen leaned back and chuckled, and it was clear he remembered the day five years before just as clearly as Lucy did.

"Between you and me both, we couldn't convince him to come down off the roof. He nearly broke 'is neck for 'is trouble. And yours, too, if I remember rightly, when you tried to catch 'im on 'is way down." Warming to his subject, Mullen leaned forward, his elbows on his knees.

"And what about the time 'e took it into his head that 'e was Long John Silver and 'e was all set to have a go at treasure hunting?" he asked. "Make no mistake about it, Miss Lucy, 'e was ready to sail the Seven Seas. And 'e would have done if I hadn't convinced 'im it wasn't right to leave you 'ere all by your lonesome what with no mother to watch over you."

"But this is different! Don't you see?" Eager to disguise the flutter in her voice that threatened to betray her, Lucy busied herself with the tea things. She poured each of the constables another cup of tea and handed them around. "Alfie's done some unusual things, I'll be the first to admit that. But he's certainly never taken it to this extreme."

With a restless gesture, Lucy pointed toward the table. On one corner of it, she had left a stack of handbills for the police to see. ALFRED E. BARNSTABLE, they proclaimed along with the address. CONSULTING DETECTIVE.

On the other side of the table, Lucy had gathered a pile of magazines. There were any number of issues of *The Strand* and one of *Beeton's Christmas Annual*, all well thumbed through by Alfie and all with one thing in common: Each contained one of Arthur Conan Doyle's Sherlock Holmes stories.

"Speckled bands! Red-headed leagues! Studies in scarlet! Who ever heard of such nonsense?" The very words soured in Lucy's mouth. "He's read them and reread them, and when he announced he was going to open his own consulting detective agency just like the one run by Sherlock Holmes, he wouldn't listen to reason."

"And you, the most reasonable woman in the world." Commiserating, Mullen shook his head. It was his small show of support and Lucy accepted it the way it was meant, as the highest praise.

She lifted her chin. She would not be so easily deterred from her argument. "The point is, Constable, that we all know he was playacting. Alfie didn't know any more about being a detective than I do. Yes, I'll be the first to admit he's eccentric. Yes, I agree that once he gets a thing into his head he's as impossible to stop as the five forty-five out of Victoria Station. But he's never disappeared before. Not for six whole weeks. Not without a word as to where he's gone."

The realization wedged up under Lucy's heart. Eager to distract herself, she collected the magazines from the table and returned them to the bookshelf next to the fireplace. She fitted them neatly between Pomenture's *History of the Indian Subcontinent* and Barton's *Narrative of the Operations and Recent Discoveries Within the Temples, Tombs, and Excavations in India*.

"Be that as it may . . ." Brushing crumbs from his hands, Constable Mullen rose out of his chair. "There ain't much we can do. You understand that, Miss Lucy, I know you do. You've 'eard the same at the station when you stopped in. And I daresay, it's what the gents up at Scotland Yard told you, for I heard you been there, too, badgerin' them for help. There ain't a thing we can do unless there's been a crime committed. And thinkin' you're Sherlock Holmes, well . . . it may be daft, but it ain't exactly a crime, is it?" Mullen laid one hand on her arm in a friendly gesture. "Ol' Alfie, he'll turn up. He always does."

"Yes. You're right." There was little else Lucy could say. Her worries congealed inside her into a painful knot of anger. She glanced at the mantel and the photograph of Alfie Barnstable that stood there in its silver frame.

In his starched white shirt and the formal dark coat he usually reserved for church services, Alfie looked stiff and uncomfortable. But even the uncompromising eye of the camera could do little to disguise the twinkle of mischief in his eyes or the way his head was cocked so that his Homburg sat jauntily to one side and his small, pointed beard seemed an exclamation mark, his commentary on life in general.

The knot of emotion beneath Lucy's heart climbed into her throat.

The moment Mullen had gotten up out of his chair, Crookston had popped out of his as well. He didn't follow Mullen to the door. He stopped near where Lucy was standing, his solemn, blue eyes trained not on Alfie's photograph, but on the bookshelves.

"Your attempts to find your father are admirable," he said. "But I must say, I'm not at all convinced you're going about it the right way. Reading Sherlock Holmes is one thing, but tell me, Miss Barnstable, how do you hope a knowledge of Indian culture might help you find your father?"

It was on the tip of Lucy's tongue to tell him the truth.

She wanted to explain about Alfie's journal, the one she had found in his bedchamber. She wanted to tell him all about the cryptic entries in it. Veiled references to infamous London neighborhoods like Limehouse and Seven Dials. Ridiculous lists of names: real names like Shadwell, and ones that were less than believable. Outlandish names like Kali and the Devil. Names straight out of the stack of penny dreadfuls she'd found in a pile under Alfie's bed.

But there were one or two things in Alfie's journal that had piqued Lucy's interest and another half dozen that absolutely astounded her.

No one could have been more surprised than Lucy when she discovered that someone had actually hired her father to work on a case. A real case.

In typical Alfie fashion, he never said a word to Lucy about it, just as he never explained in his journal what the case was all about. But there was a suggestion here, a hint there. Lucy had spent hours piecing the thing together. As astonishing as it seemed, all the information led her to one conclusion: Whatever Alfie was working on, it had something to do with India.

Constable Crookston's perceptive gaze invited her to tell him all about it.

Every logical bone in Lucy's body advised her it was the right thing to do.

Most of all, she wanted to draw her one real clue out of her pocket and show it to the constables. It was a small stone carving, a curious item she'd found by accident in a secret compartment in Alfie's desk. At first, she didn't have any idea what the thing was. But the more she read about the history and culture of India, the more she'd visited the British Museum and learned all she could about the antiquities in it, the more she was convinced that it was a vital clue to her father's whereabouts.

It was no bigger than a man's pocket watch, a square stone that contained an inscription in small, angular writing. On her very first trip to the British Museum, Lucy learned that it was a seal. The ancient inhabitants of the Indian subcontinent had used such items to mark their possessions. Very recently an entire cache of them had been found at Mohenjo-Daro, a town along the Indus River.

As far as Lucy could tell, Alfie's seal was unique. The other seals she'd seen at the museum depicted animals. Alfie's was decorated with the figure of a man wearing an elaborate turban. He was surrounded by worshiping animals—a tiger, an elephant, and a bull.

But what the significance of the Indian seal was to Alfie was as elusive and as cryptic to Lucy as was her father's disappearance. She knew only one thing: The seal was her only link to her father. It wasn't much, but it was all she had, and as much as she would have liked to show it to the police, she found that she couldn't.

She wasn't ready to share the seal with them. She wasn't ready to expose herself to any more of their criticisms. Or their condescension.

Her hand in her pocket, her fingers curled around the terra-cotta-colored stone as if to keep it safe from prying eyes, Lucy lifted her gaze to Constable Crookston's.

"Indian culture? It's a diversion. Nothing more. A way to fill the empty hours."

"And does all your work allow time for such amusements?" Absently, Crookston fingered the worn copy of Wilkinson's *Manners and Customs of the Ancient Hindu* that Lucy had bought from a used book dealer in Wigmore Street. "I understand from Mullen that you take in boarders."

It was a welcome change of subject. Lucy patted the seal into the deepest corner of her pocket. She turned away and gathered up the teacups. "I have been for years," she said. "From what you've heard about my father, I'm sure you understand why. It's a large house, and difficult to maintain when the man who should be the breadwinner is more interested in treasure hunting and flying machines." She met Crookston's surprisingly level gaze.

"If you've been listening to Constable Mullen's gossip, you know there's some small bit of money left from my mother's inheritance, but it's hardly enough to get us by. We have seven boarders at the moment, and room for more. If you know of anyone . . ."

Crookston obviously didn't, and he was just as obviously uncomfortable telling her so. He turned toward the door.

Lucy saw them out. In the distance, the last rumblings of the storm that had soaked the city faded. Lightning flickered in the night sky. She turned her back on the wet, dark street and locked the door behind her.

It was cool and when she returned to the parlor, Lucy allowed herself the luxury of standing before the remnants of the coal fire that flickered in the grate. Though she told herself it would only make the pain inside her worse, she glanced again at the photograph of Alfie.

"Alfred Barnstable, consulting detective!" Even now, the words felt odd on Lucy's tongue. They shivered through her like a winter's chill.

"You had to open a consulting detective agency. You had to pretend you were Sherlock Holmes! And whatever you were up to, you got yourself mixed up in something you couldn't handle. You are the most exasperating person in the entire Empire," she added for good measure.

"You're impulsive, Alfie Barnstable. And you're unruly. You're impractical. You're irrational and illogical." Her piece spoken, the anger drained from Lucy's voice. Her shoulders drooped.

"And I'd give anything to learn what's become of you," she whispered. "I'd give anything at all to have you back."

The jangle of the front bell jarred Lucy out of her reverie. Automatically, she glanced at the clock on the wall. A frown creased her forehead. No one in their right mind would call at this hour.

Just as quickly, a surge of expectation quickened Lucy's heart.

It could only be Constables Mullen and Crookston come back again.

Her steps suddenly eager and impatient, she headed for the front door.

Perhaps she'd judged the police incorrectly, she told herself. Perhaps they were not as insensitive to her plight as they seemed. Perhaps they'd remembered something significant, or seen something important.

Perhaps it wasn't the police at all.

Perhaps Alfie was back.

The very thought froze Lucy into place. Her hand already on the brass doorknob, she stopped long enough to take a deep breath, hoping it might still the furious pounding of her heart.

"It isn't Alfie. It can't be Alfie."

She repeated the words under her breath like a prayer, and braced herself against the disappointment that was sure to come when she opened the door and found that she was right.

She opened the door nevertheless.

There was a streetlamp farther up the road, but little of its light made its way to Lucy's front door. The darkness was nearly absolute. Still, she knew the man on her doorstep was not Alfie Barnstable.

He was too tall to be Alfie. Too broad. Even in the meager light, she could tell his hair was far darker than Alfie's, and he looked to be clean-shaven. He was wearing a rough sort of coat of the kind often favored by men of the lower classes who worked near the river and it looked to be wet and dirty, stained with something darker than the fabric itself.

A streak of lightning burst in the sky overhead. Like the blaze ignited in a photographer's flash pan, the burst of light left Lucy blinded. She squinted and backed away, but not before she registered a fleeting impression of the man. The silver light illuminated only the left side of his face, but what she saw was uncommonly striking: a strong jaw and eyes that were steady and determined, hair darker than her own and a nose that was not as straight as some and yet seemed perfectly fitted to the man's features.

It was a face the likes of which some women dream. The face of a hero out of some blood-and-thunder melodrama. Lancelot. Tristan. Ivanhoe.

Holmes?

The thought brought Lucy up short. She was not usually so fanciful a person and she scolded herself and shoved her fantasies firmly back where they belonged. She was not the kind of fickle woman who was instantly attracted to strangers. Especially strangers who had the audacity to call in the middle of the night.

"If you've come about a room . . ." It was on the tip of Lucy's tongue to send the man away with a firm lecture about making business calls at the proper time of day. She didn't. But only because she remembered the stack of accounts that sat, unpaid, on her desk.

Another boarder would not hurt, she reminded herself.

Another boarder would not hurt at all.

Lucy swallowed the sharp reply that threatened to alienate the man before he'd ever spoken a word.

"If you've come about a room, you may step inside," she said.

For a minute she thought perhaps the man hadn't heard. That he didn't understand. He swayed on his feet and lurched forward and he might have fallen if he hadn't clutched on to the iron railing that surrounded the front stoop.

Lucy had little experience with liquor. Not that she was so naive as to think Alfie never indulged in a drop or two. Of course Alfie drank spirits. All men did. But she had never been in close contact with one who was intoxicated.

With a click of her tongue and a toss of her head, Lucy made to close the door. The man shot out one hand, wedging it open.

"Barnstable," he said. The man's voice was thick and his words slurred, but Lucy could not fail to catch the hint of a Scottish burr. He rolled the "R" in the name. "Alfred Barnstable."

He had her attention now. Lucy flinched and took a step forward. Certain she was not going to try to close the door again, the man dared to draw his hand away long enough to reach into his pocket. He pulled out one of Alfie's handbills and held it up for Lucy to see.

Torn between caution and curiosity, Lucy dared to hope for more.

It came without another moment's delay.

"Alfred . . . have to . . . talk . . ."

The words hardly made any sense, but they were enough to cause Lucy's heart to jump.

In the six weeks since her father had disappeared, she had been from one end of London to the other looking for him. In all that time, she had never imagined that the information she was trying so hard to find might come to her instead. Right to her front door.

Fighting to keep her excitement at bay, she stepped back to allow the man into the house. "Come in," she said. "If you have word from Alfie—"

The stranger stumbled into the entryway and Lucy's words disappeared on the end of a startled gasp.

What the flash of lightning had only briefly illuminated, the light of the gas lamps that flickered on the wall showed in full.

The man was covered with blood.

Lucy sucked in a small breath of surprise. As much as she told herself that it was rude to stare, and that it would do the man no earthly good, she could hardly help herself. She'd never seen anything like it.

The stranger's right eye was nearly swollen shut. His lips were bruised. There was a gash on his forehead that was deep and wide and another along his right temple that was raw and grotesquely purple. His clothes were torn and soaked with rainwater. His knuckles were scraped.

Lucy could not help but feel a tug of pity. Before she could tell herself it was unreasonable, and perhaps even a little dangerous, she wound her arm through the man's and led him into the parlor.

He didn't resist and Lucy thought it no wonder. Every step seemed to cost him, both his strength and his pride. By the time she ushered him into the parlor, his face was ashen beneath its veneer of blood.

"I'll get some hot water," Lucy said. "And some bandages. Sit down." She led him to the chair closest to the fire.

The man looked at the chair. He looked at Lucy.

His eyes were dark and as glassy as a pigeon's. He didn't answer her. He didn't do anything at all.

As if trying to make some sense of everything she said, he simply stared at her.

He was still looking at her when his eyes rolled back in his head, his knees gave out, and he collapsed onto the parlor floor.

# Chapter 2

L ucy Barnstable was eminently sensible.

It was something on which she prided herself.

Before she ever went to help the man, she took care of the things any prudent woman would.

Her boarders were not usually up and about this late at night, but she couldn't take the chance. The last thing she needed was for word to go around that there was scandal in the house. Scandal in the form of a battered stranger.

Lucy hurried to the parlor door and snapped it shut.

From there she went to the tea tray and retrieved the pot of water on it. She held her hand along one side of the pot. It wasn't hot, but it was still warm.

For now, that would have to be enough.

Appropriating the linen serviette that Constable Mullen had left near the chair he occupied, she carried it and the water over to where the man lay.

Lucy knelt and carefully turned the man over. It was no simple task. He was tall and well built, with shoulders nearly too wide for his ill-fitting coat and legs that were long enough so that she had to untangle them once she had him on his back. By the time she was done, she was breathing rapidly.

Lucy sat back and wiped her hands against her

skirt. She blew an errant curl of hair out of her eyes and peered into the stranger's face.

This close, he looked worse than ever.

It was no wonder she had registered the impression of a nose that was well shaped but hardly straight. It was surely broken. There was a bulge on the bridge of it and a wicked-looking bruise that blanketed it in purple. The man was clean-shaven, just as she'd thought, but his face was slick with a devil's brew of rainwater and blood that thickened on his upper lip and rolled down his chin.

He was dreadfully pale and each of his breaths was so shallow as to be barely perceptible. The man's coat was open. His shirt was torn. So were the unmentionables he wore beneath it. With one finger, Lucy nudged the cloth aside. She could see a strip of bare skin along the right side of his body and an ugly bruise that colored him from his collarbone down to his abdomen.

She didn't dare look any farther.

A tiny thread of panic wound tight through Lucy's stomach. It would be bad enough if her boarders knew the man was here, bleeding all over the rug where on rainy Sunday afternoons they gathered to play charades. It would be worse if the man died and in the morning she had to explain about the body in the parlor.

Setting aside both her trepidations and her exacting opinions about cleanliness, Lucy dared to lay one hand against the man's chest. His heartbeat was weak but steady and she allowed herself the luxury of relaxing just a little.

He wasn't going to die. At least not yet. And if she had anything at all to do with it, not on her parlor rug.

Lucy sat back on her heels. She wondered who the

man was and what had happened to him. She marveled that any man could have suffered such terrible injuries and survived. And suddenly she was burning with curiosity.

Fighting to quell the feeling, Lucy dipped the serviette into the water and squeezed it out. Gently she wiped the man's face.

But even while she tried to concentrate on her work, she could feel Alfie's eyes on her. "I'd blame you if you were here," she grumbled, glancing up at the photograph of Alfie where it beamed at her from the mantelpiece. "I'd remind you that you are the inquisitive member of the family. Not me. I'd ask you to remember that your curiosity has landed you in a sea of troubles more than once in your time. I'd offer every piece of advice I could think to offer, and I know exactly what you'd do."

She let go a long, shaky breath and tossed the cloth aside, a white flag of surrender. "Exactly," she said, "what I'm going to do."

Lucy told herself she had no cause to be nervous, and less still to feel guilty. She reminded herself that whatever she did, it was for the man's own good.

Still, she bit at her lower lip. She scraped her palms against her dark skirt. She realized, suddenly, that she'd been holding her breath and she let it out and hauled in another, keeping it deep in her lungs for courage.

She ignored the fact that her fingers were trembling and her palms were sweating. She refused to look at the poor, battered face of the stranger, or listen to his reedy breaths, or notice the unnatural chill of his skin.

She ignored everything.

Especially the warnings of her own conscience.

She turned her back on Alfie's grinning face and

on his expression. The one that seemed to say that, all along, he knew she'd come to this.

Lucy promptly proceeded to go through the stranger's pockets.

Five minutes later Lucy sat back, feeling not unlike she imagined the man on her floor must have felt right before he collapsed. She was out of breath. Light-headed. Dizzy.

The man carried no identification, but in one of his coat pockets, she'd found a quantity of banknotes. She'd flattened each and every one and counted them all carefully. The total was staggering, enough to keep her household in luxury for the better part of two years.

The implications were obvious. Whatever had happened to the stranger, he hadn't been robbed. No thief worthy of his profession would ever have let a prize so precious get away.

But it wasn't the money she'd found in the man's coat pocket that snatched Lucy's breath and made her heart pump like a steam engine.

It was what was in his trouser pocket.

Slowly, Lucy unfolded her fingers and stared down at the object cradled in the palm of her hand.

It was no bigger than a man's pocket watch, a square stone that contained an inscription in small, angular writing. It was decorated with the figure of a man wearing an elaborate turban, a man surrounded by a tiger, an elephant, and a bull.

Slowly, as if to be sure there was no sleight of hand involved, nothing that could trick her eyes or her mind, she reached into her own pocket for the seal she'd found in Alfie's desk. She held the two side by side.

They were identical in every way.

It was too impossible to be a coincidence, too extraordinary to be ignored. It was enough to electrify her mind and kindle a flame of hope in her heart, and it led her to one conclusion.

It wasn't mere happenstance when the man mentioned her father's name at the door. The stranger had to have some connection with Alfie.

Lucy was so busy turning the astonishing thought over in her head, she nearly didn't hear the man moan.

He groaned again, louder this time. His eyelids fluttered.

Guilt and uneasiness mingled in Lucy and escaped with a little gasp. Before he could notice it was gone, she tucked the seal back into his pocket. She wasn't nearly as lucky with the banknotes.

She had them folded in her fist and was ready to return them to his coat pocket when the stranger's eyes flew open. Moving faster than a man in his condition should have been able to move, he bolted upright and grabbed Lucy's wrist. His fingers closed tight around it, grinding bone against bone. Lucy yelped and dropped the money.

"What in the name of Auld Hornie do you think you're doing?" Even through swollen lips, the man's voice held a keen edge of suspicion. He looked her up and down.

His right eye was swollen and bloodied. His left had fared better, but just barely. It should have been a pathetic look.

It wasn't.

His look was intense and searching, as pointed as the spark of mistrust she could not fail to notice in it, and as fierce and unrelenting as the hold he had on her wrist.

Fear shot through Lucy. It tightened her stomach

and tangled around her heart. But it wasn't nearly as powerful as the anger that followed in its wake.

Lucy clenched her teeth and looked the man in the eye. His good eye.

"I don't want your money," she said. "If I did, I would have been long gone with it by now. It's all there. Count it if you don't believe me."

"I will." As quickly as he'd grabbed her, the man let her go. The effort cost him dearly. His face was pasty and each of his movements was slow and painful, but he did just as he said. He gathered up the banknotes from the carpet and counted them. Satisfied they were all there, he jammed the money back into his pocket.

It only took a few seconds but by the time he was done, the man's face was as white as candle wax. He closed his eyes and sagged against the nearest chair. Lucy was thankful he was already on the floor. If he wasn't, she feared it was where he would have landed again.

All her worries rushed back at her in an instant. This time, they brought reinforcements. Yes, it would be bad if the stranger died in her home, just as she'd thought earlier. But now it would be even worse. She refused to let him die before he told her all he knew about the Indian seal in his pocket.

And Alfie.

Still on her knees, Lucy scooted closer. She reached for the wet cloth and laid it on his forehead. "How do you feel?" she asked.

The man's eyes flickered open. A cynical chuckle laced his voice. "Like I died and went to hell," he said. Being careful to move slowly this time, he looked all around the room. His gaze took in everything: the tidy and serviceable furnishings, the tasteful pictures positioned evenly if not artfully on the walls, even the ornaments arranged in precise order on the mantelpiece. "Damn!" he mumbled. "Neat as a pin and cozy as a country church. Definitely hell."

Lucy's expression soured. She backed away. "Really, sir. I will excuse your impropriety but only because of your sorry state. You obviously received quite a bump on the head. Otherwise you wouldn't talk that way in front of a woman you don't know."

"Wouldn't I?" The man cocked one eyebrow. The expression was nearly as disarming as he intended it to be. It might have had its full effect if he didn't wince from the effort.

Lucy stood and tossed the damp cloth onto the floor. With the fingers of her left hand, she rubbed at the spot on her right wrist where he'd grabbed her. "I'm sure I don't know what you would or wouldn't do," she said. "And I don't think I want to find out. I know nothing at all about you except that you're a Scotsman."

"Am I?" It was certainly a rhetorical question and the stranger tossed it out nonchalantly. He was nearly skilled enough to make it look as if he didn't care how she might answer. Yet Lucy couldn't help but notice that his head was cocked to one side. His eyes weren't so much half-closed as they were hooded. He was intensely interested, though she couldn't say why.

Setting the thought aside, she went back to the tea tray and poured the last cup out of the pot. She didn't ask the man how he took his tea. She loaded it with sugar and stirred it briskly, and when she delivered it to him, she found him wiping his hands on the cloth and wincing when it touched his knuckles.

"You sound enough like a Scotsman to me," she said, handing him the cup. "There's a burr in your words that could only have come from north of the border. But there's something else as well. . . ." She pursed her lips, trying to work it out. It was on the tip of her tongue to mention that when he paid attention to his words, the burr disappeared completely and left a proper public school accent behind. The cultured tones did not at all match his rough workingman's clothes. Or his salt-of-the-earth smell.

She didn't. But only because she remembered the seal. She couldn't afford to offend the man.

"Drink it down," she said instead, pointing to the cup of tea. "And tell me why you're here."

The man didn't argue. Holding the cup gingerly to his swollen lips, he sipped the tea until it was gone and when it was, he set the cup down on the rug beside him. "Alfred Barnstable. Consulting Detective." He glanced at the handbill that had fluttered to the rug beside him when he fainted. "I've come to see him."

So he was looking for Alfie, too.

The edges of Lucy's hopes frayed. She cursed her luck and her imagination for letting it run away with her. She cursed herself for being naive enough to think this man might have answers instead of simply more questions. But she wasn't about to give up so easily.

"Alfie is out right now," she said. Even she was surprised at how smoothly she told the lie. Like a bather testing the waters at Brighton, she ventured toward the information she desired, one careful step at a time. "He's been called away. On business. Is there a message I can give him?"

He answered her question with one of his own. "He's your husband?"

Lucy shook her head and glanced over at Alfie's photograph on the mantelpiece. "My father," she answered. "I take it you're not a friend of his, or you would have known. That must mean you're here on business. . . ." She let the tail end of her sentence trail off so that it was more of a question than a statement.

Whether to make himself more comfortable or to stall for time, the man gritted his teeth and pulled himself to his feet. He didn't stay there long. With a mumbled oath, he dropped into the chair.

"He'll be back tonight?"

"I really can't say. Why do you need to talk to him?"

"Why do you need to know?"

The memory of the terra-cotta seal was the only thing that made Lucy bite her tongue. She managed a tight smile.

She retrieved the man's teacup and took it back over to the tray, stepping as carefully around him as she was around the truth. "For your information," she said, her voice calm and businesslike, "I am my father's assistant. The Watson to his Holmes, if you will. When Alfie is not in town, I am authorized to handle all aspects of his affairs. You can discuss anything with me that you would tell him."

"Can I?" The stranger didn't look certain. He shook his head as if to clear it. "You're not one of those New Women, are you, wearing bloomers and riding bicycles?" He shivered and Lucy guessed that this time, it had nothing to do with his injuries and everything to do with his opinion of progress. He let his gaze wander over her, from the top of her head to the tips of her shoes.

It was a candid look, and as disconcerting as it was direct. It might even have been construed as indecorous if the man didn't top it off with a derisive grunt. "You don't look like a detective," he said.

"You don't look like a dockworker." The words

were out of her mouth before Lucy had a chance to stop them, before she ever had the chance to think them over and realize that they were true. She tossed her head. "You're altogether too sure of yourself. And too bold. You're no more a working-class man than I am Queen Victoria."

As if the remark touched a chord, the man flinched and a light went on in his good eye. He opened his mouth to respond. But before he ever had a chance to speak, the spark was gone. He snapped his mouth closed and sank back against the chair cushions.

Lucy saw her advantage and took it. "Whatever it is you've come about," she said, "you can trust me as you would Alfie himself." That much was true and Lucy didn't feel at all guilty about saying it. The rest, of course, was nothing more than a pack of lies. She soothed her conscience by reminding herself it was all for a good cause. All for Alfie.

"I am in touch with my father daily," she assured the man. "If need be, I can consult him about your case. May I ask who recommended our agency?"

The man seemed puzzled by the question. He looked from the handbill to Lucy and back again to the handbill. "I found the broadsheet in my pocket and . . ." With an effort that was nearly palpable, he struggled out of his seat and took a couple of shaky steps toward the door. "I'll stop by another time, why don't I?"

"No!" Lucy darted between the man and the door. She had promised herself that she would stay calm. She had vowed to remain composed so that he could not even begin to guess how important he was to her. She failed miserably.

Gathering up the tatters of her self-control, she held them close around her. "What I mean is, I really don't think it's wise. Not in your condition. I have rooms to let. You must have seen the sign in the front window. You could stay here. At least tonight. If Alfie isn't back by morning, perhaps you'd reconsider and tell me what business it is that brings you here to see him."

"Perhaps not." The man got as far as the table where the tea tray was set out. He stopped and swayed. "Perhaps you could . . . ?" His knees buckled.

This time, Lucy didn't wait for him to fall. She scrambled over and hooked one arm around his waist. He leaned heavily against her and she led him back to the chair.

"I won't allow you to leave." Lucy settled the man, and reaching for a small knitted blanket she kept on the divan, she arranged it over his knees. "There's no need for you to be shy, if that's what you're being. Or too proud to accept help. And no reason at all to think you'd be taking charity. I saw the money, remember? I know you can afford to pay. There's an empty room. On the third floor."

"You really are most remarkable, Miss Barnstable." For the first time, the man managed what was nearly a smile. It transformed his expression enough for Lucy to imagine that there might be a handsome face beneath the blood and bruises. He tried like the dickens to keep his eyes open, but it was clear from the start that he would lose the fight. They drifted closed at the same time his head rolled back against the chair cushions.

"Third floor?" This time when he chuckled, there was a hint of amusement in the sound. "I'll be damned if I could make it as far as the first. Just leave me here to die in peace."

Restlessly, Lucy adjusted the blanket. She fetched a pillow from the divan and propped it behind his head. "You're not going to die," she told him in no uncertain terms. "Not in my house. My boarders would be outraged and I wouldn't have any idea what to do with your body. Besides, the police would ask me what name to put on your gravestone and I'd be in a pretty bind. You haven't so much as introduced yourself."

"Haven't I?" The man's voice faded. He fought his exhaustion and forced himself to look at Lucy.

"Well, that's the hell of it, isn't it?" he said. "That's why I'm here. That's why I want to hire your father. You see, I remember being beaten." He closed his eyes against a wave of pain. "I would have trounced the bloody bastards if they hadn't played me dirty. Scot's pride, do you think?" For a moment the man's eyes glittered. Just as quickly the look was gone, replaced by a cynical smile. He looked down at his bruised and swollen knuckles. "At least I fought back. Raw courage, do you suppose? Or simply madness? Whatever it was, the pain in my ribs tells me it didn't work very well." He shifted in the chair, trying to settle himself more comfortably.

Frustrated, he grumbled. His expression darkened. His lips pulled into a grim line. As if he was thinking very hard, his brows dropped low over his eyes.

"There were three men. No. Four. One of them . . ." Thinking very hard, the man cocked his head to one side. "I knew one of them. A fellow with a smile as sleek as the silver handles of a casket." The stranger shivered, but whether it was from the memory, or the fact that he couldn't put a name to the face, Lucy couldn't tell. As if setting the thought aside, he hitched his shoulders.

"I woke up in a wretched alley somewhere in Whitechapel. You know, one of those filthy places where the rats are as big as racehorses and the muck is an inch deep all around." He caught himself and looked at Lucy.

"No," he said, assessing her with precision. "I don't suppose you know of places like that. Even if you do fancy yourself something of a detective. It's just as well. They aren't the kinds of places for young ladies. Not young ladies like you. When I woke up, I was alone. I went through my pockets and found your father's handbill. That's what gave me the idea to come here and see him. It's all I remember." He looked at Lucy levelly, expecting her to make some sense of the whole thing.

She didn't.

Frustrated by Lucy's obvious confusion, the man leaned nearer. "You'll forgive me if I don't make myself clear. It's been a long night. And not a pleasant one. The minute I dragged myself out of that alley, I realized I had something of a mystery on my hands. And I need a detective to help me solve it. You asked for an introduction, but I'm afraid I can't give you one. You see, Miss Barnstable, my memory is completely gone. I don't have the slightest idea who I am."

# Chapter 3

"Have you seen this?" Farleigh Atwater's sumptuous white mustaches quivered. Nonplussed, he sat back in his chair and tapped one slim but gnarled finger on the article that filled the bottom half of the front page of the *London Illustrated News*. "There are to be Sikhs at the Queen's Jubilee."

"Sikhs?" A butter knife in one hand, a pot of marmalade in the other, Harleigh Atwater looked up from his piece of toast. His eyes were as blue as his twin's, and just as dubious. "Thought we took care of them at Goojerat back in '49," he said, his sumptuous white mustaches quivering. "Must be some sort of mistake."

"Not according to this." Farleigh bent over the breakfast table and squinted at the page. His bushy eyebrows rose. They might have met his hairline if his hairline had not retreated far beyond their reach years before. "Says they'll be part of the procession and that they are to stay at the Star and Garter in Richmond. Seems unlikely, but there you have it," he harumphed, sitting back again. "Don't know what the world is coming to. Modern ideas. All one Empire and all that rot."

"Rot, indeed." Harleigh added a dollop of marmalade to his toast and crunched into it. "Not like that back in our day, I can tell you that much. Why, at

Goojerat . . ." He turned to Lucy. "I say, Miss Barnstable, have we ever mentioned Goojerat?"

Startled out of the thoughts that had occupied her
for all of the night and the better part of the morning,
Lucy glanced up at her boarders. As casually as she
could, she slid her folded copy of *The Strand* magazine farther under her plate, hiding the Sherlock
Holmes story she'd been reading. It took her a moment to focus both her thoughts and her energies
and to remind herself that she was in her own dining
room and not with Holmes and Watson, embroiled
in the case of the man with the twisted lip.

For all its romantic nonsense, she had to admit that
the story was engrossing.

"But not the least bit helpful," Lucy mumbled to
herself.

"Of course we were helpful!" Farleigh grumbled.

"We were with Lord Gough," Harleigh added as
if it went without saying. "He was simply Hugh
Gough then, of course. Field Marshal. Impressive
chap."

"He was at Goojerat."

"Have we ever told you about Goojerat?"

The overlapping voices of the Atwaters brought
Lucy out of her thoughts. She managed to offer Farleigh a smile. Or was he Harleigh?

Lucy shook the thought away. It hardly mattered.
Harleigh And Farleigh Atwater were as interchange-
able as their names, their matching dark morning
coats and high, old-fashioned collars, their superb
white mustaches and shaggy eyebrows.

"Goojerat . . ." Lucy chewed over the word. "Yes,
I do believe you have mentioned it." She added
quickly, "A time or two," because she could not bear
to break the poor dears' hearts or deprive them of

the chance to recount, yet again, the story of what they considered the British Army's finest hour.

"Back in '49. That's when it was." Farleigh took up the telling of the tale. Or was it Harleigh? "Of course it all began back in '43, when we first joined the Fourteenth Light Horse—"

The door to the dining room snapped open and Lucy was spared the further details. Much to her dismay, she realized too late that there were worse things than another blow-by-blow account of the British Army's defeat of the Sikhs at Goojerat nearly fifty years earlier.

Mrs. James Slyke was one of them.

Mrs. Slyke had been living at the house since the death of her husband three years earlier. She was Lucy's most demanding and particular boarder, a woman who seemed always to be in a constant state of dyspepsia. She was as sour as yesterday's breakfast and, Lucy suspected, as mean-tempered as any of the Sikhs the two Atwaters had ever met in battle.

With a lift of her ample upper lip, Mrs. Slyke strolled over to the table and scanned the Atwaters' plates. "You haven't eaten all the breakfast, have you?" The Atwaters went right on with what they were doing, skillfully ignoring Mrs. Slyke just as they ignored her every morning.

Mrs. Slyke fetched her own plate and went to survey what was left of the breakfast buffet. "Bacon again?" She turned a steely eye on Lucy. But though disapproval laced her voice, she piled her plate high, not only with bacon, but with kippers, and broiled tomatoes, and as much toast as she could manage to mound on it.

Completely oblivious to the fact that there had been something of a conversation going on in the room before she entered, Mrs. Slyke seated herself in the chair directly opposite Lucy's and launched into a lecture, one that might have been infinitely more effective and entirely more refined if her mouth had not been full of bacon.

"I have just had the most terrible row with that Clara Miller before she left for work," Mrs. Slyke said. "It's unconscionable. That's what it is. She lets that child of hers run wild and says he will learn manners when her husband returns from the West Indies." Mrs. Slyke leaned closer so that the shelf of her formidable breast rested on the table. She lowered her voice and gave Lucy a wink. "If she has a husband."

"Boy's no harm to anyone." Harleigh bit into another piece of toast. "High-spirited. That's all. Boys are supposed to be high-spirited."

"Rude. That's what he is." Mrs. Slyke finished her bacon and started in on the kippers. "And careless. His mother received a telegram this morning and can you believe it? On her way out of the house, she handed it to the boy with the simple instruction to put it away in their room." With a flourish, Mrs. Slyke produced the telegram from the pocket of her black bombazine gown. "He dropped it, of course, thoughtless creature. Right inside the front door."

Lucy sighed. "I shall give the telegram back to Mrs. Miller as soon as she gets home," she promised, holding out her hand for it.

Mrs. Slyke pursed her lips but even she did not have the temerity to hold on to the telegram. "You needn't read it," she told Lucy. "It's simply an order. From one of Clara Miller's customers. Some Society lady who, no doubt, has grown fatter than she should and needs her gown altered."

Holding in her exasperation, Lucy tucked the telegram into her pocket. "I'll take care of it," she assured Mrs. Slyke. "But I must say, Mrs. Slyke, I find Jack Miller a pleasant enough child. As Mr. Atwater says, he is a bit high-spirited—"

"Boys are meant to be high-spirited." This time, it was Farleigh who spoke up. At least Lucy thought it was Farleigh. "Diligent lad. Good at running errands. And he knows all about Goojerat. I say!" His eyes lighting, he glanced from Lucy to Mrs. Slyke. "Have we ever told you about Goojerat?"

Again, the door to the dining room opened. This time, it was Millicent Foxworthy who entered. Miss Foxworthy had been a boarder in the house since Lucy was twelve. At the time, Lucy had thought her the most ancient of creatures. That was thirteen years earlier, and if Miss Foxworthy had been ancient then, she was surely antediluvian by now. She was short and so frail-looking Alfie always said the first stiff wind to come by would blow her clear across the city and into the Thames. Her hair was the color of a mourning dove and today, as always, it seemed to be doing its best to escape from the bun she wore at the back of her head.

Miss Foxworthy swept a strand of hair away from her cheek at the same time she skittered into the room. She peered at the crowd around the table through rheumy eyes and offered each of them one of her small, quivering smiles.

"No use even trying to talk about Goojerat now." Deprived of his pleasure, Farleigh Atwater's shoulders slumped. He looked at Miss Foxworthy and shouted, "Deaf as a post, you know."

Lucy did know.

She knew Miss Foxworthy was hard of hearing. She knew Mrs. Slyke was difficult, and exacting, and as hard to please as anyone she'd ever met. She knew about Goojerat.

Lucy rolled her gaze toward the cracked plaster ceiling.

Dear God, but she knew all about Goojerat.

All she wanted now was a little peace and quiet to think about all the things she didn't know about.

All she wanted was some time alone to think about the stranger.

Lucy's thoughts traveled to the mysterious man who was now occupying the vacant room on the third floor. Once he'd recovered enough to walk, it wasn't hard to convince him to stay the night. As much as he tried to disregard his injuries and his resulting weakness, he was sensible enough to know it was for his own good.

What he could not possibly have known was the way Lucy's mind scrambled to make sure he wouldn't disappear before she discovered the truth about him. He had some connection with Alfie, even if he did not remember it. The Indian seal proved as much. And Lucy swore she was going to find out what it was.

Desperate for some idea as to how she might convince him that she was all she claimed—Alfie's assistant, Alfie's confidant, Alfie's Watson—Lucy had spent most of the night and the early hours of the morning reading through Conan Doyle's stories. None of them had shed any light on her problem. As far as she could tell, Watson had never been brazen enough to claim a talent he did not have, and Holmes had never had to deal with a man who did not remember his own name.

As if simply thinking about him could conjure up his presence, the door opened yet again, and the stranger walked into the room. Not two feet inside the doorway, he pulled to a stop and glanced around the dining table, and though he controlled his reaction as neatly as she had seen him master his emotions the night before, Lucy could not help but notice the expression of surprise that registered upon his face. He was obviously not expecting a crowd.

And they were just as obviously not expecting him.

As one, Lucy's boarders turned to stare.

In spite of the fact that his face was bruised, his right eye was swollen shut, and he was covered with an assortment of cuts and scratches, the stranger did not show the least bit of mortification at their close inspection. Recovering in less than a heartbeat, he inched his shoulders back enough to make the most of his better-than-average height and favored each of them with a look in turn. It was an authoritative look, Lucy could not fail to notice that. Just as she could not miss the fact that it caused both Harleigh and Farleigh to snap to attention at the same time it made even Mrs. Slyke and Miss Foxworthy flush like schoolgirls.

"Good morning." The stranger shifted his gaze from the boarders to Lucy and his dark eyebrows rose a bit, enough for her to wonder if he was assessing her nearly as closely as she was considering him. For some odd reason even she could not explain, the prospect was not a comforting one. She had no doubt how she looked.

She had seen her face in the mirror that morning. She knew there were smudges of sleeplessness beneath her eyes and her hair looked a fright. On rising, she had done little more than twist it into a long, thick braid that hung down nearly to the center of her back. Though the stranger may have been too weary to appreciate it, the night before, she had been dressed to receive visitors. She was not nearly so fashionably attired today. This morning, like every morning, Lucy wore a drab brown housedress with

bone buttons that marched up the front and over her
bosom and long sleeves whose cuffs she had Mrs.
Miller alter periodically as the old ones frayed and
stained.

The stranger, though, looked remarkably recovered
from his ordeal of the night before and, now that he
was cleaned up, not at all unattractive. Except for the
fact that the jacket was not quite ample enough to
accommodate his broad shoulders, the winter-weight
suit Lucy had borrowed from the trunk of clothing
Clara Miller kept in the attic in anticipation of her
husband's return fit him fairly well. Funny, Lucy
thought, her mouth going suddenly and inexplicably
dry, she had seen Albert Miller a time or two in that
same suit. Yet she had never thought of Mr. Miller
as quite so tall or quite so well made.

Yes, the stranger looked remarkably good.

And Lucy hated him for it.

How could he look so very well rested when all
she could do through the whole of the long, sleepless
night was think how she might live up to all the
ridiculous promises she had made him?

Carefully, Lucy laid her serviette over her copy of
"The Man with the Twisted Lip." "Good morning."
She managed to choke out the words at the same
time she scrambled out of her chair. She turned to
those seated at the table. "This is our newest
boarder," she said before she realized she could not
even begin to introduce him. How could she when
she did not know his name?

"This is . . . this is . . ." Baffled, Lucy turned to
her other boarders. "Miss Foxworthy," she said, laying one hand gently on the old woman's shoulder.
She looked across the table at Mrs. Slyke. "And Mrs.
James Slyke."

It was an innocent enough remark, yet it had an

uncommon effect upon the stranger. His head snapped up and he flinched as if he'd been slapped.

Lucy's stomach lurched in the peculiar way it always did when she realized Alfie was about to stir up some variety of turmoil. Or perhaps excitement.

Excitement. That's what it was. The spark of recognition in the stranger's good eye registered as excitement in Lucy's brain. She wasn't sure how it happened or what, exactly, it meant. She only knew it was important.

Clutching her hands at her waist, she stepped forward, and if her boarders looked at her oddly, she paid it no mind. She kept her eyes on the stranger, evaluating his reaction. Every one of her senses on the alert, she waited for his answer. "Is it the Slyke or the James that sounds familiar?"

"James." He said the name slowly, trying it on for size. "James." This time, he sounded more confident, but he did not smile or look particularly pleased.

Lucy gulped down the bubble of excitement that threatened to escape her in a giggle of triumph. It was not so hard being a detective after all!

As if to tell Mr. Sherlock Holmes she would not be needing his help, she gave her copy of "The Man with the Twisted Lip" a contemptuous look, and skirting the table, she went to stand near the stranger.

"And this is . . ." She brought herself up short. Was James the man's Christian name? Or was it a family name? Recovering her aplomb at the same time she regained her voice, Lucy launched into her introduction without another thought to its accuracy. Her boarders would not care which was correct, she told herself. They would care if she stood there blithering and at a loss for words, as if she'd been foolish enough to let a man into her home when she was not certain who he was.

Which she had.

The realization sobered Lucy. But it didn't stop her.

"This is Mr. James," she said with as much authority as she could muster, and when the stranger did not object, she went right on. "He'll be staying with us for a while."

"Sir!" Farleigh popped out of his chair. Or was it Harleigh? "Farleigh Atwater," he said, clearing up the mystery. "At your service. Good to have you in the regiment. An officer, are you?" He glanced at his brother. "Looks like an officer."

"Officer, indeed." The other Atwater brother followed suit. Rising, he introduced himself and rumbled his approval. "Fine chap. Reminds me of Field Marshal Gough. He was at Goojerat," he told Mr. James. "I say, have we ever told you about Goojerat?"

"Goojerat?" Mr. James cocked his head to one side. "Back in '49, wasn't it? The way I've heard it, Gough thrashed Shere Singh and pursued him into the Khoree Pass. Magnificent victory. Brilliant soldiering."

"I say!" Their eyes as bright as fireworks, Farleigh and Harleigh spoke at the same time. Probably far faster than the Fourteenth Light Horse ever moved, they advanced on Mr. James. They had him surrounded in an instant. Looking more than a little overwhelmed, Mr. James backed into a corner.

Lucy might have taken pity on him and saved him if she hadn't heard the sounds of heavy footsteps out in the passageway. Darting to the door, she opened it in time to see a man clad in a dark overcoat heading up the stairs.

"Mr. Grogan?" Lucy called to him and though he could not have failed to hear her, he did not stop or look over the banister toward her. "Mr. Grogan, would you like to join us for breakfast?" Still, she got no answer, and mumbling a word that was hardly befitting either a lady or the mistress of the house, she turned back into the room and closed the door.

"That Grogan fellow . . ." As if she could see beyond the door, Mrs. Slyke curled her upper lip. "A strange bird if there ever was one," she pronounced. "Never leaves his room except in the dead of the night. I know. I hear him crumping down the steps at all odd hours. And then returning in the morning . . ." Mrs. Slyke did not need to say what she thought of Mr. Grogan's peculiar habits, her sour expression said it all. "Don't see why you have the likes of him living here with decent folk."

"Mr. Grogan has never shown himself to be indecent," Lucy reminded Mrs. Slyke. "And if he is not sociable . . ." She tossed the thought aside as inconsequential. She was thankful that Mr. Grogan kept to himself in the small garret room on the fourth floor. From the little she had seen of him in the six weeks since he had come to the house as a boarder, she knew he was tight-lipped and forbidding, and she suspected he was as cold and harsh as his ice-blue eyes and his thin smile. It was just as well that she did not have to make conversation with him, just as it was fine with her that he chose to take his meals elsewhere. It saved her money at the greengrocer's and for that alone, she was thankful.

"Take a look at this, will you." Before Lucy could fully recover from her thoughts, she felt Farleigh's hand touch her elbow. "Fellow's injured," he said quite simply, turning her toward Mr. James. He laid one hand against Mr. James's brow and tisk-tisked somberly. "Must have taken a real battering at the hands of those devil Sikhs. Doesn't look like anything fatal but still, something must be done."

Harleigh obviously agreed. His eyes bright with the prospect, he stepped back and looked Mr. James up and down. "May need to cauterize those wounds."

"Or perhaps surgery."

"Surgery, indeed!"

"We must get the regimental doctor in here as soon as possible."

"Brilliant idea!" Extricating himself from Farleigh's touch and Harleigh's fervent and quite alarming look, Mr. James sidestepped the Atwaters and headed toward the door. "And isn't it a coincidence? He is waiting for me right now in the parlor. Miss . . ." Clearly a man who was not comfortable without all the facts, he shrugged away the annoying problem of not remembering Lucy's name. "She's coming with me," he said. He grabbed Lucy's arm and dragged her into the passageway.

He didn't breathe a sigh of relief until they were safely in the parlor with the door shut behind them. When it finally was, he pulled a handkerchief embroidered with Albert Miller's initials from his pocket and mopped his brown. "You might have warned me."

"You wouldn't have believed me. No one ever does." Lucy couldn't' help herself. She laughed. "They are harmless, really."

"I would sooner face the Sikhs at Goojerat than another onslaught by those two old fellows. Are they always so . . ." He scrambled for the right word. "Intense?"

"When it comes to Goojerat, yes. They are quite elderly and between them, they don't have many memories left." It was a mistake from the minute she

said it. Lucy knew as much. Reminding Mr. James
of his singular problem was both heartless and ill-
mannered. She choked over her apology.

"No need." Mr. James waved away her worries
with one well-shaped hand. With barely more than
a grimace to betray the fact that he must be in a great
deal more pain than he was willing to admit, he
eased himself against the overstuffed arm of the
divan.

"How do you suppose I knew about Goojerat?" he
asked. "I don't know my own name, yet it seems I
know a great deal about some relatively minor battle
that happened nearly fifty years ago. The names. The
places. I looked at myself in the mirror this morning
and though I admit it was not a pretty sight, I can
see past the bruises well enough. I can't be more than
thirty years old. There's no way I could have the
slightest association with Goojerat."

"Perhaps a relative might have," Lucy suggested.
"Or perhaps you are a soldier."

He considered only a moment before he shook his
head uncertainly. "I'm not at all squeamish. At least
I wasn't when I examined my own injuries this
morning. That would qualify me for a soldier, I suppose. But I have a nagging suspicion I'm far too un-
disciplined. No." This time when he shook his head,
it was with conviction. "There's nothing in what's
left of my memory that suggests the military."

"A historian then?" Lucy tried to narrow down
the list. "A writer of scholarly texts? Or an artist who
paints sweeping canvases of battle scenes?"

This time when Mr. James shook his head, it was
with disgust. "We could spend the rest of our lives
guessing, until we were as old as those gents in the
dining room. I'm afraid it will get us nowhere." Still
looking at the closed parlor door, he tried to narrow

his eyes. It might have worked if he didn't wince at the pain. He laid one hand gently against the right side of his face. "You don't suppose I know those two from somewhere, do you?"

It was Lucy who dismissed this question. "You would surely remember two such as that," she said. "And if you knew them, they would surely know you. Though their hold on reality is somewhat tenuous, Harleigh and Farleigh Atwater really do have a remarkable capacity for recalling names and faces."

"And I suppose if I knew them, I'd know you." For a moment, his good eye lit. It was the same mischievous spark she'd seen the night before and it made her just as uncomfortable.

Nearly as uncomfortable as the look he gave her.

His head tipped, his body still propped against the divan with his long legs out in front of him, he looked Lucy up and down, and if she thought she felt self-conscious about the close scrutiny he'd given her in the dining room, she had surely been wrong. It was impossible to compare that casual look to the thorough way he appraised her now. His dark gaze skimmed Lucy's worn house shoes. It surveyed the shape of her hips beneath her gown, and the size of her waist. He kept his gaze on her bosom so long, she swore he was carefully counting each of the buttons along the front of her dress. For one moment she actually considered crossing her arms over her chest to prevent him from continuing.

He didn't give her time. Satisfied, though Lucy could not say with what, Mr. James moved his gaze from her bosom to her chin and from her chin to her lips. He kept his eyes there a bit too long and Lucy found herself holding her breath, waiting, though she could not have said for what, wanting, though she had no notion that she was lacking anything at all.

Recovering with what was almost a guilty start, Mr. James slid his gaze to her eyes and from there to the top of her head.

"Oh, yes," he said, his voice warming in the same alarming way as his smile. "I would remember you."

It was ridiculous to be rattled by such a look, yet Lucy could not seem to help herself. She felt heat rise through her, following the path of his gaze. It pooled in her bosom and shot up her neck and into her cheeks. It made her head whirl. It made her lips tingle.

Unwilling to let him observe the impact of his potent gaze, Lucy looked away. "The Atwaters have lived here as long as I can remember," she said. Her voice sounded breathless, even to her own ears. "If you knew them, then you would surely know both me and my father."

"And I don't." He rose from his place on the divan and took a step nearer. "You must certainly have told me last night, but I'm afraid I don't even remember your name."

"It is Lucy," she replied. She clenched her hands into fists at her sides, fighting to check the unbounded pulsing of her heart. "Lucy Barnstable. And you? Do you suppose we've hit upon something? Are you really Mr. James?"

"The James is right. I'm certain of that. But not the Mister. You can call me James. And I . . ." Before Lucy could even think to move away, he snatched her right hand in his. "I shall not call you Miss Barnstable. It's far too fussy a name for a woman as braw as you." He smiled, pleased it seemed by his own use of the Scottish word for beautiful. "I shall call you Lucy."

His look was bad enough. His touch was infinitely worse. It prickled through Lucy like the heat of the summer sun and left her feeling as light-headed as she had the time Alfie brewed a batch of his own ale and insisted she be the first to sample it.

His hands were large, his fingers long and square-tipped. Though Lucy had not forgotten the rough working clothes he'd arrived in, his hands belied the fact that he engaged in menial labor for a living. They were bruised and his knuckles were scraped, but his skin was smooth, not soft like a woman's, but well cared for. His skin was nearly as warm as the spark of devilment that flashed in his dark eyes.

Lucy's voice caught behind a knot of some unfamiliar emotion that wedged up in her throat and made her heart bang against her ribs. "It appears we've learned something else about you, James." Her voice was no steadier than the pounding of her heart, but she forced herself to raise her eyes to his. Bolstering herself against the rush of disturbing sensations, she gave him a smile that was tight enough to disguise her discomfort and cold enough to convey the outrage she couldn't help but feel.

Walking the tightrope between putting him in his place and trying not to offend him, she fought to keep her voice as light as possible. "You are, apparently, altogether shameless and used to being quite a heartbreaker, if I am not mistaken. I'm afraid in this instance, your charms are wasted."

As quickly as she could, Lucy snatched her hand away. She tucked it into the safety of her pocket, fighting for some semblance of control and something—anything—that might change the subject and save her from the heat of his penetrating gaze. She found it the minute her fingers touched Clara Miller's telegram.

"I've contacted Alfie about your case and I heard from him this morning." She wasn't sure where the idea came from, but she was grateful for it. The words tumbled out of her before she had a chance to think about them. Drawing the telegram from her pocket, she flashed it before his eyes. She tucked it back into its hiding place before he could see who it was addressed to or where it came from. "He's a bit reluctant to accept your case."

"Reluctant? You mean he won't investigate and find out who I am?" As if stung, James took a step back, and Lucy congratulated herself.

She had succeeded. At least this much. She had taken him by surprise and turned his mind back to the problem at hand—and away from her.

In less than a heartbeat, the spark of deviltry was gone from James's eye as well as from his manner. He watched her closely, struggling against an onslaught of emotion that streaked so quickly through him, Lucy might have thought it her imagination if she didn't see him clench his jaw against it.

Worry.

Desperation.

Fear.

The feelings played across his handsome face, each in turn.

He deserved every one of them, Lucy told herself, hardening her heart at the same time she turned away from his pain. He deserved a moment's worry in exchange for what he'd put her through. He deserved it for tempting her with his smoldering looks. And his fiery touch. But though Lucy liked to think of herself as being as unsentimental as she was level-headed, she couldn't let him suffer.

James was her only hope. He was Alfie's only hope. And as much as she would have liked to see him as uncomfortable as he had made her, she found she could not.

Uneasy with the thought that he might be able to read through the lies that fell so easily from her lips, she kept her back to James. "Not investigate? I didn't say that, did I? No, no. That wasn't what I meant at all. It's simply that Alfie is busy. Very busy indeed. You see, he is in . . ." Lucy's mind went blank. Her voice faltered. "He is in Lee. In Kent." It was the first place that came to mind, though she could not say why, not until she remembered "The Man with the Twisted Lip" in which Holmes traveled to Lee to look into the strange disappearance of Neville St. Clair.

"Lee?" Behind her, she heard James dismiss her flimsy excuse with a snort. "Lee cannot be more than ten miles from here. Surely Alfie might return easily enough."

In for a penny in for a pound.

It was the one clear thought in Lucy's head.

She was already in for a penny.

She might as well toss in her pound.

Whirling to face him, she threw back her shoulders and looked James in the eye, interrupting him with a disdainful lift of her chin that would have done even Mrs. Slyke proud.

"You simply don't understand the detective business," she told him. "The case Alfie is working on is . . . well . . ." Lucy lifted her shoulders in a dismissive little gesture. "The case is quite sensitive." She lowered her voice to nearly a whisper and hoped she sounded more mysterious than ridiculous. "Alfie is not free to come and go as he pleases. There are certain confidences that must be kept. Certain secrets that must be protected."

"But he is willing to take my case?"

Lucy smiled. It wasn't a friendly smile. And it certainly wasn't a flirtatious smile. She liked to think of it as her Watson smile: thoughtful, slightly detached, professional, and sympathetic. It did not offer too many promises, but then, it didn't leave the client without hope, either.

"Yes. Of course he is willing to take the case." Again she pulled the telegram from her pocket. "For now, he will direct the investigation from afar. He assures me we'll hear from him daily."

"And . . . ?"

"And?" Lucy was so busy building a structure around the framework of lies she'd constructed she hadn't thought as far as the next step. She settled on a plan in an instant. "And," she said, poking the telegram back into her pocket, "we are to begin in earnest tomorrow morning."

"But—"

She held up one hand for silence when he began to protest. "Really, James, think of how wise Alfie's advice is. In the little I was able to convey in my telegram to him, he deduced the serious nature of your injuries. He realizes the truth even if you are not willing to admit it to yourself. You are not as strong as you should be. Not if we are to be successful at our investigation. You need to rest. At least for the remainder of the day. By tomorrow, we'll hear from Alfie again. I know we will. And I trust he already has a theory about who you are and why you found yourself here."

Forcing a look of esteem and awe onto her face, Lucy glanced at the photograph of Alfie. "He is a brilliant man," she said. "One of the truly great minds of our time. He knows what he's doing."

She wished she did.

The thought snuck up on Lucy and she banished it as quickly as she could. Her framework was sagging under a structure of lies that was becoming too preposterous even for her to believe. Before James could discover as much, she marched to the far side of the room and retrieved her sewing box, effectively dismissing him. She seated herself on the divan and made a great show of threading a needle.

James may not have had much of a memory, but he was very good at taking a hint. He crossed the room and paused at the door, his hand already on the knob. "Very well. I do think I should tell you, Lucy . . ."

Her name resonated from his lips, as soft as a prayer and as compelling as poetry. Try as she might to keep her gaze on her needle and thread, Lucy looked up. She was just in time to see James smile.

Like the sun peeking out from a bank of thunderheads, it was a look that transformed his face. One that held her spellbound.

"I do remember enough about last night to know I would have ended up dead in the street if you hadn't talked me into staying here," he said, his voice as warm as his smile. "Thank you."

"You're very welcome." Lucy's hands trembled. She convinced herself it was because the light was weak and threading a needle in it was difficult. She pulled her gaze from his and concentrated on her needle.

But James wasn't done. He shuffled his feet against the worn carpet, and Lucy was forced to turn her attention to him again.

"I'm sorry about what I said." He was either a practiced liar or especially smooth at apologizing. The words flowed from his lips like warm honey and left Lucy feeling uncommonly pleased, both with herself and with him.

"Sorry?" Her voice trembled over the word. "I cannot imagine why. I—"

"I said it was hell." James looked all around, at the tidy and serviceable furnishings, the tasteful pictures positioned evenly if not artfully on the walls, and the ornaments arranged in precise order on the mantelpiece. This time when he smiled, the corner of his good eye crinkled with amusement. "That was ill-mannered beyond belief and though I may not know much about myself, I am certain I am not ill-mannered. Or insensitive. I hope you'll understand. I was tired and not thinking clearly. I was—"

"Of course." Lucy excused him with a look at the door. She had no choice. If she let him carry on much longer with his angel's voice and his devil's smile, she was very much afraid he might observe the peculiar effect he was having on her. "I'm sure I will hear from Alfie this evening as I do every evening. We'll talk later, why don't we?"

As soon as James was gone, Lucy slumped back into the thick cushions of the divan. She tossed her sewing down on the seat beside her, absently rubbing at the spot where James's hand had rested against hers.

"Now see what you've gotten me into?" She turned to glare at the photograph of her father. "This is impossible. Maybe even dangerous. I'm in over my head this time. I don't have the slightest idea what I'm doing and here I am playing at it as if I do."

But even Lucy was not sure if she was talking about the detective business.

Or about James.

# Chapter 4

"**D**amn!" James winced and threw down his razor. It landed with a clatter into the bowl set on the chest of drawers and sent up a geyser of hot water and soap bubbles that splattered the front of what he suspected was one of Albert Miller's best shirts.

"Did I hear a call of distress?"

Before James had time to recover, Harleigh Atwater stuck his head into the room. Or was it Farleigh?

"Just passing by, sir, when I heard you." Whichever of the Atwaters it was, he made himself at home easily enough. He pushed open the door and stepped into the third-floor room, examining the wreckage of soap suds and puddles with one quick look. "Having a problem, are you?"

"Yes." James didn't sound any more pleased than he looked. He scowled at himself in the mirror and dabbed at the trickle of blood that streamed down his chin. "I was trying to have a shave but . . ." He blotted the wound and peered at his misshapen face. In the two days since he'd been at the Barnstable home, the swelling had come down considerably and his bruises had gone from brilliant purple to muted green. But he still looked like something the cat dragged in from the gutter. It didn't help his face or his disposition to realize that his attempts at shaving were making things worse.

"It's damned near impossible to shave with one eye swollen," he grumbled. "My coordination is off, damn it. I think I'm shaving whiskers and I'm really slicing skin."

"Well, Farleigh Atwater can help you there, sir. You can be certain of that." Farleigh threw back his shoulders. He fished the razor out of the bowl and wiped it against a nearby towel. Glancing around, he spied a chair across the room and went to fetch it. He positioned the chair across from where James was standing and gave the high wooden back of it a good-natured pat. "Have a seat, why don't you," he said. "I'll have you as neat as ninepence in an instant."

There was something less than reassuring about the thought of Farleigh at his neck with a razor, no matter how dull it happened to be. James glanced uncertainly from the old man to the razor. "Well, I . . ." Just as reluctant to hurt Farleigh's feelings as he was to have his Adam's apple carved in two, he cleared his throat. "That is, I . . ."

"Now don't you go trying to let me off easy, sir. My bones may be old but there's a good deal of vigor left in here." Farleigh pounded his chest with one fist. "I was good enough for the best of the Fourteenth Light Horse, don't you know. Batman to Sir Digby Talbot."

"You were a batman?" James could hardly help himself. Batmen were legendary within the services. They were the personal servants of officers and, as such, had responsibility not only for the officer's saddle and horse, but his clothing and appearance as well. The thought of Farleigh as a batman brought a smile to James's face.

"Of course, he wasn't Sir Digby," Farleigh went right on, "not back at Goojerat. I say . . ." His blue eyes lit. "Have I ever told you—"

James didn't give him a chance to ask the inevitable question. Darting between Farleigh and the chest of drawers, he retrieved the razor strop and handed it to the old man. "Sir Digby's with the Foreign Office, isn't he?" The question was out of James's mouth before he had a chance to think about how he knew the information. He pulled to a stop, wondering what it meant.

"That he is." Farleigh didn't notice James's hesitation. He contentedly spanked the blade against the strop. "Has been since '78," he said. "The same year he was raised to the peerage. He was a real brick, I can tell you that much about him, sir. The best subaltern the army ever had."

"Second best."

Harleigh must have been listening at the door. He strode into the room and joined the conversation.

"Palmerston Temple. Now there was the finest lieutenant in the Fourteenth Light Horse." Harleigh clicked his heels together and offered James a quick bow from the waist. "I was his batman."

"Temple!" Farleigh sniffed with derision at the same time he steered James into the chair. He fluffed out a towel and draped it around James's neck. "Couldn't hold a candle to Sir Digby. Rose through the ranks," he added as an aside to James. "Knighted." He glanced at his brother. "Temple was never knighted."

"Temple was killed, you'll remember. At Goojerat. I say"—he glanced down at James—"have I ever told you—"

Scrambling to change the subject, James brought

up the first thing he could think of. "What you can tell me about," he said, "is Lucy."

His choice of a topic should have come as no surprise to James. He'd said the first thing that came to mind and today, like every day since he'd met her, Lucy was the first thing on his mind.

James may not have been surprised by the thought, but he was uncomfortable with it. He twitched it aside.

"Miss Barnstable?" Farleigh expertly frothed the shaving soap and lathered James's face at the same time Harleigh retrieved his jacket—or, James corrected himself, he should say Albert Miller's jacket—and began brushing it thoroughly. Farleigh passed the razor in front of James's eyes and James held his breath.

"She's a handsome woman, isn't she, sir?" Farleigh glided the razor down James's left cheek and in spite of his misgivings, James found himself relaxing. He didn't feel a thing, not even when Farleigh slipped the razor over his assortment of injuries, not the slightest pull or tug from the dull edge of Albert Miller's razor. James leaned back in the chair.

"I know it isn't proper, us discussing a young lady in such a way, sir, and I know you'll understand I mean no disrespect. But there's no denying facts." Farleigh sighed. "As the enlisted men say, sir, she is a stunner."

Across the room, Harleigh echoed his brother's sigh. "It's all that lovely dark hair of hers."

"Mmm." James agreed. Lovely, dark hair. He'd noticed it, of course. Though he could barely stand straight at the time, he'd noticed it the first time he met Lucy. And yesterday at breakfast . . .

James's eyes drifted shut. Yesterday, Lucy had all that lovely, dark hair twisted into a single braid that hung down her back. Damn, but he'd been tempted to run his hands over it when he'd talked to her in the parlor. He could imagine how it would feel, heavy and warm. Soft as silk. He could picture himself unwinding it and watching it cascade over her shoulder. He'd curl a strand of it around the tip of one finger and—

"And of course those eyes of hers." Harleigh's voice roused James from his thoughts. He flinched back to reality and Farleigh jerked his hand away.

"Careful, sir," he said, peering down into James's face. "You're likely to cause a mishap."

"Yes. Yes. Of course." Banishing the thoughts that had no business in his head in the first place, James settled back again.

"As I was saying, sir . . ." Harleigh came into his line of view. He was done brushing James's jacket and had begun to work on his boots. "It's her eyes, I think, that are the most striking. Dark eyes. And she doesn't spend time batting them at a man like some of those scatterbrained young coquettes do. You must know the kind of women I mean, sir. A soldier can't seem to help himself. He's likely to meet them now and then."

James warned himself against allowing his imagination to get the better of him again, but try as he might, it was impossible to keep the memories at bay. He thought about Lucy's eyes. They were dark, just as Harleigh said, but not nut-brown like his own perfectly ordinary eyes. Lucy's eyes were the color of autumn, brown with flecks of gold like sunlight through a canopy of October leaves.

"Of course, there are those who say she has a good deal too much intelligence for a woman," Farleigh went on, drawing James out of his thoughts as expertly as he drew the razor across James's right cheek.

"And that she hasn't learned to hide it well enough to suit them," Harleigh added.

"Oh?" James popped open one eye. "Who?"

The Atwaters exchanged knowing looks, but they didn't answer his question. Harleigh took a long look at Albert Miller's rather sparse collection of shabby ties and shook his head sadly. Farleigh rinsed the razor. He mysteriously produced a warm, damp cloth and laid it over James's face at the same time he got the conversation back on track. "She's a sensible young woman," he said, admiration evident in his voice.

"Not flighty like some," Harleigh added.

"Or eccentric."

"Head on her shoulders."

It was James's turn to sigh. For the last twenty-four hours, he'd been prudent enough to not even dare think about those shoulders, or about the delightful body they sat upon. But now that the Atwaters had brought it up, how could he help himself?

Lucy was a handsome creature, no doubt of that, even if she did seem a bit straightlaced and remarkably unimaginative for a young lady in her peculiar line of business. Thinking about her caused James's mind to drift back to the previous morning and the picture she had made standing in the parlor in her plain housedress. She looked a brown hen, no doubt of that. But James had not failed to notice the supple movement of her body beneath her simple dress and the gentle curve of her hips.

Against his better judgment, he wondered what kind of raw beauty he might find beneath her brown hen trappings. Lucy's hands were work-worn and no wonder, doing for a house full of boarders. But when he'd been so rash as to take her hand in his, it had been warm. He wondered if her cheeks would be, too. Would she blush if he stroked a finger along her jaw?

He thought about touching her, about letting his hand drift over the smooth column of her neck and down to her shoulders. About trailing his fingers even farther, across her collarbone and down to the secret and shadowy place between her breasts. He would feel her heartbeat, quick and erratic against his fingertips. He would—

"Damn!" The oath exploded out of James at the same time he ripped the cloth away from his face and bounded out of the chair.

Astounded, Farleigh blinked. "I'm so sorry, sir," he said. "Was the cloth too hot?"

"Cloth?" Battling to regain his composure, James stared down at the damp cloth in his hand. He shook away his discomfort along with his thoughts of Lucy. "No," he said, looking from the cloth to Farleigh and forcing a smile that was no more heartfelt than it was substantial. "It wasn't too hot. Not at all. I'm sorry, I—"

"No need to explain, sir. Not to me." One hand raised, Farleigh cut off his apologies. He glanced over James's shoulder toward his brother and headed for the door. "If you won't be needing us any further, sir . . ."

James reprimanded himself, not because of his errant thoughts but because he'd taken advantage of the Atwaters' good natures. What was even worse was that he hadn't had the sense to show them how much he appreciated it.

"Wait." James stopped them. Fishing into his pocket, he brought out a gold sovereign. "You must certainly let me—"

One look at the coin in James's hand and Farleigh's grizzled eyebrows climbed up his forehead. Harleigh's shoulders shot back. The Atwaters exchanged outraged looks before they trained their collective disapproval on James.

"Sir!" Harleigh's voice was nearly as rigid as his shoulders. "Since when do enlisted men accept money from officers?"

"We were doing our duty, sir," his brothers added, "as Her Majesty's' soldiers and batmen. There's certainly no need for you to—"

"No. No. Of course not." James quickly tucked the coin back into his pocket. He scrambled for something that might redeem himself and make amends.

But before he could, Harleigh came to the rescue. "Understandable, sir," he said in that tone of voice that told James that he didn't understand at all but he was willing to forgive, just as he'd forgiven countless other young officers countless other offenses before this.

"Understandable, indeed." Farleigh backed into the passageway outside of James's door. His brother followed. "You'll call us if you need us, sir?"

"Of course." It was the only answer James could give. The only one either of the Atwaters would accept.

"Fine fellow." James heard Harleigh comment as the brothers retreated down the passageway. "Even if he does forget to act like an officer now and again."

"Could be the head injury." Farleigh replied in hushed tones and glanced surreptitiously over his shoulder, a look James was not meant to see. "Been known to make men peculiar. Remember that Wilding chap at Goojerat? Struck by a Sikh bullet just above the left ear. Never was the same again. Mad as a hatter until the day he died."

James closed the door but the Atwaters' words still sounded louder than cannon shot in his ears.

"Mad as a hatter until the day he died." His own voice fell dead against the silence that surrounded him and James leaned heavily against the chest of drawers, his arms braced, his hands flat against its pitted surface.

The Atwaters had put into words the same thoughts that had haunted him since he'd woken in the filthy alley in Whitechapel with a mouth full of blood and his head filled with nowt but a pounding pain.

He might never be the same again.

"The same as what?" James looked up at the stranger's face that stared back at him from the mirror. "The same as you used to be, you bloody fool," he answered himself. "Now if only you knew who that person was."

He frowned into his own eyes.

"James." He tried the name again, as he had down in the breakfast room, and was satisfied enough with the fit of it to know it was accurate. "James." He said it again, watching his face as he did, searching his mind for the memory of some other voice speaking his name.

Was there a mother somewhere who had crooned the name to him? If there was, he had no recollection of her, no vivid mind pictures of rollicking holidays with a houseful of brothers and sisters or solitary nights at the expensive public school where he had surely acquired his proper accent and enough good taste to know that Albert Miller's clothes were a far cut below what he was used to wearing.

Was there a man somewhere who'd cursed his name? The men who beat him certainly must have, James told himself. If they knew his name at all. Was theirs a random assault? Or a well-planned ambush? He thought the latter, though he could hardly say why. He thought there was at least one man there who was a long-time enemy.

The thought caused a shiver to snake its way up James's back and over his shoulders.

"James." He gave the name another go. Was there some woman out there who had wrapped her honeyed voice around his name? He snorted at the thought. He trusted there had been at least one! But had there been a special woman? One who even now was waiting for him, worried and wondering?

He hoped not, as much for his own sake as for the woman's. He might easily have been able to forget any number of casual romances, but he didn't like to think he could ever forget the woman he loved.

Countless questions.

And no answers.

Feeling more empty than ever, James set them aside. He dismissed the things he did not know and concentrated on the things he had learned.

He was a Scotsman. He agreed with Lucy on that much. There was no mistaking the accent, no matter how expertly he managed to make his tongue maneuver its way over a suitable English equivalent.

"Very well," he muttered, his gaze still fixed to the mirror. "That's number one, then. You're a Scotsman sure enough." His mind drifted back to his conversation with the Atwaters and he added to the list. "A Scotsman who knows a thing or two about obscure battles like Goojerat and recognizes at least one name from the Foreign Office." There was one more thing he should add and reluctant as he was to do it, James knew he had to be honest with himself. No matter how vexatious it might be, it was his only hope of discovering his identity.

"You're a Scotsman who knows a thing or two about obscure battles like Goojerat and recognizes at least one name from the Foreign Office and . . ." He sucked in a breath, steeling himself against the rest of his confession. "And knows a pretty woman when you see one," he admitted, his thoughts traveling back to Lucy.

Eager to get rid of the picture of her that formed in his head, James closed his eyes and forced himself to breathe deeply. He let the breath out slowly and took in another, allowing his mind to drift.

"Damn," he grumbled, his eyes popping open. It was no wonder he spent his waking hours thinking about Lucy. There wasn't another damned thing in his head that made the least bit of sense.

There was nothing left of his past, nothing but a void so great, it seemed he needed to fill it with idle and inappropriate thoughts of a woman who was clearly not interested. A woman he could not afford to offend.

The thought sobered James but it offered little comfort, and hoping to banish it, he did a turn around the room. He stopped long enough at the window at the far end of it to nudge aside the faded draperies and stare out at the fog that clung to the city, a mist as thickset as the disturbing thoughts that had taken up residence inside his head.

His fate and any hope he might have of discovering his identity rested in the hands of Alfie and Lucy Barnstable, he reminded himself. People he didn't know. And though he had no recollection of his life prior to his arrival on the Barnstable doorstep, he knew one thing about himself instinctively: there were few people—even ones he knew—whom he trusted.

It was an ugly thought, and traitorous in light of

all Lucy had done for him, but there it was. No matter how hard he tried to tell himself to set aside his doubts, he found that he could not. There was something scratching at the back of his mind. Something that told him to watch his tongue and guard his actions. Something that warned him to take things slowly, and to be discreet, and thoughtful, and very, very careful.

Perhaps that's why he hadn't shown Lucy the seal.

Reaching into the pocket of his trousers, James took out the object and held it toward the window for a better look.

He'd known what the small stone carving was the minute he found it in his pocket and that in itself made him wonder. It wasn't every man who would know an ancient Indian artifact when he saw one.

"But what does it mean?"

The silence that met James's question mocked him. He turned the seal over in his hands, running his fingers over the intricate carving. Was he a history professor or an archaeologist? Or perhaps he was the reincarnation of some great maharajah?

James's cynical chuckle broke the silence, and shaking his head, he tucked the seal back into the safety of his pocket.

Why he was in possession of something so ancient was as much of a mystery as who he was, and he was convinced that finding the answer to one would lead to the answer to the other.

And there was only one way to begin.

His fingers still aching and not at all as cooperative as he would have liked, he struggled to knot one of Albert Miller's ties around his neck. The result was not perfect, but it would have to do. Grabbing his jacket, James went in search of Lucy.

\* \* \*

"I told you to leave and never come back."

Just when James had given up all hope of finding Lucy, he heard her voice in the back garden. Torn between curiosity and courtesy, he paused on the crumbling stone path that connected the back of the Barnstable property with the house. He craned his neck, trying to look as if he was not eavesdropping; at the same time he did his best to see through an overgrown tangle of newly sprouting rosebushes and a brittle curtain of last year's morning glory vines.

Miss Foxworthy was the one who'd suggested to James that he might find Lucy outside. But the old woman had neglected to mention that Lucy was with someone. And from the sound of it, it was someone she wasn't happy to see.

"I said out!" Even through the blanket of morning fog, Lucy's voice rang with displeasure and from up ahead, James saw a flash of color as she darted across the path. The next second he heard a muffled thwack and a shriek that sounded for all the world like Lucy had had the wind knocked out of her.

Courtesy be damned!

His head down, James pushed through the rose-bushes and stopped at the edge of an open space no bigger than the Barnstable parlor where he found Lucy sprawled in the center of the grass.

She wasn't hurt. James could tell that in an instant. She'd taken a spill on the dewy grass and it was obvious from the string of invectives that fell from her lips that the moisture had not damped her temper.

Too furious to notice James, Lucy braced herself against the broom she held in one hand and pulled herself to her feet, her brown housedress gathered around her ankles.

They were remarkably attractive ankles.

The thought was completely inappropriate, but that didn't stop James from having it. Keeping to the shelter of the concealing undergrowth, he gave himself to the appreciation of Lucy's ankles. Even though they were encased in thick, black stockings, they looked delicate and slim. So did her shins when she raised her dress enough that he caught a glimpse of them. And her knees.

Another, even more inappropriate thought flitted through James's head and it was just as well that Lucy decided at that moment to fluff her skirts back into place. It saved him the trouble of choosing between banishing the thought or simply enjoying it. Before James could do either, Lucy raised the broom over her head and dashed into a tiny brick outbuilding that looked to be a sort of garden shed.

In an instant, she was back out again, waving her broom, hot in pursuit of a large and quite brutish-looking rooster. "Out! Out! Out!"

James controlled a chuckle that threatened to betray him. Keeping to the far side of the clearing, he nursed a fresh scratch on his knuckles caused by a rose bush, and watched the battle, his mood improving even as the fight between Lucy and the rooster escalated.

"Off with you!" Lucy waved the broom, shooing the black-breasted rooster toward the stone wall that separated the Barnstable property from the house next door. But the plucky bird would only go so far. He planted himself on the ground next to the wall and glared up at Lucy, his dark eyes shining with defiance.

"So that's the way it is to be, is it?" Lucy tossed down her broom and made a grab for the bird. She wasn't nearly fast enough. In a shower of feathers, the rooster fluttered over her and Lucy found herself empty-handed.

She grumbled a word a lady never should have used.

James smiled.

Her hands on her hips, Lucy turned on the bird. Sometime during the skirmish, the pins had come loose from the tight knot of hair at the back of her head. A long strand of dark hair hung over her shoulder. Another one floated before her eyes. She puffed her cheeks and pursed her lips and blew the curl away.

Her lips were even more appealing than her ankles.

His imagination was running as wild as the rooster and James reined it in, too engrossed to dare miss Lucy's next move.

She did just as James expected her to do. She made another grab at the rooster. Unfortunately, the rooster expected it, too. He flapped around her in a wide arc and settled at her feet.

Lucy glared at the bird. The bird glared back.

But it seemed that roosters, like too many human males, were not good judges of female character. The rooster thought he was out of Lucy's reach and, thus, safe from being caught. James might have thought the same.

If he hadn't seen Lucy smile.

It was a smile he recognized, though he could not have said from where. But he was glad to know it when he saw it, and he was sure that his ability to recognize it had stood him in good stead a time or two. It was an utterly female smile, all sweetness and understanding, and it could only mean one thing: She was up to something.

As if to prove his theory, Lucy flicked her wrists

and raised her gown, trapping the rooster beneath her wide skirts. Her mission successfully accomplished, she smiled broadly.

"Good show!" James could no longer control himself. Applauding, he stepped forward. "A formidable opponent, but it looks as if you've vanquished him."

Surprise shot into Lucy's face and drained the color from it. She recovered quickly enough. "You might have helped," she said and bent to retrieve the rooster. It was then she realized she couldn't easily get at it without lifting her skirts and taking the chance of its escape.

James saw her predicament and always the gentleman, or so he liked to think, he offered assistance. "I could help now," he said. Crossing the clearing in three strides, he dropped to one knee in front of Lucy. He glanced up and gave her a smile. He wasn't at all sure where he'd learned such a smile or how many times he'd used it to equally satisfying results, but it must have been as devilish as he intended. Lucy blushed mightily.

James raised his eyebrows at the same time he made to raise Lucy's skirts. "May I?" he asked.

Lucy was trapped as effectively as was the rooster. She lifted her chin and looked away, eager to hide her mortification. "Please," she said through clenched teeth.

James lifted her skirt a fraction of an inch. He should have known the rooster would not accept imprisonment readily, not even imprisonment in so interesting a place. He had no chance to see any more than the tips of Lucy's shoes before the bird lashed out and pecked his hand.

"Damn!" James dropped Lucy's skirt and sucked at the wound, but he wasn't about to give up. Firmly ignoring the cheery giggle that escaped Lucy, he set his jaw and tried again. This time, he raised her skirt higher.

And was rewarded for his efforts.

Her ankles were as slender as he'd thought, delightful in their dark covering. Her legs looked longer than he'd expected and—

"Devil take it!" James bellowed when this time, the rooster drew blood—right before it flapped out from beneath Lucy's skirt. Startled out of his pleasant thoughts, James went down on the seat of his pants.

It was bad enough listening to Lucy chuckle, but even the damned bird thought the whole thing funny. It stood not two feet from James, its long neck straight, its elegant head high, its wattles trembling with the equivalent of rooster laughter.

While James and the bird were busy glowering at each other, Lucy reached down and scooped the bird up under her arm.

"Got you!" It flapped its wings and did its best to escape, but she held it tight and looked down at James. "It seems you're the one who needs help now," she said, and offered him a hand up.

He pretended not to notice. His pride hurting nearly as much as his backside, he climbed to his feet and brushed off the seat of his pants, eyeing the rooster carefully. "Is he always so disagreeable?"

The excitement of the chase still gleaming in her eyes, Lucy looked at the rooster. "Always," she assured him. "This is Hercules. He belongs to the Blighs." She glanced briefly toward the nondescript house next door before she tipped her head toward the tiny brick outbuilding on the Barnstable property. "Alfie used to keep chickens in there, you see, and . . ." Try as she might to contain a wicked smile, Lucy could not. Her eyes sparkled. "Well," she said, "hope springs eternal. The chickens have been gone for a good long while, but Hercules hasn't given up."

"Persistent devil, eh?" It suddenly occurred to James that he and Hercules had a good deal in common. He took a step closer to Lucy and was driven back again by a nasty look from the rooster. He thought it expedient to change the subject. "You remind me of Sherlock Holmes," he said, glancing from Lucy to Hercules, "in the story of the blue carbuncle. Detective and . . ." He chose his words carefully, eager to keep in Hercules's good graces. "Detective and fowl."

Lucy's dark brows rose. "You read Sherlock Holmes?"

"Well, I suppose I must have at one time or another," he admitted, though he couldn't remember ever doing it. "But it wasn't a rooster in the story, was it? It was a goose."

"It was stuff and nonsense. That's what it was." Spinning toward the waist-high wall, Lucy tossed Hercules over the top and watched him disappear toward home in a flurry of feathers and outraged squawks. She brushed her hands together. "Stuff and nonsense," she said again, louder this time, in case James had not heard her properly. "Blue carbuncles and red-headed leagues. Speckled bands and twisted lips. It's romantic nonsense. That's what it is."

"And you don't believe in romantic nonsense?" He supposed it was cruel to tease her so, but now that Hercules was gone, James felt uncommonly brave. There was a single one of Hercules's feathers snagged in the lock of hair that caressed Lucy's shoulder, and carefully he slid it out. He smoothed the feather over her cheek.

Automatically, Lucy's eyes drifted shut and a

shiver ran through her. She caught her breath, her breasts straining against her brown dress.

James knew he was acting just as intuitively. The burning in his blood. The pounding in his chest. The rush of desire that pooled in his gut. They must all be nothing more than instinctive, surely, yet each felt so right at the same time the whole encounter seemed so deliciously irrational. He leaned nearer. "Which part is it you have a problem with?" he murmured. "The nonsense? Or the romance?"

He had been a fool to speak. His words broke the spell. As if remembering herself, Lucy opened her eyes and took a step back. As soon as he was done cursing himself for spoiling the moment, James wondered if she was so virtuous as to object to his advances, or if perhaps she was not nearly as bewitched by the moment as he had been. Either way, he was left with nothing but a feather and a scathing look from Lucy that would have put Hercules to shame.

"Both," Lucy said, her voice as tight as the way she curled her fingers into her palms. "I don't appreciate foolish whims any more than I appreciate the fact that Dr. Doyle makes the detective business seem so . . . so . . ." Lucy's eyes flashed. There was something more than merely outrage there. James could sense it though he could not say how. He could feel it in the unspoken words that trembled on the air between them.

Lucy drew in a ragged breath. "He makes it look so easy," she finally said. "As if it were all nothing more than a game. A game that anyone can play, even a man with no more knowledge of what he was getting into than—"

She arrested the remainder of what she was going to say, her cheeks suddenly as pasty as they had been flushed only a moment before. Collecting herself, she gathered her skirts in one hand and headed for the house.

"Wait!" James grabbed her arm to hold her in place. "I didn't mean to offend you. I thought we were to begin our investigation today, that's all. If you'd rather not . . ."

Though she did it politely enough, Lucy was sure to remove her arm from his grasp. She raised her chin and met his eyes. "Of course. Our investigation. It's time we got started. I'm ready anytime you are."

# Chapter 5

Lucy wasn't ready.

She wasn't sure she ever would be.

Standing in her bedchamber, she glowered at herself in her looking glass and tucked the last of her hairpins back where they belonged. She pivoted, glancing over her shoulder to be sure the back of her hair was presentable.

"Of course you're ready," she told herself. "You have to be. You haven't any choice." She swiveled back the other way, sucked in a breath and squared her shoulders, giving her reflection the kind of no-nonsense look she had always reserved for use on Alfie.

It was unwavering. Determined. Decisive.

And it worked no better on herself than it ever had on Alfie.

Lucy's shoulders slumped and the air rushed out of her lungs. In the face of her decision to carry through not only with convincing James that she was a proper detective but in actually conducting an investigation, she couldn't help be worried.

She wasn't a detective. No one really was. Detectives were the figments of writers' frenzied imaginations. They were no more real than dragons. Or fairies.

"Or mysterious strangers who appear out of nowhere and bring excitement and romance into a woman's life." The words were out of Lucy's mouth before she could stop them, and she scolded herself for being uncharacteristically fanciful at the same time she congratulated herself for recognizing that while she might say the words, she knew better than to believe them.

No matter what Alfie said or how he tried to live his life, she knew there was no excitement and romance in the real world. There couldn't be. Where would logic stand in the face of such foolishness? Who would look after the day-to-day obligations of life if everyone's head was in the clouds?

No. Lucy was sure of it. There was no more romance in a life such as hers than there were real detectives. Years of living with Alfie had proved as much. There were no pirates, though Alfie claimed there were. There were and never would be flying machines, though he had tried to make her believe in those as well. There was no Sherlock Holmes.

She had never had to remind herself of such indisputable facts before and she wondered why she did now.

"I don't know what's wrong with you, Lucy Barnstable," she said. She reached for her straw boater and settled it on her head, all the while glaring at her reflection. "You were never so whimsical before. You've always been sensible. And logical. The most clear-thinking woman in London. That's what Alfie used to call you. And that's what you are."

The words sounded confident, but they weren't nearly as reassuring as she would have liked. Lucy was grateful she was alone. At least she didn't have to convince anyone else of the merits of her argument. She was enough of a realist to admit it. She couldn't even convince herself.

"You *were* the most clear-thinking woman in London," she grumbled. "Before James landed on your doorstep."

Reluctant to acknowledge the blush that crept into her face, Lucy secured her hat in place with a foot-long hat pin and turned from the mirror.

The moment she was out of the garden and away from James, she had promised herself to put the encounter with him well and truly behind her. She still meant to do it. And she would, she vowed. Just as soon as the rugged burr in his voice stopped causing shivers to ripple up her spine. And the disturbing nearness of him stopped throwing her usually well-ordered thoughts into a whirl. And the memory of his touch stopped burning through her blood.

Despite her best intentions, Lucy couldn't keep herself from bringing her hand to her cheek. Slowly, she followed the path James had laid. She had never dreamed that so brief a contact could set her head reeling or that any man's touch could quicken her heart and make her knees weak. Yet James had accomplished all. With little more than a feather.

Disgusted at her own lack of willpower, Lucy clenched her teeth, fighting against the sensations that skittered up her back and sent her heart racing.

"It might be easier to think yourself a detective if only you'd start acting like one," she told herself in no uncertain terms. "And stop acting like a fool."

Brave words.

If only she could persuade herself to believe them.

With one last glance in the mirror, Lucy slipped a dark jacket over her white blouse. But try as she might to avoid looking into her own eyes, she found she could not. She was too honest to let the truth go unspoken.

"You're not a detective," she told herself, her voice

dipping along with her spirits. "You're not a detective now and you never will be one, and here you are playacting at it as if you were. You wouldn't know how to be a detective if your life depended on it."

She stared at herself a moment longer, and the inescapable truth of her own words chilled her soul.

Her life didn't depend on her being a detective.

Alfie's did.

Without another thought for either the folly of her actions or the consequences, Lucy headed downstairs to begin her investigation.

Whatever else James knew—or didn't know—he certainly knew London.

Though reluctant to spend the money, Lucy had ordered a hansom cab to collect them at the house. A growler would have been cheaper, of course. But the lumbering four-wheeled growlers were less comfortable and far less fashionable than the smart and quick hansoms. It wasn't much of a reason to spend the extra money, but if there was one thing Lucy had learned from reading Doyle, it was that Sherlock Holmes always traveled by hansom. It must have been the proper thing for a detective to do.

Because the hansom driver sat in back and above his passengers, they were afforded a clear view of the road, and James took full advantage of it. As they inched through the abominable traffic, he was quick to point out landmarks and comment on points of interest both familiar and obscure.

How he knew so much about the great city was as much of a mystery as who he was, but Lucy didn't bother to question it. James did not spring fully formed on her doorstep. She knew that well enough. He had to have come from somewhere. And wher-

ever that somewhere was, whatever had happened
to him along the way, it seemed it had taken him
straight through the heart of London.

As if to prove her theory, no sooner had they
turned from Oxford Street onto Gower and from
there to Great Russell Street than James knew exactly
where they were headed.

"The British Museum?" He gave her a sidelong
glance, his gaze sliding from Lucy to the imposing
neoclassical building. His eyes narrowed and she
wondered if it was with suspicion or curiosity.
"Why?"

He was bound to ask. Lucy expected it. For once,
she was ready with an answer. "It was Alfie's suggestion," Lucy said, smoothing one gloved hand over
her black, close-fitting skirt. "I heard from him again
this morning. He has a number of theories, of course.
A great detective such as he . . ."

Though it occurred to Lucy that Alfie didn't have
a humble bone in his body and that he never would
have stopped in the middle of such shameless praise,
she felt it was her duty to temper the statement with
the right amount of humility. She brushed away the
remainder of her words with the wave of one hand.

"Alfie thought, perhaps, a visit to the museum
might prove fruitful to our investigation," she said.
"Apparently, there are certain items of . . ." She
paused. "Certain items of interest . . ." She nodded,
satisfied at her choice of words. "He'd like us to take
a look."

"And what items are those?"

Damn him for being so curious!

The oath rumbled through Lucy's head. She had
planned to whisk James into the Indian Gallery before he could even begin to suspect her purpose. She
was hoping to catch him off guard, so that she might

gauge his reaction when she showed him the gleaming glass-fronted case of stone seals.

She might have known he wasn't the type of man who'd let himself be led around, not even if he knew where he was going, why he was going there, and what, exactly, was expected of him when he got there.

Stalling for time, Lucy watched carefully as they pulled to the end of a line of cabs waiting to allow their passengers to alight. She kept her voice even and her gaze focused on the museum—and away from James. She didn't dare give herself away. Not yet. She did all she could to keep from glancing toward the pocket of his trousers, but she couldn't stop herself from wondering if he had his seal with him.

The thought crossed Lucy's mind at the same time her own hand stole into the pocket of her skirt. Just as it always was, Alfie's seal was there. It felt warm to her touch and heavy with the weight of its secrets.

"Alfie suggested we might take a look at the Indian Galleries." She hated to give even this much ground but she knew he would never be satisfied with less. There was some consolation in reminding herself that he would have found out soon enough at any rate, as soon as they went inside and she led him up the broad stairway to the upper floor.

As nonchalantly as she could, Lucy glanced at James, measuring his reaction to the news.

He didn't return the look. His eyes half-closed, he sat very still, his forearms resting on the waist-high half door of the hansom, his long legs cramped by the close quarters, and if he was surprised either by their destination or by the reasons she offered, he didn't show it.

After what seemed too long a moment, he glanced

her way, the look both cursory and searching, casual and earnest. "You never cease to amaze me, Lucy. Are you telling me that in addition to your talents as a detective, you are also a collector of Indian antiquities?"

The question was innocent enough. As innocent as the look he gave her. But he had hit dangerously close to the mark. Lucy squirmed in her seat.

She couldn't admit to her ultimate sin. She wasn't about to let him know she'd seen his seal. If she did, it would mean confessing that she'd' gone through his pockets while he lay unconscious on her parlor floor. Besides, she didn't want James to know about her seal. Not until he explained how he'd come by its twin.

"Me? A collector?" Flustered, she forced a laugh and pressed one hand to her heart. "I assure you, I know nothing about India or its antiquities," she said, and though she tried to stop herself from prattling on like a jobbernowl, she could not seem to keep the words from tumbling from her mouth. "I haven't even been here to the museum for years and years. I wouldn't be here today if not for Alfie's advice. You seem to know so much about London, you may have to help me out. I'm not sure I'll even be able to find my way to the Indian Gallery."

Lucy wasn't sure what was worse: the lie itself or the fact that he might actually believe her to be as inept as she was trying to make herself out to be.

She was spared from finding out. The cab pulled to a full stop, and anxious to escape, Lucy pushed against the door and hurried out. She was already paying the cabman when James scrambled out of his seat, and she was on her way into the building by the time he caught her up.

Though she had never visited the British Museum

before Alfie's disappearance, by now, the cavernous building was as familiar to Lucy as her own home. In the days since her discovery of the stone seal in her father's desk, she had haunted the Indian Galleries too many times to count. She knew every statue of every deity by name, every carving by sight, as if they were old friends.

Still, she paused at the top of the stairway and glanced around, trying her best to look a little lost. "Alfie said the exhibit was around here somewhere," she mumbled just loud enough for James to hear. A reverent silence stilled the air and Lucy automatically lowered her voice to a whisper. "Ah, there!" She pointed to a passageway straight ahead. "That looks Indian, doesn't it?"

Before James had a chance to answer, they heard a voice behind them.

"Miss Barnstable?"

Lucy froze in place. This was the last thing she needed. Someone who knew her.

"Miss Barnstable, it is you, isn't it? How lovely to see you again! It's me, Ardath Meerchum."

Lucy let go a long, ragged breath. All was not lost, she told herself. Not yet. If she chose her words carefully, James would never have to know that Miss Meerchum was the woman Lucy liked to think of as her Museum Friend.

This was, after all, the place where she'd first met Miss Meerchum, and although she did not seem at all the type whose tastes would favor the ancient or the exotic, each time Lucy came to the Indian Galleries, she found Miss Meerchum already there. She could picture her now as she'd seen her the first time, her long, thin nose pressed to the glass case where the stone seals were displayed, her eyes behind her wire-rimmed spectacles round with the wonder of it all, eager and breathless to catch every detail.

It was a tactical error not to anticipate that she would be here today, but Lucy had to make the best of it. She had no other choice. Pasting a smile to her face, she turned.

Ardath Meerchum was far taller than Lucy and terribly thin. As always, she was swathed in black from head to toe. The effect was rather startling, not unlike seeing a long-legged waterbird dressed in a nun's habit. Behind her spectacles, her eyes were colorless. So was her face. Although she couldn't have been more than a year or two older than Lucy, her mouse-colored hair was streaked with gray. It was parted in the middle and pinched into a severe bun at the back of her head.

Despite her painfully plain appearance and the fact that she was rather too inclined to tell stories about her aged father and the three cats she lived with, Miss Meerchum was pleasant enough. The first time Lucy had come across her in the galleries, they had traded polite greetings. The second time, they spoke a few friendly words. By the third and the fourth times they happened upon each other, they realized they had a great many interests in common, not the least of which was the study of Indian antiquities.

Together, they had spent hours poring over the exhibits, and once or twice they had shared tea afterward in the small shop across from the museum's main entrance.

"Ah, Miss Barnstable. It is you!" Clutching her handbag to her chest, Miss Meerchum beamed her watery smile at Lucy. She turned to James, but couldn't quite get up enough nerve to meet his eyes. Instead, she kept her gaze focused on his shoes. "This must be—"

"This is Mr. James." Hoping to put an end to the meeting before Miss Meerchum could give away the fact that she was, indeed, a frequent visitor to the museum, Lucy supplied a hasty introduction. "He's a new boarder at my home and he was kind enough to accompany me here today."

James shook Miss Meerchum's hand. Miss Meerchum smiled down at the floor. "I'm pleased to meet you, Mr. James. Has Miss Barnstable shown you—"

"We've only just walked in." For once, Lucy was glad that Miss Meerchum was so timid as to be afraid of her own shadow. She hoped it meant Miss Meerchum would take no notice of her rudeness. "As a matter of fact, we were just on our way into the Indian Galleries. Perhaps we'll see you another time."

"Yes. Of course." Miss Meerchum might be timid, but unfortunately, she was not insensitive to the fact that Lucy couldn't wait to be rid of her. She blinked, not unlike a nocturnal animal caught in the glare of a light, and tried her best to hide her hurt.

Her best wasn't good enough. Miss Meerchum's eyes filled with tears. Her lower lip quivered.

A wave of guilt spread through Lucy and she promised herself she would make up for her thoughtlessness. She swore she'd pay for the next round of tea and biscuits. She promised that the next time they were together, she would allow Miss Meerchum all the time she wanted to gaze longingly at the incredibly intricate Indian jewelry that so interested her. She vowed to never again complain about listening to Miss Meerchum's cat stories. ·

None of it made Lucy feel any better.

"We really have to be on our way." Lucy curbed her remorse. Determined to make a hasty retreat, she slipped her arm through James's. He didn't' seem at all put out by the intimacy of the gesture—damn him. In fact, he seemed uncommonly pleased. He drew her closer and gave her hand a pat.

Lucy clenched her teeth around the smile she sent James's way. She softened it considerably when she turned back to her friend. "Good day, Miss Meerchum," she said.

Miss Meerchum sniffed. "Good day to you, Miss Barnstable. And you, Mr. James."

Miss Meerchum turned to head into the room where the sculptures were displayed, and Lucy found herself relaxing. Her relief didn't last long. Before she even had time to extricate her arm from James's, Miss Meerchum turned back to them. The light of the gas jets on the walls reflected against Miss Meerchum's eyeglasses. The light winked and spluttered. It glinted and gleamed. For a fleeting moment, Lucy had the impression that Miss Meerchum's eyes were shooting sparks.

As quickly as it came, the image was gone. Miss Meerchum turned just enough to give James a quick look and the fire went out of her eyes. She was the same Miss Meerchum she'd always been, quiet and kind and very considerate, even in the face of Lucy's ill-mannered treatment. "Do have Miss Barnstable show you the stone seals," Miss Meerchum said. "She knows ever so much about them."

"Does she?" James's eyebrows rose. He watched Miss Meerchum walk away before he turned a shrewd look on Lucy. Was it amusement that glittered in his dark eyes? Or suspicion? Whatever the emotion, he hid it quickly enough, slipping a veneer of light sarcasm over his words as easily as some men shrugged into their morning coats. "And here I thought you hadn't been to the museum in years and years."

Lucy did her best to control her reaction, but she was afraid it came out sounding very much like a "harumph." She frowned. "I thought your memory was bad."

He turned his smile up a notch. "Only my memory of everything that happened before I met you."

Lucy wasn't at all pleased with the subtle change of subject. Or with the smile. Both made her feel exactly as she'd felt in the garden earlier that morning. A little light-headed. And out of breath. And while both sensations might be intriguing in their own, curious way, neither was the least bit comfortable.

She untangled her arm from James's and stepped back. "Just because a person has knowledge of a certain subject does not mean that person is a frequent visitor to the museum," she told him.

"You have knowledge of Indian stone seals. A rather esoteric pastime, don't you think?" He looked at her knowingly but he didn't volunteer any information about his own seal. "It must be especially frustrating to have such an interest and not visit the museum for years and years."

"Years and years." Lucy offered him a tight smile.

"Years and years," James confirmed.

She might even have been willing to think he believed it if one of the guards didn't happen by.

"Good morning, Miss Barnstable," he said with a tip of his hat. "Good to see you again."

His lips pursed, James watched the man disappear down the passageway. "Years and years," he said, almost to himself. He turned to her, an exasperating little smile tickling the corners of his mouth. "You must have been a remarkable child to have changed so little."

He was irritating and he didn't deserve an answer.

Instead of giving him one, Lucy hurried along. James followed readily enough, past row upon row of glass-fronted cases filled to overflowing with jewelry and pottery, fertility figures and stone statues, and breathtaking objects cast from solid gold.

Though it was Wednesday and there was no charge for admission to the museum, Lucy imagined that most of the patrons were downstairs, admiring the Elgin Marbles or gathered around the Rosetta Stone. The galleries on the upper floor were nearly empty. The swish of Lucy's skirts provided a muffled accompaniment to the echo of their footsteps against the marble floor. Along the walls to either side of them, gas jets hissed and sizzled, their light throwing odd shadows across their path.

Once or twice, Lucy dared to glance at James out of the corner of her eye. The flickering light cast shadows like dark fingers over his face and made his hair look as if it had been poured from liquid onyx. The odd combination of light and darkness made it impossible to try to read the emotion in his eyes, and not for the first time since she'd met him, Lucy wished she could conjure up the talent to read his mind.

Had James reacted when Miss Meerchum mentioned the seals? Lucy didn't think so but then, what did she want? She was enough of a pragmatist not to expect an out-and-out admission. She had no delusions, no fantasies that he would produce the seal from his pocket with a flourish and explain to her, chapter and verse, what exactly it meant and what connection it had to the one she'd found in Alfie's desk. But she had hoped for at least some reaction. A sharp intake of breath. A muffled word of astonishment. A hand pressed, aghast, to his mouth.

She had been reading far too many Sherlock Holmes stories.

Lucy faced the dispiriting consequences of her runaway imagination.

She might have known that James was not the kind of man to betray his emotions. Or his secrets. She would never surprise the truth out of him, or deceive him into betraying it. Her only hope lay in waiting for him to reveal it. Or in uncovering it herself.

The glass-fronted case full of seals came into view, and Lucy paused. James stopped at her side and assessed the display with one keen look. "I know you'll think me impertinent," he said, "and I know you'll remind me that your father, the great detective, is far more experienced than either of us and that he obviously knows what he's doing. But as fascinating as all this is, I have to remind you that we are supposed to be investigating. I don't think a room full of musty antiquities holds any clues to my identity."

"Don't you?"

It was a challenge of sorts, as much of one as she was willing to risk so early in the game. Lucy knew it. She was not used to speaking so openly, or so indiscreetly, and she did it now only because she felt she had to. He had learned more than she wanted him to know. Well, it was her turn. Could she flush him out? Would he admit to owning the seal? And if he didn't?"

Her stomach knotting, she braced herself for James's response.

"I do love cat and mouse." There was no mistaking the subtle note of danger that suddenly edged James's voice. He took a step forward, closing the distance between them, and though he was close enough to rest his hand on her arm, his face was still lost in shadow. She could see no more of him than the glimmer of his eyes and a smile that was not the least bit warm and not at all friendly.

James's fingers closed over her arm, burning Lucy's flesh even through her black jacket. Before she had time to react, she found herself close enough to catch the scent of the good, plain soap she'd given him.

"I suppose you think my love of wordplay tells you something about me," James said. "You'll say I must be a barrister. Or a vicar, speculating as to the sins of his congregation and watching in rapt fascination as they try to deceive him into thinking they're saints instead. I would say you're wrong, dear Lucy. I think, rather, that I have a perverse sense of humor and a certain delight in puzzles and politics. I enjoy fencing with words rather the way I enjoy a good game of chess. But I suggest you learn the game before you try to play it."

Lucy refused to retreat. At least not yet.

"I don't know what you're talking about," she said. "I am merely following my father's orders. He told me to bring you to the Indian Galleries of the British Museum, so that is where I've brought you. I don't know—"

"Well, bless my soul, and isn't it good to see you again!"

Lucy's shoulders sagged. James grumbled a curse. He removed his hand from her arm and stepped away. "For a woman who hasn't been near this place in years, it's amazing how many friends you have."

Together, they whirled to look at the guard who was beaming at them in turn.

No. Lucy amended the thought. He was not beaming at *them*.

He was beaming at James!

The guard was a heavyset man with a nearly bald

head and a face as round and red as pomegranates. He stepped forward and pumped James's hand. "I was beginning to worry about you, sir. And for good cause, by the looks of you. Gor blimey and if you don't look like you been to an Irish wedding! Look at them bruises! And a mouse!" Examining James's eye, he let go a long, low whistle and shook his head.

"Not that it's any of my business, sir, but a bloke can't help but worry when a fellow says he'll be around to pick up something important and then don't appear for days and days and don't send no word or nothing." He stopped only long enough to catch his breath.

"Lord lumme, but I do swear," he said, "it's good to see you again, Mr. Smith!"

# Chapter 6

"Smith. James Smith."

Not for the first time, James tried the name aloud. But no matter how many times he said it, it simply didn't sound right. It sounded . . .

He grumbled, searching for the right word.

"Foreign," he said. "It sounds foreign."

"Don't be ridiculous." Sitting at his side in the hansom cab, Lucy adjusted her skirt. "It sounds like the most English name in all the world."

"But I'm not English," James reminded her. His voice was edged with resentment. He didn't quite understand it, no more than he understood his strange reaction to the name, but he wasn't about to argue with it. The emotion was too powerful to deny. "I'm Scottish. You said so yourself."

Though she was usually the most logical of creatures, Lucy was beyond listening. She was too pleased with herself, and had been since they'd left the museum.

Smug and serene, her eyes bright and her face glowing with the thrill of success, she laughed. The sound was as enchanting as church bells though James would have been hard-pressed to admit it. He was too worried, though he couldn't say about what, and Lucy's cheery nonchalance wasn't helping matters.

"All right then," she conceded. "Not the most English name in all the world. The most British. It isn't foreign-sounding at all. James Smith. As British as the Union Jack."

James wished he could be so certain. He wanted to believe it, of course. More than he'd ever wanted to believe anything in his life, he wanted to believe he'd found a name for the face that stared back at him from the mirror. But . . .

"But it doesn't feel right." Ill at ease, he shifted in his seat. "We found the answer to our mystery nearly before we started looking. It seems awfully simple, doesn't it?"

"Elementary," Lucy corrected him. The quip was amusing enough, but James didn't rise to it. He had a queer feeling down deep in his stomach, the kind of peculiar sensation that told him something wasn't quite right.

Uneasy at the thought, James turned over the parcel he was holding and examined it from every side. The affable guard—whose name, it turned out, was Horace Peck—had fetched it from a back room where, apparently, it had been stored for some time, waiting for James's arrival.

The moment Peck handed it to him, James had been half-inclined to tear into it, the way Lucy wanted him to. But he'd refrained. Though he wasn't sure why, he suspected it was the kind of thing that was best dealt with in private.

The package was wrapped in brown paper and secured with ordinary twine. The name "James Smith" was written across it in a hand that was literate and precise. That in itself led James to believe that Peck was not the one who'd prepared the package. The man's own admission confirmed his theory.

"Can't rightly say who left it for you, sir," Peck

said, scratching one finger behind his ear. "But there it was. Just like you told me it would be. Sitting right over there on the floor." He pointed to a spot across the room. "One minute it wasn't there. I turned my back and the next thing I knowed, there it was. Right there behind that statue of that there god, Vishnu. That's where I found it. Just like you said I would last time you was here at the museum."

"Last time?" James's ears pricked. Finally, he'd found someone who knew something about him, someone who had at least some knowledge of where he'd been and what he'd been doing before the night he'd come to his senses and found himself bruised and bloodied on Lucy's parlor rug. He fought to control the rise of excitement in his voice. "When was the last time I was here?"

Peck had the good manners not to look dubious about the odd question. He scrubbed a finger along his top lip. "Can't rightly say. On account of because me and the missus, we've been right busy, what with her old dad up and dying on us the way he done. And her mum's been no help, I can tell you that much. The old dragon, she—" Remembering himself, Peck sniffed aside his observations.

"That was well on to a fortnight ago," he said, getting his story back on track. "And it seems to me . . ." He paused, thinking very hard. "That's right. That's it. You stopped in the very day afore the old fellow shuffled off the mortal coil, as they say. Told me about the parcel, you did. And dropped me a right proper sovereign to keep it for you. Mighty generous of you, sir. Me and the missus, we had ourselves a special dinner after the funeral, thanks to you. But I'm getting away from my story again. You stopped in that morning. You remember, sir. You must, because it was raining trams and omnibuses that day and you was telling me—"

"How hard it was to find a cab in the rain." James answered without thinking, the memory flowing through him effortlessly. He listened to the echo of his own words die away and his blood surged and his heart beat a lively two-step inside his chest.

Lucy caught the significance of his words instantly. Her head snapped up and she stared at him, eager for more.

"I was wearing my new black overcoat," James said. As if it might disappear if he charged in flat out, he waded through the memory carefully. Like the pictures in a dream, the images were hazy. He concentrated on them, letting them ebb and flow, watching them coalesce into something that was nearly tangible. "Not the coat I was wearing when I arrived at your house," he told Lucy. "I had my umbrella when I walked out of the hotel but—"

Peck laughed and slapped his knee. "Can't tell you how many times I told the missus that story, sir! Imagine, you giving your umbrella away like that! You said as how you walked out of your hotel and there was a young lady getting all drenched. Her hat was soaked and her hair was all dripping."

"She was crying." James remembered now. As clearly as if it was happening before him. The girl was respectable enough from the looks of her. She was upset because she had an interview with a potential employer for the post of governess, and in her haste, she'd left her umbrella at home.

"I thought I'd catch a cab fast enough," James explained. "I didn't think I'd need my umbrella."

"But then you couldn't. Catch a cab, that is, sir. At least that's the way you told the story." As hard as he tried to be respectful, Peck couldn't keep from chuckling. "You was a sight by the time you got here, if you'll pardon me saying it, sir. Wet around the edges and mad as a buck. I almost didn't pay you no mind when you asked me to watch out for that there parcel. But when you passed me that quid, well, I knowed then that you was a real gentleman. I'm gladder than I can say that you finally showed up for it." He'd already handed the parcel to James, and he indicated it with a tip of his head that made both his chins quiver.

"I was beginning to think I missed you, sir, what with the funeral and all. Thought maybe you'd left town. Or forgot."

"Mr. Smith? Forget?" Hot on the trail of more information, Lucy stepped forward, laughing away the suggestion. Her nose twitched like a terrier's with the scent of game in its nostrils. Her eyes glowed with the excitement of the chase. "Tell me, Mr. Peck, when did your father-in-law die?"

Peck considered the question. "That must have been . . . Yes, it were a Saturday. Two weeks ago. And you, sir," he said, very satisfied with himself, "you was here Friday. The day before."

"And today is Wednesday." Thinking hard, Lucy bit her lower lip. She turned to James. "You arrived at my house on Monday. That gives us ten days to account for."

"Ten days." His mind a million miles from the hansom and the strident sounds of city traffic, James repeated the words. Ten missing days. And a lifetime before that.

"It shouldn't be hard to put the pieces together now." As if she could read his mind and the riot of thoughts pounding through it, Lucy offered her opinion, pulling James out of his thoughts. There was a dray with a broken axle blocking the street ahead of them and she settled in to wait. "We have a name. And that parcel." She slid her gaze to the package in James's hands. "It could tell us a great deal."

"It could," James agreed, and he knew she was right.

He hefted the parcel in his hands, running his fingers over its contours. It was a book, he could tell as much from its size and shape, but why anyone would leave him a book, and what that book might be about, was a complete mystery to him.

He suspected it might not be as much of a mystery to Peck.

After he'd handed it to James, Peck tried hard to look at everything but the parcel. It was the first clue James had that while Peck might have been conscientious enough to collect the package and put it in safekeeping, he had not been strong enough to resist the lure of a mystery. His second clue was far more mundane. He'd noticed that one corner of the paper wrappings was not tucked in as neatly as the others, as if someone had taken a look, then tried to wrap it up again.

"This Indian gubbins . . ." Clue number three. When there was a lull in the conversation, Peck had tried his best to fill it. "I don't rightly understand it, if you catch my meaning, sir," he said. "All this to-do about them blokes what's living on the other side of the world! Goes in and out of fashion, don't you know. And right now, what with the Queen's Jubilee coming up and all them representatives from all over the Empire coming to honor the old girl, it seems all the rage, don't it?"

Lucy, of course, had the advantage, and she wasn't at all shy about pressing it. Like everyone else in the

Empire, James imagined she had kept herself up-to-date with news about the festivities planned for the celebration of the Queen's sixtieth year on the throne. He'd probably done the same. But he couldn't remember any of it. And Lucy obviously could.

Still beaming from the triumph of discovering his name, she had given James a dismissive little look, as if telling him she'd take over from there. She sidled closer to Peck. "There's to be quite a large contingency representing India at the festivities, am I right?" she asked.

"That's right, miss. And one of them raja types, he's giving the grand old girl that famous diamond what everyone's talking about. In honor of the Diamond Jubilee. The Eye of the Devil it's called." Peck's nose twitched. "I seen pictures of it in the London *Times*, I have, not that I usually read *The Times*, I can tell you that, miss. I fancy the *London Illustrated News* myself. It's got more sketches, you see, and they make the stories seem to come to life and—"

"And you saw pictures in *The Times* you say?" Gently, Lucy turned the conversation back in the right direction.

"That's right." Chastised, Peck cleared his throat. "One of the blokes here brought *The Times* in for us to take a gander at, and I'll tell you what. That there Eye of the Devil, that diamond is finer than anything we have here in this museum. Big as a cat's skull, it is, and it twinkles like a thousand stars!"

The hansom started up again with a jolt that shook James out of his reverie. He saw that Lucy was still watching him—and the parcel—carefully.

"We'll open it later," he said, and even as he did, he knew he had no intention of keeping the promise. *He* would open it later. When he was alone. And after he'd evaluated it and found whatever it was he was supposed to find inside, he would decide if he wanted to share the information with Lucy and her father. He wanted more answers before he did, answers as to who he was and why this book was waiting for him behind a statue of Vishnu, left by some mysterious person who for whatever reason could not meet him face-to-face. He wanted answers about James Smith. And about why the name didn't feel as if it belonged to him.

He wanted answers about Lucy.

James glanced her way, hoping to hell that his look didn't betray the rumblings of doubt he felt eating away at his insides.

Was Lucy as innocent as she seemed? If she was, why had she taken him to the museum to see a display of Indian stone seals?

James's hand made its way to his pocket. He patted it, feeling the hefty weight of the stone inside, and though he tried to quell the questions running rampant through his head, they could not be curbed.

Was there more going on behind that pretty face of Lucy's than even he could guess at?

Uncomfortable with the thoughts, James set them aside. The answers, it seemed, lay more with Alfie than with his daughter. As she was careful to point out, Lucy was simply her father's assistant. It was Alfie himself who had instructed them to go to the museum. Where a package waited. A package with James's name on it.

Like the fleeting glimmer of memory that had assailed him inside the museum, the thought made James's heartbeat quicken. The situation was certainly a jumble, but it was slowly sorting itself out, and the tangle seemed to lead in a surprising direction. Perhaps the mysterious Alfred Barnstable knew a great deal more than he was willing to say.

"We should telegram your father," James suggested, eager to pursue the idea. "He'll be interested in everything we've learned. The name. The parcel."

Her lips pressed into a thin line of irritation, Lucy traded him look for look. "And whatever you find inside that parcel, you won't share the information with me, will you? You'll wait for Alfie." Lucy sniffed, dissatisfied, but her eyes flashed with some emotion that had nothing to do with disappointment. There was more desperation than anything in the look and in the instant it flickered in her eyes, James wondered what it meant.

Before he had time to think about it, Lucy turned away, effectively shielding her emotions. She tugged at her gloves. "I have explained before, I am my father's agent," she said. "I have his full confidence. How do you expect me to report our progress to him if you won't share a vital clue?"

James laughed. "A clue? Is that what you think it is?" It wasn't fair to tease Lucy when she was being so terribly serious, but he could hardly help himself. She had a tendency to interpret events to fit her needs and he owed it to her to point that out. "How can there be a clue when you think the mystery is solved? You said so yourself. You said you believed Peck. You said you were willing to accept that very British-sounding name. You said I am James Smith." He gave her an abrupt nod, as if introducing himself. "Since that is precisely what I hired your father's consulting detective agency to find out, I'd say the case is closed."

"Closed? No. It can't be!" Lucy leaned forward and laid one hand on James's arm. The baffling emotion he'd seen in her eyes trembled in her voice, honing it with desperation. "You can't sack me! I mean *us.* You can't sack us. You can't say the case is ended. Not before we find—"

Lucy caught her breath. All too late, she realized that though she'd brought her words under control, her actions were anything but. Appalled by the familiarity of her own impulsive gesture, her eyes widened and she stared down to where her hand clutched James's arm.

James stared, too. Lucy's hand in its dark cloth glove made a curiously appealing package. One that was as mysterious as the parcel Peck had delivered. One that was tempting enough nearly to make James forget that only a short while ago, he had questioned her innocence and her motives.

He was a lunatic, surely, whatever else he was. James was certain of that. For one mad moment, he thought about drawing the glove from her hand.

Slowly.

One finger at a time.

He wanted to touch the flesh beneath. To trace the shape of each finger and measure the heat of her skin against his lips.

Though he may have had doubts about his identity and his past and the puzzling role of Lucy and her father and the British Museum in it all, there was no doubt as to this feeling. This was desire, pure and simple.

No. James corrected himself.

It might be simple, but it was anything but pure.

It settled in his gut where only minutes ago, doubts and uncertainty had taken up their lodging.

James twined his fingers through Lucy's. "Would it be so awful if the case was at an end?" he asked. "I would know who I am and we would be free to concentrate on other things." He quirked his eyebrows, the gesture conveying his message more than his words. "Things that have nothing to do with your father's consulting detective agency."

"I promised myself this wouldn't happen." Lucy's voice was breathless. As if the effort cost her dearly, she tore her gaze, and her hands from James's and stared straight ahead of her, repeating the words like a prayer. Or a plea. "I promised myself. After this morning. I promised myself. I told myself—"

She was so earnest, James couldn't help but laugh. "Why? I confess, I've seen my face and I may not be the most bonny lad, but am I so much of a scunner?"

She might not have understood the Scots word, but she grasped its meaning. Lucy's good manners won out over her embarrassment. "Oh, no! It isn't that at all! I don't mean to be cheeky, but when you're not black and blue and your face isn't swollen, you really must be quite a handsome gentleman. And you are usually quite well behaved. When you're . . . when you're . . . when you're not carrying on with a girl and chicken feathers and such." Lucy swallowed hard.

"But I . . ." She fought to extricate herself from the situation. "What I mean is, it would certainly jeopardize our working relationship, wouldn't it? I mean, if I . . . that is, if we . . ."

"Yes." He had no choice but to agree with her. "It would certainly jeopardize our working relationship. But if that relationship were over . . ."

"And if it were, we wouldn't be on our way to the London *Times* now, would we?" It was obvious the explanation had just occurred to Lucy and just as obvious that she thought it the perfect argument. Sounding very sure of herself, she clutched her hands together in her lap.

"If we thought the case was closed, we wouldn't be checking out that newspaper item Mr. Peck told us about. The one about the Queen and the Eye of the Devil. No. Don't bother to answer." She staved off his reply with a cast-iron glance. "You are far too glib-tongued. You'll turn my words around on me and have me believing I've said things I never did. Alfie could do it, too."

"Then I take it as a compliment." James chuckled. If nothing else, he had to admire her powers of deduction, and her mettle, and he had to admit that deep down inside, he was just as relieved as Lucy appeared to be. It was just as well she'd steered them clear of the dangerous terrain where James had been foolish enough to think they might tread unharmed.

Unfamiliar terrain frequently contained land mines. He'd learned that somewhere, sometime in his life. It wasn't good to go charging in. Not when you could tread carefully. And take your time. And avoid disaster.

Though he couldn't say how he knew, he was aware that the advice about land mines also applied to women.

He also knew that in many cases, they were one and the same.

James had the uncomfortable feeling he'd learned that lesson somewhere in life, too, and that he'd sustained far more damage learning about women than he'd ever encountered from land mines. It might be interesting to remember it all someday. If he ever remembered anything.

For now, what seemed important was to remember that it was foolish to let his desires rule his head. Even desires that were so intriguing as to make him discover temptation in a woman's glove.

The thoughts spinning through his head, James watched the cab slow as it neared the office of *The Times*. When it stopped, he climbed out and helped

Lucy down. He had insisted on paying for this portion of their excursion and while he did, she crossed the pavement to be out of the way of the crowds swarming down Fleet Street.

No sooner had he joined her there than he saw Lucy's eyes pop wide open.

"Miss Meerchum!" Lucy's voice contained all the astonishment of her look. "What on earth are you doing here?"

James turned in time to see Ardath Meerchum looking just as surprised. A silly smile brightening her amazingly unattractive face, she pulled to a stop there on the pavement and clutched her handbag to her chest. "Miss Barnstable? Mr. James? What a fortunate happenstance!" She gave a little laugh and stared down at her boots.

"Imagine! Meeting you again so soon," Miss Meerchum said. "It is surely a happy coincidence! You're not . . ." She ran her tongue over her thin lips. "You're not stopping for tea, are you?"

"Not today." Far more polite than she'd been at the museum, though James could not have said why, Lucy gave her friend a fleeting smile before she headed up the steps of *The Times* building. "Good afternoon, Miss Meerchum."

"Good afternoon, Miss Barnstable. And you, Mr. James." Miss Meerchum dared to glance up at them before she collected herself and continued on her way. "I do hope you both have a very good day."

Pausing on the wide stone steps, James watched her go. "Odd, that," he mumbled.

"Miss Meerchum?" Lucy laughed. "She's very odd indeed."

Except it wasn't at all what James was thinking.

The thought came and went so quickly, he barely

had time to reflect on it before they were inside the building.

The main offices of the London *Times* were as imposing as James expected them to be. Though there were dark-suited, somber-faced men coming and going from every direction, a silence as reverent as the one they'd encountered at the museum filled the entrance hall. Ahead of them, an austere fellow sat behind a desk. His hands clenched together on the desktop, he looked James and Lucy up and down.

The one look was apparently enough for him to size up Lucy's tasteful but inexpensive clothing and James's borrowed suit.

"Admission only by order of the editor," he said, his lips pinched. "Unless, of course, you have business here."

"Of course." As dignified as a duchess, Lucy glided forward. She excused herself around a tall fellow with iron-gray hair who was carrying a stack of papers. Lucy stepped to her right. The man stepped to his left.

Again, Lucy excused herself. The man did the same. They might have gone on that way forever if James hadn't caught the man's eye.

The man froze. His mouth working over a string of silent words, his eyes suddenly narrowing to slits, he stared at James, and something told James the man's astonishment had nothing at all to do with James's injuries. And everything to do with James's mere presence.

Just as quickly, the man remembered himself. Glancing over his shoulder toward the man at the desk and seeing that he was watching, he affixed a smile to his face. He tucked his stack of papers under his arm and hurried forward, offering James his hand

and clasping it in a hold that was calculated to look far friendlier than it felt.

Instantly James smelled danger. He could feel it on the small currents of air that tickled along the back of his neck. He could sense it in the tall man's handshake, and instinctively he glanced a warning toward Lucy. She was canny enough to catch his meaning. She stepped closer.

Unaware of the look that had passed between James and Lucy, the man spoke just loud enough for the man at the desk to hear. "How good to see you again."

James didn't answer. For once, he was glad he wasn't able to. He reminded himself about the land mines. And about the importance of patience. He stopped, and waited for the other man to make the first move.

The scheme worked. For all his stiff formality and the smile that was just as rigid, it was obvious the man was uneasy. He shifted slightly from foot to foot. He had eyes the color of faded blue draperies, and they darted from side to side as if he were afraid someone might be watching. "You'll have to excuse me for a moment, if you don't mind," he said. "I simply must deliver these letters to the editor's office." He paused, and James had the uncomfortable feeling that he was supposed to say something. When he didn't, the man grumbled.

"I have everything you asked for," he hissed. He recovered in an instant and raised his voice in a passing imitation of warm congeniality. "Wait in my office, why don't you," he suggested, pointing toward a passageway that led from the main entry. "Three doors down on the left. Have a seat. I shan't be but a moment."

James wasn't about to argue. Offering Lucy his

arm, he went into the cramped room where the man
had directed them to wait.

Lucy took a seat in one of the stiff-backed wooden
chairs along the far wall. "I don't like that man," she
said simply.

"Neither do I." James didn't waste a moment's
time. Being careful not to disarrange the stacks of
papers that were piled on the desk, he went through
them one by one.

They were items that were apparently intended for
an upcoming issue of *The Times* and there was nothing telling among them. Nothing that was any help
in explaining who the man was who worked in the
office or why he and James might have had some
contact in the past.

"That's very rude," Lucy mumbled, watching
James leaf through another stack of papers. "And
probably illegal."

"Probably." James was hardly listening. There was
a blank piece of paper in the center of the desk and
he picked it up and examined it. "He must have had
another paper over this one when he was writing,"
he mumbled. "And if the fellow has a heavy
hand . . ." James held the paper up. There was one
window high up on the wall and just enough sunlight filtering down through it to allow him to see
the impressions made by the nib of the man's pen.

"Ah!" He purred a sound of satisfaction and set
the paper down exactly where it had been. "His
name is Canaday," he told Lucy. "Pollard Canaday."

There was some small sense of satisfaction in
seeing Lucy look astonished. She rose from the chair
and leaned over the desk, eyeing the blank page.
"And how do you know that?"

James offered her a mischievous smile. "Elementary!"
Lucy grumbled a response and had he been less

of a gentleman, he might have asked her to repeat it. Instead, James gave her the same kind of look she had been practicing all day. The smug one. The one that had exasperated and infuriated him.

He was pleased to see it had the same effect on her.

But even though she was annoyed, Lucy was shrewd enough to think through the problem and see what he'd done. She looked down at the blank page, then over at the window. "Where did you learn to do that?" she asked.

James shrugged. "I haven't the slightest idea." There were a number of other interesting items on Canaday's desk, a silver cigarette case he would have liked to have a closer look at, a carriage clock inscribed from Blanche, and stacks of notes that were, obviously, being turned into stories for *The Times*. He knew he didn't have the time to examine them all, so he glanced through the papers.

It was a full minute before he realized Lucy was staring at him in disgust.

"Don't look so righteous." He set down the last stack of papers and went through the desk drawers. The bottom one on the right was locked and James mumbled to himself. "Don't detectives do things like this all the time?"

"Not detectives who like to stay within the boundaries of the law," Lucy countered. Her words caught over a tiny gulp of surprise. "Or detectives who don't wish to be caught," she added quickly. "Here he comes!"

By the time Canaday opened the door, Lucy was again seated in the chair across from the desk. James was lounging casually at her side.

Canaday snapped the door shut behind him and leaned against it. It took him a moment to collect himself and his thoughts. "I told you never to come here," he said.

His voice was rough with worry. His body was tense. Canaday had enough bottom to keep his chin up and his gaze on James, but James couldn't help but notice that a muscle at the side of his jaw clenched.

Again, warning bells went off inside James's head, and he reminded himself to be careful. He'd been right earlier when he'd decided that there was something dangerous about Canaday and now, he knew why.

Canaday was dangerous because Canaday was afraid. Very afraid. And James reminded himself that there was nothing more dangerous than a frightened man.

Sensing that James was watching all too carefully, Canaday snapped to life and scrambled behind his desk. With it firmly between himself and his visitors, he regained at least some of his confidence. "The usual place would have been much more appropriate," he said. "It would have been safer."

From somewhere deep within the labyrinth that was his mind, a memory rose in James's head: chess. He didn't remember individual games or who he'd played against, but rather the sensations. The challenge. The carefully orchestrated moves. The meticulously planned strategies.

Just as quickly, another thought replaced it, and James found himself smiling. This was nothing like chess, he told himself. This was more of a game of cards.

Less subtle than chess. Far more daring in its own way. Just as skilled.

Just as in a game of chance, James knew he had

to play the cards he'd been dealt. As far as he could tell, he had only one.

He hoped it was an ace.

"Yes. No doubt. It would have been far more convenient. For you." James lounged against the wall, his left shoulder tucked up under a picture of Her Majesty the Queen. "But I went to the usual place. And I waited. You weren't there."

Canaday might have found the words to answer if James had given him time. Instead, he interrupted the man's sputtered protest.

"I won't tolerate ineptitude," James said. At the same time he propelled himself away from the wall, he kept his voice even and so quiet, Canaday needed to lean forward to hear. "If you can't keep your portion of the bargain, Mr. Canaday—"

"You weren't supposed to know—" As if he'd been struck, Canaday blanched and dropped into his chair. A thin band of sweat suddenly circling his brow, his hands trembling, he reached into the pocket of his waistcoat and drew out a tiny gold key. He unlocked the bottom desk drawer and pulled out a large, square envelope. "Here," he said, thrusting the envelope toward James. "Take it."

James accepted the envelope and turned it over. There was a line of writing across the top of it in a clear, legible hand and he read it. He was surprised enough to catch his breath. And far too canny to let Canaday notice his reaction.

His strategy worked. Canaday mistook his silence for anger.

"It's all in there," Canaday said, his anxious, uneven breaths a staccato accompaniment to his words. "You'll see when you look through it. And if you don't believe me, let me tell you, I went through every one of the old files." That much said, Canaday stood. "You paid me handsomely and I've done my job. Now get out. Please. And don't come back. If anyone ever finds out I was the one who went through those files or why . . ." The consequences were, apparently, too much for Canaday to even consider. His face ashen, he went to the door and opened it. "Good day, sir."

James didn't answer. He offered Lucy his arm and escorted her out the door.

Once outside, Lucy hauled in a breath of crisp spring air and gave James a smile. "It really is most remarkable," she said, her mood as giddy as when they'd left the museum. "Alfie's advice, his suggestions . . . Not that I'm surprised," she added quickly. "He is, after all, one of the great thinkers of our time. But it is most remarkable, don't you think? First, we followed his advice and discovered your name. Now . . ." Glancing at the envelope, she suppressed a little squeal of delight. "Who knows what interesting things we will discover in that envelope. Alfie's intuition is, as always, unerring. And his powers of deduction, incredible!"

"The devil you say." Eager to put as much distance as he could between himself and Canaday, James hailed a cab and when one wasn't quick to stop, he threaded his arm through Lucy's and hurried her down the street and toward St. Paul's. "Seems like a damned incredible piece of luck to me," he told her. "And none of it good."

He might have known that Lucy would not take the comment lightly. She stopped and pulled her arm from his grasp.

Her cheeks were deliciously pink in the light of the afternoon sun. James reminded himself that he wasn't supposed to notice. "Our luck? Bad? Surely not! We've been successful. Incredibly successful."

"We are also causing something of an obstruction." James offered an apology to the people who were trying to make their way around them. He decided that taking Lucy's arm again was far too subtle a way to capture her attention and settled instead for a less courteous but far more serviceable course of action. He grabbed her hand and hauled her toward the doorway of a nearby building.

James held the envelope out to her. "Here," he said. "Take it." He couldn't quite control the tremor of irritation that crept into his voice.

He'd told Lucy he didn't believe they'd been as incredibly fortunate as she seemed to think. He'd told her he wasn't sure they'd found the secret to his identity. He'd told her that the name James Smith was wrong. All wrong.

But saying it all was one thing.

Admitting he was still nowhere near discovering the elusive secret of his identity was something else.

Lucy looked at him uncertainly. She glanced at the envelope. "You want me to open it? Here?"

"I want you to read it." He thrust it into her hands. "Go ahead," he instructed. "Take a look at what's written on the front. Then you can tell me how bloody lucky we've been. You can tell me all about how far we've come today."

This time, Lucy didn't argue. In his haste to give it to her, James had handed her the envelope face down. She turned it over and scanned the name written in a clear, legible hand. Her face went pale.

"Dear Lord!" Lucy held the envelope in her trembling fingers. "I don't suppose there's some mistake, is there?" she asked.

James answered her with stony silence.

"No. No mistake." Lucy continued to stare at the envelope. "Canaday knew you. That much is certain.

And yet this envelope . . ." She looked up at James, doubts melting the splendid confidence that had shone in her eyes so short a time before. "This envelope," she whispered, "is addressed to Mr. James Jones."

# Chapter 7

Smith and Jones.

Jones and Smith.

The names tumbled through Lucy's mind, mixing and churning. Much the same as her stomach.

Though she did her best to ignore the queasy feeling caused by the bitter taste of defeat, it wasn't as easy to dismiss the small voice in her head that was a constant reminder of her failure.

Lucy's steps dragged. Too overwrought to climb into a cab and sit quietly and helpless, she had insisted that they walk home from the offices of *The Times*. James was game enough to agree and sensible enough to remind her that they would be walking for quite some time.

Perhaps he'd been right. Perhaps they would have been better off in a cab. In a cab, she would be home sooner and the demands of her tenants would soon have occupied her mind. Then she might not have had as much time to think about what an utter failure she'd been at her first attempt at playing detective.

She had been certain. So certain. Certain she'd discovered James's true identity. Certain that by doing it, she was closer to finding out what had happened to her father. She had done everything Holmes would have done. She had investigated. And inquired. She had analyzed. And deduced. And what was she left with?

A man whose name was as much a mystery now as when they'd started out that morning.

And two important clues.

Lucy's spirits rose. In the press of pedestrian traffic that crowded the pavement, James had gotten slightly ahead of her, and she let her gaze move from his broad back down to where he had the parcel and the envelope clutched in one hand.

She had something, she reminded herself. It might not be James's name, but it could just possibly be something more important. Two vital clues that could help in her search for Alfie.

"Are you tired?"

Lucy had not realized she'd stopped in the middle of the pavement until James came back to fetch her. The brim of his tall top hat shading his eyes, he looked down at her. "I'm sorry, was I walking too fast? You probably couldn't keep up and—"

"Of course I can keep up." Lucy brushed off his apologies at the same time she declined the offer of his arm. The last thing she needed was for James to believe her fragile.

"I was simply thinking. That's all." She quickened her pace and smiled to herself, vindicated somehow when he needed to hurry to catch her up.

For a man whose hopes of discovering his identity had just been dashed, James looked none the worse for wear. Debonair even in Albert Miller's castoff clothes, he walked down the street as if he owned it, meeting the eyes of passersby, glancing at everyone and everything with an intense curiosity, one she could attribute only to the fact that each small detail of city life must seem quite fresh to a man who remembered nothing at all of his past.

About to cross a street, they stopped to allow a carriage bearing a coat of arms to pass. James used the opportunity to turn and study everything around them.

"It's a remarkable city, don't you think?" His gaze intense and searching, he took it all in, from the stately facade of St. Paul's Cathedral across the street to the crush of humanity behind them. "I never tire of it. Look there!" He pointed toward a vendor hawking newspapers. "And there." He pivoted again, this time showing Lucy a flower peddler selling her wares on the street corner.

Lucy might have rolled her eyes if she wasn't in public. There were far more important things for them to worry about than newspaper vendors and flower peddlers, and it was on the tip of her tongue to tell him as much.

They might talk about the parcel instead, she would have told him. Or the envelope delivered by the disagreeable Mr. Canaday.

Or they might talk about the fact that in the carriage on the way to *The Times*, James had been bold enough to take her hand.

The thought crept up on Lucy and left her wonderstruck. She knew well enough to scold herself for it. She also knew there was nothing she could do to keep it at bay.

They *might* talk about a thousand things, she told herself. They *should* talk about the parcel and the envelope. But how she wished they *would* talk about the touch of his hand against hers and how it took her breath away.

Bewildered by the thoughts that scrambled through her head and left her feeling weak-kneed, it was impossible for Lucy to think of even one of those thousand other things they could have talked about.

It was just as improbable to think she might have been clearheaded enough to begin a discussion about the parcel and the envelope. And as much as she would have wished it, she couldn't for the world find the words to explain how his touch still resonated through every last inch of her body.

Instead, she summoned a smile and the words to mask her emotions. "Perhaps you are a country gentleman," she offered. She avoided his gaze, sure he would somehow read the thoughts that shimmered behind her words. "It would explain why you find such wonder in things so common." She looked up and down the street to see if it was clear to walk on and when it was, she turned to head up Ludgate Hill.

James stopped her, his hand on her arm. "Let's go into St. Paul's."

Lucy's discomfort dissolved in a rush of exasperation. The British Museum. The London *Times*. She'd had enough sightseeing for one day. And enough investigating. She ignored his request.

Ever so slightly, James tightened his fingers around her arm and pulled her toward the church. "I would like to see St. Paul's," he said.

Lucy grumbled her dissatisfaction. "I really must be getting home. I—"

"And I would like to see St. Paul's." There was no arguing with his tone of voice, or with the steely glint of tenacity that suddenly lit his eyes as his gaze slid from Lucy to the crowd all around them. He glanced at the cathedral. "St. Paul's," he said quite simply. Through the sleeve of her jacket, his fingers pressed her flesh. "Now."

With each step up the broad stairway that led into the church, Lucy's vexation rose. "What's it to be?" she asked as they walked through the doorway and into the church. "Lord Nelson's memorial? The Duke of Wellington's crypt? If we are playing tourist, then surely you—"

James wasn't listening. In one quick movement he whisked his hat from his head and glanced around. Without a word or a thought for the fact that he was holding so tightly to her arm that it ached, he dragged Lucy up the center aisle toward the altar.

"Would you mind telling me what you're doing?" Lucy inquired below her breath. They scurried around a group of tourists staring up at Wren's dome and Lucy tried to catch James's attention at the same time she tried to catch her breath. She grumbled with frustration when neither worked. "This is hardly the right way to see the cathedral. For four shillings you can buy a guidebook and see the entire place. You can't—"

With one last look over his shoulder, James yanked her toward a side aisle and pushed his way through the nearest exit door.

After the tranquillity of the church, the streets of the city seemed especially boisterous. Lucy paused on the stairs to get her bearings. James didn't.

Half dragging, half leading her, he took the steps two at a time and when they were back on the pavement, he headed up the street as fast as he could.

"James!" Lucy scrambled to keep up. "James, what on earth is going on? You can't expect me to—"

Lucy tripped over her own feet. The world tipped and twirled. The pavement rose to meet her. Just as suddenly, she felt an arm around her, a rough embrace, and the air rushed out of her lungs.

By the time she caught her breath and her head stopped spinning, she found herself pressed against a nearby building with James's arms around her and his face only inches from hers.

Their ragged breaths mingled. Their eyes met. And

suddenly Lucy found her head in as much of a whirl as when she was about to go down, face first, in a heap.

"I'm sorry." She had a good reason for being winded, she reminded herself, and she was glad. Otherwise, she might have sounded artless and unsophisticated. And James might think the fact that his lips were so near had something to do with it. "I'm not usually so clumsy. I—"

"It's my fault." James was just as breathless. His hat was cockeyed and perhaps for the first time since she'd picked him up off her parlor floor, his guard was down, his face free of the wariness that seemed to shadow each of his expressions. It was an engaging combination and it made him look so devilishly handsome, she nearly forgot that they were out in public and that, no doubt, people were staring.

"I shouldn't have kept up such a quick pace." James was talking logically enough, but his eyes were on hers. They glinted with a distracting light that made it completely impossible to concentrate on what he was saying and far more pleasant to think about how good his hands felt against her waist. "I should have slowed down. I should have paid more attention to where we were going. All I could think was that we had to get away from there as fast as we could."

"We did?" Lucy wished she could have mustered the least bit of cynicism. Or even something that sounded like interest. Instead, her words were as dreamy as her look. She saw herself reflected in James's eyes, her lips parted, her eyes as wide and as startled as his.

James leaned nearer. He tilted his head. His gaze was on her. On her eyes. On her lips.

He was going to kiss her.

The realization rocketed through Lucy's head. It made her breath catch in her throat. Her heart hammered. He was going to kiss her, and she wasn't at all sure what she was going to do about it.

She knew there were a hundred reasons he shouldn't. A thousand.

But she couldn't think of one.

And she wasn't sure she wanted to try.

James's eyes held hers. They were heavy with emotion, dark with a secret she didn't understand. His look invited her to tip her head back. To close her eyes.

Lucy did. Feeling as disoriented as she had when she stumbled, she held her breath, waiting for the warm press of his lips against hers. She felt him move closer. His breath was warm against her cheek. It brushed her ear. His voice was low and soft.

"We're being followed," he whispered.

"What!" Lucy's eyes flew open. Mortified as much by her own behavior as she was by his bizarre pronouncement, she sidestepped her way out of James's arms and glanced at the crowd. Now that the commotion caused by Lucy's near fall and James's rescue had subsided, the people along the street continued on their ways. They were a typical crowd, the well-heeled and the ordinary man, the occasional servant on an errand from his master, the prim and proper chaperons carefully watching their young charges.

"Followed?" Lucy's gaze moved from the crowd back to James. She tugged at her jacket and straightened her hat. She pulled her gloves more firmly into place. "That, sir," she said, "is ridiculous."

"Is it?" James wasn't so sure. He stopped only long enough to scan the crowd again and before Lucy could collect herself further or protest at all, he wound his arm through hers and continued down the street.

Lucy puffed with exasperation. She huffed with aggravation. James didn't care. He zigzagged in and out of the crowd. He crossed the busy street not once, but twice, barely avoiding an omnibus the first time and nearly getting them killed by a hansom the second.

By the time they got as far as St. Botolph's Church, Lucy had had enough.

"Followed." The word hissed out of her like steam from a teakettle. She had looked over her shoulder a dozen times since they'd started out again and never seen a thing. "How do you know?"

James didn't answer. He pulled her into the churchyard. This time, instead of going into the church, they skirted the building and headed into the graveyard beyond. "It's a feeling more than anything," he said.

"A feeling." Lucy could only speak for her own feelings, and right now, they were neither charitable nor tolerant. "You've dragged me from one end of London to the other. You've nearly gotten us killed. For a feeling. Mr. Smith—" She caught herself. "Mr. Jones—" She screeched with frustration. "Whatever your name is . . . how dare you—"

"I know what I'm doing." There was a monument up ahead that marked the site of the plague pits and James hurried to the other side of it. The stone marker was far taller than either of them and wide enough so that they could stand in its shadow and not be seen from the street. He pushed her behind it ahead of him and slipped in beside her, his voice hushed to a whisper. "I remember once in Prague—"

The words caught him as unprepared as they did Lucy.

Suddenly his foolish fantasies about being followed did not seem nearly as important as this flash of memory. "You've been in Prague?" Lucy asked.

A fleeting smile brightened James's expression. "I suppose I must have been," he conceded. "I don't remember a thing about it. Except being followed. I wonder why." He tipped his head, thinking through the problem.

"No matter," he said, just as easily shrugging it away. "At least not now." Carefully, he peeked around the monument. Apparently not liking whatever it was he saw, he ducked behind it again. "You get a sense of it, I think. Of being followed. The way a hunted animal must. You feel the eyes on you in a crowd. You have the notion that every move you make is being mirrored by someone else."

Lucy wasn't so sure. From what she could see, there wasn't a soul in the graveyard and hardly any people out on the street outside the iron fence that surrounded the church and its environs. The place was as desolate as the mossy gravestones that surrounded them and as quiet as . . . well, as quiet as a tomb.

The awareness was enough to bring Lucy to her senses.

Snatching her arm from James's grasp, she rubbed the spot where he'd been gripping her. "Followed, indeed! You've been reading too many penny dreadfuls. Real people don't get followed. Besides . . ." She stepped out from behind the stone marker. "There isn't a soul around and—"

Something smacked into the side of the monument. Something hard spattered all around her, stinging Lucy's cheeks and tapping against her straw hat like hail. The rest of what she was going to say vanished in a squeal.

"Get down!"

Lucy heard James's directive at the same time she felt him hit her full force. The next thing she knew, she was lying on her back on the ground with James atop her.

If it wasn't for the fact that her teeth rattled together, her hat was askew, and her backside ached, she might actually be enjoying herself.

It was a ridiculous thing to think of and an odd time to think it, and Lucy wondered if she hadn't hit her head and, perhaps, was not responsible for the thoughts that were swirling through it. She might actually have believed it if her head was the only part of her anatomy that was affected.

But this was more than a simple trick of the mind. This involved more than just her head. Her lungs must surely be part of the conspiracy for in spite of the fact that James was far taller and heavier than she and that his weight should have pushed the air right out of her, she was breathing fast and heavy. Her heart must be implicated, too, for it was pumping with all its might. There was a queer sort of nervousness built up somewhere between her heart and her stomach and an even more unusual heat that originated at her core and spread warmth through her entire body.

James's broad chest pressed against her breasts. His hands were hard on her shoulders. His legs and hers were entwined.

It was an altogether inappropriate situation, and thoroughly delightful. At least it might have been, if James hadn't begun to curse.

"Of all the bloody, stupid . . ."

James raised himself just enough to have a quick look around, and if his voice was soft before, he obviously thought there was no reason to be quiet any longer. His words rang through the churchyard, echoing off the ancient stone, frightening a flock of pigeons that perched in the bell tower so that they took flight. "Do you suppose I was standing in back of this bloody gravestone for my bloody health?" He bounced up and peeked around the monument.

Lucy couldn't imagine what he saw, she only knew that whatever it was, it caused his mouth to fall open. "Damn!" He pounded a fist into the monument and dashed into the open, watching something out in the street, and Lucy heard the sounds of clattering wheels, nickering horses, and a cabman yelling to his team.

James stalked back to where she still lay and scowled down at her. "Did I tell ye to be careful? Did I tell ye we were being followed?" His top hat had gone flying when he threw her to the ground and he stooped to retrieve it and shoved it back on his head. "What the bloody hell did ye think ye were doing?"

The desire that had streaked through Lucy as she lay with James might have been a trick of the mind. The anger that filled her now was anything but.

"What the bloody hell I'd like to do," she told him through clenched teeth, "is get the bloody hell off this bloody ground. If you'd help—" She raised one hand and waited for him to assist her to her feet.

James didn't notice. Wincing, he clutched his side and spun to stare again into the street. "How could I have been so bloody dull-witted?" He grimaced and ran his hands over his ribs. "I knew we were being followed. I told you we were being followed." He spun around toward Lucy and, seeing that she was struggling to her feet, offered her a hand.

With an icy glare, Lucy declined it.

She got to her feet and leaned against the monument, brushing off her skirt and blowing a lock of hair out of her eyes. "You're a madman," she told him. "I said as much before and now you've proved it. You're imagining things, surely. People watching us. Following us."

In answer, James grabbed her elbow and showed her around to the other side of the monument. There, where Lucy had heard something smack the stone, the granite was splintered.

When he was sure she'd had a close look, James yanked Lucy's arm, turning her to face him. "Someone took a shot at us," he said.

Relief swept through Lucy. This proved it. It proved everything she'd suspected. He had been talking nonsense before. And he was talking nonsense now. Nonsense was something she was used to dealing with. After all, she had spent her life with Alfie.

She lowered her voice and gave him the kind of smile she had always used to soothe her father when his flights of fancy got out of hand. "Really, James, you must think things through. It might be amusing to pretend at such things, and it is most certainly exciting, but why would anyone—"

"Damn it!" James's words were as hard-edged as the granite memorials to every side of them. He gripped her shoulders and bent to look her in the eye. "I don't know why anyone would want to shoot us. I don't even know who I am. Perhaps the answer to the one mystery is the key to the other. Then again, perhaps who I am has nothing to do with it. Perhaps they knew you from someplace or another and they know you can be as haughty as a devil-dodger. Perhaps that means they were shooting at you. I only know that someone took a shot at us. The carriage was draped. I didn't get a good look, but damn, if I don't think it was your friend Miss Meerchum."

"Miss Meerchum!" Fury wiped the smile from Lucy's face. She glanced at the empty street. There was no carriage and no one watching them. And if by some twist of fate there ever was, it had certainly not been Ardath Meerchum.

Realizing as much made anger shoot through every inch of Lucy's body. "How dare you? How dare you accuse poor Miss Meerchum? How dare you try to include her in your distorted imaginings. That is . . . it is unconscionable, sir. It is . . . It is . . ."

Just the kind of story Alfie might have concocted.

The thought settled in Lucy's head and turned her blood to ice water. Though she could not have said why it mattered, she had thought James different from her incorrigible, irresponsible, unpredictable father.

It hurt to realize he was not.

Anger and disappointment mingled inside her, thickening into a tight ball of outrage that robbed her of her ability to speak. Unable to even begin to put her emotions into words, she turned on her heels and stomped away.

It was a long walk from the graveyard at St. Botolph's to the Barnstable home near New Kent Road, but Lucy did not pause once along the way. Her pace was fueled by her anger as well as by the fact that she knew that James was right behind her.

To his credit, he kept his distance, but that hardly made Lucy feel any better. By the time she got to her front door, her hair was in her eyes and her hat was in her hands. The inside of her collar was damp and sweat trickled between her shoulder blades and made her itch. Too anxious to keep ahead of James, she had paid little attention to her surroundings. She wanted to arrive home. She didn't care how she got there. Now she saw that her boots were caked with muck, the hem of her gown was wet, and her gloves were ruined beyond repair.

She hardly cared.

Throwing open the front door and not bothering to close it behind her, Lucy stalked into the house and strode into the parlor.

She stopped cold when she saw Freddy Plowright waiting there.

"'Freddy!" Lucy nearly cried with relief. It was such a comfort to see Freddy. Reliable, stalwart, dependable Freddy. Freddy with his flaxen hair parted down the middle and slicked close to his head. Freddy, every inch of him pressed and pleated and brushed to perfection, his spectacles sparkling in the last of the afternoon sun that filtered through the parlor curtains, his mustache bright and fuzzy, like a golden caterpillar.

Freddy was not at all as handsome as James but that didn't matter. Not a bit.

Freddy was Freddy and though Lucy's heart may not have warmed at the thought, her intellect responded as it always did. Her emotions did not appreciate Freddy, and she was glad. This was not a matter for emotions. It was a matter for common sense.

And her common sense told her Freddy Plowright was the best thing that had ever happened to her.

Freddy would never land on her doorstep with his eyes blackened and his clothes bloodied. Freddy would never take it into his head to build a flying machine or go treasure hunting in the South Seas. Freddy would never envision himself a detective or think that someone was following him. And he would certainly not, never in his wildest dreams, even begin to imagine that someone had taken a shot at him.

Freddy was predictable and trusty. From the cut of his clothes to his topics of conversation, from his sensible aspirations to his thoroughly practical outlook, he was completely without excitement. He was not the least bit impulsive or spontaneous. He had never had a reckless thought in his life.

It was what made him so agreeable and so nice to be with. It was why it was so easy to carry on a conversation with him.

Freddy was nothing like Alfie. Nothing like James.

Freddy was everything Lucy ever wanted her life to be. Stable and solid and secure. No fancies. No eccentricities. And absolutely no detectives.

"Lucy, you're . . ." Freddy stared at her in astonishment. "You're tousled. Why is your hat off? And why is your gown filthy? What's happened? What—"

Freddy's questions dissolved in the light of James's arrival. Without ceremony or the least scrap of civility, he pushed into the room behind Lucy and traded Freddy wary look for wary look. But while everything about James, from his expressions to his thoughts, were closed to scrutiny, Freddy's mind was an open book. Lucy knew exactly what he was thinking.

There was no question that he wondered who James was and what he was doing in Lucy's house. There was no mistaking the fact that he was appalled at James's lack of manners and stunned by his blackened eye and his swollen lip. There was no denying that poor, dear Freddy seethed with curiosity. He was dying to know if James's general state of dishevelment had anything to do with Lucy's. However he would never be ungentlemanly enough to ask.

There was also no question that Freddy's unexpected appearance would have been easier to deal with if James had the good sense to go away and leave them to their privacy, and no doubt at all in Lucy's mind that James was not about to do it.

Eager to send James on his way and put him firmly out of her thoughts, Lucy stepped to Freddy's side. She wound her arm through his and turned to James.

"I do believe an introduction is in order," she said. "Freddy, dear, this is our newest boarder, Mr. James. Mr. James . . ." As if daring him to object, Lucy raised her chin and kept her gaze firmly on James. "Mr. James, this is Freddy Plowright. Freddy and I are engaged to be married."

# Chapter 8

"Engaged to be married." Too annoyed to keep still, James muttered and tromped across to the bath, pulling at the buttons on Albert Miller's shirt at the same time. The shirt was too snug and he tugged at it rather more vigorously than he should. Three buttons popped and pinged against the blue and white tiled floor. The fabric across the back tore in not one but two places.

James swore.

Not that the damned shirt was worth much. The tumble James had taken in the churchyard had done more than left every inch of him aching. There were a number of abrasions on his chest, souvenirs of the beating he'd taken, and he'd aggravated them all. The shirt was caked with dried blood and wet with fresh blood, and grumbling with exasperation at the same time he groaned from the pain, he tore it and the singlet he wore beneath it the rest of the way off and used what was left of the shirt to dab at his wounds.

"Engaged to be married. What the bloody hell is the bloody woman talking about? Lucy? Engaged to be married to . . ."

He thought of Freddy Plowright, his stiff posture and his limp handshake, his finely polished manners and his complete lack of personality. It wasn't a pretty picture, not by any stretch of the imagination, and it caused a weighty sensation to churn through James's stomach.

"Lucy, engaged to be married to that?" He tossed the shirt down and kicked it into the farthest corner before he leaned over the bath to test the temperature of the water.

It was hot, much too hot. James hardly noticed. Ever since he'd dragged himself into the house in Lucy's formidable wake, he'd been looking forward to a good, long soak. He'd relax, he'd promised himself. He'd pamper his sore muscles. He'd do his best to forget that someone had followed them and try, at least for a while, not to wonder who it was or why they should take the trouble to trail after a woman detective and a man who had no name.

He'd vowed that for as long as the hot water held out, he'd set aside the curious pieces of a puzzle that was getting more and more jumbled by the hour. Pieces that included the parcel and envelope he'd tucked into the wardrobe in his bedchamber for safe-keeping. And Lucy's knowledge of Indian stone seals. And Ardath Meerchum, a woman as mousy as any he'd ever met and one who he'd swear he'd seen speed away in a draped carriage, a pistol in her hands.

But how could any man sit back and relax in the face of such astounding news?

"Lucy and Freddy," James grumbled while he stripped off his trousers. He supposed he shouldn't have been surprised. After all, Lucy was an attractive woman. Hell, she was perfectly handsome, even if she was too headstrong and far too stubborn for her own good.

But Lucy and Freddy Plowright?

It was absurd, that's what it was. Clearly, Lucy

would never be happy with a man who was no match for her, and just as clearly, Freddy was no match.

He was too proper by far. Too prim and quiet. Too . . .

"Too ordinary." James sent his trousers into the corner with his shirt. "Too damned ordinary. That's what he is."

Lucy would never be challenged by a relationship such as that. She would never be excited by it. James might not know a great deal about himself, but he did fancy himself a good judge of character. He'd appraised Freddy Plowright the moment he met him. Appraised him and passed judgment.

There wasn't a spark of passion in Freddy. Not an ounce of imagination. Not one shred of originality.

To think that a man such as that might even dream of teaching Lucy the fine art of making love . . .

The thought brought James up short and he yanked out the stopper at the bottom of the bath, drained some of the hot water, and replaced it with cold.

Not that he needed to cool off, he told himself. Not by any means. The heat that shot through his body was a result of the steam building in the room. It had nothing to do with the pictures of Lucy that flitted through his mind: visions of Lucy with her hair down around her bare shoulders, images of Lucy with her lips parted and her head back and her eyes closed, waiting for his kiss.

It was the heat of irritation. The result of surprise. Surely, that was the only reason his heart slammed against his bruised ribs. The only explanation for the tightness in his gut.

It couldn't possibly have anything to do with Lucy. Or what Freddy might or might not teach Lucy. Or with the fact that he might be teaching it to her even now down in the parlor where James had left them together.

It was a surprise. That's all it was. That's all he would allow it to be.

Still reminding himself of the fact, James fetched a bar of soap from a side table and set a towel out where he could reach it from the bath. He was still shaky from the beating. Still a little unsteady on his feet. Had he been himself (and had he been able to remember who that self was), he knew there was no way he would be disturbed by the idea of Lucy finding satisfaction in Freddy Plowright's arms. Or in the thought that she deserved far more than a milksop like Freddy could ever offer.

"Damn!" James threw the soap into the bath. No matter how logical he tried to be, his reasonings all brought him back to the same place.

Lucy.

James cursed. He cursed himself and Freddy Plowright. He cursed whatever strange twists of fate had plopped him down in the middle of the lives of these people and left him standing, naked, in the middle of Lucy's bath wondering what she was doing down in the parlor.

And what Freddy was saying to her.

And what she was saying back.

He cursed the fact that though his good sense and every instinct warned him it wasn't wise, he cared about Lucy's happiness.

And he knew that a man like Freddy would never understand the passions that seethed beneath her veneer of respectability, just as he would never be able to awaken them, to share them, to . . .

James added more cold water to the bath.

He had no business entertaining such thoughts, he

told himself, stepping into the water, just as he had
no business trying to make Lucy's decisions for her.
Of course she'd chosen Freddy Plowright. From what
James had learned when they were introduced,
Freddy was from a good family. He had a fine job
as a bank clerk.

"And at least he knows his own name." If the
thought wasn't enough to sober him, the cool water
was. James lowered himself into it, wincing when the
water stung his cuts.

Freddy Plowright had more than James. He had a
name, a past, a family, and while James might not
remember, he told himself he might have the same.
A name. A past.

A family?

The thought cooled his fantasies about Lucy far
more effectively than the cold water ever could.

His one arm half-lathered, James paused.

Was there someone, somewhere, waiting for him
to come home? A fiancé? A wife? A woman who
paced the floors waiting for his arrival and cried herself to sleep when there was no word from him?

And if there was that possibility, how could he
look into Lucy's marvelous dark eyes and pretend to
give her even a fraction of what Freddy offered?

James shivered. "No wonder," he mumbled,
watching the cold water pour into the bath. He
closed the faucet and opened the hot-water tap, lean-
ing back to allow the warmth to penetrate his sore
muscles. But even that was not enough to relax him.

His thoughts raced and his head whirled. He
closed his eyes and tried his best to find something
that would occupy his mind, but all he could see was
Lucy one moment and some other, nameless woman
the next. A woman who watched. And waited.
And wondered.

Fighting to keep both his doubts and his demons at bay, James did the only thing he could think to do to occupy his mind. He raised his voice as loud as he could and sang the first song that came into his head.

It was a German drinking song, and though he never stopped to wonder where he'd learned it, he wished to hell that he had a drink to go with it.

Freddy was gone before the singing ever began.

Too testy to deal with him and too tired to even begin to wonder why, Lucy sent him on his way with a quick apology and a story about how much work she needed to do around the house.

It was not quite a lie, but Lucy felt guilty nonetheless. Hoping to assuage her conscience at the same time she lightened her load of housework for the next day, she collected the bundle of fresh linens that had been left by the washerwoman and started up the stairs with it. She supposed she'd heard the voice long before, but it never quite registered in her mind. It was a household noise, a steady hum that provided the melody to which her thoughts droned through her brain.

It wasn't until she was on the first-floor landing that she realized someone was singing and not until she was all the way at the top of the stairs that she recognized the voice.

She glared at the closed door of the bath.

"You have a lot of cheek sounding so relaxed and carefree," she grumbled. "After what you put me through."

After what she'd put herself through, she corrected herself. After all, she was the one who was foolish enough to think James wanted to kiss her. She was the one who was idiotic enough to enjoy the tumble in the grass and the feel of his long, lean body stretched out against hers.

"That'll teach me." Lucy stomped down the passageway. She left clean linens for Miss Foxworthy.

It would teach her, right enough, and she vowed not to forget. It would teach her never to trust her heart over her reasoning. It would teach her to value her logic far more than her emotions. It would teach her that no matter how attractive a man happened to be, he could still be as peculiar as her father, and just as prone to incredible fantasies.

"Followed" Lucy snorted. "Shot at! Shot at by Miss Meerchum!" She repeated the words, using them to mask the rich rumble of James's voice and the sounds of splashing that accompanied it. They helped remind her that she was angry and terribly disappointed. And helped her forget that if James was in the bath, that splendid, lean body of his was . . .

"Oh, bother!" Lucy scattered the disturbing thoughts with a shake that sent the rest of the linens flying. She retrieved them one by one, reminding herself as she did that it was neither polite nor wise to think about one of her tenants so. Especially when that tenant happened to be a man whose secrets seemed as impenetrable as his vexatious personality, one whose motives were as tightly closed and as carefully sealed as the parcel and envelope he'd been given that afternoon.

The thought hit Lucy like a thunderclap. Standing stock-still outside the door to the bath, she held her breath and listened. James finished one song and when he started in on another, she whirled around and headed for the stairs.

With any luck, she'd be long finished before he ever got all the way through the next chorus.

\*     \*     \*

Her gaze sliding from the name "James Smith" to the name "James Jones," Lucy weighed the parcel in one hand, the envelope in the other.

What she was doing wasn't dishonest, she told herself. Not really. After all, she was in James's room to deliver fresh linens and if she just happened to come across the parcel and the envelope he had received earlier in the day . . .

"Just happened to find them? At the bottom of the wardrobe?"

With a grunt, Lucy silenced her words as well as her conscience. What she was doing wasn't stealing, nor was it unscrupulous. She didn't mean to make off with either item. She simply wanted to get a look at them, and if James wouldn't cooperate . . .

Again, her conscience pricked, and again, she suppressed it with a hearty dose of pragmatism.

If James insisted on waiting for Alfie before he opened the parcel and the envelope, they might not get opened for a very long time.

And by then it might be too late.

Her conscience soothed, her determination renewed, Lucy congratulated herself. It wasn't a bad plan at all. Unless she got caught.

She had no choice but to be quick about her work.

Ignoring the way her stomach jumped and her fingers trembled against the brown paper, Lucy examined the parcel. Even a cursory look told her it would be far too difficult to rewrap without leaving telltale signs that it had been tampered with. She set it down on the bed and went to work on the envelope.

James had left a single gas jet burning and she turned her back to the door and tipped the envelope toward the light. Holding her breath, she slid her finger beneath the flap.

"Hello, what's this?"

At the sound of the voice, slightly annoyed and more than a bit wary, Lucy sucked in a shriek of surprise and spun around.

James stood in the doorway.

She thought that being caught in his bedchamber pilfering his possessions would be the worst thing in the world.

She'd been wrong.

The worst thing in the world wasn't being caught in his bedchamber. It wasn't even realizing that she'd been so busy rationalizing she hadn't been listening and hadn't known he was done with his singing and with his bath.

The worst thing in the world was having him come upon her when he wasn't expecting her, and discovering that he wasn't wearing anything at all except a knee-length smoking jacket that was open and untied.

And a towel wrapped around his waist.

Heat shot through Lucy's cheeks. As if it might exonerate her guilt, she dropped the envelope on the bed alongside the parcel and in the same motion scooped the pile of linens into her arms. She held them tight against her chest, hoping she might stop the runaway hammering of her heart and somehow disperse her sudden and disturbing awareness of James's nearly naked body.

That was not as easy as it sounded, or as simple as she knew it should have been.

Try as she might, she could not keep her gaze from James. Too unnerved to consider the implications of all she was feeling, she had no choice but to focus on details.

The towel was one of Lucy's best, she noted, and it looked especially white in the faded light. James had it knotted on one side. It was slung low across his hips to reveal a trim waist and a fine mat of dark hair that dusted his stomach.

Lucy didn't allow her gaze to wander farther downward. She had already seen a scarce strip of James's naked thigh where the towel met edge to edge. She didn't dare think what else might be revealed by the snug-fitting towel. Or how much her suddenly far-too-active imagination might visualize.

Because she didn't know where else to look, Lucy allowed her gaze to drift upward to the dark hair sprinkled across James's broad chest. She watched the way the light shifted, caressing his muscles, defining them in lines of flickering gold and muted gray.

He had been hurt far more by the beating than she'd suspected. She could see that now, and her heart warmed at the thought. Where the smoking jacket hung open, she could see that there were patches of purple on his chest and along his ribs and an assortment of cuts and scratches that looked fresh and far more painful than she knew he would ever admit.

"Well, what do you think?" As if daring her to take a closer look, he rounded the bed. His voice dipped at the same time his eyes brightened. "You must have an opinion, Miss Barnstable. You have an opinion about everything." He held out his arms and if he meant to give her a better look, he succeeded. The smoking jacket gaped open farther and she saw even more of his bare skin. "You're interested enough to stare. Interested enough to wait for me in my bedchamber."

"Hardly waiting." Lucy gulped down her mortification. She pressed the armful of linens closer to her body and firmly refused to glance at the parcel and envelope that lay on the bed. In the dim light, it was just possible he hadn't seen them. Not yet. It was just possible he hadn't guessed the real reason she was here where she had no business. With a man she had no business being alone with. A man whose state of undress she had no business appreciating nearly as much as she did.

Dashing the thought from her mind, Lucy hurried through an explanation. "I was bringing clean linens," she said. "As I do every day. I was—"

"You were waiting." James did not seem the least bit disconcerted by his lack of attire. As a matter of fact, he seemed to be enjoying her uneasiness. He kept his arms at his sides, allowing her a perfect view, and Lucy could no more keep herself from drinking in the sight of him than she could help enjoying it: the rakish tilt of his chin, the solid line of his shoulders, the unyielding plane of his chest. The cuts and bruises that marked his skin did nothing at all to make him look wounded or vulnerable. If anything, they made him look formidable and solid, as imposing as the Greek gods whose statues she'd seen at the British Museum.

Except that the light in his eyes fired a smile that was positively disarming.

"Delivering linens," Lucy insisted. Captured by the charm of his smile, she tripped over the words, and feeling far more vulnerable than she had when the bed was between them, she scrambled to save herself from succumbing to the power of it. "Freddy left and—"

"Ah, Freddy." As if the mere mention of her fiancé was a talisman powerful enough to deter him, James stepped back. The disarming smile thinned just enough to give it a cynical edge.

"Freddy's a real brick, isn't he? A cut above the

rest. So damned respectable. Imagine what he might say if he could see us now."

The idea was too horrible to even consider, and Lucy refused to do so. "Freddy would never think to embarrass a lady so," she said.

"You? Embarrassed?" James laughed. "What about me? I'm the one standing here nearly as naked as a worm. But perhaps that's what you were hoping to see?"

Before she could even think of an objection, he closed the space between them.

Before she could even think to hang on tight to them, he stripped the linens out of her arms and tossed them on the bed.

Before she could move, or try to think of all the reasons he shouldn't, he stepped even closer, close enough for her to smell the scent of the soap he'd used in the bath and to feel the heat that rose from his body.

Automatically, Lucy's hands came up. She rested them flat against his chest and even she wasn't sure if it was to hold him at a distance or to take advantage of the feel of his body through the silky smoking jacket.

He would have liked to pretend he was immune to her touch. Lucy could tell as much from the shadow of self-reproach that darkened his eyes. But even he could do nothing to disguise the sharp breath of wonder that made his chest rise and fall beneath her fingers. His body moved against hers, and when she found neither the courage nor the willpower to step away or to prevent the contact, James's surprise dissolved into the heat of a heart-stopping smile.

"You're not the least bit embarrassed," he said, and it wasn't a criticism. "You're far too practical to ever be embarrassed. Embarrassment is for swooning young ladies and romantic gentlemen. It's time to face the facts, Lucy my love, you're no swooning young lady and I . . ." He turned his smile up a notch. "If the thoughts I'm having are any indication, I think it's safe to say that I am no gentleman. So you see, you're not embarrassed and I'm not sorry. The only thing I'm apologizing for is that I didn't think to do this sooner."

He dipped his head and his mouth came down on hers. His kiss was probing and tentative and her head and her heart warned her to resist, but Lucy didn't listen. She had no thoughts of anything except the effervescence that bubbled through her veins and the heat that built in her core and left her wanting more.

"You're not the least bit embarrassed," James whispered. His voice was husky, his Scots accent more pronounced than ever. He trailed a series of shivery kisses along her jawline to her ear. "You're not embarrassed to be kissing me when you're engaged to Freddy. You're not embarrassed to set a trap for a man when he's fresh from the bath and least expecting it. It's amazing! Amazing what a woman will do to cover up the fact that she's a thief."

"What!" Lucy pressed her hands to his chest and pushed him away as hard as she could. Caught on the thin wire between outrage and complete humiliation, she felt the color drain from her face and the heat from her body. She glanced at the parcel and envelope that lay on the bed and from there to James. Every trace of desire was gone from his eyes. They were clear and steady, and, damn him, they glittered with amusement.

"How could you?" Lucy's voice broke over the

words. "You saw that I had the envelope. The moment you walked in. You knew what I was doing here and you—"

"Took advantage of the situation?" James's smooth laugh rippled the air between them. "Of course I did. Why not? You weren't being entirely honest with me. I saw no reason I should be any more sincere. You don't think I'm fool enough to believe you were lying in wait to seduce me, do you?"

The idea was too preposterous to even consider. That's why Lucy couldn't understand why it caused a deliciously uncomfortable ripple to vibrate through her body. She gulped down her mortification and hid her reaction behind a healthy dose of outrage. "You don't think that I—?"

"Of course not." Chuckling, James held up one hand as if in surrender. "All right," he said, "we both win. I got to pay you back for looking through my things. And you got the kiss you wanted."

Lucy spluttered over a protest.

"Don't deny it," James went right on. "You know I'm right. It's what you wanted this afternoon. Right there in the street outside of St. Paul's. You thought you were going to get it, too. You made a pretty picture, I'll tell you that much. Your eyes were closed and those precious pink lips of yours were puckered and waiting. Lucky for you there's a bit of a gentleman inside me and—"

"A gentleman?" This time, Lucy wasn't about to let him ride roughshod over her protest. She stepped up to him and raised her chin. "No gentleman would ever treat a lady the way you've treated me."

"And no lady would try to steal from one of her tenants." James raised his eyebrows and met her, eye to eye. If he was angry, he didn't show it. He was so satisfied with himself, he couldn't keep a smile from his face. He leaned closer and whispered, "I won't tell Freddy if you won't."

Lucy curled her fingers into her palms and tucked her thumbs around them. "There's nothing to tell Freddy," she said through clenched teeth. "Not unless you're willing to admit that you're an utter cad."

"Yes. I am," James admitted matter-of-factly. "But I am not completely without scruples. You've heard from your father this evening?"

The question caught Lucy off guard. "No," she answered honestly and waited, wondering what he might be getting at.

He glanced at the bed. At the parcel. And the envelope. The packages that might contain some clue to her father's disappearance. "Then we'll go over the papers tonight. Together." James backed away, opening a path that would allow her to circle the bed and get to the door. "The parlor in twenty minutes?"

"Yes." Lucy was too relieved to question his motives. Her mind already racing over all the possibilities, she headed for the door. It wasn't until she was past him that she felt James's hand capture hers. In one smooth movement, he spun her around and, like a fisherman, reeled her closer.

"One other thing," he said. He smiled down into the surprise that filled her eyes. "One more kiss. Just so we have something to keep from Freddy."

He didn't wait for her to agree or disagree. He didn't wait for her to do anything. He pulled her against him, his hands pressed to the small of her back.

His first kiss was probing and tentative. This one was anything but. He kissed her long and hard, his tongue tempting and teasing and tickling hers. It was an incredible sensation. Incredible and impossible to resist.

In one second, Lucy's common sense deserted her. Desire rushed in to fill all the empty places it left in its wake. As if the sound came from a long way off, she heard herself moan. James was far taller than she, and he bent closer at the same time she rose up on her toes, longing to deepen the contact.

He stroked her and caressed her, his fingers hard and sure against her white cotton blouse. He glided his hands to her ribs and back down over her hips, caressing her waist, grazing her breasts.

Sensations swirled with sounds, tastes with touch. Lucy floated on a cloud of desire. She couldn't have said where his hands explored—any more than she could account for what her own hands were doing— she only knew that her body tingled and ached and that James felt the desire as surely as she did. She heard him groan her name at the same time his lips left a trail of fire along her neck. They seared the skin in the hollow at the base of her throat where he pressed one last, lingering kiss before he let her go.

There was nothing to do, and certainly nothing she could say. Dazed and weak-kneed, Lucy retreated as quickly as she could.

It wasn't until she was halfway downstairs that she realized she was holding his towel.

# Chapter 9

"It was a mistake. I shouldn't have kissed you."

Pacing the parlor from one end to the other, James practiced his apologies. He had never been very good at this sort of thing. He was sure of it. Never very good at repentance, and he gave it another go, hoping that when Lucy finally joined him, he'd have the backbone to sound as damned awful as he felt.

If he had to eat crow, he might as well eat it off a silver platter.

"It was a terrible mistake to act the way I acted upstairs," he said his shoulders rigid and uncomfortable inside another of Albert Miller's shirts. "I apologize. I never meant for things to get so out of hand and—"

Hadn't he?

The question gnawed at his mind in much the same way as the feverish flush of desire still tickled his body. Truth be told, there was nothing in the entire world that he'd wanted more than he'd wanted things to get out of hand.

He'd wanted to kiss Lucy, he confessed that much to himself, just as he confessed that he'd hoped she would react exactly the way she did. He'd yearned to feel her melt against him, her body soft and inviting, her lips moist and parted. He'd wanted to prove that there was more passion in her than even she had ever imagined. And to prove to himself that he was completely impervious to succumbing to it.

It was hell admitting he was wrong.

His shirt collar felt suddenly too tight and James ran one finger around the inside of it.

It did matter. He'd acknowledge as much to himself though he'd be damned if he'd ever let Lucy know it. It mattered far too much. And there was nothing he could do for it. Nothing he could do about it. Except apologize.

His mind made up, the words ready in his head if not on his lips, James linked his hands behind his back, squared his shoulders, and faced the door.

"Like a bloody criminal in front of a firing squad," he told himself. He heard Lucy's footsteps out in the passageway and he tensed. He watched the brass doorknob twist and he held his breath.

The words tumbled out of him before the door was all the way open. "You took my towel."

Startled, Lucy paused inside the doorway. But only for a moment. Gathering her composure, she carefully closed the door behind her, and firmly refusing to meet his eyes, she went to the table and sat down. Her movements were brisk and businesslike, as crisp and unemotional as her voice.

"I'm sorry I've kept you waiting," she said. "I had to finish delivering the rest of the linens. I took Mr. Grogan's up to him and—"

"I hope he was dressed." It was unfair to make light of the subject, especially since Lucy seemed as determined to put it behind her as James was. Perhaps that was precisely why he found himself teasing her.

The incident obviously had not affected Lucy, not nearly as much as it had him. She didn't stumble over lame apologies or stammer through inept excuses. She didn't look as if the memory of every touch, every kiss, crawled through her like the prickle of the midsummer sun, heating a course through her body that burned her blood and seared her brain.

She looked unruffled. Unmoved.

Unimpressed.

James's pride was wounded. His self-esteem was crushed. It was less painful to laugh about their encounter than it was to own up to the truth. He shrugged, as if to say he couldn't help himself. "I'd hate for you to have something else to keep from Freddy."

Lucy raised her eyes to his and in a flash of memory that was far more distinct than any he'd had in the last few days, James remembered his childhood governess, a woman named Miss MacDonald, whose steely eyes could stop a lad cold at a hundred paces.

Lucy gave him the same kind of look. A Miss MacDonald look. She had that same flinty glint in her eyes. That same lift of her chin that told him whatever else she might be feeling, she was definitely not amused.

"I never see Mr. Grogan," Lucy said. "No one does. He's out late most nights and he doesn't join us for meals. I have no idea if he was dressed or undressed. I don't even know if he was there. Nor do I care."

"No more do I." As chastised as he had been years earlier by Miss MacDonald, James sat down at the table next to her. Neither of them said a word. Neither had to. There was an unspoken pact between them, a tacit understanding that they would keep their distance.

As if to underscore it, Lucy scooted her chair a

fraction of an inch farther from his. James kept his arms close to his sides. Together, they looked at the parcel and envelope he'd left at the center of the table.

"I—" Her hands on the table, Lucy hesitated. She drew in a deep breath. "I must admit, I didn't think you'd be so reasonable about this. If I knew you were agreeable to letting me take a look at the packages, I wouldn't have . . ." She didn't need to put the rest of it into words. They both knew precisely to what she was referring. Lucy wiped her palms on her dark skirt.

"You said you were going to wait for Alfie. Remember? In the cab on the way to *The Times*. You didn't know about the envelope then, of course. But you said you would open the parcel on your own. And you would share the information you found inside it with Alfie when he returned. Quite frankly, James . . ." She shifted her gaze to meet his. "I am surprised at your change of heart."

So was he.

James turned the thought over in his head. When he'd received the packages, he had no intention of sharing them with Lucy. Or Alfie. No intention of sharing them with anyone. Like the Indian stone seal he'd found in his pocket, the two mysterious packages seemed enigmatic reminders that there was more to his life than he suspected, certainly more than he remembered. As much as he wanted to find out the truth, about the packages and about himself, some instinct told him to use caution every step of the way.

Yet sometime between the cab ride and that moment in his bedchamber when he'd agreed to show Lucy the packages, he'd changed his mind.

He didn't like to think he was thinking with his

heart—and other even more sensitive portions of his anatomy—and not his head. He refused to believe it had anything to do with Lucy's marvelous eyes or her lustrous hair. He was by far too sensible a man to think it had anything to do with the infinite softness of her lips. It was because he felt guilty for the way he'd treated her upstairs. That was the reason. Realizing it and feeling much relieved, James sat up a little straighter.

"I see no reason to delay our investigation pending your father's arrival. As you've pointed out, you are his Watson. Well, Watson . . ." For the first time since their unnerving encounter, James managed what was almost a smile. "The game's afoot. Where shall we start?"

Her eyes sparkling with anticipation, Lucy glanced from the parcel to the envelope. "The parcel, I think," she said, shifting her gaze back to it. "You received it first and though that is probably not significant, one never knows."

James agreed. It probably wasn't significant. But this wasn't the time to argue the point. His hand flat against the package, he slid it over to Lucy.

"Go ahead," he said. "Show off your detecting skills. As your father's assistant, you must have seen him do this sort of thing any number of times."

"Hundreds of times," Lucy added a little quickly.

"Hundreds of times." James indulged her. "Very well then, you must have learned something from watching him all those hundreds of times. Can you tell me anything about the package and the person who left it for me?"

He didn't dare speak the other question foremost in his mind: From the evidence before her, could she tell him anything about himself?

Every muscle tensed, every nerve tight with anticipation, James waited. And waited some more.

Expelling a murmur of displeasure, he swiveled in
his seat to find Lucy still staring at the parcel. If he
didn't know better, he would say she was not nearly
as excited by the prospect of deducing its significance
as he might have thought she'd be. As a matter of
fact, she looked positively terrified.

Lucy's dark eyes darted back and forth, studying
the parcel, searching for the answers to its secrets.
She ran her tongue over her lips, and James tried not
to notice the way it left them looking moist and inviting. He concentrated on her hands instead, watching
the way her fingers hesitated over the wrappings.

"The string is extremely fascinating," she said. The
words rushed out of her and again James had a recollection of his childhood. He'd been coerced into reciting
a passage of Milton to a roomful of adults—probably
by a look from Miss MacDonald—and he remembered how uncomfortable he was at the whole thing,
and how the words had whooshed out of him in one
quick breath. The same way Lucy was talking now.
"And the knot is distinctive."

It did not look at all distinctive to James, but then,
he wasn't the detective. Watching Lucy trace the
name "James Smith" with one finger, he waited for
more.

"The hand is well educated," she said. "Written
with a broad-pointed pen. The writing is very mascu-
line, don't you think? It seems obvious the parcel
was sent by a man."

"Yes. Of course." James couldn't help but be awed.
He supposed that on some level, he'd realized all the
same things, but he hadn't been nearly clever enough
to form his impressions into so coherent a theory. He
leaned forward, eager to learn more.

Feeling him move nearer, Lucy glanced at him out
of the corner of her eye. Not until she was certain
that he was going to keep his distance did she go
back to her study of the parcel.

She slipped the string from around it. "Now for
the wrappings," she told James. "Brown paper. Very
ordinary. There's nothing more to be learned from it,
I'm afraid."

"And from its contents?"

Again, Lucy licked her lips. Again, James had the
nearly uncontrollable urge to help her along. Her
mouth was remarkably sweet. He'd learned that
much up in his bedchamber. He wouldn't mind taking her in his arms and having another taste.

And he knew he couldn't risk it.

Keeping his hands at his sides, his mouth where
it belonged, and his thoughts to himself, James
waited while Lucy tore the wrappings from the
parcel.

"It's a book," she said, exposing the binding.

James himself had deduced as much earlier, but
now that the wrappings were off, he bent closer for
a better look. "*The History of the Art of the Indus Val-
ley*." He read the title aloud and watched as Lucy
flipped through the pages. "It looks to be a ponder-
ous tome, doesn't it? Complete with maps and
photographs."

"The entire history of the art of the Indian subcontinent laid out in one volume." Lucy slapped the
book shut and turned to him. "Why do you suppose
it's important?"

James couldn't answer. This time, it had nothing
to do with the fact that Lucy's eyes were bright in
the reflected light of the lamp or that her face was
touched with color. There was a pattern forming at
the back of his mind, like one of the tartans he re-

membered from his boyhood in Scotland. He couldn't see its colors yet. Nor could he recognize the clan. And until he knew full well what it meant and what it stood for, he wasn't about to commit himself.

Peck, the guard in the Indian Galleries of the British Museum. The book of Indian art that had been left for him behind a statue of one of the Hindu gods. The stone seal.

He had no idea what it all meant, or why it was all important. He only knew it was. He suspected that Lucy did, too.

"Indian art." He dared to say the words, hoping they might trigger some stimulus inside his brain. They didn't, and he shook his head. "I have no idea why I'd care about Indian art. Except that the Indian Gallery is where we ran into Peck. You're the one who dragged us there," he told her. He fixed his gaze to hers, challenging her. "You tell me. Why should Indian art be important to me? Or to you?"

Lucy hesitated. Far too long. She fussed with the sleeves of her white blouse and thumbed through the pages of the art book. She fidgeted in her chair and skimmed her hands over her hair.

She glanced at James, her eyes uncertain. But still, she didn't say a word, not until she looked over her shoulder toward the mantelpiece and the photograph of her father that sat on it. Only then did she haul in a breath and when she let it out again, James suspected that even she did not know what she might say.

"I think, perhaps, we should take a look at the envelope delivered by Mr. Canaday, don't you?" Lucy asked. Before James had a chance to answer, she had the envelope in her hands. She ripped it open and spilled its contents onto the table.

There wasn't nearly as much as James had hoped there would be, just some articles clipped from old issues of *The Times*.

"More on India," James said, scanning the papers. He lifted the first article and held it to the light. "This one's nearly a year old. It concerns an archaeological excavation at Mohenjo-Daro." Though he could not have said why, he glanced up at Lucy, expecting some reaction to the name. He didn't get one, nothing but an even look that met his. Her look was an invitation, though he could not have said to what. It dared him to say more.

He hated to disappoint her, but there wasn't anything more to say.

James set the first article aside and went on to the others, passing them to Lucy as he finished.

Each and every article had something to do with India, its history and its art. By now, a good deal of it was starting to sound familiar and he wondered how much of it was because he'd heard it from Peck and Lucy, and how much was the echo of suppressed memories, things that had happened long before today's visit to the British Museum.

It wasn't until he came to the last article that another small piece to the puzzle fell into place.

The article told the story of the Maharajah of Rangpoon, a man of incredible prestige and power on the subcontinent whose wealth was renowned and whose opulent lifestyle was the stuff of legends.

"Rangpoon." James said the name below his breath, and though he thought it was nothing but an idle slip of the tongue, it must have contained a good deal more emotion than even he imagined. In the middle of reading one of the articles, Lucy paused and turned to him.

"You know the man?" she asked.

James shook his head. It was neither a yes or a no, but some answer in between. He scanned the rest of the first page of the article. "They say he will be here in London for the Jubilee. He's presenting the Queen with a statue, the—" The article must have taken up more than one column. James flipped to the next clip.

"The Eye of the Devil!" James stared at the page and at the drawing that illustrated the article, and somewhere in the back of his mind, a memory flared. Though he could not have said how it was possible, he recognized the brass statue instantly.

It was Kali, the Hindu goddess of destruction. Her fierce fangs were tipped in blood. Her eyes were aglow. In the center of the headdress she wore was the Eye of the Devil.

The Eye of the Devil was one of the largest diamonds in the world and certainly the most perfect: two hundred eighty-three carats of flawless, fiery ice. Like most famous jewels, its past was cloaked in mystery and shadowed with a trail of deceit, treachery, and blood. Word had it that the Maharajah of Rangpoon had obtained it years earlier. Some stories said it was part of a marriage settlement, others that it was booty from some war between Indian princes. Whatever its source, the eye of the Devil was not destined to stay in India much longer.

As a show of loyalty, Rangpoon was coming to England in the middle of June to present the diamond to Victoria on the occasion of her Diamond Jubilee.

"Rangpoon is making a great show of the gift," James commented, still studying the drawing. "He's certain it will generate a great deal of goodwill between himself and the British government in Delhi, and from what I've heard, goodwill is exactly what he needs right about now. The old scoundrel likes to play

both ends against the middle. Rumor has it he has
sympathies for the Indian National Congress, the
group that supports independence for India. The
viceroy will never put up with that for long, of
course. There's been talk of taking away Rangpoon's
power and giving it to his nephew, a fellow who was
educated at Oxford and whose loyalty is without
question."

Even in a pen and ink sketch, the beauty of the
diamond was undeniable, yet it was difficult for
James to picture the gem in black and white. He envi-
sioned it full of color, instead: flickers of intense blue
and sparks of silver that burst upon the eye like lightning, glimmers of yellow as brilliant as the Indian
sun and red, clear, and bright like blood.

"Rangpoon will miss the Devil," he said. "It's his
pride and joy. But they've got him between hell and
high water. Give the old girl the diamond, and he
might be able to curry a little favor with the government. Refuse to present it . . ."

James considered the implications.

"Refuse to present it and Rangpoon isn't the only
one whose loyalties are in question. He's acting as a
representative for all of India. If Victoria doesn't receive the Eye of the Devil at the Jubilee, it could
spark an international incident. It would fuel the independence movement, that's for certain, and that
could mean an all-out war."

"Does it say all that there in the article?" At the
sound of Lucy's voice, James's head snapped up. He
didn't answer her. He couldn't. He had no idea how
he knew about Rangpoon. Or the Eye of the Devil.

The knowledge burned through his brain, as bright
and as deadly as the diamond itself. It filled his blood
with heat at the same time it left his stomach icy cold.

Impatient for an answer, Lucy reached for the newspaper and snatched it out of James's hand. She scanned it quickly. "It doesn't say a word about the Indian National Congress," she said. Her voice was tight with excitement. Her gaze moved up to James and stayed full on him. "It doesn't say anything about how Rangpoon is trying to court favor with Delhi, either. How do you know all that?"

James shrugged, a gesture that surely must have looked as impotent as it felt. He rummaged through his mind, but whatever door had opened on seeing the Eye of the Devil, it was firmly shut again. There was nothing there. Only the empty, lonely blackness of oblivion.

Her frustration mounting, Lucy sighed, but while James expected her to say something, she looked over her shoulder again at the photograph of her father. When she turned back to James, her eyes were solemn. She studied him, as if measuring his worth.

Like the kiss they'd shared, James could not imagine why her opinion of him mattered nearly as much as it did. He held his breath, waiting for her to pass sentence.

Her mind made up, Lucy nodded. "I have something to show you," she said.

She retrieved something from her pocket, something small enough to cup in one hand. Her palm down, she set it on the table. When she moved her hand away, there was an Indian stone seal.

James knew in an instant that the seal was a duplicate of the one he carried in his pocket. The angular writing, the man wearing his elaborate turban, the worshiping animals, they were all familiar and so different from the seals they'd seen at the British Museum, he knew there was no mistaking the fact that his seal and Lucy's must have some connection.

What he didn't know was what it meant.

James watched Lucy watch him, watched her stare at him wordlessly. She leaned as close as she had dared come since their encounter above stairs, close enough for James to see her face full in the light, and to realize that it was bright with expectation.

His heart skipped a beat. If he didn't know better, he would say that Lucy knew about his seal. That she knew about it, and was waiting for him to produce it.

If he didn't know better, he might actually have done it.

But whatever else James didn't know—about himself and his past—he recognized the whispers of danger, the tingling along his arms and at the back of his neck that told him to be careful.

A man never knew who his friends were.

Like a voice from the past, the words filled his head.

A man never knew who his enemies were, either, and if he was wise and wanted to live into his old age, he was never reckless enough to confuse the two. He was never so trusting that he dared take chances with his life. Or his secrets.

Yet he had already given his life into Lucy's hands. If he needed a reminder of that, James need only look over to the rug in the front of the fireplace, the place where he'd fainted dead away within minutes of meeting Lucy. He need only look at the chair where she'd settled him with a blanket over his knees or the table, now empty, where she'd gotten water to clean a stranger's wounds.

If he closed his eyes, he could still feel her hands the way he'd felt them that night. They were quick and assured, so gentle that even through the pain that stabbed his body and clouded his mind, he could feel her there. When the nature and the extent of his injuries should have killed him, Lucy was the one who had kept him alive, and thinking about it, he realized she was the only thing that had kept him going in the days since.

Lucy, with her unbounded energy and her enthusiasm for her father's work. Lucy was the one who helped drive away the black despair when it threatened to swallow him in the nothingness that had already claimed his past. Lucy was the one who replaced it with a shining glimmer of hope.

He didn't need to remind himself, but even so, James shifted his gaze to her. Lucy was still watching him, still waiting. She couldn't have known about the Indian stone seal in his pocket, yet instinctively, he knew she wanted him to produce it.

She wanted that and more.

Usually full of restless energy, Lucy sat perfectly still. Her hands were folded on the table in front of her. Her head was bent forward. Steady and patient, she waited, and James knew if she had to, she would wait forever.

She waited for proof. Waited for him to show he trusted her. Waited for him to open his secrets to her. And his heart.

No, a man could not take chances. James reminded himself of the fact. He could not risk confusing enemies and friends. He could not trust those he didn't know, or get to know those he did not trust.

It was good advice, and James damned it to perdition along with his doubts and fears.

He forced his eyes from Lucy's, down to the stone seal that lay upon the table, and reaching into his pocket, he drew out his seal and laid it next to hers.

"We have a connection, you and I." His words were as full of the sudden and quite inexplicable relief he felt at opening his secrets to her as was his heart. "I wish I understood. I wish . . ."

He was not a man who was prone to wishing. He knew it instinctively. It was that, surely, that made the words catch in his throat.

He knew just as well that he was not a man who depended on wishes to make his way through life, but one who, for good or ill, relied on actions.

James kissed Lucy's cheek.

He didn't wait to see what her reaction might be, to the stone seal or to the kiss. He left the room as quickly as he could.

Before the weight of the emotions that stirred his blood and warmed his heart could cause him to make another mistake.

# Chapter 10

It was well past midnight when Lucy finally went to bed and later still before she fell asleep. Even then, it was a restless sleep at best.

Perhaps that is why she woke so quickly when she heard the sounds.

Lucy's eyes popped open. Silence filled the house, pressing close against her ears, and she listened harder, straining to hear the elusive sound that had shattered her sleep. She heard her own heartbeat and the swish of the blood inside her veins. She listened to the steady beat of the clock on her bedside table. From a very long way off, she heard a solitary church bell chime the hour: three o'clock.

And she heard something else.

Lucy held herself stiff and still. In the darkness, it was hard to tell where the noise came from, just as it was impossible to say what it might be. She only knew that it was wrong somehow, that it did not fit with the normal sounds of the house at night.

Carefully, Lucy raised herself on her elbows and cocked her head. She never left a light burning in the passageway outside her bedchamber, but as she looked toward the closed door, she saw a slender sliver of light slip across the floor outside. The floor-boards creaked, the sound as loud as a scream in the thick silence.

Suddenly wide awake, Lucy sat up in bed. She swung her legs over the side and watched the light come and go, sweeping across the floor on the other side of her door.

Lucy's heart thumped. She told herself she was being foolish and appallingly romantic but she could hardly help herself; for one moment, she thought it might be James outside her door.

Automatically, her hand traveled to her cheek. Her skin wasn't hot. It couldn't have been so many hours after James pressed a kiss there. Yet she swore she could still feel the warmth of his lips.

Lucy's face burned. Mesmerized by its mystery and its promise, she watched the light come nearer. Her heart pounded at the same time it beat out her most secret wish.

She wished it was James outside her door and if it was, she wished he was on his way to finish what he'd started in his bedchamber that evening, what he'd continued in the parlor with a good-night kiss.

This time, there was no mistaking the fact that Lucy's face was fiery hot, just as there was no mistaking its cause. It was the heat of embarrassment. The heat of shame.

Bewildered by a side of her personality she never knew existed—a flighty, impulsive, positively lusty Lucy—she held her breath and watched the silver stripe of light inch under her door. Her heart stopped. Her breath caught. But her brain refused to be cowed into submission as easily as her body.

It was completely unlike her to act the way she'd been acting, it reminded her. She was a rational woman. Or at least she was supposed to be. And rational women did not throw themselves at men, nor did they welcome the advances of strangers, towel-clad or otherwise. They didn't melt at a touch.

Or shiver at a glance. They didn't force themselves to spend the better part of the night reading Sherlock Holmes to keep their heads occupied. They didn't spend the rest of the night tossing and turning because they couldn't get a man's face, or his kiss, out of their minds.

The reprimand did not drift through her brain the way the light drifted outside her door. It marched through in heavy boots and left her feeling decisive and unwavering. She lifted her head and threw back her shoulders, glaring at the door in righteous indignation. It would not happen again, she promised herself. Not even if James was outside her bedroom door. Not even if he'd come to finish what he'd started.

Despite her resolve and all her good intentions, she was strangely disappointed when the light slid past her door and the sounds of stealthy footsteps continued farther down the hallway.

It wasn't James.

Lucy wondered if she should feel relief or disappointment. She didn't have time for either before another thought took up residence in her head. If it wasn't James outside her door, it was someone else. Someone who dared roam the house in the middle of the night with a stealthy step and a bull's-eye lantern.

Anticipation turned to curiosity and Lucy grabbed her dressing gown from the end of the bed and threw it over her nightgown. She slid her feet into her slippers, and being careful not to make a sound, she went to her door and inched it open.

To her left was Miss Foxworthy's room and the stairway that led either down to the entryway or up to the second floor where Mrs. Slyke, Mrs. Miller, and the Atwaters had their rooms. It was completely dark.

To her right, the passageway turned at a sharp angle. At the turn, the hallway led to Alfie's room and the adjoining snuggery he liked to think of as his study and workshop. Against the worn wallpaper with its faded pink roses and white camellias, Lucy saw the faint reflection of light.

On tiptoe, she followed the flicker. She paused where the passageway turned and peeked carefully around the corner. The door to Alfie's room was open. From inside, she heard the telltale squeak of floorboards and the ruffle of objects being moved on Alfie's desk.

Too curious to be apprehensive and far too puzzled to think of the whole thing as anything more than a peculiar mental exercise, Lucy crept closer to the doorway. She peered inside. In the pitch-darkness, even the meager light of the bull's-eye lantern seemed blinding.

In the days immediately prior to his disappearance, Alfie had brought home from who-knows-where an enormous and enormously garish plaster bust of the Queen and installed it in one corner of the room. It was at least three feet high and covered in a glittering gold paint that couldn't help but appeal to a man with Alfie's flamboyant tastes. As Lucy watched, the light traveled over Her Majesty's visage, illuminating the regal eyes, the aristocratic nose, the chins that were so majestic they could only have belonged to a queen.

From there, the beam swept over Alfie's desk. It was no more well ordered than his mind, and in the dazzling sweep of light, Lucy saw the jumble of books that littered the desk, the mountains of papers and magazines and what Alfie liked to call his "detective tools." It was chaos, plain and simple, a mess so daunting as to prevent Lucy from even thinking about taking the time to put the room in order.

The light moved again and Lucy better saw the man who was holding it.

His back was to her, but even from where she stood, Lucy could see that he was of average height. He had stocky shoulders and short legs. He swung the light toward the far wall in front of him and against it his silhouette showed her he was wearing a long overcoat and a Homburg hat.

Lucy's throat clenched. Tears sprang to her eyes. She expelled a shaky breath and stepped into the room, her voice wavering between a sob and laughter.

"Alfie!"

The man swung around. The light came with him. It shined full in Lucy's face. Blinded, she squinted and turned her head, but it didn't matter. She didn't need her eyes to tell her she was wrong.

It wasn't Alfie. This man swore at her in phrases Alfie would never utter. His voice was as uncouth and unfamiliar as his words. Keeping the light in Lucy's eyes, he lumbered forward, and before she could get her bearings, he grabbed her arm.

"Damned, ruddy female." He gave her a shake, emphasizing his point. The light moved with him and for the first time Lucy caught a glimpse of his face. He was clean-shaven and heavy-jowled, with small, vicious eyes and a smile that showed an empty space where his front teeth should have been. He smelled of bacon and onions and a good deal of beer. His fingers drilled into Lucy's arm.

"He told me no one would bother me, damn 'is eyes! He said as 'ow there weren't no one 'ere but some ol' biddies and them simpleton brothers. Forgot about you, did 'e? Or was 'e just hopin' I wouldn't find you and get distracted?" The man's gaze traveled the length of Lucy's body and his voice warmed.

It wasn't a comfortable kind of warmth, not the kind she'd heard shine through James's words now and again. Lucy shivered. Her right arm still caught in the man's grip, she tightened her dressing gown with her left hand and looked him in the eye.

"Who are you?" she asked. "What are you doing here? How did you get in? I know I locked up before I went to bed and—"

"Never you mind none of that," the man said. His top lip curling, he looked around the room. "Now that you're 'ere, you can help me through this goddamn mess." With the tip of one worn shoe, he kicked at the closest pile of books.

It wasn't so much his words that infuriated Lucy as it was his actions. He kicked the books—Alfie's books—and as she watched him, her temper soared. Too angry to be afraid, she wrenched her arm from his grasp and rubbed the spot where his fingers had been.

"Get out," she said. "Now. Get out or I'll—"

The man's chuckle stopped her. It was as cold as his look was hot, as chilling as the ice that formed in Lucy's stomach. He turned his lantern a fraction of an inch, just enough for her to see the long-bladed knife he had tucked into the waistband of his trousers. 'You'll what? Scream for the police? They ain't gonna help, I can tell you that much. But you . . ."

He let his gaze leave her for a second. It roamed the room, glancing from the bookshelves behind Lucy's left shoulder to the bow-fronted china cabinet on the other side of her.

Too late, Lucy realized it was a critical error to let his casual scrutiny of the room distract her. The man darted forward and grabbed her. He whirled her around and hurled her away so quickly, she didn't have time to brace herself. She slammed against Alfie's desk and only the reflexive act of holding out her hands to steady herself kept her from toppling over it head first.

"Now that you're 'ere you might as well make yourself useful," the man said. "You live in this rat's nest. You know where things is kept. Go ahead. Get it for me."

Lucy flattened her hands against the desktop. The man was behind her and she wasn't sure what he could see. Whatever it was, she hoped it looked convincing. She hoped she looked dizzy and disoriented enough to buy herself some time.

She hung her head and managed a noise that sounded enough like a sob and scolded herself when it sounded all too convincing, even to her.

"Oh, please, sir!" Stalling for time, Lucy swigged back tears that were only partly simulated. Her mind worked furiously. The man was a full hundred-weight heavier than she and accustomed to violence, if the size of his knife and the look in his eyes meant anything. There was no use screaming; Miss Foxworthy would never hear and everyone else was too far away. There was no use fighting, either. Her only hope lay in joining the game. With any luck, she could find out who the man was and what he was so intent on finding.

"It . . . it will take some time," Lucy said. Hoping to distract the man, she raised one hand to her eyes as if to wipe away tears. With the other, she felt around the desktop. "It isn't easy to come by, you know."

In the weird half-light and with all the clutter, it was difficult to see exactly what was on Alfie's desk. The one and only thing she found that seemed solid enough to be a weapon was a beaker that Alfie used in his chemical experiments. Most of his equipment was down in the parlor but Lucy clearly remembered when he'd cooked up this concoction. It was so malodorous, she'd ordered it out of the room, and for Lord knows what reason, Alfie brought it up here. Whatever the reason, she was glad for it now.

Wrinkling her nose, Lucy closed her fingers around the heavy glass beaker. "You might have to help me," she said, stumbling over the words while her mind raced double time. "I've only heard about it, you see. He talked about it all the time. But he never shared it with me. Not with anyone. I've never . . . never seen it." She held her breath, waiting to see if the man would recognize her words for the desperate lies they were. Her hands clutching the beaker behind her back, she turned. "Could you describe it?"

"Describe it?" The man growled. "What do I look like? Some blinkin' tour guide? Wait a bloody minute." The man cocked his head, as if he was unused to having ideas, and now that he'd had one, he wasn't quite sure what to do with it. "If he talked about it all the time, why do I need to describe it?"

He took a step toward Lucy and his expression changed from bewilderment to fury. With an agility she would not have expected from a man his size, he set his lantern down on the nearest table and whipped out his knife. Graceful as a dancer, swift as a street fighter, he closed the distance between them. "I ain't playin' games," he snarled. "Not with you, my little miss. Get it for me. Now. Or I'll—"

Lucy didn't want to hear what he would do. She planted her feet and braced herself. Her aim was straight if nothing else. The contents of the beaker hit the man full in the face but it didn't stop him. At the same time he roared in outrage and in pain, she saw the flash of his knife. It came straight at her.

James knew exactly how danger felt.

Though he could not have said where or how he'd come by the information, he knew it was true. He recognized the smell of danger. He knew its texture and its touch. Even in his sleep he could sense a hint of it in the air. It crawled along his skin and settled like frost in his stomach, intruding on the pleasantly provocative dream he'd been having about Lucy.

There was no use fighting the feeling and reluctantly he let the dream fade, promising himself as a kind of compensation that he would conjure it again, some other time when he could fully savor the delicious images that had filled his head.

Fully awake now, James scraped one hand through his hair and opened his eyes. He had no idea what woke him. It may have been a sound, but he didn't think so. He thought it more of a feeling.

A feeling that something wasn't quite right.

Grumbling when Albert Miller's pajamas twisted around his thighs, he sat up and cocked his head. There wasn't a sound inside the house or out, nothing but the solitary peal of a church bell tolling the hour.

The quiet was not nearly as reassuring as it should have been. There was something unnatural about it, as if the house itself and all its occupants were poised unwittingly on the edge of some great peril.

For a minute he sat perfectly still, thinking through the problem. All was quiet. There seemed no earthly reason for him to leave his bed, no purpose to be gained from having a look around the house to make sure everything was all right. He could, of course, make certain. He could stop by Lucy's room and check to see if she was sleeping safely.

The thought brought him up short and before he even realized what he was doing, James found himself already out of bed and heading for the door.

"Oh, no!" He stopped himself before his body could lead him where his head knew he had no business. "You might just as well walk into a lion's den," he reminded himself, marching back to the bed. "You'd probably come out less scathed."

He plopped back down on the thin, uncomfortable mattress and was just about to tuck himself under the blankets when he heard a roar.

It was a voice he didn't recognize, a man's voice. The commotion was coming from the first floor where Lucy and Miss Foxworthy had their rooms.

This time there was no hesitation in James's steps. He shot out of bed and raced across the room. He hauled open the door.

James took the steps two at a time. He went even faster when, a moment later, he heard Lucy scream.

Instinctively, Lucy raised her hands to shield herself from the knife blade, but it was hardly protection enough. The man's outraged bellow roared through her ears at the same time he fell upon her. Blinded by the mixture in the beaker, he howled and kicked and lashed out. His aim wasn't good, but his odds of hitting something weren't bad at all. His knife met flesh, slicing the side of Lucy's hand.

Screaming more from the surprise than the pain, she clutched the beaker and her bleeding left hand to her chest and did her best to retreat. But with Alfie's desk behind her and the man in front, there was no place for her to go.

The knife flashed past her eyes, closer this time,

and Lucy winced. Blood covered her left hand and soaked into the sleeves of her nightgown and her dressing gown. Her blood. Just looking at it made her head reel and her stomach tumble. She couldn't feel the fingers on her left hand at all, couldn't feel anything but the heat of the blood. It saturated the front of her nightgown, weighing down the delicate lace, gilding it with crimson.

Her fingers were numb and Lucy realized she was quickly losing her grip on the blood-slicked glass. It was the only weapon left to her and if she was going to use it, she knew she would have to move quickly.

Gathering her last bit of strength, Lucy forced herself to gulp down her nausea. Ignoring the knife when it streaked past her eyes, she slid her right hand under her left. With it supporting both her wounded hand and the beaker, she raised her arms and brought the beaker crashing down on the man's head.

Sounds overlapped. Curses and shattering glass. Screams that might have been her own. Shouts. Footsteps pounding on the stairs.

The noise filled Lucy's head. It was the last thing she remembered before her knees gave out and darkness claimed her.

# Chapter 11

The next thing Lucy knew, there were lights burning against her closed eyelids. She squeezed her eyes tighter and turned away. It was only then she realized her head was pillowed on someone's lap.

Moving slowly against the brightness, she opened her eyes.

"James." Her voice rasped out of her, its brittleness a strange contrast to the warmth that flooded through her when she realized she was safe. She didn't stop to wonder if the feeling had anything at all to do with James, she simply luxuriated in it. It was as comforting, somehow, as the rough texture of James's green and pink striped pajamas against her cheek.

"Dinna fash yersel' with talking." His accent as pronounced as she'd heard it at other times when he was moved by some powerful emotion, James didn't look at her. He concentrated on her hand instead, and on the cloth he had pressed to it. It was quickly turning bright red, and watching it made Lucy's stomach jump. She moved her gaze back to James.

"Relax," he said. "Don't move. You're fine, I think, provided this blood all over the front of you is from your hand and not from some other wound." He didn't ask permission to examine her and it was just as well. Lucy wasn't sure she had the strength to refuse.

Loosening the ribbon tie at the neckline of her nightgown, James spread the fabric apart. His touch was gentle, his examination blessedly quick. Even injured, Lucy wasn't sure how long she could endure the warmth of his hands against her skin. A second too long and she was sure he would notice the way her heart beat in furious response to his touch.

James trailed his fingers down her neck and Lucy held her breath. He nudged the nightgown open farther, his fingers brushing her breasts, and she closed her eyes. She didn't dare open them again until he settled the nightgown back in place, his fingers lingering through the lace as if he could rid it of its bloody coating. When she did, she found James looking remarkably relieved.

"You're fine except for your hand. I know it stings like hell," he said, letting go a ragged breath and shifting his gaze back to Lucy's hand, "but I don't think it's as bad as it looks." He removed the cloth and refolded it, applying pressure with the side that wasn't already soaked with blood. "If I had to guess, I'd say the other fellow did not fare nearly as well as you."

It was an innocent enough reminder of all that had happened, but it made Lucy's fears rush back at her. She glanced around.

"Don't worry," James said, and from her singularly comfortable vantage point, Lucy couldn't help but notice that his eyes sparkled with something very close to admiration. "He's long gone by now. The last I saw of the poor blighter, he was headed out the front door as if the devil himself was on his tail. What did you do to him?"

"Do? To him?" Lucy made a move to sit up, but

James wouldn't allow it. His one hand still holding the cloth, he put the other on her shoulder, keeping her in place. It was an awkward movement at best and he couldn't accomplish it while looking at her hand. He shifted his gaze to her face.

"You're a right fine fighter, Miss Lucy Barnstable," James said. A smile glimmered in his dark eyes, but his voice was rough and curiously thick. "I would be glad to have you at my side in a battle, and no mistake."

The warmth inside Lucy squeezed around her heart, making it impossible for her to respond. It was just as well. She wasn't sure what to say.

She didn't have a chance to say anything. There was a commotion out in the hallway and the Atwaters rushed into the room with Harleigh—if it was Harleigh—leading the charge.

It was neither Harleigh's short nightshirt nor his bony shins that astounded Lucy as much as it was the battle saber he dragged alongside him with both hands. From its elaborately decorated sheath to the fringe of crimson hanging from its haft, it was the kind of weapon Lucy had seen in paintings of the Charge of the Light Brigade: old-fashioned and cumbersome and positively romantic. It was as impressive as the pistol Farleigh came in carrying.

"Reporting for duty, sir!"

Both their mustaches quivering, the Atwaters snapped to attention and offered James a pair of crisp salutes.

His eyes suddenly as steely as the blade, Harleigh hauled his sword from its scabbard and brandished it right and left. "Was it the Sikhs, sir? The bloody scoundrels. They've penetrated our defenses, have they? I'll show them a thing or two." He swung the sword around and James ducked and tucked one arm around Lucy's shoulders, instinctively shielding her. "I'll dice them, sir!" Harleigh vowed. "I'll slice them! I'll run them through!"

"No need!" Farleigh stepped to the fore and laid his pistol against his cheek. He shut one eye, lining up his shot. "I shall take care of the Sikhs, sir. Don't you worry. Nasty devils. Every one of them. Just give me the word and I'll discharge a volley. Send them running for the hills."

Farleigh squeezed the trigger and Lucy caught her breath at the same time she felt James flinch. Fortunately for them all—and for the bust of the Queen for which Farleigh was inadvertently aiming—James recovered in a heartbeat.

"Good work, men," he said. James's voice was brusque and authoritative enough to distract the Atwaters from their lethal intentions. They stood at attention.

"The area is secure, gentlemen," James went on. "The Sikhs have retreated. But we can't afford to let down our guard. I'll need you men to patrol the perimeter."

As one, the Atwaters offered James another salute. As one, they turned to head out of the room. Before they could get that far, James reached up and snatched the pistol out of Farleigh's hands.

"That won't be necessary," he told Farleigh, setting the gun down on the floor beside him. "Or that." He appropriated Harleigh's sword and put it far out of the old man's reach. "Secrecy is of the essence, gentlemen," he told them. "And quiet." He gave them a broad wink. "We mustn't let them know we're on to them."

Harleigh's eyes sparkled with excitement. Farleigh gurgled with exhilaration. He clapped one hand over his mouth and followed his brother out of the room and down the stairs on tiptoe.

"Good Lord!" James withered and Lucy could not keep herself from smiling. "You don't suppose they'll hurt themselves, do you?" He craned his neck, checking on the Atwaters' progress. "I wouldn't want that on my conscience, that's for certain. That or—" James's relief dissolved into an annoyed grumble and a moment later Lucy saw why.

The commotion in Alfie's study had done more than rouse Harleigh and Farleigh. The rest of the house was up as well.

Clara Miller stood out in the passageway and peered into the room. Her mouse-brown hair was atumble, her eyes were sleepy. Her son, Jack, was anything but. Wide-awake and eager for excitement, he scampered into the room, his lightweight slippers swishing against the floor. He took one look at the blood that soaked the front of Lucy's nightgown and his eyes grew as round as saucers.

"Cor, Miss Barnstable! Have you been killed?"

"No, Jack." With James's help, Lucy sat up. "I'm fine. Really. The blood on my nightgown . . ." She looked down at the front of her gown, then over at James as if to be sure she wasn't lying to the boy. "It is from my hand. I cut myself on a piece of broken glass. And then I became so upset, I fainted. Silly of me, wasn't it? Mr. James was nice enough to help."

"Help, indeed!" From the tone of voice and the indignant sniff that accompanied the last of the words, Lucy knew Mrs. Slyke was out in the hallway. She loomed in the doorway like a thundercloud over a church picnic. "How a respectable woman is supposed to get her proper sleep in a place such as this . . ." Mrs. Slyke clicked her tongue and shook her head. "It's unacceptable. That's what it is. Why, if I wasn't a poor widow . . . if I had the strength to look for residence elsewhere—"

"What an excellent idea!" Clara Miller had run back to her room for more cloth and James discarded the first piece and reached for a fresh one, pressing it carefully to Lucy's hand. He didn't bother to look at Mrs. Slyke. "Elsewhere. There's a fine thought. Why don't we all go elsewhere. Jack—" He gave the boy a look. "You need to get back to bed."

"But, Mr. James—"

"Because Miss Barnstable is going to need a good deal of help around here in the next few days, that's why." James patted Lucy's shoulder and after he was certain she could sit on her own without his support, he rose to his feet. In spite of his ill-fitting pajamas, his bare feet, and the night's growth of beard that shadowed his face, he looked oddly self-possessed and in charge, a fact that was not lost on Jack Miller. The boy backed toward the door instantly.

"No questions," James said. "The best thing you can do for Miss Barnstable is get some rest. She'll need some help in the morning, fetching and carrying things. Will you be ready?"

"Yes, sir."

Jack responded to the authority in James's voice as instinctively and as completely as the Atwaters had. Lucy wouldn't have been at all surprised if he saluted. He didn't, of course. He dashed off the way he'd come with promises to be up bright and early and offers to help.

"Mrs. Miller . . ." James turned to the boy's mother. "Perhaps you could assist Miss Barnstable with changing her clothes. And you—"

James gave Lucy a pointed look while he helped her to her feet.

"This is getting to be a habit . . ." When he was

sure he could entrust her safely to Mrs. Miller's care, James stepped back to let them out of the room. "The parlor," he said, his eyes flashing with the same authority he had aimed at the Atwaters and at Jack Miller. "Twenty minutes."

Restlessly fingering the edge of the faded draperies, James stared out the parlor window at the street. Though he'd asked Lucy to meet him in twenty minutes, it was long past that time and there was no sign of her.

It was just as well.

If she walked in this instant, he wasn't sure what he would say. What he would do.

Not in light of what he'd learned since he, himself, came into the room.

Still too staggered to think his way past the anger that churned his stomach and pounded through his blood, he tried to calm his breathing and focus on the wisps of fog that writhed over the pavement outside the window. A hansom cab plodded by and he told himself to concentrate on the rhythmic beat of the horses' hooves.

He had little success.

Despite his best efforts, his gaze traveled from the view outside to his own face, a ghostly reflection in the glass. There was no need to mask his feelings. Not this time. He was alone and alone he could let down his guard. His eyes flinty, his lips pulled into a thin line, he met the expression that stared back at him from his reflection.

And faced the stark pain of betrayal.

"Damn!" Teetering on the edge between raw fury and bleak disappointment, he spun away from the window and the sight of the emotions that shone all too clearly in his eyes. Automatically, his gaze moved to the table set before the fireplace.

When he'd left the room earlier in the evening— what seemed days ago instead of hours—the table had been empty except for the Indian art book he'd received from Peck, the newspaper articles that had come from Canaday, and the two stone seals, his and Lucy's. Now, it was piled with issues of *Strand* magazine and littered with cheap editions of Dr. Doyle's Sherlock Holmes stories. Just as he found it when he came into the room a few minutes ago.

A sour taste filled James's mouth. Fitfully, he fingered the magazine at the top of the pile, the one that included the story "The Cardboard Box." Again, he skimmed through the story, listening as Doyle's words echoed inside his head, annihilating his naive fancies, crushing his last shreds of hope.

He might have gone on that way forever if he hadn't heard the rustle of Lucy's skirts against the battered carpets. As if to put distance between himself and the ugly truth, he set down the magazine and backed away from the table. He looked up just in time to see Lucy pause on the threshold.

James's emotions congealed into a knot that blocked his breathing and robbed him of his voice. In silence, he stared at Lucy.

Though it was still two hours before dawn, Lucy had changed out of her bloodied nightgown and into her brown housedress. James was just as glad. His head still full of the picture she'd made lying with her head cradled on his knees, his fingers still tingling from the touch of her bare skin, he had decided on the safe course, too. He'd returned to his room and changed from Albert Miller's absurd pajamas into a pair of black trousers and a clean, if not especially comfortable, shirt. The sleeves were a tad too short and not quite wide enough to accommodate his arms, and even though the house was not in the least bit warm, he'd rolled them above his elbows.

He fingered them silently, checking each sleeve to make sure it was in place, his gaze roving from Lucy's dress to her hair. When he'd found her after her encounter with the burglar, Lucy's hair was wild, a dark halo that framed her pale face and tumbled over her shoulders and down her back. Now it was carefully combed, not pinned up as she usually wore it but tied at the nape of her neck with a thin blue ribbon.

The style was as artless as it was sensible. It made her look younger, somehow, fragile and fresh. Or perhaps the impression came not from her, but from some trick of his own memory.

Even now, James could feel his heart speed and his blood quicken when he remembered how he'd run into Alfie's study and found Lucy unconscious on the floor. The front of her nightgown was wet and crimson and for one horrible moment, he was sure she was dead.

Hardly dead.

A cynical voice inside James's head intruded, forcing him to face the truth.

Lucy was hardly dead. And hardly fragile.

If the fact that she'd fought off a burglar wasn't enough to destroy any fantasies he had about her, what he'd found out in the time he'd been waiting for her certainly should have.

The thought sobered James and he faced Lucy as he faced the reality of what he'd just learned, head-on and in silence.

He watched her move into the room, her gaze fixed somewhere over his left shoulder, and it took him a moment to figure out why. She was acutely embarrassed, not only because James had seen her in her nightclothes but, no doubt, because she had needed rescuing, and she was fighting the stark honesty of the emotion as only Lucy could.

Any other time, James might have been charmed by the realization. Tonight, it left him cold.

"Can you believe it?" Lucy shook her head, babbling to cover her uneasiness. "Mrs. Miller thought I should change into another nightgown." She capped the comment with a distinctive laugh, one so musical, it nearly melted James's defenses. He didn't let it. Not this time. He promised himself he never would again.

Lucy came as far as the table and stopped, seemingly more comfortable with it between them. "Mrs. Miller had the most curious argument," she continued, "about why I should stay in my nightclothes. She said that now that I'd had an encounter with a burglar, it was obvious that I was an invalid. Or at least that I should act like one. As any truly conscientious invalid knows, I should not appear in street clothes for a good long while. I should look as helpless as possible until such time as I recovered. Or at least until the rest of the household was well and truly tired of the whole thing."

Her eyes sparking mischief, she paused, waiting for James's response.

He wished to God he could give her one, but he could not seem to force the words past the leaden taste that filled his mouth.

The twinkle of amusement in Lucy's eyes evaporated. Her pleasant mood chilled by his icy reception, she looked past James to the window. "It is nearly dawn. Or it will be soon enough. I thought it best to be dressed and ready for the day. It seems you thought the same."

James didn't reply. He couldn't. He let his gaze wander from the eyes he had thought so guileless, to the mouth that had curved so enticingly beneath the pressure of his own. It would take a stronger man than he was to pretend none of it had happened. To imagine that now that he knew the truth, it didn't hurt as much as it did.

Lucy was not at all happy about his silent reception, and as usual, she was not the least bit shy in letting him know. Barely smoothing the irritation from her voice, she cradled her injured left hand in her right. "It's difficult getting dressed without the use of one hand," she said, pointing out what should have been obvious to James. "I'm sorry it took so long."

"I'm not." After so long a silence, his words sounded like a rumble of thunder. It was a poor opening gambit and he should have known better. Somewhere in his murky past, he knew he'd learned to handle delicate situations more skillfully than this. He wished he'd learned other things as well. Like how the devil he was supposed to handle the kinds of feelings he had for Lucy and what he was supposed to do now that he'd found everything he believed about her to be lies.

"Mrs. Miller brought tea." It was a poor way to try to salvage the situation, but it was the only thing James could think to say. He glanced at the teapot and cups that had been set on the table. "And bandages. Before we talk, we best take care of your hand."

For a moment he thought Lucy might refuse. Still smarting from his apathetic welcome and indignant as only Lucy could be, she flashed him a look that was as defiant as it was conclusive. But her hand must surely have hurt. She sat at the table and laid her arm on it, pulling away the cloth that had been cushioning the wound.

As careful to keep his distance now as he had been earlier in the evening after their encounter in his bed-chamber, James took the chair beside hers. But where before, the air around them had crackled with electricity, now it was still, as cold as the stilted words that passed between them.

"It isn't nearly as bad as I thought," James said. He peered at the cut, pleased to see that either Mrs. Miller or Lucy had been sensible enough to cleanse it thoroughly. "With proper care, it should be healed well enough in a few days." James reached for a roll of clean gauze. He made a move to take Lucy's hand and hesitated.

He hardly needed a reminder of how soft her skin was. About how smooth it felt against his. Each time he drew near enough to feel the heat of her body, his own body responded instantly and so fiercely, it never failed to astonish him.

James set his jaw, steeling himself against the inevitable shiver of awareness. He wouldn't let it happen, he vowed. Not this time.

Not ever again.

James's hands were capable, his fingers skillful. His care was not as gentle as it was both efficient and quick. As if he could not stand to touch her.

The thought stabbed at Lucy and she winced.

"I'm sorry." Thinking he'd hurt her, James glanced up from his work. It was the first time he had dared meet her eyes since they'd sat down and Lucy was just as glad. This close, it was impossible to lie to herself any longer. She had not imagined the frosty bite of his gaze when he looked at her from across the room. It was there still, and at this distance, it was more potent and disturbing than ever.

Stunned and chilled through to the bone, she sat in silence and waited for him to finish. It might have been a good deal easier to endure his touch if her memory were less accurate. Then, she might not have thought back to everything that had happened in Alfie's study. She might have told herself that she was wrong, that James's eyes didn't glitter with exquisite emotion when she came to and found her head on his lap. She might have convinced herself that the warmth of his hands against her skin was nothing more than the product of her overactive imagination.

At least then, his stony silence would not be so puzzling. Or so painful.

Lucy watched him finish with the final bandage and secure it in place. When he was done, James didn't sit back. He hunched forward in his seat, his hands at his sides, his gaze fixed on Lucy's injured hand.

"I know what you're thinking," he said. "You're going to have another go at that ridiculous guessing game you've been playing all these days. A soldier. Or historian. A painter of battle canvases. You've tried them all, haven't you? Now you're going to suggest that perhaps I am a doctor. Not tonight, Lucy." He sat up and raised his eyes to hers, their chill melting beneath the intensity of the emotions he had been trying to keep in check. Like a touchstone igniting, his brown eyes sparked with bronze, a fire that matched the sudden burst of intensity in his voice.

"Tonight, I don't want to talk about what I am," he said. "I want to talk about what you're not."

Hoping that he wouldn't notice that her hands were suddenly trembling, Lucy pushed her sleeve into place. She looked from James to the books and magazines she'd left scattered on the table and her stomach turned.

He couldn't know.

The words pounded through her head much the way her heart crashed against her rib cage.

It was too soon to panic. It had been a long and eventful night and her imagination was running away with her. He couldn't know.

She wouldn't allow it.

"I'm afraid," she said, her voice far more breathless than she liked, "that I haven't the slightest idea what you're talking about."

"I was here. In twenty minutes. I waited here for you long enough to send Harleigh and Farleigh back to bed." It was hardly an explanation, but Lucy indulged James, hoping against hope that she had jumped to conclusions and that he would prove her wrong. "I see that you were reading before you went to your room."

Lucy's gaze followed James's over to the magazines. She could hardly dispute it. She had been reading. After he'd left her in the parlor, she had to do something to keep her mind off his good-night kiss, and she decided to read some of the Holmes stories, hoping they would offer her some clue as to where she might take her investigation.

"Yes, I wasn't very tired. Not after . . ." Lucy nearly mentioned the kiss. She might have had she been able to interpret his odd mood. Something told her it was better to leave well alone. She stopped herself just in time and offered him a stiff smile instead of the truth. "It never hurts to tackle a project full out, does it? I thought I'd get a start on tomorrow. The news of your stone seal is certainly significant and I shall telegram Alfie first thing in the morning about it. I wanted to—"

"I saw the books." It was a masterful attempt at prevarication at its finest but unfortunately James wasn't listening. He moved his hand over the piles of books and magazines on the table. "And you know, for a minute, I thought that's exactly what you were doing. Getting a jump on tomorrow. I assumed you were studying that Indian art book. Searching for clues. Investigating possibilities. Detecting all the while."

He looked her way and the cynicism that edged his smile made her blood run cold.

"Yes. Well . . ." The book on Indian art sat closed in the center of the table. With her good hand, Lucy reached for it and slid it closer. "There's a good deal we need to learn," she said. "Not the least of which is how we both happened to come by seals that are very valuable and very unusual."

"And yet you weren't reading about Indian stone seals." James reached for the magazine that sat open atop the pile. "You were reading Sherlock Holmes."

Lucy's mouth went dry. "You make it sound like a crime," she said with a little laugh that came out sounding much too harsh. "We all need diversions from our everyday duties. The stories are romantic nonsense, of course, but they help fill the empty hours."

As if he hadn't heard, James glanced through the pages of the magazine. "I remember this Holmes story. And that's saying a great deal for a man who can't even remember his own name. But I was passing the time, waiting for you to come down. I saw the magazine open on the table and Paget's illustrations caught my eye. Suddenly it all came back to me. I remembered a day a few years ago. I remembered hearing that the latest Holmes story was available. I had some empty hours to fill myself . . ." He paused as if to let her know that he had, indeed, been listening to every word she said.

"I went out and bought the magazine. I have a vague memory of a blustery cold day and coming back to a cozy room. Not my own home, I don't think. A hotel room. I remember pouring a glass of brandy and settling down to read 'The Cardboard Box.' It became one of my favorites." The pages ruffled beneath James's fingers. "Has to do with a murderer who sends a severed ear to a woman as a warning." He looked up from the pages, measuring Lucy's reactions to his words.

"Nasty little gift, that. Grisly as all hell. If I remember my Doyle, it arrived by post. A neat parcel all tied up with twine."

His words were far more casual and innocent than the knowing look in his eyes. Too late, Lucy realized where the conversation was headed.

Determined not to let it get there, she forced a laugh. "You'll have to forgive me. I've left such a mess. If you'll just let me—" She made a move to snatch the magazine from James's hands.

"Oh, no!" James swiveled in his seat, keeping the magazine neatly out of reach. "Not yet. Not until you explain." He ran his finger down the columns of print and though he apparently found what he was looking for soon enough, he didn't begin to read right away, and Lucy couldn't help but think that he was trying to get a grip on some powerful emotion before he could trust himself to speak.

"Let me read a line or two," he finally said, his voice as tightly reined as his emotions. " 'The string is extremely fascinating.' 'The knot is quite distinctive.' 'The hand is well educated.' 'Written with a broad-pointed pen.' All things Holmes says about the parcel that arrives in the cardboard box."

He looked from the magazine to Lucy.

"Precisely the same things you said about the parcel given to me by Mr. Peck."

He was far too close to the truth for Lucy's liking. She sprang from her chair, fighting to put some distance between herself and the validity of his reasoning.

"Well, that proves it then doesn't it?" She circled the table, straightening the piles of magazines and books as she went, her hands fluttering as much as her heart. "Dr. Doyle must certainly be a fine writer! And far more skilled than a good many of his critics give him credit for. Imagine, he knows exactly how an experienced detective works."

"Does he?"

Lucy's circuit had brought her dangerously close to James. He reached out a hand and snatched her right arm, holding her firmly in place. "I asked you a question, Lucy. Does Dr. Doyle know what it's like to be a real detective? Or do you know what it's like being a detective from Dr. Doyle?"

It was a question Lucy could not answer and her hesitancy spoke volumes. In one quick movement, James was out of his chair. His eyes sparked impatience. His voice was a growl deep in his throat.

"What kind of game are you playing, Lucy? You don't know any more about being a detective than I do."

Lucy squeezed her eyes closed, shutting out the sight of the pain that flashed so eloquently in James's eyes. She might have known he would never let her hide so easily from the facts. His fingers twisting around her wrist, he yanked her nearer, until her breasts were pressed against his chest and his words were hot against her cheek.

"Damn it, woman, answer me!" As if it might jar

loose the truth, he gave her a shake. "You claim you're working with your father but I've yet to see hide nor hair of the man. It's just a ween o'blethers, isn't it? All smoke and gammon and spinach. Do you often go through such an elaborate ploy to fleece the occasional madman who can't remember his name out of his money?"

"Money?" The word tasted like ashes in Lucy's mouth. She swallowed around it and twisted her arm, but it was impossible to break loose of the hold he had on her. She raised her eyes to his, forcing herself to meet his wrath.

"I've kept my end of the bargain," she said, her teeth clenched around her own rising anger. "I said I'd investigate and I have."

"You said your father would investigate." James glanced at the fireplace and the photograph of Alfie and his top lip curled. He returned his gaze to Lucy and fixed it there, holding it steady. "Is there an Alfie?" he asked. "Or is that all part of the game, too?"

She could meet his anger and his scathing glances. She could hold her own beneath his cruel words and his rough touch. She could not listen to him talk that way about Alfie.

Lucy's eyes filled with tears. "There's an Alfie, right enough," she assured him, her words as distinct as a slap. "At least there was. He disappeared weeks ago and I haven't heard a word from him since."

It was enough of a surprise to catch James off guard. He loosened his hold and Lucy saw her opportunity and took it. She snatched her arm from his grasp and retreated to the other side of the table.

"You said you communicated with him every day. You showed me telegrams. You—"

"Smoke and gammon and pickles." There was no

satisfaction in the shrift. Lucy dug into her pocket for the telegram that she had waved so frequently and so cavalierly in front of James's eyes. "One telegram," she admitted, her voice as heavy as her heart. "And it wasn't even sent to me. It was Mrs. Miller's and I used it—"

"To dupe me."

When he put it that way, it was impossible to deny. Still, Lucy did her best. "Not dupe." She shook her head, struggling to find the words that might explain away his anger and her own guilt. "You never would have hired me. I'm only a woman, after all, and that first night, you made it more than clear that you didn't approve of modern women. If I told you I was conducting my own investigation, trying to find Alfie, you wouldn't have cared a fig."

He didn't contradict her. He stepped back, his weight against one foot, and crossed his arms over his chest, holding in the anger and hurt that simmered below the surface of his words. "And how does that concern me?" he asked. "I was just some poor fool who happened to stumble onto your doorstep."

Lucy realized the only way to deal with his anger was to meet it head-on. She speared him with a look, doling out the truth the way she dispensed oatmeal at the breakfast table, the way she dealt with all unappealing tasks, quickly and efficiently, without too much concern for the mess left behind.

"Some poor fool who happened to know Alfie's name," she told him. "You knew his name. You had his handbill. And you had—" She nearly choked on her shame. "You had the twin of the stone seal I found in Alfie's desk. I went through your pockets while you were unconscious, you see, and I found more than your money." She confessed quickly, before he could reason through to the same conclusion and have yet another offense to heap onto her assortment of sins.

"I had no other choice. I thought you might be able to lead me to Alfie so I—"

"Led me down the primrose path." There was nearly a hint of admiration in his voice. James shook his head, and a sarcastic smile pulled at the edges of his mouth. "All this time, I thought you knew what you were doing. And you were getting it all from a book!" His smile disappeared and though he held himself stiff and tall, Lucy knew his words cost him his pride. "I thought you were trying to help me find out who I am."

Finally, he had given her an opening, a way to justify her sins and make amends. "We've done a good deal toward finding your identity," she reminded him. "We have the stone seals and the book from Peck. We have the newspaper articles about the Eye of the Devil."

"And I have two names. Am I James Smith or James Jones?" James's control cracked. "Damn it, Lucy, I trusted you. I knew I should have listened to my head instead of my heart. This ridiculous charade of yours has gotten us nowhere at all. If you just would have admitted from the start that you didn't have a chance in hell of finding out—"

"Is that what I should have done?" Lucy's anger burst, a shield against his bitter words. "And where would that have gotten us? You would have gone on your merry way and I would be no closer to finding my father."

"At least I might have found a way to get on with my life, instead of hanging on to hope that was no hope at all. Didn't you see what you were getting us into? Didn't you even care?"

"All I cared about was Alfie." Too overwhelmed by the truth to face him a moment longer, Lucy turned her back on him. She found herself face-to-face with the photograph of her father. She stared at it, the edges blurred by the tears that filled her eyes.

"You were a stranger," she said, her voice choked with the same tears. "Why should I care about you? How could I? All I knew was that there had to be some connection between you and Alfie. The stone seals proved it. I thought you could lead me to him and I knew I had to say anything and do anything to keep you from leaving. I thought that through you, I could find out what's become of Alfie. You're right . . ." Her voice dropped and she hung her head. "I didn't care if you ever discovered your identity. All I wanted to do was find my father."

Tears spilled over Lucy's eyelashes and rolled down her cheeks, but she didn't bother to wipe them away. She listened to the last echoes of her shameful admission fade away and tried to find the words— and the backbone—to explain the rest. It took longer than it should have, but finally, she found the courage to put voice to the feelings that had filled her head and strangled her judgment, her wits—and her heart.

"I didn't care," she said her voice no more than a whisper. "I didn't care about you at all. Not at first. It wasn't until I got to know you that I realized how very much I cared."

But by the time Lucy worked up the courage to speak the truth and turn around to face James with it, he was gone.

# Chapter 12

"Here, put this on."

The sound of James's voice, and the fact that without warning he strode into the parlor and laid what looked to be an elaborate evening gown onto Lucy's lap, startled her enough that she pricked her finger with her sewing needle.

Sucking at the tiny puncture, she looked up from her mending. It was nearly a week since they'd stood in this very room and she'd confessed the ugly truth to James: the truth about Alfie and about her own dubious expertise as a detective; the truth about her feelings for James.

With a grunt and a small shake of her head, Lucy dismissed the disturbing memory.

James had heard only what James wanted to hear. He'd heard her confess her treachery. He'd heard her admit indifference. And if he hadn't heard a word she said about how much she'd come to care for him, it was just as well.

If James knew the way she felt about him, she could never have survived the embarrassment or endured the glittering sparks of anger that still shimmered like fire in his dark eyes.

During the long, miserable week, he had not spoken a word to her. He left the house early each morning, and as far as Lucy knew, he was not back by the time she went to bed. He didn't take his meals with the other boarders.

Perhaps he was out looking for another place to live. Perhaps he was conducting his own investigation.

Whatever he had been about, she would never have guessed that it had anything at all to do with elaborate evening gowns.

Concealing her surprise and the instinctive and quite automatic response that he could consign the dress, his sudden need to communicate with her, and himself to perdition, Lucy looked from the gown to James. "I beg your pardon."

"I said, put it on. There's a cab coming around to collect us in an hour."

"Is there?" Lucy's surprise grew in exact proportion to her annoyance. She did her best to control both, concealing her emotions behind the kind of neutral expression she generally reserved as a response to one of Alfie's lunatic schemes. "And would you be so kind as to tell me where we might be going."

James had just come in from the outside and he was still wearing one of Albert Miller's spring-weight morning coats. It wasn't buttoned, probably because it didn't quite span his chest, and when he moved away from Lucy in exasperation, it flapped around him. "We are going," he said, turning back to her, "to the opera."

Lucy could not have been more surprised if he had said they were going to head to South America on one of Alfie's flying machines. As if she wasn't sure she'd heard correctly, she leaned forward. "I'm afraid I must have misunderstood. What did you say?"

James puffed out his annoyance. "You heard me well enough," he said. "Now get above stairs and get ready, woman. The curtain goes up in just under three hours."

"Does it really?" Until that very moment, Lucy had not recognized the emotion that had been churning through her all week. She knew she was wretched about losing what she had come to look forward to each day: James's companionship, his conversation, his stimulating if not always comfortable presence. She knew she was humiliated at having bared her soul to him and grateful just the same that he had not heard a word of her confession. She knew she was disheartened at the turn of events and so discouraged to have lost the thread that might lead her to Alfie she could taste disappointment morning, noon, and night.

But she had not recognized the anger.

All the while, it had bubbled just beneath the surface of her hard-fought indifference. She realized that now. And now, it threatened to overflow.

For once, Lucy didn't even try to damp the irritation in her voice. She let it snap through her words and found a perverse sort of pleasure in the bittersweet relief. "Three hours, eh? In that case you have plenty of time to tell me why you're going to the opera. And while you're at it, you may as well explain how you can possibly be so arrogant, so pompous, and so thoroughly idiotic to think that I might, by any stretch of the imagination, wish to accompany you there."

It was far more satisfying than she would have imagined to let her anger go, particularly because James was not expecting it. He flapped further from her, and for the first time, Lucy realized he was not as confident as he pretended to be.

There was more going on here than he would have her think—she was sure of it—and whatever it was, it was enough to cause a tremor even in James's formidable self-control.

Far more interested than was wise and far too irritated to let it pass, Lucy casually laid aside her needle and thread. The dress was still in her lap and she ran her hands over it.

It was difficult to see the entire gown without holding it at arm's length, but what she could see was incredibly beautiful. The dress was made of white satin. The sleeves were short and puffed, the bodice cut straight and low over a jabot of satin that cascaded down the front to the pointed waist. The skirt was without ornamentation except for a design that soared from the hem, a single iris embroidered entirely in white pearls.

It was the most splendid gown she had ever seen, and probably the most expensive thing she had ever had in her hands. Lucy's eyes narrowed. She looked from the dress to James. "And where did this come from?" she asked.

"Does it matter?" His anger rising in response to hers, James stepped forward and Lucy had the distinct impression he might have kept coming at her if he hadn't stopped himself just in time. His arms close against his sides, he took a slow, calming breath.

"I won't play games Lucy. I haven't forgotten that you admitted to going through my pockets. You know I have money and to spare. I talked to Mrs. Miller. Had her choose something appropriate." With one hand, he made an impatient gesture toward the dress. "She found it at the shop where she works. Apparently it was something made for some Society dazzler and for whatever reason, never collected. Mrs. Miller had to make some adjustments, of course, but apparently, that wasn't a problem. She said she knew your size and your . . . your shape." He looked away long enough to convince Lucy that though he was trying hard, he was not altogether impervious to all that had passed between them in the previous weeks.

The realization should have made her feel worse. It would, Lucy promised herself. When she was alone and she could think it through, she vowed that she would wallow in embarrassment and chagrin. She would be appropriately appalled at her complete lack of reason. She would be sufficiently horrified at her absence of judgment and the fact that for the weeks James had been here, she seemed to have lost her wits as well as her heart.

But for now . . .

Lucy did her best to control the tiny smile that threatened to betray her.

For now, James wanted something. He wanted it badly. Enough to make him speak to her after a week of uncomfortable silences. Enough to make him come to her with an invitation that he was handling so poorly she knew it must be very important, indeed. Enough to make him forget himself, and remember that before he discovered that she had exaggerated her own inadequate abilities enough to deceive him, there had been something between them, the echoes of which still resonated in the air and shivered through Lucy like the tingle of electricity.

The awareness made her bold. Her daring only served to intensify her anger. It sharpened her tongue.

"Your invitation is certainly charming, but I'm afraid I shall have to refuse." With both hands, she gave the gown a little push, as if dissociating herself from it. "Freddy is coming by this evening. We're going for a drive."

The mention of Lucy's fiancé was enough to distract James, at least for the moment. "Freddy!" He rolled the "R" through his teeth and bit off the syllables as if they tasted bad. Color rose in his face. "Freddy is a milksop. He's a tedious chap, you have to admit, and though he might like to think he'll have a lifetime to learn it, he'll never know how to satisfy a woman like you."

"Though I do not see it as one, I take it you mean that as a compliment." Lucy tucked her hands beneath the evening gown her right hand automatically smoothing over the nearly healed wound on her left. "I have to remind you, you are talking about the man to whom I am engaged. I'll have to ask you to be polite." She shifted her gaze from James to the door. "Or to leave."

Too flustered to keep still, James did a turn around the room and for a moment she thought he might actually heed her warning and leave her in peace. Instead, he stomped from the sofa to the fireplace and from the fireplace to the bookshelves that lined the far wall. He marched over to where Alfie's chemistry supplies were laid out on a table and ran a finger over the beakers and vials. Halfway back over to where Lucy was seated, he seemed to remember his coat. Uncomfortable, he stretched and stripped off the coat, grumbling when the sleeves pinched around his forearms. He tossed the coat onto a chair and crossed the room, stationing himself firmly in front of Lucy.

"You don't really think you'll ever be happy with a man such as that, do you?" he asked. He didn't wait for her to reply. It was clear he thought he already knew the answer. "I'd wager a dozen of claret and a side of beef that the only thing the man ever talks about is bank accounting."

His words were closer to the mark than he realized. Chafing beneath the truth, Lucy sat up straight and tall. She picked at the row of beading on the skirt of the gown. "There is nothing wrong with bank accounting," she told him. "It can be quite fascinating. Especially the way Freddy explains it."

"Right." James knelt on the floor in front of Lucy. "There's been enough lies between us," he said, his voice husky. "Let's not add to it. How can you think of spending the rest of your life—"

"The way I spend the rest of my life is certainly none of your concern. If I decide to explore Africa or to join a convent—"

"Convent?" The fact that James snorted the word did not do him the least bit of credit. His eyes flashed. "I'd sooner see you in a convent than tethered to Freddy. Don't get me wrong. I'm sure he'll be the perfect husband. Kind and considerate. Polite and reserved. He'll peck you on the cheek now and again and expect you to be happy with it just as he'll be happy to have the same in return. Good God, woman, don't you see? He'll bore you to death!"

While James was prophesying her fate, he grabbed her right hand. He gripped it tightly in his own, his eyes as fierce as his hold on her, his words drumming through her head.

Lucy's heart drummed along with them. Her breath caught. She stared into James's eyes and the waves of emotion that rippled through his words tugged at her heart and pooled deep within her, stirring her blood.

It was frightfully hot.

Lucy gulped down a mouthful of air, fighting to recover her composure. It was not so easily done.

James's fingers were locked over hers. His eyes bore through to her soul. His breathing was ragged, torn by the emotions he'd held close for so long.

The same emotions she felt. The ones she'd tried to confess. The confession he hadn't waited around long enough to hear.

Odd how anger could curb even hotter emotions. Lucy held the thought. She looked from James down to where their fingers were entwined. "I thought," she said, "that we were talking about going to the opera."

"We are talking about going to the opera."

"Then why are you holding my hand?"

As if it were on fire, James untangled his hand from hers. He sat back, and Lucy was glad. With some distance between them, she found it far easier to breathe.

"I'm sorry." There was just enough of a tremor in James's voice for her to know he was sincere. "I didn't mean to—"

"Of course you didn't." Lucy cut short his explanation. With her head still feeling light and her heart pulsing quick and hard, it was just as well to put the subject behind them. "But you still haven't explained why you want to go to the opera."

The reminder was enough to bring James to his senses. He jumped to his feet. "I've been investigating," he said and Lucy would say this much for him, he managed to keep most of the cynicism from his voice. "I've spent a good deal of the last week thinking and trying to work things out. In spite of the fact that I told myself it would do me no good, I couldn't help but think about you." It looked as if he might start in again, and Lucy wondered if she could hold her own against another rush of his ardor. Fortunately for her peace of mind as well as her fragile emotions, she never found out. Sensing the danger as surely as she did, James was wise enough to keep to the subject at hand.

"I was thinking about the way you've been reading the Holmes stories," he said. "It really isn't a bad idea, you know. I decided to do the same. Thought I might learn a thing or two from the master."

The explanation made little sense and when Lucy did not respond, James pulled a copy of the day's newspaper from the pocket of his coat. "You've read all the stories," he said, waving the newspaper in front of her. "You know that Holmes religiously reads the newspapers and that he is especially fond of music."

"Yes. Of course. But—"

"But though it might work for Holmes, it didn't quite work for me. Until I saw this." James unfolded the newspaper and pointed to an item that took up a good deal of the Society page.

"Opera," he said quite simply. "Tonight, at the Royal Opera House. As part of the festivities in honor of the Queen's Jubilee, they're doing *Aida* and you and I . . ." He paused as if waiting for her to object and when she kept silent, he went on. "We're going to be there."

It still made little sense. Setting aside the gown, Lucy rose from her chair and crossed the room to take the newspaper from James's hand. She scanned the article. "Why? Why *Aida*? Why Covent Garden? There isn't anything—"

Her gaze caught on a familiar name mentioned in the article.

"That's right," James said. "They go on and on as only the London Society pages can do, pictures and lists of who will be there, what they'll be wearing, who is being seen with whom. So you see, we won't be the only ones attending tonight's performance. Sir Digby Talbot is going to be there."

"Digby Talbot." The name was vaguely familiar,

though Lucy could not have said why. She glanced from the newspaper to James, waiting for an explanation.

"It all started with Harleigh," he said. "Or was it Farleigh? No matter, soon after I arrived here, one of them mentioned Sir Digby. I knew who he was."

He said the last words as if they had some great import and Lucy could well imagine why. "You recognized the name?"

"Yes. Well . . . That is, I think so. As soon as I heard the name, I responded. I knew Sir Digby was with the Foreign Office though I cannot say how or why. I'd forgotten all about the incident. Forgotten there might be some connection. Until this week." He turned away from her, nudged aside the draperies, and looked out the front window. There was little to see beyond the occasional dray that lumbered by and the foot traffic that was characteristically sparse this late in the afternoon, but he kept his gaze fixed there.

"I haven't been thinking clearly," James admitted. "I suppose I could ascribe it to the beating. My mind hasn't been working quite right. It took me until this week to realize that there might be some connection, some reason that I know Sir Digby. Some reason he might know me." He dropped the edge of the curtain and turned back to her, wounded Scots pride shining in his eyes.

"I tried to see him earlier in the week," he said. "They wouldn't let the likes of me past the front door of the Foreign Office."

Lucy kept silent. It would only have embarrassed him further if she sympathized. She glanced through the newspaper item again. "So you decided to try to talk to Sir Digby at the opera." She didn't need James to confirm her theory. It made a great deal of sense. At least on the surface.

Thoughtfully, she tapped the newspaper against her chin. "It isn't a bad plan, of course. You'll casually bump into him at the bar before the opera begins or you'll manage, somehow, to have a word with him at intermission. Yes, indeed. A fine plan." She slid her gaze to James. "Then why do you need me?"

James hesitated just long enough for her to realize there was more to the plan than he would admit.

"You said, no more lies," Lucy reminded him. "You said there'd been enough deception between us."

"Yes . . . well . . ." James looked away. "Sir Digby has something of a reputation," he finally said, noticeably bracing himself against Lucy's reaction. "An eye for the ladies, you might say. If I can't get near him, I thought you might—"

"You thought you could use me as bait, like a worm dangling from a fisherman's hook!" Outraged, Lucy slapped the newspaper onto the table. "That is disgraceful!"

"Is it?" James could not so easily be put off. He hurried over to where she stood and being careful to keep a safe distance between them, he fixed her with a look. There wasn't the least bit of desperation in his eyes, and for that, Lucy was sorry.

She might easily have turned from desperation. She just as easily might have disregarded a look that held a threat, or one that was pleading.

She couldn't ignore reason.

James set his mouth in a grim line. "You're forgetting the stone seals," he said.

Lucy groaned, her anger crushed beneath the weight of the memories that crowded her brain. "I haven't forgotten," she said. "I won't ever forget. Just as I won't ever stop trying to find my father."

"Then come to the opera with me." James caught her arm when she turned to leave. This time, he didn't hold on to her as if his life depended on it. He held her firmly but gently and his voice dropped. It was edged with the same intensity that glimmered in his eyes.

"You said it yourself the other night," he told her. "You said there had to be a connection between Alfie and me. The seals prove it. I think you're right. If Sir Digby knows me . . . if he can give us some clue to my identity . . . Don't you see, Lucy, the closer we get to finding out about me, the closer we'll get to finding Alfie."

He was right. Damn him, but he was right.

Lucy swallowed her pride. Closing her eyes, she nodded her acceptance.

"You'll do fine." She didn't have to look at James to know he would say anything to make her feel better. His voice held the kind of false bravado that told her he was trying as hard as she was to believe that somehow, his plan might help both the causes.

"There's one thing for certain," he added, his voice warming at the idea. "Sir Digby will notice you right enough. Everyone will. You're certain to be the most beautiful woman in the place."

Lucy was grateful that her eyes were still closed. Something told her she wouldn't have liked to see the way James smiled when he said it.

# Chapter 13

"**Y**ou've never been to the opera, have you?"

James already knew the answer to his question, but he could hardly help asking it. One look at the expression of wonder on Lucy's face was enough to make him forget himself.

Like a child on Christmas morning, her face was flushed. Her eyes were wide. Her lips were parted in a smile that was half astonishment, half unabashed delight. She stood in the massive and sumptuously decorated vestibule of the Royal Opera House, her ecstatic gaze gliding from the grand staircase to the Grecian lamps to the gloriously gilded ceiling so quickly, James wondered she wasn't dizzy from it all.

He was feeling a bit dizzy himself.

James stopped to consider the astonishing notion. The grandeur of the stately old theater on Bow Street did not impress him at all and that could only mean one thing: He'd been there before. Neither was he awed by the fashionable crowd. He kept an eye out for Sir Digby Talbot but other than that, he had no concern for the elegantly dressed ladies and stylish gentlemen, no interest even in the courtesans who strolled the building, their brightly painted cheeks and rouged lips blatant advertisements.

His head had begun its whirl back at the Barnstable house, the moment he saw Lucy walk down the stairs in her new gown. It continued now as he watched her watching the crowd. It was just as well that the wealthy woman for whom the gown was originally designed had never come around to collect it, he decided.

The dress was made for Lucy.

The creamy color of the gown was a perfect accent to her peaches and cream complexion. The simple neckline showed off her shoulders and was cut just low enough to show a good deal more of her than he had ever been fortunate enough to see before. James stepped nearer. From this angle, he could catch just a glimpse of the tops of her deliciously rounded breasts, just a hint of the soft, secret shadow that lay between them.

"Marvelous, isn't it?"

Lucy's question seemed to have something to do with the crowd in general, but it caught James off guard.

Hoping to hell he wasn't blushing, he pretended to be studying the detailing on the brass staircase just to the left of Lucy's shoulder.

"Marvelous," he agreed, wondering what she might say if she knew his comment had nothing at all to do with staircases.

"I can't help but think I'm imagining it all." Lucy stepped aside to let a stately dowager by. "It's like a scene from a fairy tale, isn't it? Or a dream. A dream all spangled and sparkling with light."

She was the one who was sparkling.

It was hardly something he could say out loud, but at least it was a good deal more suitable than thinking about portions of Lucy's anatomy that he had no business thinking about. James settled for it. His mood mellowing as his gaze dropped, he glanced from the top of her head to the tips of her satin shoes.

The petal-soft fabric of the dress hugged Lucy's hips. The pearls that made up the intricately beaded flower on the front of the skirt winked at him in the glistening light of the overhead electric chandeliers.

A smile tugging the corners of his mouth, he let his gaze glide up once again. With Mrs. Miller's help, Lucy had done up her hair simply and effectively, sweeping it up from her neck and pinning it back in the mysterious way that women sometimes did, so that while it looked neat and stylish and ever-so-proper, it gave the impression that just the right impassioned touch might bring it tumbling down around her shoulders.

James felt his smile waver. Lucy's delectably bare shoulders . . . Lucy's hair cascading down, tangling in his fingers . . . Lucy's radiant eyes and shining smile and the scent of the rose water that she'd dabbed on before they left the house . . .

It was enough to make any man lose his train of thought.

James pulled himself back from the brink. He had to remember to control himself. He had to remind himself why they were here. He hadn't forgotten his anger. He couldn't. He'd never forget that Lucy had offered the false promise of hope, that she'd deceived him, and misguided him. That while what she'd done had been done with the intention of finding her father, it was rash and foolish. She'd taken James's trust and turned it around upon itself, until it was no more than a mockery.

But he was a man, after all—his gaze drifted to Lucy's slim waist—and no man could look upon such a vision and not be moved.

As if she could feel his eyes on her, Lucy tugged at her elbow-length white satin gloves. "I feel as out-of-place as a halibut in Piccadilly Circus. I never realized—" She blinked in amazement, watching as a young woman wearing far too much makeup and not nearly enough dress to cover her substantial bosom walked in on the arm of a young man James recognized from the newspapers as the Duke of Armagh.

Lucy blushed to the roots of her hair. "You must think me terribly provincial. I'm afraid I am, rather, even though I've lived in London all my life. Of course, I know such things go on . ." She watched the young lady and the duke disappear up the stairs. "But . . . Well, it isn't often a woman of my class is exposed to quite so much . . ." She searched for the words that might even begin to explain the excitement that buzzed all around her. "So much spectacle."

It was impossible for James not to laugh in warm response. "If you think this is spectacular, wait until you see the opera. You'll love it, Lucy. I know you will. There's a triumphant procession in Act Two that—"

"You've seen it before?"

His head cocked, James considered the question. "I suppose I have. At least I seem to remember a good deal about it. But not here." He looked around. "This place is familiar, but I don't associate it at all with *Aida*. I first saw *Aida* at La Scala in Milan," he said, sure of himself though he could not say why. "And again, the next year, in Paris."

"Then perhaps you can tell me what to expect. I have to admit, the thought of listening to an entire opera sung in Italian is more than a little daunting."

James laughed again, a full, throaty sound. "I can't imagine you being intimidated by anything, especially something as harmless as Italian!"

Their eyes met and held.

Lucy's were clear and bright. Her pupils were

enormous dark pools. The kind a man could get lost in.

The kind this man was getting lost in.

James knew he should be the first to look away. It was the only prudent thing to do. Not that he was in any mood to be prudent. Hell, he was feeling reckless enough to kiss Lucy right here, in front of the cream of London Society.

The thought sparked a sudden and quite inappropriate response from his body. As pleasant as the sensation was, it brought him to his senses.

James forced himself to glance away, giving his imagination a reprieve from the heady feeling of staring into Lucy's eyes. Feeling far more unsure of himself than he liked, he searched his mind for some safe topic of conversation. Some issue that had nothing at all to do with dark eyes, luminescent skin, or warm—

"Opera!" The sound of James's voice surprised even him. He managed to stumble onto the subject as if he'd intended it all along. "The opera is about an Ethiopian princess named Aida," he said. "She's the soprano. And she's been captured by the Egyptians and made a slave to the Egyptian pharaoh's daughter. Aida is young and beautiful. She's—"

It was a mistake to look Lucy's way again, especially when he was talking about a young, beautiful woman. For a moment James lost his place in the story. He brought himself back around, but though he was able to recapture the narrative, he could do nothing at all about disguising his emotions. His words came out sounding far too husky, far too blunt. "She's very much in love."

Catching her lower lip in her teeth, Lucy glanced up at him. "Is she?" The words trembled like the smile that came and went across her expression. "Is it wise for her to feel that way?"

"No." James shook his head, more sure of himself than he had been since the night he woke up in an alley with a head full of nothing but pain. "It isn't wise at all. But you see, she can't help herself. She's in love with a young man, Radames, the tenor. He's an Egyptian, you see, a soldier who's been ordered to crush Ethiopia. That puts them in a fairly impossible situation, and they know it. '*Amore amore!*' they sing. '*Gaudio tormento, soave ebbrezzana, ansia crudel*! O love immortal! O joy and sorrow, sweetest delirium, dark doubts and woes!'"

Lucy laughed rather halfheartedly. "Not a very happy sentiment, that. But at least they seem a sensible duo." As if drawing the rationality around her, she tugged again at her gloves. "They are wise enough to realize they have no future together."

"They realize it. But they hardly care. Radames . . . Well, he is the tenor, after all, and tenors have a way of being hopeless romantics. Even though Aida is his enemy, he is in love with her. He calls her '*Celeste Aida.*' Heavenly Aida."

Ignoring the warnings of head and heart, James crooked a finger under Lucy's chin and tipped her face toward his, his words a rich undertone to the buzz of noise around them. " '*Celeste Aida, forma divina, Mistico serto di luce efior, del mio pensiero, tu sei regina, tudi mia vista sei lo splendor.*' " James smiled, pleased at the way the poetry of the foreign words had made their way so effortlessly from his lips. " 'Heavenly Aida,' " he continued, translating for Lucy's benefit. " 'Beauty resplendent, Mysterious blending of flowers and light. Queen of my soul, you reign transcendent. Thou of my life art the splendor bright.' "

Lucy blinked. It was hardly a proper response. Considering their sophisticated surroundings, she

should have laughed carelessly or given James a co-
quettish smile. She should have answered with some
esoteric Italian verse of her own. Or at least acted
enough of a cabbage-head to bat her eyelashes at him
and proclaim his brilliance for all the crowd to hear.

Instead, all she could do was blink and stare.

What had he called Italian? Harmless? Hardly so.
If it was, why did it seem such a deadly weapon
when it fell so musically from James's lips?

"Your Italian is splendid." She managed that much
and hoped it didn't sound like a croak from a mouth
that was suddenly too dry. "You never told me you
speak Italian."

"I didn't know I did!" James's eyes lit with the
realization. He thought through the problem another
moment. "I do," he said, the smile in his eyes traveling to his lips. "I'm sure of it. Italian. French. German, of course. A smattering of Danish. Russian.
Even a little Polish!"

"Good heavens!" Lucy pressed one hand to her
heart, honestly taken aback. "All those?"

Not as proud of his accomplishment as he was of
the simple fact that he'd remembered them, James let
his smile dissolve into a devilish grin. "I imagine it
comes in quite handily," he said, one eyebrow sliding
up. "I might come to the opera . . ." He looked all
around. "And meet a beautiful woman. . . ." He
shifted his gaze back to Lucy. "I might say anything
at all to her and she wouldn't know if she should
smile dreamily or slap my face!"

Lucy laughed at the absurd notion. "That doesn't
seem a very efficient method of communication. If
the lady doesn't know what you're saying, why
bother saying anything at all?"

James looked pensive. "Then I could translate for
her," he said. "And she could decide for herself if

she should smile dreamily or slap my face." He lowered his voice, his gaze searching Lucy's face as he spoke.

"I could tell her she was beautiful in Danish. *Du er virkelig smuk.* Or that she had the prettiest eyes I've ever seen in French. *Vous avez les plus beaux yeaux dans tout le monde!* I might even be feeling bold and tell her that her lips were as luscious as strawberries. *Deine Lippen sind süsse wie Erdbeeren.*" He pulled a face. "That sounds awful in German, doesn't it? Rather as if I'm telling you that you have some dreadful disease."

Perhaps she did.

Lucy considered the thought.

Perhaps she did have some terrible ailment. It was the only thing that might explain the feelings that assailed her. The only thing that might possibly justify the fact that at any other time, in any other place, she would no doubt have been successful at ignoring them.

Tonight, trying to convince herself of the fact that she didn't feel every one of James's words melt through her defenses and heat her through to her soul was as futile as trying to silence the hum of excitement that permeated the air all around them.

Despite her objections—about attending the opera and wearing a dress she had not bought and paid for herself, about being even a small part of James's distasteful plan—Lucy could not help but be captured by the magic of the moment. The gown was the stuff of dreams and though she had never fancied herself a particularly fetching woman, she knew she looked handsome in it.

The theater itself was remarkable, the kind of place where light and sound mingled, assaulting the senses at the same time it heightened them, filling her eyes and her head, immersing her—if only for this one night—in sensory delights that tingled through her body and made her feel drawn tight with excitement.

And James . . .

Lucy looked into his eyes.

For the first time since she'd known him, James was dressed in clothing that had been made especially for him. He looked remarkably dashing in formal attire. For once, he wasn't uncomfortable, merely a temporary lodger in another man's clothes. His perfectly tailored cutaway coat fit close enough to show off the width of his shoulders but allowed him the luxury to move freely. The coat was dark, as were his trousers, complementing his hair. His shirt, waistcoat, and tie glowed snowy-white beneath the light of the lamps.

It was, apparently, the requisite outfit for all of the men attending the opera, but on James, it was more than simply tasteful. He stood out in the crowd. It may have been because he was so tall, but Lucy thought rather it was because he wore not only his clothes but a certain air of quiet sophistication so very well. He didn't need to be flashy and pompous like so many of the aristocracy who surrounded them.

The well-dressed ladies who turned their eyes and their smiles in his direction could never have guessed at the extent of his injuries that fateful night he had stumbled into her home. He looked every inch the man about town, and far more at home here among the elegant crowd than he had ever looked in the shabby surroundings of the Barnstable household.

"Well?" James seemed to be waiting, and Lucy wondered if she'd been so lost in her fancies that she'd missed a goodly portion of the conversation.

"Are you going to smile dreamily?" he asked, "Or slap my face?"

"Don't be silly." Lucy snapped open her white satin fan. It gave her trembling hands something to do and took her mind off the fact that she was very much tempted to smile dreamily. "I'm not going to do either. I'm going to be practical and logical."

"Of course."

Lucy ignored James's groaned response. "I am simply going to point out that it tells us something very important about your past. The fact that you speak any number of languages tells us—"

"Odd, the way things come back to you." James wasn't in the mood to listen to her reasoning. He shook his head in wonder. "Until this moment, I hadn't given it a thought. Thinking back on it, I remember a school in Heidelberg—" He broke off and turned slightly so as better to scan the crowd. "It hardly matters right now, of course. If Sir Digby is able to identify me, there'll be no more need for speculation."

He was right.

If Sir Digby Talbot knew James, if he was able to put a name to him, to give him a family and a history, all the pieces of James's past would come together. It was what James wanted, after all. More than anything. Or anyone.

And Lucy could hardly blame him.

The weeks he'd spent with no memory must surely have been more than difficult. Sir Digby just might be James's one chance at salvation, and Lucy's one chance to locate Alfie.

The idea should have cheered her—finding her father was still uppermost in Lucy's mind—but there was the matter of James, and she could not be so blind as to think her feelings for him might disappear without a trace the moment he regained his life.

Once he knew who he was, would she ever see him again? Or would he bid her a hearty and heartfelt good-bye, as grateful as he could be for the mess she'd made of trying to discover his identity and just as eager to get on with his life?

Though the gaiety around them continued, Lucy felt a sudden tug of melancholy. "Something tells me this story won't have a happy ending," she said.

"*Aida?*" James gave the crowd another quick inspection before he turned back to her. "You're right, I'm afraid. Because of Aida, Radames betrays his country and he's sentenced to die. They seal him beneath the altar of one of their gods, burying him alive. But as he sits there in the darkness, he realizes he's not alone. Aida comes to him. They die in each other's arms."

The very thought brought tears to Lucy's eyes.

"Stuff and nonsense!" She waved her fan in front of her face to hide her reaction. "Opera, I mean. I'm sorry to say, but I have a feeling that I will find it as silly as I do the Holmes stories. Romantic claptrap."

"Perhaps it is." His eyes glinting with mischief, James smiled down at her. "But did you ever stop to think that perhaps there's nothing wrong with a little romantic claptrap?"

Lucy was an honest woman. At least she'd always thought herself to be. Fortunately, this time, she did not have to decide between lying and telling the truth. Beyond James's shoulder, she caught sight of a group of impressive-looking older gentlemen entering the theater.

Lucy recognized one of them from the picture that had appeared in the newspaper. "Sir Digby!"

She had James's attention instantly. Following her gaze, he turned and watched with interest.

Sir Digby Talbot must have been nearly seventy. But though the years had turned his hair white and lined his face so that it reminded Lucy of a well-used blanket, they had diminished neither his vigor nor his manner. A man who was obviously as used to wielding power as he was to swinging his silver-tipped walking stick, he swept into the vestibule wearing his dignity as effortlessly as he wore his flawlessly tailored and obviously expensive clothing.

Intent on the conversation he was having with a large, bald man who'd come in with him, Sir Digby hardly noticed when the crowd parted before him to let him by. And when James appeared at his elbow, the old fellow went right on talking.

"Sir Digby." James's interruption was as polite as possible. "Excuse me, sir. I—"

"See my secretary," Sir Digby growled, and without giving James a look, he kept right on walking.

Stunned, James hesitated for a second. It was one second too long. Before he had a chance to recover, Sir Digby was already by him and on his way up the staircase.

Like the Red Sea around the Egyptian hordes, the crowd closed behind him, making it impossible for James to follow. Lucy knew that in a matter of minutes, Sir Digby and his friends would be ensconced in their private box and there would be little chance of seeing him again the rest of the night.

She acted almost without thinking.

Lucy nibbled her lips to redden them. She pinched her cheeks. Sliding passed a gaggle of well-dressed spinsters, she hurried to the stairway.

"Sir Digby!" She had not meant to speak so loudly.

She had not even realized she'd done it until a good many people turned to see what was going on.

Lucy realized she hadn't needed to pinch her cheeks. They must surely be flaming. She ignored that detail as well as the fact that she saw James, with a horrified look on his face, pushing his way through the crowd to try to get to her side. Lifting her chin, she sauntered over to where Sir Digby stood, one foot poised on the bottom step of the staircase, his white eyebrows raised halfway up his forehead.

"Now don't tell me you've forgotten." Lucy tapped Sir Digby's arm lightly with her fan and did her best at giving the old fellow a little pout and a seductive wink. "You promised you wouldn't. Not ever." She felt James fall into place behind her and thanked her lucky stars. She wasn't sure how long she could keep up this absurdity.

"I have someone you simply must speak to." Without shifting her glance from Sir Digby's slightly stunned expression, she reached around for James's arm and dragged him to her side. "I know you remember him as well as you do me. This is James—"

Sir Digby made a choking sound. He looked from Lucy to James and back again to Lucy.

"Young woman, I don't know what you are talking about." Again, he turned his gaze to James and for an instant Lucy thought she saw a flicker of recognition in his eyes. It was gone as quickly as it came and she decided that it was, rather, a flash of anger.

"Who are you people?" Sir Digby demanded, his voice soaring along with his temper. "What do you want? I've never seen either one of you in my life! I shall have the management eject you. I shall—"

"No need, sir." One of Sir Digby's companions came to the rescue. Taking the old man's arm, he led him up the stairs, but not before he threw Lucy and James a flinty look. "Just an unpleasant misunderstanding," he assured Sir Digby. "And hardly worth getting yourself upset about. Why don't you come along and we'll have someone bring up a bottle of champagne."

The fire in her cheeks turning to the ice of mortification, Lucy watched them go. She didn't dare look around. Dozens of people poured up the stairway toward the private boxes and she was sure every one of their eyes was on her.

It wasn't until silence filled the vestibule and the strains of Verdi's overture could be heard coming from inside the theater that Lucy dared to look up.

She found James staring at her.

He opened his mouth. Snapped it shut again. One hand out, he moved toward her as if to say something and not being able to find the words, he pulled back and stood stock-still.

Finally, he burst into laughter.

"Damn them all!" He wound his arm through Lucy's and led her up the stairway. "Come on. Let's go watch the opera!"

# Chapter 14

"Do you still think it's all a lot of romantic claptrap?"

It was completely inappropriate for James to take advantage of the moment, but he could hardly help himself.

He was feeling bold.

The scent of Lucy's perfume was enough to make any man feel brazen. And if it wasn't, the fact that he'd spent the entire cab ride home surreptitiously watching her exquisite profile silhouetted in the flickering gaslights would surely have done the trick.

He handed Lucy down from the hansom and before she could settle herself on the pavement or remove her hand from his, he asked the question that had been foremost in his mind since the curtain went down on the opera and the houselights went up.

"Whatever are you talking about?" Lucy looked past James toward the darkened Barnstable house. It was a weak evasion at best and he was not about to let her get away with it. Half hoping that the rhythmic clip-clop of the hansom had caught in his bloodstream and was, therefore, the cause of his heart throbbing unrelentingly, he waited until the sounds of the departing cab faded into the night.

The throbbing did not fade with it.

"I'm talking about the opera, of course," he said.

Even with Lucy so near, it was difficult to read her expression. There was a streetlight farther up the road, but it provided little illumination. Her face was bathed in soft shadows, a pale oval above the high, ruffled collar of her black satin evening cloak. "'I'm talking about the fact that when the opera ended, you had tears in your eyes." Gently, he touched a finger to each of her eyes and was rewarded with the brush of her lashes, a caress as ethereal as a butterfly's wings. He glided his hands over her face. "And on your cheeks."

As stoic and stubborn as ever, Lucy dismissed the observation with a tight smile. "You must surely be mistaken. Me? Cry over a story? Impossible! Of course I realize it was romantic claptrap. Young lovers, jealous rivals, all that nonsense about—how did you translate it for me at intermission? Intoxicating love?"

" *'Inebbriata io sono,'* " James supplied the words Lucy could not remember. " *'Dall'inatteso guibilo, Inebbriata io sono. Tutti in undi si compiono I sogni del mio cor.* By the unexpected joy, I am intoxicated; All in one day are fulfilled the dreams of my heart.' "

"Indeed!" Lucy's protest might have been far more convincing if she did not catch her breath. "Romantic," she said, "claptrap."

James laughed. It may have been because her excuses were far too feeble to take seriously, but he suspected his mood was affected more by the fact that she had yet to make a move to dislodge her hand from his. "Admit it, Lucy, you were moved. The music . . . the singing . . . the pageantry of it all!"

"The music and the singing and the pageantry, yes. I will admit that much. It was majestic and very stirring. And I can never thank you enough—" She snipped off the enthusiasm that had crept into her words. "I'm grateful," she said quite simply at the same time she moved past James and headed toward the house. "But that doesn't mean I have to agree with you, does it? Romance? If that is what you call romance, I must beg to differ with you. What woman in her right mind would ever do what Aida did and sacrifice herself for a man?"

"You did." James let her get as far as the first step. Her hand still caught in his, he pulled her to a stop and turned her to face him. With James still on the pavement and Lucy on the stairs, they were eye to eye. "You put on that ridiculous performance for Sir Digby simply so that I might have a chance to meet him. Why?"

Lucy shrugged. The movement caused her satin cloak to shift. The polished fabric caressed James's free hand. He sucked in a breath, reveling in the fact that a pleasure could be so simple and yet so sensual. The cloak was fastened at Lucy's neck and open down the front and he slid his hand inside, resting it against her satin dress at the waist.

Lucy didn't protest. And she didn't move away. She met James's eyes. "I . . . I knew how you were looking forward to meeting Sir Digby," she said. "I knew you would be disappointed if you didn't have a chance to speak to him, and then when he was so rude . . . When he refused to even acknowledge you . . . I . . . well, I'm afraid I rather lost my head. I don't know what came over me. It was very unlike me."

She could believe such nonsense if she chose. James did not. He threw his head back and laughed. "It was very like you," he assured her. Releasing her hand, he slipped his other hand inside her cloak and drew her closer. "Only you don't know it yet."

"Don't I?" He wondered if his own voice sounded

as breathless as Lucy's, and if she realized that as
determined as she was to try, she could not hide her
body's response to his. Her words might be nonchalant, but her eyes were luminous. Her heart beat
wildly against his.

"I do believe I know my own character," she said.
"And I admit that I'm sorry about Sir Digby. Honestly, I am. I know you think me a poor detective
and a terrible liar and a dreadful annoyance but you
have to believe me, James, I did hope that Sir Digby
might give you some clue as to your identity."

"And you risked embarrassing yourself to get it.
Or worse. If it wasn't for that chap who talked Sir
Digby into a glass of champagne, the old blighter
might have had you tossed out on your fashionable
and quite lovely little bum." James gave her a
squeeze, his fingers drifting ever so lightly over that
portion of her anatomy under discussion.

Even in the dark, he saw her face flush. Her eyes
drifting closed, she moistened her lips. "Being
thrown out of the theater is hardly the same as being
buried alive inside a tomb," she said, her voice a
whisper. "So you see, I'm not anything at all like
Aida."

"You're just as brave. Just as beautiful. Like her,
*'T'areva il cielo per l'amour creata.* Heaven created thee
for love.' "

"Oh, my!" It was Lucy's last attempt at regaining
her senses as well as some semblance of control, but
it was a halfhearted one at best. When James kissed
her, even that lukewarm objection vanished, inciner-
ated as suddenly and as completely as the last ves-
tiges of her resistance.

She tilted her head back, basking in the heat of
James's mouth on hers. His kiss was not at all tentative. Neither was his touch. Inside the cloak, his

hands slipped over the satin gown, stroking her hips, encircling her waist. He flattened his hands at the small of her back and pressed her closer.

Lucy couldn't say which of them came to their senses first or who suggested they would have far more privacy, and a good deal more comfort, inside the house, but the next thing she knew, she was fumbling with the front door key. She didn't bother to turn up the lights. She didn't have the chance.

Once the front door closed behind them, James's mouth came down on hers, hungry and searching. Her body tingling with each new sensation that spiraled through her, Lucy returned kiss for kiss. Locked in each other's arms, they danced a stammering figure across the entryway, clattering into the hall table and nearly upending the umbrella stand. Somehow, they managed to make their way as far as the parlor.

Her back to the door, Lucy groped for the knob. It was a simple enough task. Or at least it should have been. It was made completely impossible by the feel of James's mouth against her throat. He trailed a line of fiery kisses from her jaw down to where the ruff of her collar tied around her neck. He made his way back up again, his tongue touching here and there.

Savoring the sensations and too reluctant to break the spell, Lucy held her breath. She might have gone on that way forever if James hadn't kissed her again. He parted her lips and nudged her mouth open bit by bit, until his tongue met hers. Delight lingered, a delectable undercurrent that shivered through her. Desire sparked, and Lucy knew if they didn't get into the parlor soon, she would surely shatter from the need that filled her.

She made one last attempt to find the knob. Her

fingers closed around it and she twisted, and when she felt the door give way behind her, she whirled into the room.

Along the wall, the gas jets were turned so low, the light was no more than a muted glow that washed the scene with gold. The soft light glinted in James's eyes as he followed her inside. It caught on the hint of a smile that lifted the corners of his mouth when he kicked the door closed behind them. He tossed his tall top hat on the table and peeled off his coat.

"No!" When Lucy made to untie her cloak, he stopped her. His eyes on hers, he reached out a hand and took one end of the tie that held the cape closed. He curled the ribbon around his finger and pulled.

The bow yielded to his touch. Capturing one side of the cloak in each hand, James slid it from her shoulders and dropped it on the floor, an inky puddle of satin that pooled around their feet.

"I never thought—" James's gaze wandered over Lucy, from her face to her throat to the neckline of her dress, and his thoughts seemed to drift along with it. "That is, I never presumed . . . But I always hoped. I never dared dream but—" His hands roaming along with his words, he let the satin jabot at the front of her gown drift through his fingers. "I always imagined it would be this way." His gaze slid to her satin gloves and his eyes lit with what was surely roguishness of the most delightful sort. "And speaking of imagination . . ."

He hooked a finger at the top of one of her gloves. "I have a confession," he said. He returned his gaze to hers momentarily. "When we barely knew each other . . . The day we visited *The Times*. You were wearing gloves and I . . . I was wondering . . ."

Without further explanation, he tugged at the

glove. It glided over her elbow. It slid down her forearm. It slipped to her hand. The smile on James's face brightened. Slowly, he pulled the glove the rest of the way off, one finger at a time.

When he was finished, James murmured his approval. He tucked the glove in his pocket, and taking her hand in both of his, he traced its shape with one finger. His finger dipped between her thumb and forefinger, then up and over the other fingers in turn. It coasted and lingered. It sailed and soared.

Lucy's desire soared with it. Though she felt she would swoon from the heat of James's touch and the feel of his body so close to hers, she managed a smile. "Did you? Imagine, I mean. If that is the case, sir, I suppose I might be obliged to ask why you were imagining anything at all about me."

"That's easy enough to explain." He busied himself removing her other glove. "It's because you have the most beautiful eyes." He touched a kiss against each eyelid. "And marvelous ears." He nibbled on an earlobe. "It's because you're tenacious and hardheaded . . ." He kissed her brow. "And because I've come to find out that beneath it all, you're caring and sensitive and very softhearted, indeed."

Watching James's gaze slide to the front of her dress, Lucy caught her breath. He glanced at her briefly, as if offering a final chance for her to change her mind. When she didn't, he slid two fingers beneath the satin, shifting her dress and corset just enough to caress the bare skin beneath. Holding the fabric aside he bent and pressed a kiss between her breasts. He parted his lips and his tongue touched her skin, spreading liquid fire.

Lucy groaned. It seemed a poor response to a sensation so exquisite yet it was the only thing she could do. She was hot and cold, wound tight with apprehension at the same time she felt freer than she had ever felt in her life. She was frightened and feeling so brave, she dared to glide her hands to James's shoulders and slip off his jacket. It joined her cloak on the floor.

James smiled his approval. "You're a rare fine woman, Lucy Barnstable," he murmured, drawing the pins from her hair. "As braw as the finest flower and as strong as the Cairngorm Mountains."

"Am I?" Lucy would have liked to believe it, but she was not so sure. Over James's shoulder, she caught sight of the photograph of Alfie. She turned her face away, her head tipped back to receive James's kisses, but even the warmth of his mouth wasn't enough to relieve the doubts that plagued her.

Was she strong?

She was sensible enough to know that there were no actions without consequences, and confident enough to know that no matter the consequences, she was ready to give herself to James, body and soul.

But she was not strong. Not strong enough to find her father, or to learn how to expose the secrets that were buried so deep within James's mind that even he could not uncover them.

Did it take some special strength to admit her feelings for James and surrender to the overwhelming sensations he provoked in her? Or had she simply convinced herself that she had taken all the chances she would take? That she was ready to give up, and forget herself and her self-doubts in the heat of passion?

"Not as strong as you think, perhaps." The words felt like ice on Lucy's lips. The same ice that suddenly filled her insides. Gently, she pushed away from James, far enough to try to take the measure of his expression. "You were talking like a Scotsman again," she explained. "And I'm sorry, but when you do that, I am reminded of your past."

"A past? Do I have one?" He barked a laugh, fighting to recapture the mood at the same time the look in his eyes told her he realized it was lost forever. "Does my past matter so much at a time like this?"

"Yes." Lucy pressed a hand to her lips. The heat of James's kisses still simmered there and as quickly as she could she dropped her arms to her sides. "I told you that when I approached Sir Digby this evening, I wasn't acting like myself. You disagreed. But you see, you were wrong. My real self is a great deal less daring than you think. And a good deal more afraid to take chances. Especially chances . . ." She looked to where her cloak and James's jacket lay in a tumble on the floor. She looked at her hands and swore she could still feel James's touch against her skin. "Chances," she said, "like this."

"Are we taking a chance?" James reached for her arm and held it, and when she did not make a move to pull away, he stroked her cheek, drawing her gaze back to his. "Tell me, how is it dangerous for two people who care for each other to express their feelings?"

Lucy couldn't answer him. Not when he was so close. Not with the heat of his body still igniting an answering heat in her. She backed away and turned from him, wrapping her arms around herself. "We should talk," she said.

James laughed, a sound that was brittle in the air. "I'd say it's a bit late for that, wouldn't you?" He came up behind her but he knew enough to keep his distance. "I'd have thought we've already said everything there was to say."

Outside the window, Lucy watched the moon float

from behind an embankment of fat clouds. Its silvery light sugarcoated the pavement and the houses across the road. She shivered.

"How can we pledge our love to each other," she asked, "when there might be someone else?"

James grumbled. "Blast Freddy! If you really feel—"

"What I feel for Freddy is friendship. Nothing more." For the first time, Lucy realized it was true, and she wondered that she hadn't worked it through before. "I mistook that feeling for something stronger," she admitted. "I convinced myself it would be enough because I wanted everything Freddy represents. Security and safety. Wonderful, mind-numbing routine. I know it's hard to understand, but after years of living with Alfie, all those things seemed so important. I just wanted . . ." She rummaged through her mind, trying to produce the right mixture of words. "I just wanted to be the same as everyone else. I'm afraid I've treated Freddy very badly. I didn't know enough to realize that friendship isn't love. Now I've learned that sometimes, even love isn't enough." She turned to James and took his hand.

Already, there was a barrier between them. She could feel it there. It cooled the air that had been so heated, enclosing him in a distant place she knew she would have to fight to reach.

"I'm not talking about Freddy," she told him, her eyes pleading for understanding. "I'm talking about you. And until we know who you are . . . don't you see?" Her question vanished on the end of a sob and it was a minute before she could bring herself to speak again. "Until we know more about you, we can't say that you don't have a family and a—" She couldn't manage to put her fears into words. "There might be someone waiting for you."

James, apparently, didn't need the reminder. His face as rigid as his bearing, he nodded. "Yes. Of course. It isn't as if the thought hasn't occurred to me, I just seemed to have put it out of my mind in the face of more pressing matters." He gave her a smile that kindled a bittersweet response, and took her hand in his. "If there's someone to whom I've made a promise—"

"I know you would keep it." Lucy was sure of it. James was an honorable man. He would keep his word, just as he would keep faith with some woman who might, even tonight, be staring out her window, watching the moonlight against the pavement. Watching, and wondering where he might be and when he was coming home.

Lucy's throat tightened. "You might think me strong, James, but you are wrong. At least when it comes to this. If there's someone else, someone you are pledged to return to . . ." She blinked away the tears that filled her eyes. "If we make love, things will never be the same. Not for you. Not for me. And if someday you must leave . . . It's too much of a chance for me to take. I'm not that strong. I'm not that strong at all."

"Don't cry. Please." James wiped the tears from her cheeks with his thumbs. "You're right, and you needn't worry that I will try to convince you otherwise. But, Lucy . . ." He cupped her chin and raised her face to his, looking deep into her eyes. "Don't think that I'm worried about hurting some nameless woman who may or may not exist. I'm not. It's probably wrong of me, I know. If she exists, I surely owe the woman more regard than that. But it's difficult to muster emotion for a face I can't see when I close

my eyes. As I do yours. A voice I don't hear inside
my head day and night. As I do yours. You resonate
inside me, Lucy my love, like my heartbeat and the
air inside my lungs. Like the echo of my own self."
He dropped a kiss on Lucy's brow and the tip of her
nose. He pressed a tender kiss against her lips. "I
swear, it's you, Lucy. It's you I can't risk hurting."

James promised Lucy he would go right to bed.
He swore that as soon as he heard her climb the
steps and knew that she was settled safely behind
the closed door of her room, he would go up to his
own room and try to get some sleep.

Yet he hadn't moved a muscle. All night long, he
sat on the divan in the pitch-dark room, thinking
through everything Lucy had said.

She was right, of course. No matter how hard he
tried or how many ways he attempted to look at it
he couldn't deny that everything she said was the
absolute truth. As much as they both might be
tempted, he couldn't risk his honor—or her heart—
for one night's pleasure.

But what a night it would have been!

Even now, a thrill rocketed through James's body
at the thought. He shifted in his seat, trying to settle
himself more comfortably. Knowing there wasn't a
feather's chance in hell.

James took a deep breath. He swore he could still
smell Lucy's perfume. It lingered in the air like the
disturbing images that played their way across his
mind, tickling his nose and his fancy. He didn't need
to close his eyes, he could picture Lucy, radiant in
her white gown, eagerly responding to his kisses. The
taste of her skin had made him as squiffy as a sailor.
Her going had left him feeling empty and wanting,

and hours later he still ached with the bitter mingling of abstinence and regret.

And the painful realization that no matter the cost, he had done the right thing.

James glanced at the clock on the mantelpiece. All night long, he'd listened to it tick away the endless minutes. Now, a thin stream of gray light drizzled through the curtains, showing him that it was nearly six o'clock.

"Time for the household to start stirring." James stretched his arms over his head and forced himself to his feet. It wouldn't do for the other tenants to find him here in the parlor, he reminded himself, especially dressed in the clothes he'd left the house in the night before. He collected his hat from the table and his jacket from the chair where he'd tossed it once Lucy had gone to bed. He was about to open the parlor door and head upstairs when he heard the front door open and close. Footsteps crossed the floor.

James thought of the burglar who had challenged Lucy so boldly, and dismissed the notion instantly. No burglar would dare enter a home in daylight with so little regard for the noise he was making.

His curiosity piqued, James inched open the door.

From where he stood, he could see the man who had just come in the front door, but only from the back. He was of average height, his hair an indeterminate color in the watered-down light. His coat was spotted with rain and he was busy shaking off his umbrella and tucking it away in the stand near the front door.

"Grogan." The answer to the little mystery came out of nowhere, and James found himself feeling a bit foolish. Many times, Lucy had mentioned Mr. Grogan, the boarder who lived one floor above

James, a solitary and none-too-friendly individual who came and went at odd hours and largely kept to himself. James should have thought of Grogan immediately. He could only attribute his slow wits to lack of sleep. And want of Lucy.

Yet if he was so sure of himself, why did James hesitate?

The question skipped through his mind at the same time he stepped back, keeping the door open only enough to see and not be seen. A second later, James knew the answer.

Even from this not very helpful angle, he realized there was something vaguely familiar about the man who stood in the entryway. Something about the set of his shoulders, and the tilt of his head, and the cut of his coat. Something that called up long-dormant memories.

The awareness churned through James's stomach like the remnants of a bad meal. It prickled at the back of his neck.

While James watched, Grogan finished with his umbrella. He shook the rain from his shoulders and turned to head up the stairway.

"Hell and damnation." The words escaped James in a startled whisper. He stood stock-still, frozen by the realization that he knew the man all too well.

He should, James reminded himself bitterly.

The man Lucy called Grogan was really Michael O'Connor, a soulless bastard who sold his services, if not his loyalties, to the highest bidder.

O'Connor had tried to kill James not once, but twice. The last time, just weeks ago in a Whitechapel alley.

Listening to the tramp of O'Connor's boots as he made his way up the stairs, James cursed himself for his dull wits and a head that was so soft that a beating could drive the memories from it, and so hard that he'd been unable to see the truth that had been staring him in the face.

His vision blurred and sweat broke out on his forehead. His breath tight, his heart pumping so hard he swore it would burst, he snapped the door closed and leaned his head against it.

As blistering as the lightning that had torn through the sky that night, light exploded behind James's eyes, opening a floodgate of memory.

He remembered it all. His history. Himself. The night he and Michael O'Connor had come face-to-face again.

It was the night he'd forgotten himself and his past. The night all memory of his mission had been blotted from his mind.

The night Michael O'Connor—mercenary, madman, and one of Lucy's lodgers—had tried his damnedest to beat James to death.

With a stout lad gripping each of his arms and another with fists like hams directly in front of him doling out the blows, there was little a man could do.

Not that James hadn't tried.

He had a gash in his forehead to prove it. His right eye was swollen so badly he could barely see out of it, and he was certain his ribs were broken. Each breath he took tore through him like fire. Each futile move he made to try to avoid the next hammering blow shot pain through his chest.

A brutal punch to his gut made James forget all about his ribs. He coughed and spat blood. Black and slick, it flecked the ground around him, as glossy as glass in the flash of lightning that ripped through the night sky.

The burst of light flooded the grimy alleyway,

throwing the brick walls and dustbins that surrounded them into strange silhouette. The brightness
burst behind James's eyes, one flash, then another,
until his head was full of fire.

If he'd had only one opponent, some thug hired
for the occasion whose greed was the only driving
force behind his fist, James was sure he would have
bested the man.

If it had been only one of O'Connor's gillies, he
would have beaten him with no problem.

And if it had been just O'Connor himself?

The thought clattered through James's head with
much the same delicacy as the punch that caught
him square in the jaw. His teeth rattled and he
tasted blood.

If it had been O'Connor and only O'Connor, James
knew he would have had a time of it. Yet even then,
he would have stood at least a chance at victory.

But, damn it, it was all of them. All at once.

Like the devil he was, Michael O'Connor stepped
up behind the brute throwing the punches, and taking a long draw on his slender and expensive cigar,
he looked James up and down.

The last time they'd stood this close, O'Connor had
been at the business end of a gun barrel. And James
had been at the other.

In those few seconds before the gun exploded
against James's chest, he'd committed O'Connor's
face to memory.

The only question now was, did O'Connor remember him?

With a barely perceptible shake of his head,
O'Connor signaled to the man in front of James. His
arm still cocked, the bullyboy stepped back, a satisfied smile on his pug-ugly face.

Like the suffocating hand of a strangler, silence

closed around them, broken only by the drumming of the rain, the rumble of thunder overhead, and each rough breath James fought to take.

O'Connor took another step nearer. He narrowed his eyes.

If the blood that covered his misshapen face wasn't enough to hide his identity, James prayed that the changes of the last twelve years would be.

It seemed his prayers were answered. There was no spark of recognition in O'Connor's ice-blue eyes, no sign of anything except hatred. It was as chilling an emotion as any James had ever encountered, not because it was so potent, but because it was so completely impersonal.

"I'm a patient man. You've seen as much for yourself." O'Connor was a Dublin man born and raised, and his accent might have been musical if it wasn't for the hint of malice that edged his every word. He dropped the stub of his cigar onto the pavement and ground it beneath his boot heel.

"But I'm sick to death of wasting my time, boyo. I don't know who the devil you are or where they found you. I don't know how they talked you into this fool's errand. I do know you've been a royal pain in the arse. And I'm dreadful tired of it. You have information. I know that for certain. You know about the Eye of the Devil." As casually as if he were simply passing the time of day, O'Connor drew a flick-knife from his pocket. He flipped his wrist and the blade snapped open. Its well-honed edge gleamed in the odd half-light. "Is there anything you're wanting to tell me?"

There was. There was a great deal James would have liked to tell the man. He would have liked to tell him to go to hell.

For good or bad, the words wouldn't make it past his swollen lips.

Tired of waiting, O'Connor clicked his tongue and turned away, but not before he waved one hand, signing to the bully that he could have another go at James.

The man delivered another blow with relish. It was a punch to the midsection that knocked James's head into the brick wall at his back. It left him with a mouth full of bile.

He didn't stand a chance. James knew it. He supposed he should have been saying his prayers, or at least wondering what might become of his body after it was found in this filthy place.

But it wasn't what he was thinking at all.

The thoughts that filled his head were as daft as any. They were crazy. Like the bright balloons of light that exploded behind his eyes.

They were fey. The last pathetic thoughts of a lunatic. As mad as the notion that he might still get in a lick or two if for no other reason than for old times' sake.

Bracing his weight against the fellows who held his arms and the wall at his back, James steadied himself against the pain that shot through his body. He tensed the few muscles that didn't hurt and every one of them that did, and he jumped.

His feet left the ground just enough for him to get one leg in the air. He didn't have time to aim. He didn't have the strength. He kicked out as hard as he could.

He caught the man who stood in front of him unprepared. With an expletive that nearly drowned out the roll of thunder over their heads, the ruffian fell back clutching his groin.

A sure as he knew his own name, James knew

what would happen next. The two men who were holding him tightened their grips, their hands like steel bands around his arms. Furious that a situation he'd thought well under control had gotten out of hand, O'Connor spun around. He stepped up and faced James eye to eye.

"So that's the way it's to be then, is it?" O'Connor spat the words at James along with a string of obscenities. "It's a poor place to die and a foolish thing to give your life for. But you're leaving me no choice. You're—"

O'Connor's words were interrupted by the shrill blast of a police whistle.

There was no way the police could have been coming to rescue him. James knew that. No one knew he was there. Hell, no one even knew he was in London.

But even the hint of police presence was enough to make a man as canny as O'Connor know he was in danger. His head cocked, he darted a look at the mouth of the alleyway, gauging the sound of the whistle against the time he had left. In that instant, another flash of lightning shredded the sky, and James knew O'Connor didn't need any more time.

James braced himself for the sting of the knife meeting his flesh. But instead of the knife, O'Connor used his fists.

The savage punch he aimed at James's gut was enough to knock James off his feet. Already lightheaded from the loss of blood, he hit the pavement face first and even before his cheek sank into the muck, O'Connor kicked him in the stomach.

What little air was left in James's lungs exploded out of him with a sickening sound that was half wheeze, half gurgle. Struggling against the realization that he was drowning in his own blood, James lifted his head. He pushed against the wet pavement.

He might have succeeded in heaving himself off the ground if O'Connor hadn't struck again.

He got in one more kick, this one to James's head.

For an instant the world was a blur of bright color. James watched the blazing lights behind his eyes turn bloodred. He saw them fade. Even before his head hit the ground for the final time, everything went black.

# Chapter 15

"Good morning!" A tea tray in her hands, Lucy ventured a few steps into the parlor. As Harleigh and Farleigh had promised after the reconnoiter of the premises she had persuaded them to conduct, James was there. And he was alone. She offered a smile and hoped the smudges under her eyes didn't betray just how long and sleepless the night had been.

Six hours of tossing and turning had done nothing for her appearance, she was sure. It had done as little for her composure as spending those hours thinking about James and all they had shared the night before.

Even now, Lucy could feel her skin tingle and her blood quicken. Even now, she could feel the heaviness that had settled in her heart, a constant reminder that no matter how heady and tempting the seduction, no matter how appealing the man, she and James would never have a future. Not until he found his past.

She paused, uncertain that she was ready to face James and the reality of all that they'd said—and done—the night before.

"I thought," she said, "that we might talk."

He didn't answer immediately and Lucy did not have to wonder why. Though it was well into the morning, he was still wearing the evening clothes he'd worn to the opera. His face was shadowed by a night's growth of beard that made it look angular and more rugged than she remembered it. His eyes were unreadable, heavy with an expression that, a few weeks ago, she might have attributed to suspicion. Now, she was sure it was simply the product of too little sleep.

Lucy's heart squeezed with sympathy. As restless as her own night had been, at least she had spent it in the relative comfort of her own bed. James must have fallen asleep here in the parlor. She was glad she'd thought to seek him out, and happier still that she'd thought to bring breakfast.

"I've brought you a pot of tea and some toast." She laid the tea things out on the table. "You didn't join us for breakfast this morning, and I suspected that you might be wanting something by now." She poured a cup of tea, added sugar and cream, and held it out to him. He didn't accept it. He didn't even acknowledge it.

Lucy looked at the tea uncertainly. "I could make coffee if you'd rather—"

"You're awfully canty this morning." James turned an expression on her that was not quite a smile. "Are you always so chipper when the rest of the world is feeling so damned forfochen?"

"Well, I can't say what—what is it you said?— forfochen might mean, but if it means weary, I will confess, I am no better rested than you. That's what I wanted to talk to you about." Tired of holding his cup and waiting for him to fetch it, she took it to him.

"I was up all night thinking," she said, dropping into the seat across from James's. "About—" She could hardly tell him everything she'd been thinking about. She couldn't possibly mention the fact that she'd spent a good deal of the night reliving each and every one of his caresses, remembering the way his hands left a nearly unendurable heat in their wake. Neither could she tell him that she'd spent more time still dreaming of the taste of his kisses, and the way his mouth slid over her skin.

The thought nearly upended her and Lucy set it aside. "I've been thinking about the things we talked about last night," she said. It wasn't a lie, merely a half-truth. "I think we should continue our investigation."

"Do you?" James set aside his cup of tea untouched. He sat back, assessing Lucy. His gaze was direct. It always was. But this morning, something about it made her stomach lurch.

Had James's ardor cooled now that she was just plain Lucy again, and not the woman in the white satin confection of a dress? Had his passion been a product of the moment? A passing fancy he regretted or, worse still, one he regarded merely as a lost opportunity for a conquest that would be forgotten as soon as it was consummated?

The questions battered Lucy's heart, but she refused to let them deter her. She adjusted the skirt of her brown housedress and clasped her hands together on her lap. "I won't lie to you, James. I am still determined to find my father and I still think you are the one who can help me do it. Besides . . ." She unclasped her hands. Rearranged her skirt. Latched her fingers together again.

"If we can find out who you really are—"

It was a simple enough statement, and it should hardly have come as a surprise to James after what they'd discussed the night before, but Lucy wasn't prepared for his reaction. With a grunt of disgust, he rose from his seat and crossed the room. He poured a cup of tea, then thought better of it. Setting the cup on the table, he turned to Lucy.

James leaned back against the table, his arms over his chest, his legs crossed at the ankles. He looked far more at ease than she had ever seen him look. And far more dangerous.

Lucy wondered at the thought. If she didn't know better, she would swear there had been some transformation in James overnight. The tender expression that had softened his eyes as they stood wrapped in each other's arms was gone. His lips were hard. His shoulders were rigid. In all the time they'd known each other, she had seen him angry, and annoyed, and vexed beyond tolerance. She had seen his tender side and experienced the melting glances that told her there was more to the man than even she had ever imagined, a side to him she would willingly explore, if only fate would give them the chance.

But she had never seen him like this.

It was as if the air of sophistication and elegance that had surrounded them at the opera had never left him, and it had nothing to do with the fact that he was still in his evening clothes. His trousers were rumpled. His shirttails were out. His tie and collar were gone, and Lucy had the vague recollection of being the one who'd stripped them from him. In spite of it all, James looked comfortable and completely in control, a commanding presence in the tatty little room, certainly, but, she suspected, he would have been just as self-assured and confident had he been standing in Buckingham Palace itself.

"Find out who I really am." James said the words rather like he was proposing that man might visit the moon. "Do you think it's possible?"

"If you would allow me to continue with my investigation—"

"Continue with your investigation. Is that what you think we need to do?"

The question was not nearly as unnerving as the way he asked it. "You make it sound like a riddle." His gaze was far too nerve-jangling. Lucy rose from her seat and busied herself fluffing pillows. "I've given it a great deal of thought. I even spent some time early this morning reading over Alfie's journal and—"

"Journal?" For the first time that morning, James's voice betrayed emotion. He reined it in, but not quickly enough. "You never told me Alfie kept a journal. You never let me—"

"Read it?" The audacity of the statement surprised even Lucy. "Is there a reason you should? There's nothing in it about you, I can guarantee that much. There's nothing in it that's the least bit helpful except . . ." She hesitated. All these weeks, she'd chosen to keep the meat of Alfie's journal to herself. Her secrecy had gotten her nowhere. Would her honesty pay better dividends?

"Alfie was working on a case," she told him. "A real case. Not one of the ones he concocted inside his head. Someone had actually hired him to conduct some detective work."

"Not me."

How James could sound so certain, Lucy didn't know. She hardly paid him any mind. "I know it may sound rather farfetched . . ."

Farfetched? Inside her head, Lucy wondered at the word. The idea that had come to her that morning, the idea she was about to propose to James, wasn't simply farfetched. It was insane.

She refused to listen to the voice. "Do you remember what Holmes says in one of the stories?" she asked. "He says something about taking all the evidence in a case and looking at it carefully. He says that after all the impossibilities are eliminated, whatever is left, no matter how improbable it seems, must be the truth. I've spent the morning trying to follow his advice."

Lucy held a pillow in front of her, a shield to protect her from the logical argument she was certain James would use to poke holes in the deduction she had so painstakingly formulated. "I told you, I found this Indian stone seal in a secret drawer in Alfie's desk." She pulled the seal from her pocket and held it up for James to see. "The seal by itself doesn't mean a thing. I must admit, originally, I thought it might be something Alfie had made himself. A kind of stage prop, if you will. But I've learned enough at the British Museum to know I was wrong. It is certainly authentic. And rare. Keeping that in mind, I read the journal over again this morning, and looked at it with a new perspective . . . There are one or two things that strike me as interesting."

"Such as?"

Lucy fought the urge to keep her theory to herself. She went on with her narrative. "Alfie mentions visiting a warehouse in the vicinity of the river in the area known as Limehouse. It is a place run by a certain Mr. Shadwell."

Was it Lucy's imagination, or did James react to the name? She might have paid it more mind if she wasn't so worried about looking foolish. She rushed on, eager to finish and face the consequences. "From what Alfie says about Shadwell and his associates they are, on the outside, legitimate businessmen. They are involved in importing tea from India. But Alfie believed that the business was simply a camouflage, a facade if you will, for some other enterprise that is not quite legal. Antiquities smuggling, perhaps. Or art forgery. Again, it's something I thought Alfie imagined when I read about it the first time, but now I don't think so. I think that, and the seal . . ." She looked at the stone seal in her hand one last time before she tucked it back into her pocket.

"The stone seals and Shadwell's connection with India and Alfie's disappearance . . . by themselves they don't mean much. But put them together with what we learned from the Indian art book and the articles we received from *The Times.* I think it tells us that the case Alfie was working on had to do with something truly extraordinary. I've eliminated all the impossibilities. I'm left with only one deduction. It seems improbable, to be sure, but . . . I think Alfie's case had something to do with the Eye of the Devil."

There. She'd said it. She'd blurted out the most ridiculous idea she'd ever had. She'd said it aloud, and opened it, and herself, up to James's criticism and, possibly, his scorn. She knew it was outrageous, and all she had to do now was stand there and wait for James to tell her as much.

He didn't. He didn't say a thing.

As disappointed by his reaction as she was nervous about obtaining it, Lucy grumbled. "The Eye of the Devil," she said, slower and louder, just so he was sure to understand. "We read about it in those articles from *The Times.* It's the statue that contains the fabulous diamond that's supposed to be presented to the Queen next week. I can't imagine what Alfie would have to do with it. Perhaps someone hired him to guard it, or to sneak a peek at it and draw a picture so that it might be copied and sold by the souvenir vendors on the Queen's Jubilee day. I don't know." She gulped down the note of desperation that had crept into her voice and raised her eyes to James's.

"I know it sounds incredible to think that Alfie might be mixed up in something so wildly romantic," she said. "The idea occurred to me before, but I was never willing to accept it. If you could look at things the way I have, if you could believe—"

"Do you?"

Again, the maddening questions. Again, the exquisite manners and the slightly amused, almost disinterested tone of voice. It was enough to make Lucy want to scream.

She punched a pillow instead, defending herself instinctively. "I do. I know it sounds crazy. It sounds crazy to me, too, and far too like something straight out of one of the Holmes stories. I know what you've heard about Alfie. I am, after all, the one who told you. I told you he was the finest detective in the country. I told you he had the best skills and the quickest, most astute mind. I was not entirely honest with you."

Lucy wasn't sure if it hurt more to tell James the truth, or to admit it to herself. Either way, she was obliged to speak the words, for James's sake and her own.

"Alfie is a bit eccentric," she said plainly. "He is capricious, a dreamer who creates wild fantasies for himself as easily as some other people brew tea." She looked over at the cup that James had left on the table. "But whatever else my father is, he is not a liar. He wouldn't have lied in his journal and he would never lie to me. I believe that's why he never spoke to me about the case. He didn't want to lie and he didn't want me to worry. Again, I think that points to a case that is far different from the usual detective fare. I doubt he would have gone to such trouble if he was simply following an unfaithful wife or looking for some spinster's missing cat. But how you are connected with it—"

"What do you plan to do?" Suddenly as animated as he had been relaxed, James snapped to attention. He lifted the cup of tea and drank it down, then poured himself another. "Where will you go?" he asked. "Who will you talk to?"

"I can think of only one thing to do," Lucy admitted. Raising her chin, she stood straight and tall, as if daring James to try to stop her. "I have contacted Mr. Shadwell and asked for an appointment tomorrow. I'm going to Limehouse."

He didn't look surprised. In fact, if Lucy had been forced to put a name to the expression that darted across his face, she would have said it was disappointment. It came and went quickly, leaving him thin-lipped. "It is a dangerous part of town," he said.

"I know." Lucy moistened her lips. "I was hoping you might come with me."

"Of course."

Relieved, Lucy smiled. "Thank you." She swept toward the door. "I have a great deal to do before tomorrow. If you'll excuse me . . ."

James watched her leave the room. The brief time they'd spent together had left no questions in his mind about last night and what had nearly happened between them. He still wanted Lucy. God, how he wanted her! His body tightened at the very sight of her. His heartbeat raced. His fingers itched to touch her silky flesh.

Amazed that his response to Lucy could still be so strong after all he'd learned, James laughed at his own gullibility.

No, there were no questions about his needs. Or his desires. The only questions he had now were about Lucy.

James wondered, not for the first time that morning, if things hadn't been better before he regained his memory.

Before he knew who he was and what he was doing in London, he'd had far fewer questions about Lucy's sincerity. Or her loyalty. If he was still in that dark place where his identity and his past were nothing more than ciphers, he would never have had to wonder if Lucy was telling the truth.

Now, of course, all that had changed, and wanting Lucy so much he could taste it was the least of his problems.

By accompanying her to Limehouse, was James walking into a trap?

It wasn't the only question that pounded through his head.

Did Lucy know who Michael O'Connor really was? And if she did, did that mean that James had been lured to the Barnstable home simply to be a pawn in their dangerous game?

Questions. Questions.

And none of them more important than the ones that twisted around his heart as he stood staring at the empty space where only minutes ago Lucy had been.

Was Lucy what she seemed, the woman he'd come to know and love?

Or was Lucy the enemy?

The next day it was raining stair-rods when they went outside for the cab.

Lucy darted out of the house under cover of her umbrella and while James gave the driver the name of Shadwell's business and its address on Garford Street near Limehouse Pier, she scrambled into her seat. James climbed in beside her. Using the handle of his own umbrella, he pounded on the ceiling of the hansom, signaling the cabman to proceed.

For a June day, it was cool and damp, and inside her black coat, Lucy shivered. She was enough of a pragmatist to realize that her trembling might be as much a product of her nerves as of the weather, and sufficiently irrational when it came to anything that had to do with James to know it was just as likely to be caused by his nearness.

It was hardly a comforting thought.

Although James had gone out of his way to be polite while they waited for the cab, it was clear that some barrier had come between them. His manners were as strained as the smile he shot her way. His answers to her questions were as clipped and as dispassionate as they had been in the parlor the day before when they'd arranged this excursion to Shadwell's.

He was exceedingly reticent for a man who, just two nights ago, had been willing to accept more than simple conversation from her.

The thought was unworthy of her and Lucy repressed it, along with the sigh that threatened to betray her. Still, there was no harm in trying to engage James in conversation, she told herself. It would pass the time and, with any luck at all, relieve the unbearable tension stretched between them.

She plunged precipitately into the first bit of household gossip that came to mind. "Mr. Grogan moved out last night."

"Did he?" James seemed genuinely surprised. "Where has he gone?"

"He didn't leave an address. Not that it matters. He never received anything in the post, and no one ever came to visit him."

"Did he say why he was leaving?"

"Did I ask?" Lucy clicked her tongue. "He didn't say why he was going, and I don't want to know. He was a thoroughly unlikable man and I, for one, am glad to be rid of him." She might have said more about Grogan and what she thought of boarders who were so churlish, if the cab hadn't slammed into a hole in the pavement. Lucy squealed her surprise, and reaching for the door, she tried to brace herself. Before she could, the cab bounced out again, rattling her thoroughly.

Automatically, James reached out a hand to steady her. His arm brushed her breasts and Lucy held her breath. She didn't dare let it out again until the cab had rocked back to its steady pace and James removed his hand.

"Sorry, guv." The cabman called down his apologies.

James grumbled an oath. He turned enough in his seat so that he was looking into Lucy's eyes. "You aren't hurt, are you?" he asked, and for a moment, his eyes shone with the old, familiar intensity. It flowed over Lucy like sunshine, seeping through to her soul.

She shook her head, though she wasn't at all sure if she'd been hurt or not. If she was injured, she wouldn't feel it. All she could feel was the heat of James's gaze, the warmth of the emotion that had been missing for only a day but had left her feeling as if she'd been lost in the cold for years.

James bent his head closer to hers. "You must be very careful," he said. "The next time you let Grogan's room."

"Must I?" Lucy wasn't so sure caution was what she was thinking about right then and there. Though her head counseled prudence, her heart advised otherwise, and her body fairly screamed that indiscretion might be better still. She eyed James's lips, remembering the delicious sensations they roused when he pressed a kiss between her breasts.

James's gaze moved down Lucy's face, all the way to her lips. His eyes darkened to a color that reminded her of smoke. "You wouldn't want to put yourself at risk," he said. "From anyone."

"I have never felt at risk from my boarders. Not any of them." Lucy was a poor liar. She was at risk right now. At risk of making a fool of herself in front of a man who had shown all too clearly that he was no longer interested in her.

She fought to save herself from the inevitable embarrassment. "Are you advising me to stop letting rooms altogether?" she asked. "Or to stay away from men named Grogan?"

"Is that his name?" With a snort, James sat back in his place. His retreat broke the spell, and Lucy supposed she should be just as glad. She might have been even more satisfied if the air around her didn't chill at his going.

She sniffed her displeasure, taking in a breath of the air that was growing more and more pungent as they got nearer the river. "Of course that's his name," she said. "Why wouldn't it be? I have a limit, you know," she added acidly, just to confound him. "I only allow one boarder at a time who isn't sure of his own name."

Her sarcasm was lost on James. As the hansom clattered over Southwark Bridge and on to the north side of the river, he sat up in his seat. "We need to go east on Upper Thames Street," he said, looking around. "Not west. What the devil—?"

Lucy shrugged off his alarm. "The streets are always crowded so near the river," she reminded him. "And there have to be a hundred different ways to get to Limehouse. Perhaps our cabman is more astute than most and knows an easier route."

"Perhaps." James conceded the fact, but he did not seem to fully accept it. From that point on, he didn't speak another word. He kept his gaze on the road, scrutinizing every twist and turn. When the cab turned left, then right and left again, James rapped the ceiling with his umbrella.

"You're going the wrong way," he called up to the cabman. "You're headed north into the heart of the City."

There was no reply.

"Damn!" James pounded the top of the half door that closed over their knees. Traffic here was lighter than it had been close to the water. The thoroughfares were wide. The cab picked up speed and careened through a series of hairpin turns until Lucy was no longer sure which direction was which.

"He won't be stopping anytime soon," James said. He gripped the handle at the side of the cab and held on tight. "We may have to jump."

"Jump?" The cab jostled its way around an omnibus stopped squarely in the center of the road and Lucy's teeth rattled. "What on earth are you talking . . . talking about?" She tried her best to give James a look that told him she thought he'd gone completely mad, but it was impossible. The driver whipped his horse around St. Mary-le-Bow and sped down another street, knocking her off balance. She pitched into James and he hooked an arm around her shoulders to keep her upright.

"Don't you see?" he yelled to her over the sounds of the city whizzing past them. "We're not going to Limehouse."

"Not going to Limehouse? Wherever else would we be going?"

"Wherever else it is that your friend Grogan wants us to go. And from the looks of things, I'd say it isn't somewhere I want to be."

Lucy had neither the time nor the inclination to ask what he meant. Much the same way as the cold claw of fear clutched at the back of her neck, she clutched the cab doors in front of her until her knuckles were white. "Stop it. You're frightening me."

The cab turned again, into a street that looked as if it had no outlet. "I do believe," James said, "that it is time to be frightened."

Ahead of them, a large group of men shielded by their umbrellas stepped off the pavement and hurried across the road. The driver had no choice but to rein in his horse.

Above the horse's whinnied protests, Lucy heard the cab screech to a stop on the rain-slicked street. Her body lurched forward, then back again. Her head slammed into the back wall of the cab. The air rushing from her lungs, she ricocheted forward. She would have gone headlong over the doors of the hansom if not for James. By the time she finally came to a full stop, he had both his arms wrapped securely around her, keeping her on her seat.

He waited only long enough to be sure she wasn't hurt before he punched the door open and was out of the cab.

He splashed into a puddle and nearly went down on his knees, but it didn't stop him. Recovering, James righted himself and headed for the back of the cab, pushing his way through the crowd of curious onlookers that had gathered on the pavement.

Lucy grabbed her umbrella and followed.

One of the cab's axles was split and the cab listed at an angle. Holding on to her umbrella with one hand and the side of the cab with the other, she lowered herself onto the street. From somewhere in the heart of the crowd, she thought she heard someone call her name. She paid it no mind. She was too busy staring at James in horror.

The cabman had been thrown from his perch by the jolt. He lay in the middle of the street, but there didn't appear to be anything wrong with him.

At least not yet.

James had the unfortunate fellow by his collar and was in the midst of hauling him off the ground with one hand.

"Good Lord!" Lucy hurried over just in time to see James give the fellow a shake.

"Who?" he asked him. "Who paid you? And where in the hell were you taking us?"

The cabman might have been able to answer if he could breathe.

"Really, James!" Lucy came to the man's rescue. Laying one hand on the driver's shoulder, she looked across at James. "He could have been injured," she reminded him. "Or worse. And here you are ill-treating the poor fellow." She wrenched the collar of the man's coat from James's grasp and helped him to his feet. "Are you all right?" she asked. "Are you hurt?"

"No, ma'am. Thanks to you." The man's voice was muffled by the scarf he wore wound around his face to the bottom of his nose. He had a hat pulled low over his head, nearly to his eyes, but Lucy could not fail to read the glance he shot James's way. "The 'orse got away from me, sir," he said. "I swear that's what 'appened. I don't know what comed over 'im."

"Yes. Well." James ran a hand over his jaw. His eyes still dark with suspicion, he looked at Lucy. "If your incompetence has caused this young lady any harm—"

"Please, guv!" Above his scarf, Lucy saw the driver's eyes fill with tears of alarm. "You can't report me to the authorities. They'll take away me license. That's what they'll do. And I won't 'ave any way whatsoever what to provide for my family."

"No one's going to take away your license." Lucy turned from the driver to James. "I'm fine," she assured him. She looked back at the cabman. "Really. I'm fine. There's no reason for you to worry. Accidents happen, after all, and I think we all recognize that this was an accident." She looked at James pointedly.

He didn't look convinced. Annoyed with the cabman's incessant chatter and Lucy's indulgence of it, he stepped back and looked around. Lucy had no doubt, he was trying to get his bearings and figure out where they were.

"Thank you, miss." The cabman scooped his hat off his head and held it to his chest. "You're a saint, that's what you is. A saint and no mistake." He set his hat back upon his head. "Who would ever believe such wild talkings?" he asked, following behind James to the pavement. "Paid to do that?" He looked over at the damaged cab. The cabman snorted. "Who ever in 'is right mind would think what a man would do that to the thing from what he made his living?"

Lucy shook her head in agreement. Side by side with the driver, she walked toward where James stood with his back to them, grumbling his responses to the questions being thrown at him from the crowd.

That's when she saw the knife.

In a flash of insight, Lucy realized the cabman must have had it hidden in his hat. It wasn't thick or long, but it was more than sharp enough to do damage.

Her heart catching in her throat, she watched the man raise his arm. The blade flashed like lightning through the rain. The knife arced toward James's back.

"James!" She screamed his name though she knew James would never register her fear and react in time.

There was only one thing to do.

With a stroke worthy of the strongest cricketeer, Lucy lifted her umbrella and brought it down with a smack on the top of the cabdriver's head. The man's body went limp. The knife clattered to the ground.

James was at her side in an instant. He stared down at the cabman who had landed with a splash in the gutter.

"Do you still think it was all an accident?" he asked.

"You have a peculiar way of showing your gratitude," Lucy told him. Her knees were beginning to tremble rather violently and afraid that she might land in the muck right next to the would-be assassin, she clutched her umbrella with both hands and leaned against it. It was bent in the middle, but it did the job.

"You might at least thank me for saving your life before you start lecturing. If not for my umbrella, you might be . . ." She blinked away tears. "You might be . . ." She didn't have a chance to say more.

There was a commotion at the back of the crowd. It parted to allow a pasty-faced Freddy Plowright through to the street.

"Freddy!" Lucy stared at her fiancé in wonder.

"Lucy." Freddy acknowledged her quite politely, as if they had met nowhere more peculiar than at a friend's tea. He gave James a cursory look, then glanced at the cabman. His face paled. "Lucy, you . . . you struck down that man!"

"Yes, Freddy, I did." Lucy faced him squarely. "With my umbrella."

"But, Lucy . . . I . . ." Freddy's lips twitched. He looked over his shoulder. The excitement had attracted attention, even here in the self-important area of the City where money was the usual meat of any conversation and banking procedures and practices the wine that washed it down. The crowd on the pavement was beginning to grow, and Lucy saw any number of faces pressed to the glass in the windows of the building directly in front of them.

Freddy looked with dismay at the gathering throng. "This is where I work," he said. "There are men here who know me. Men I work with closely. This won't look good for me, I can tell you that much. There will surely be rumblings within the bank. Rumors of your behavior. I'm sure you don't understand the workings of the business world and I'm certain you don't realize that your childish behavior will have ramifications. What you've done here . . ." Freddy shivered noticeably. "Well, it can't do anything but hurt my position."

"And what about my position?" Lucy's voice rose, loud enough to attract even more attention. The crowd gathered closer, eager to see what new excitement was afoot.

"Shhh." Freddy grabbed her arm. He threw an apprehensive smile at his fellow workers and an even more anxious one at James who didn't take to the idea of him holding on to Lucy's arm. "Please, Lucy," he begged her. "Don't make a scene. If we're lucky, I will be able to convince them that your behavior was the result of the strain caused by this unfortunate accident. I will tell them that it isn't at all your usual behavior. I will explain about your father. That's what I'll do." Convinced of the genius of the idea, Freddy's expression brightened. "I shall tell them you couldn't help yourself, you were acting like your father."

"Was I?" Suddenly Lucy's coat felt all too warm. She glared at Freddy. "And what the bloody hell is wrong with that?"

Freddy's face went from pale to ashen. He swallowed so hard, his Adam's apple bounced. "Please, Lucy. You mustn't. However am I going to justify your conduct if you only compound it with more irrational behavior?" Involuntarily, his gaze traveled back to the cab and over to its unfortunate driver.

"How will I ever begin to explain your involvement in so shocking a situation? Some of these men are my superiors," he hissed, trying to silence Lucy with a look that was filled with disgust. "How shall I tell them that the woman they've just seen attack a full-grown man is actually the woman to whom I am engaged to be married?"

"I'll tell them for you." Lucy had no intention of doing anything of the sort, she simply wanted to see Freddy's horrified reaction to her statement. He didn't disappoint her.

Pulling away from Freddy's clammy grasp, she looked him in the eye. "You've got your facts a bit turned around, I'm afraid, Freddy, my boy," she told him. "I am the daughter of Alfie Barnstable, consulting detective, and you're right, I am a good deal more like my father than you—or I—ever suspected. But I'm not the woman to whom you're engaged to be married, Freddy. I am the woman to whom you *used* to be engaged to be married."

# Chapter 16

Sniffing back tears, Lucy dabbed her apron to eyes that burned. The fumes of the onion she was chopping to add to the pot of soup that simmered on the stove were strong enough to make her head ache. So strong, it was impossible for her to think clearly.

And that was exactly what she wanted.

In the last twenty-four hours she'd done everything she could to keep busy. To stop herself from thinking.

At the chance that she might offend Lizzie, the maid-of-all-work who came in to do for them three times each week, she'd spent all of the evening before sweeping the floors and dusting the furniture. At the risk that her boarders would rebel at her lack of culinary skills, she'd sent Mrs. Grey, the cook, home this afternoon to sit with her son, Tom, who had the ague. And though she'd warned herself it was a fool's errand—and she'd been proved more than correct—she'd tried to relieve her anxiety by spending the morning working on her investigation.

"Investigation!" Lucy harumphed the word, or at least she might have if not for an onion-induced sob. "Investigation" was hardly a fitting word for a morning filled with frustration and humiliation, and it hadn't helped keep her mind any busier than had the tidying and the scrubbing, the dicing and the peeling. Much to her annoyance, neither had the noxious fumes of the onion.

It seemed that nothing she did could get rid of the pictures that played over and over inside her head.

Lucy snuffled and ran her sleeve across her eyes. No matter how busy she kept herself, she couldn't forget the terror of the day before. The flash of steel. The murderous intent that gleamed in the eyes of the cabman. The knife. Aimed directly at James.

Even in the heat of the Barnstable kitchen, the thought caused a shiver to snake its way up her back. Though James apparently considered the subject closed and demonstrated as much by refusing to discuss it further, she could not escape from the disturbing memories.

Had she been more sensible and less impetuous, had she hesitated or her blow been less sure, James would surely be dead.

Lucy's lower lip trembled, but she refused to allow her tears to fall. With a whack, she chopped the onion into smaller pieces, then minced those pieces into tinier bits still. She might have gone right on until there was nothing left of the onion but pulp, if the kitchen door hadn't swung open. If James hadn't walked into the room.

"I've been looking all through the house for you." He let the door go. It snapped closed behind him and he let his gaze wander from her watery eyes to her red nose. "Not crying about Freddy, I hope."

Lucy was not at all in the mood to respond to his feeble attempt at humor. She swigged back tears. "I am making dinner," she said, as if he needed an explanation when the facts were so conspicuous. "I am not thinking about Freddy. I'm thinking about onions. And about the roast that is in the oven. And if I was thinking about Freddy and everything that happened yesterday . . ." She cleared her throat and blinked away tears. "If I had nothing better to do than think about Freddy . . ."

"No regrets?" James crossed the kitchen and stood on the other side of the table, opposite from where she was working. She'd already pared and chopped a bunch of carrots. They were on the table, and James reached for a piece, but he didn't take a bite. "You aren't sorry you called off the engagement?"

"Sorry?" Lucy squinted at him through the haze of tears in her eyes. "I should say not. It was a mistake to think that a man like Freddy could ever—"

"Exactly what I told you the day I met the fellow." James attempted a smile.

In that instant, she saw a glimmer of the old James, the James who'd existed at the opera and before, the man who still haunted her imagination and her dreams. There was more than a touch of affection in the expression that lit his face. And a hint of admiration. There was a fire behind the flicker that sparkled in his eyes.

As quickly as it came, the smile was gone, and the James who had inhabited her house, but not her heart, these past days was back. The silent James. The brooding James. The James who when he looked at her at all had so many doubts in his eyes, she could not bear to meet them.

"We need to talk," he said. He set aside the piece of carrot and leaned forward, his hands on the table. "Why did you go to see Sir Digby Talbot this morning?"

The last thing Lucy needed was a reminder of what a dolt she'd been. Hiding her discomfort, she scooped the onions into a bowl and carried it to the stove. "What difference does it make?" she asked. "I didn't see him." Away from the table, the air was clearer and she gulped it in, welcoming the cleansing breath.

"The man is as unreachable as the stars. He has clerks and personal assistants and aides all around him. Like a human shield." She dumped the onions into the soup pot and returned to the table for the carrots. "There I was at the Foreign Office, waiting and waiting and waiting some more. I waited for hours on the hope that I might actually be allowed in but I—"

Her hand poised above the carrots, she looked at James in wonder. "How did you know I tried to see Sir Digby?"

"Ah, one question at a time. And I asked the first one. I asked why you went to see him."

Lucy was tempted to take the carrots and run back to the stove and away from James. Far from where he could see the emotion that must clearly be betrayed in her expression. She didn't. She stood and faced him, though she did allow herself to hide behind her bowl. She held it to her chest, her arms around it.

"I thought I might talk to Sir Digby," she said. "I wanted to ask him about his behavior at the opera. It may sound daft, but I do believe he knew more than he was willing to say. Did you see the way he looked at you at the theater? Not the first time when you tried to speak to him, of course. He was too absorbed in his own conversation to notice you then. But when I pulled you over to meet him and he really looked at you . . . I swear there was a flash of recognition in his eyes. I still can't understand it, no more than I can fathom why he was so abrupt. Unless he was trying to hide something. That is the reason I tried to meet with him this morning."

"But why?" James's question quivered with the same barely restrained emotion that gleamed in his eyes. "I need the truth, Lucy. For once. All of it."

"All of it." This close to the table, the bite of the onion still drifted in the air. Lucy wiped her eyes. "You have to admit, yesterday's adventure was very peculiar. The cabman . . . he wanted to kill you. And I am sure you will agree, it was not a random act. He wanted to kill *you*, whoever you are."

"But you saved my life." A tiny smile tickled James's lips, and Lucy wasn't sure if it was from amusement or ridicule. Either way, she defended herself instinctively.

"I had no choice!" she told him. "I acted on impulse, almost without thinking. Anyone would have done the same had they seen another person in mortal danger. It was a natural reaction to a fellow human's peril. A . . ." Even Lucy did not believe a word of her own poor excuses. She laid them aside along with her bowl, and squaring her shoulders, she clutched her hands at her waist.

"I had to do it," she admitted to him and to herself. "As much for my sake as for yours. I saw the knife for only a second, but it only took me that one second to realize that I couldn't live without you."

It must have been the onions. James's voice was choked. "So you went to see Sir Digby."

"Yes." It was easier to admit to her absurd plans than it was to her feelings for James. "You may not agree with me, but after yesterday I do believe that discovering your identity is more important than ever."

"And what about Alfie?"

Just when she thought she was safe, just when she thought she could steer the conversation onto her investigation and away from her feelings, he brought

# DEVIL'S DIAMOND 263

it back around to her heart. She wanted to believe that he didn't realize what he was doing, but she knew him better than that.

"I still want to find Alfie, of course," she told him. "But it seems whether I wanted it or not, my concern for you has taken its place right beside my worries about him. I can't help but think about the night of the opera. About all the things we said . . . and did. Don't you see, James? Sir Digby may be our only chance to find out who you really are."

He nodded, confirming something to himself. "And so this morning you went far out of your way, didn't you? And you endured a good bit of indignity waiting like a tradesman for an appointment that never materialized. You did all that, just to learn the truth about me?"

His observations came fast and furious, his questions made her head spin. But Lucy would not be so easily deterred from her own inquiries. "You haven't answered my question. How did you know? I didn't tell anyone where I was going. How did you know I tried to see Sir Digby?"

"I was there."

"At the Foreign Office?"

"With Sir Digby."

He might as well have told her he'd spent the morning in Australia. Lucy's mouth dropped open.

James chuckled. It was a contented, weightless sort of sound. The kind of laugh a man gives when he's been eased of a heavy burden and a worried spirit. "There are some things you need to know," he said. "Sit down."

Lucy did as she was told. Too stunned to speak, too anxious to hear what he had to say, she watched James put his hands behind his back and hitch his fingers together. Collecting his thoughts, he paced to the other end of the kitchen and back. At the table again, he faced her.

"The man you knew as Grogan is really named Michael O'Connor," he said. "No questions. Not yet," he added quickly, holding up one hand to stem the tide of her curiosity. "It's complicated and a bit confusing, but if you'll hear me out . . ." He drew in a long breath.

"O'Connor is the devil incarnate, a man who has no loyalties to anyone or anything other than his own purse. Twelve years ago, he was in the pay of the Fenian rebels in Ireland. Under their direction and with their financing and their protection, he arrived in Balmoral, Scotland, where he tried his damnedest to kill the Queen."

"What?" Astounded, Lucy sat back. "How do you—"

"I was there." James's eyes darkened. "I saw him."

"You remember?"

"I remember. That, and other things. I caught sight of O'Connor the morning after the opera and it was like a floodgate opening. It came back to me. All of it."

Lucy could hardly believe what she was hearing. A giddy smile lit her face and her mind raced, dizzy with excitement. "You remember?" The words trembled on her lips. "Your name?"

He looked Lucy in the eyes. "My name is James Dungannon," he said. "I am the eldest son of John Dungannon, the physician who attends to Her Majesty when she is in residence at her home in Balmoral." He dropped into the chair across from Lucy's and reached for her hands. He grasped them in both of his.

"For the last few years, I have been in the employ of Her Majesty," he told her. "A kind of attaché who handles various delicate"—he searched for the proper word—"situations. That's why the book was left for me so mysteriously at the museum. It's why Canaday and I had a clandestine arrangement, information in return for money. I am not supposed to be in the country, you see, and we couldn't risk certain people finding out that I was. If I had marched into the Foreign Office, they would have known I was back. Instead, I received all the information I needed in bits and pieces. Right now, one of those delicate situations involves O'Connor."

"The Eye of the Devil." It wasn't a question. Lucy was so sure of James's answer, she did not need for him to tell her she was right.

"The statue has been stolen," he admitted. "It isn't something that's public knowledge, but it will be soon enough. The Jubilee celebration is in just a few days' time. When Rangpoon doesn't present the diamond to the Queen, it will cause something of an international incident. Things could get quite ugly. The flames of rebellion in India will certainly be fanned. A good many people will die."

"And O'Connor?"

"He's behind it, of course, the bastard, and I think he neither knows nor cares about the consequences. It hardly matters to him. Ideologies are not his concern. Banknotes are. He sells his services to the highest bidder. I was hot on his trail when we renewed our acquaintance in that alley in Whitechapel."

Lucy's heart squeezed. "He's the one who beat you? And yesterday? He's the one who sent the cabman to—"

James's eyes narrowed to slits. "Oh, I don't think O'Connor knew it was me. I saw him that morning after the opera. But he didn't see me. I made sure of it. I think I was simply unfortunate enough to be a sort of inconvenience. The man who just happened to be accompanying you yesterday afternoon. He wanted me out of the way." He glanced at Lucy, gauging her reaction to his words. "I'm guessing he was after you."

The words settled like frost between them. Lucy held tight to James's hands. "Then Alfie was onto something, wasn't he?"

"It's the only thing that might explain why O'Connor was so anxious to resort to abduction. And murder. It might also explain why he was here in your home. He let the room after Alfie's disappearance?"

Lucy thought back. "The next morning."

"There's something O'Connor needs to find out, and he thought he could do it here. Once he'd decided to kidnap you, he knew he didn't need to stay in the house any longer. That's why he moved out."

"But if he needs me—" Lucy's voice clogged. The tears she'd been able, until now, to keep in check broke free and streamed down her cheeks. "That means that Alfie—"

"Shhh." James chafed her hands between his. "Alfie's fine. I'm certain of it. And we'll find him. I've already spoken with Sir Digby about him this morning and—"

"Then you do know Sir Digby!" The surprises were too many and they were coming too fast. Lucy's head reeled. "Did Sir Digby know you, then? That night at the opera?"

James laughed. "He did, indeed, and the poor old fellow nearly had apoplexy when you tried to introduce me in front of a few hundred people!" He glanced away for a second. "I am a sort of confidential attaché to the Foreign Office, you see. I am not supposed to go about in public trumpeting my connections."

"Oh, dear. And I nearly ruined it for you."

"It's all right, really." James's good humor was restored in an instant. His laugh contained all the warmth of a day in August. "I've been out of the country a good deal in the past few years. Heidelberg, Rome, Vienna. No one recognized me. And Sir Digby is canny enough to know how to play the game. By the way, he says he owes you dinner and a bottle of champagne when the time is right. As an apology for causing you such embarrassment."

Lucy cared about neither the champagne nor the dinner. She was still trying to work her way through the puzzle of all James had told her.

"There's still so much I don't understand." She smiled at James through her tears. "You were so cold yesterday. So distant." The truth dawned on her with all the delicacy of a thunderstorm. "You thought I was working with O'Connor." She cut James off before he could say a word. "It was a logical deduction on your part. In your position, it would have been incredibly foolish of you not to question my loyalty."

Loyalty.

The word stood like a wall between them. It chilled the edges of the warmth that surrounded them. Her heart in her throat, Lucy asked the one question she had not dared put into words.

"You know who you are. I'm glad. And now—" Her smile wavered. "Now we can know once and for all if there's a woman somewhere who has a claim on your heart."

James looked solemn. Too solemn. "Aye," he said. "There is."

Lucy's stomach lurched. She held her breath, fighting back the blackness that froze her through to her soul. "Yes. Of course." Her own words echoed through her head, as if they came from a long way off. "I understand, of course. I am a reasonable enough person, after all, to—"

She stopped short when James started to laugh. He stood, drawing Lucy up from her chair, and in a few quick steps he circled the table. He took her into his arms.

"You're as fine a woman as there ever was, Lucy, my love," he said. "And it's lucky I am that you are the one who's captured my heart."

"Me?" Lucy smiled through her tears. She laughed. "I thought—"

"That's your problem." He squeezed her in a ferocious hug. "You think too damned much."

"Do I?" Lucy sniffed back her tears. When James wiped them with his thumbs, she nuzzled her face into his hand. "Would you like to know what I'm thinking about now?" she asked.

"No need. For the first time ever, I do believe we're thinking the same thing." A shiver ran through James's body. The vibrations trembled against Lucy's hands where she flattened them to his chest. They traveled through her, warming her heart, heating her blood. Unprepared for the potency of the emotions that swelled within her, she sucked in a breath.

"Still thinking about onions?" James asked. He didn't wait for her answer. He lowered his head and brought his mouth down on hers.

Lucy could well understand why James's kisses affected her body the way they did. Each touch of his lips was exquisite. Each taste of his tongue, dazzling.

His kisses made her feel remarkably content even though they left her incredibly hungry. They stirred her senses and caused her body to feel the kinds of inordinate, irrational, illogical things she'd never even imagined. They sent her temperature soaring at the same time they stoked it even higher, and made her desperate to feel more of his heat.

What she couldn't fathom was why kisses that were so capable of completely engaging her body had not had the same sort of paralyzing effect on her mind.

She wished they had. If so, she wouldn't be so thoroughly furious.

Lucy rammed her umbrella into the stand in the front entryway. Hauling off her coat, she flung it over the banister and took the steps two at a time. Today was the day the Atwaters had offered to take Miss Foxworthy, Mrs. Slyke, and Jack Miller to the Crystal Palace at Sydenham to see the fireworks. The house was empty, and would be until well into the night, and it was just as well.

She didn't need an audience, prying eyes and eager ears and imaginations that were far too active and sure to supply the details, fanciful as they might be, to fill in the blanks to an incident she would rather they had no part of. What she had to say to James was better said in private. Lucy pounded past the first-floor landing and headed up the next flight of stairs, and the next. At the door to James's room, she knocked even though she had no intention of waiting for an answer. She pushed open the door and stepped inside.

She caught James by surprise. Dressed only in his trousers with a shirt hanging open and showing bare flesh beneath, he was sitting in the overstuffed chair near the window, a book open on his lap. Startled, he jumped, and seeing Lucy, he scrambled out of the chair. He reached for the pearl studs on the chest of drawers nearby.

"What's happened?" His fingers sure and quick, he slipped the studs into the shirt one by one, keeping his eyes on Lucy. "Have you heard something? Something from Alfie?"

Faced with his questions—and the all-too-disturbing sensations he always elicited from her—Lucy found she had to collect her thoughts. She hesitated. But only for a second.

She took another step into the room and smacked the door closed behind her. "You tell me what's happened. Why did you lie to me?"

"Lied? Did I?"

"Stop it!" Too exasperated to keep still, Lucy marched to the bed. "Stop responding to my questions with questions of your own. I don't want questions. I want answers. I want to know why you lied to me."

James looked ambivalent but he knew better than to try to mollify her. Finished with the studs, he shoved his shirttails into his trousers. "I'm afraid you'll have to be more specific," he said, slipping into the casual manner she knew all too well. The one that so expertly disguised his emotions and concealed the fact that behind it, his mind was coolly calculating each and every word. "At the risk of stirring your wrath with another question, can you tell me what, exactly, I've lied to you about?"

Lucy nearly screamed with frustration. "About everything. All of it." She pounded the bed in helpless fury. "All of yesterday was a lie."

"Yesterday." Though it was certain he remembered it as clearly as she did, James repeated the word. "You mean the things I told you? About Sir Digby? And myself?" He shook his head in astonishment. "You can't possibly be talking about what happened between us in the kitchen, because if you are—"

"Yes! I'm talking about the kisses. I'm talking

about Sir Digby. I'm talking about the fact that we spent the evening together in the parlor, with you telling me stories about your idyllic Highlands childhood and me hanging on your every word. You kissed me good night at the door to my bedchamber, dammit! I'm talking about that. About all of it!" Lucy's breaths came in great, painful gasps. She hauled in a sob that threatened to burst through her anger. "How could you lie to me?"

The fact that James looked clearly confused only made her anger soar. He was clever. That was certain. Just as certain as the fact that though he might be imaginative, she was resourceful. A detective had to be.

There was enough satisfaction in knowing she'd outsmarted him to make her anger subside, at least for the moment, and she faced him with her chin high and her voice steady. "I've been thinking, you see," she told him. "After all, it is my business to be curious. And I spent a good part of last night and this morning thinking about all the things you told me yesterday. There was something about your story that didn't quite ring true. Not that you aren't a consummate actor," she added, almost as an apology. "I think you might have convinced anyone else. But . . . well, I do believe it is harder to deceive someone who loves you."

He might have responded to her declaration if she had given him the chance. She didn't. She raced on with her explanation, her easy manner camouflaging the misery that weighed heavy on her heart.

"If it is any consolation at all to you, let me tell you that I'm sorry I did it. I wish I hadn't. I wish I could have been content with your kisses. And your lies." She brushed away a single tear that splashed down her cheek. "But I knew if I didn't put my wor-

ries to rest, I would always wonder. So I investigated.
I spent the morning at Somerset House."

"Oh." It was no more than a sound from James,
but it told Lucy everything she needed to know.

"That's right," she said. "I went through the records. You had part of your story right, I will give
you that much credit. James Dungannon was born in
Balmoral, Scotland, thirty years ago. He was the eldest child of John, a physician, and Florence. Subse-
quent records show that James had three younger
brothers and two sisters. The big happy family you
told me all about last night. The one I was all too
eager to believe in."

James didn't respond to the information. He didn't
react at all. He crossed his arms over his chest and
settled his weight back against one foot. "Then
where's the lie?"

"The lie is in the fact that you didn't look far
enough into the facts. But as you may have noticed,
I am rather resolute by nature. Some might even say
stubborn. I checked more than just the birth records.
And I found out . . ." The words wedged in Lucy's
throat. She cleared them away with a cough. "I found
out that you cannot be James Dungannon. James
Dungannon died twelve years ago. He was killed by
Michael O'Connor when he stepped between O'Connor and the bullet that was meant for the Queen."

# Chapter 17

"The world is meant to think that I am dead."
James sounded so convincing, Lucy nearly believed him. She shook her head in disgust. "I might have known you'd say as much."

"Only because it's the truth." With one hand, he kneaded the back of his neck. "The chaps at the Foreign Office thought it best and Her Majesty's generosity made it all possible. They feared that if O'Connor learned that I survived the assassination attempt, he would retaliate against my family. Those three brothers and two sisters you heard about last night. My parents." He watched her carefully, trying to evaluate her reaction.

She refused to give him the satisfaction of one. She met his gaze, waiting for more.

With a half shrug, James yielded. "That's why I was schooled on the Continent," he explained. "It's why I've been living out of the country all these years. And why I've got a dozen different names. Not only Mr. Smith and Mr. Jones," he added, thinking, as she was, of the British Museum and their visit to *The Times*. "If we had made it to Shadwell's in Limehouse—and by the way, it wouldn't have done a bit of good, there's nothing there you would have found out—I would have been greeted as Mr. Witherspoon. In Paris, my associates know me as Monsieur Rocard. In Germany, I am called Herr Brandt. It's a damned confusing way to live, I can tell you that. No wonder I couldn't remember who I was when O'Connor got done with me."

Lucy drew in a breath that was no more steady than the beating of her heart. "It's a convenient explanation and if I was feeling a little more indulgent and a lot less skeptical, I might be tempted to believe it. I'm too practical to be taken in by all that, remember? It's difficult enough for me to imagine that the man I love might be some sort of spy who not only works for the Queen, but knows her personally."

Lucy's self-control shattered. Her questions escaped on the end of a sob. "Do you have any idea of how you've broken my heart? Do you even care?"

James hurried to the other side of the bed. When Lucy made to walk away from him, he grabbed her forearms, and when she turned her face away, he pulled her to him, forcing her to meet his eyes. "Care? For you? Like my life. More. I swear it."

"Then for God's sake, tell me the truth."

"The truth?" James's voice was as rough as the hold he had on her. "You're the only one in the world who knows the whole of it. The only one I've ever trusted with my life. If that isn't good enough for you . . ." He let go of her long enough to rip the studs out of his shirt. They tapped against the wooden floor, one after the other, and when he was done, he tore away his shirt. "Here's the truth."

Too stunned to move, Lucy stared in horror at James's chest and left shoulder.

On his shoulder, a jagged-edged scar followed the line of his collarbone and ended just over his left breast. Not three inches away, a matching scar twisted the flesh just above his heart. It was smaller than the one on his shoulder, but no less terrible.

"Dear God!" Lucy pressed one hand to her lips, holding back tears. The anger that had bubbled inside her so short a time before mingled with the tenderness that hugged her heart when she thought of all James must have suffered. She brought one hand to his chest. For the measure of a dozen heartbeats, she rested it there, her hand against the pearly flesh of the scar. With her other hand, she touched the right side of his chest. The skin there was softer, smoother. But just as warm.

Lucy skimmed her hand over James's left shoulder. She traced the outline of the scar, across his breast, down to his heart. Her gaze captured by the rise and fall of his chest, she breathed in the scent of him, and closed her eyes, not because she couldn't endure the sight of the horrible scars, but because she couldn't bear the thought of James's pain. "I'm so sorry, I—"

"Don't be sorry." James's voice softened. He pulled her into his arms, the heat of his touch coaxing her eyes open. "If it wasn't for the fact that I was impulsive enough to step between Her Majesty and that bastard, O'Connor, I never would have been in the Queen's service," he said. "And if I was never in the Queen's service, I never would have been chasing around after that damned diamond."

Tears sprang to Lucy's eyes. "And never would have been beaten nearly to death."

"And never been beaten nearly to death," James agreed. A flame kindled in his eyes. "And never would have met you." He kissed her, his mouth lingering over hers, his words a whisper against her lips. "I'd say a few scars are worth the price."

Lucy was not so easily convinced. She tipped her head back so that she might see him better. "But you might have been killed!"

"But I wasn't." He pressed closer, and linking his arms around her waist, he tucked one leg between hers, and Lucy felt him move against her. "As a matter of fact, I think you'll agree that I'm very much alive, indeed." James smiled. "Do you need more proof?"

A thrill of anticipation ran through Lucy's body and she found herself smiling up at him. "Detectives are, by nature, skeptical creatures," she reminded him. "We always need proof."

James barked a laugh. "The proof is elementary, my dear detective." The laughter still sparkling in his eyes, he scooped her off the floor and carried her to the bed. He lay her on the pillow and sat beside her. He leaned over her, his lips nearly touching hers, his hands skimming like a summer breeze over her breasts. "I do believe this will give new meaning to the word 'investigation,' " he said.

Lucy could not bring herself to speak. Her blood sizzled through her veins. Her heart beat wildly. She gave him her answer with her kiss.

James's fingers worked free the buttons at the front of her white cotton blouse. He had a bit more trouble with her black skirt but with Lucy's help, he managed. When she lay back in her underskirt and corset, James sucked in a breath of wonder.

He traced the line of her corset top, his finger sliding beneath the lace that edged it. He trailed his hand down the right strap, across the straight bodice, up again at the left side. "A bonnie lass, and no doubt," he murmured, his tongue following the path laid by his finger. "And quite delicious! For a detective."

Lucy could not keep from smiling. Her heart soared and her head whirled. Her body tightened with anticipation. She linked her hands around James's neck, tickling her fingers through his hair

and down his neck, gliding them across his broad
shoulders and over his back.

"Oh, Lucy! You've made me so happy."

She cupped her hand around his jaw, her thumb
stroking his chin. "Which you?" she asked, her voice
teasing. "Is it Mr. Smith? Or Mr. Jones? Or is it
Herr—" She giggled. "Herr—"

"Herr Brandt." He smiled, joining in the game.
"You should know, he isn't the most attractive fellow. Wears spectacles. And a mustache." James laid
one finger across his upper lip. It was a poor imitation of a mustache, but it made Lucy laugh.

"He's an unpretentious sort of chap. Very quiet
and rather reserved." James slipped so effortlessly
into Herr Brandt's formal manner that Lucy stared
at him in amazement.

His back straight, his gaze steady, he looked Lucy in
the eyes, his own eyes suddenly those of a stranger.
"Herr Brandt does not go out much," he told her, and
even his voice was different. There was just a trace
of a clipped, foreign, and formal-sounding accent to
his words. "Herr Brandt tries not to be the center of
attention. He watches mostly, keeps his eyes open
and his mouth shut. He listens and learns. If he was
here right now . . ." James paused, considering the
possibilities.

"He's the sort of chap who would kiss you thoroughly and quite efficiently, but not with a great deal
of feeling." He proved it with a demonstration.

It was thorough. And quite efficient. But though
James might not have approved of Herr Brandt's
technique, Lucy found it more than emotional
enough. By the time James sat back, she was
breathless.

"Monsieur Rocard on the other hand . . . He is
something more of a rascal." He saw her objection

coming and stopped it, one finger on her lips. "Well, one has to be when dealing with the French!" he told her.

As easily as some men change from one shirt to another, James changed his demeanor. He was no longer Herr Brandt. Nor was he James. His accent now was that of a cultured Frenchman; the glint in his eyes that of a roué.

"Monsieur Rocard would not be formal at all, or the least bit shy." To prove his point, he hooked his fingers around the straps of Lucy's corset and pushed them down. *"Très bon!"* he whispered, his gaze raking her bare shoulders. There was a bow of pink ribbon at the top of the corset and another at her waist and he untied them. His thumbs beneath her breasts, he pushed the fabric apart. "If Monsieur Rocard didn't appreciate the sight of you, he'd be a fool! But you know how the French are, they are not the least bit happy just looking at a thing. They have to touch. To taste."

He trailed a finger over one breast, then the other, smiling when her nipples hardened beneath his touch, then bent and took her into his mouth.

Lost in a storm of pure sensation, Lucy heard herself groan. She dug her shoulders into the pillow, arching her back, encouraging him. James was only too happy to comply.

His mouth laid a path of fire between her breasts and down her stomach, tempting and teasing her. He nibbled his way back up again and suckled her at the same time his fingers found the fastening on her underskirt. He slipped it over her hips and tossed it on the floor at the same time he stood and unbuttoned his trousers.

"No! Wait!" Lucy stopped him, her hand on his. "You've forgotten the most important person of them all," she said, smiling up at him. "You've forgotten to tell me what James Dungannon would do."

"Dungannon? That cabbage-headed fellow?" James laughed, himself again. He gazed down at her, his expression so filled with love and longing it touched Lucy's soul. "Dungannon isn't a thing like either of those other fellows. He isn't always good with words but . . ." Taking Lucy's hand, he sat her up and knelt on the floor in front of her.

"He would tell ye you're braw," he murmured. "And that means you're beautiful." With one hand, he reached around to the back of her head and unfastened the pins that held up her hair. He loosened them one by one, his fingers combing through each curl as it tumbled over her shoulders.

"He would tell ye you're douce." He skimmed his lips down her neck to her breasts and back again. "And that means ye are sweet." With both hands, he traced the length of her right leg down to her boots. "Lang-shankit," he said, his fingers trailing back up to her thigh. "And that's long-legged." He kissed a path down the inside of her thigh to her ankle, all the while unlacing her boot. When he was finished with the right boot, he tugged it off and dropped it on the floor, then went to work on the left.

"He would tell ye that you're as bonnie as the flooers and that you've made him as happy as ever a man can be." Sitting back, he drew off her stockings and put them down with her boots, and when he was done, he knelt again and took both her hands in his.

"I would tell ye that ye already have my heart," he said. "I would ask ye, will ye take the rest of me as well?"

"Yes." The word trembled on Lucy's lips. "I will."

James stood and she helped him discard the rest

of his clothing. He knelt over her, and Lucy stroked her hands across his body.

James closed his eyes, reveling in her touch. "Oh, Lucy, my lass!" He brought his mouth to hers.

Lost in a place where taste and touch melted one into the other, enveloped in a circle of pure sensation, Lucy let the magic take hold, riding on the waves of passion that grew more feverish by the moment. When James slipped inside her, she drew in a breath, startled by the feel of him and the splendid, lingering movements that rocked his hips against hers, staggered that pleasure could be so pure and so simple at the same time it was so overwhelming.

Their rhythm quickened and the pleasure spiraled. At the same time she felt James move against her, the delicious tension inside Lucy burst. Their rough breaths overlapping, their arms and legs tangled, their lips melded as surely as their hearts, they tumbled together into sweet oblivion.

"Do you suppose O'Connor knew it was you that night in the alley?"

James wished Lucy would stop asking questions. He wished she'd stop talking completely. He wanted to lie there—simply to lie there—and enjoy the thrill of pleasure that still sang through his bloodstream like liquor in the veins of a drunkard.

"Mmmm." He mumbled a sound he hoped she'd accept as an answer and rolled to his side. He smoothed a long curl of her hair over her shoulder.

"I mean, did he know you were the one he nearly killed twelve years ago?"

"Mmmm." His eyes half-closed, his body heavy with satisfaction, James twisted the strand of hair around his finger and tickled the end of it across her chin.

Lucy sucked in a tiny breath of delight, but she was obviously not so easily distracted. After two hours of the most extraordinary lovemaking, all he wanted to do was relax and enjoy the pleasure that hummed through him.

All Lucy wanted to do was talk.

"It would change things considerably if O'Connor knew you were alive, don't you think? And if he knew you'd been here in the house all this time and that you'd seen him—"

"Do you always talk so much?" With an exaggerated groan, James collapsed onto his back. He knew defeat when he saw it, and he gave in with as much good grace as a man in his exhausted state could manage. He propped one arm behind his head and forced his eyes open only to find Lucy smiling at him. She was on her side, one arm cocked, her head cradled in her hand.

He couldn't help but smile back. "Aren't you the least bit tired?"

Even in the gray light of evening that filled his room, he could see Lucy's cheeks turn a pretty shade of pink. "Not really." She stretched, moving as sinuously beneath the linen sheets as she had moved beneath him only a short time ago. The sheets shifted, uncovering her breasts. Lucy didn't notice, or if she did, she didn't care. She looked James in the eye, daring him to keep his gaze from wandering from hers. "Actually," she said, "I am feeling rather . . . invigorated."

Suddenly, so was he.

James turned back to his side but try as he might to keep his eyes on Lucy's, he lost the battle. He let his gaze roam over her, from her breasts down to where the gentle curve of her hip disappeared beneath the rumpled sheets. He knew he was too dead-

tired to even consider anything more physical than
the appreciative look he gave her, and just so he'd
be certain, he reminded himself of the fact. Yet it
seemed his head had one idea.

His body another.

Almost before he knew what was happening, he
found his hands trailing after his gaze and his mind
preoccupied with a series of tantalizing thoughts. He
marveled that Lucy could have so quickly learned
the ways of a temptress. He thought of all the years
ahead, years they'd spend together, and he wondered
how much else she would learn. And what glorious
ways she'd apply that knowledge.

"Mmmm." This time, James's commentary had
nothing to do with weariness and everything to do
with the silky feel of her thighs. He scooted closer,
letting her feel the evidence of his arousal.

Lucy's smile widened. Her eyes lit with mischief.
"Good," she said quite amiably. "I finally have your
attention. Now we can talk."

"But I don't want to talk!" James's protest fell on
deaf ears. Lucy sat up, a pillow propped behind
her back.

"Perhaps not, but we really have to, don't you
think?" She tugged the sheet up around her shoulders and crossed her arms over her chest. "There are
a good many questions we need to answer and we
need to answer them soon. Not only for Alfie's sake.
The Queen's Jubilee is in two days' time and as you
so ably explained, if the Eye of the Devil isn't presented—"

"Yes. Yes." James hated when she was right. Especially at a time like this. His passion nipped by the
cold light of reason, he sat up beside her. "I've been
over it a thousand times, of course, and I never get

farther than I have before. The only consolation is that O'Connor apparently doesn't know where the Devil is, either. If he did, he wouldn't be trying so hard to get hold of information."

Lucy shook her head. Her hair spilled over her shoulders. With one hand, she scooped it back impatiently. "I'm sorry, but that makes little sense. He let a room here. That means he thinks he can find out something here. But there isn't a thing I can tell him about the Eye of the Devil. I never even heard of it until you came here. Imagine, that O'Connor would think I would know anything."

"Not you."

"Alfie?" Lucy bolted upright. The sheet sagged. She pulled it back into place. "You agree with me, then. He was working on a case. He does know something about the diamond."

James concurred. "It all comes back to what you said the other day. About Holmes. You said if we eliminate all the impossibilities, then what's left—"

"No matter how improbable—"

"Has got to be the truth." He scraped a hand through his hair. "I think it's very possible that Alfie knows something about the diamond. It follows that O'Connor might think that Alfie told you something, gave you some clue or some hint. He thinks you might know where the Eye of the Devil is. It's why he's been watching you."

This was obviously a turn of events Lucy had never considered. Staggered, she stared at James. "Then the burglary . . . it wasn't a random sort of thing at all, was it? You think that terrible ruffian really wanted to talk to me? To ask about—"

Her logic was well intentioned, if not accurate. Amazed that the truth had been staring him in the face and he'd been blind to it, James dropped his head into his hands. "I've been stupid," he mumbled. "So incredibly stupid." He raised his head, almost afraid to ask what he knew he should have asked weeks ago. "The burglar wasn't after common household plunder, was he? Was he . . . do you think he was looking for something specific?"

Thinking back, Lucy squeezed her eyes shut. "At first I thought he was simply your everyday, garden-variety burglar," she agreed. "It was the only thing that would explain his presence here. But then, when I found him in Alfie's study, I assumed he was looking for Alfie. I must admit, my head was not as clear as it should have been, but then you don't think too clearly in that sort of situation," she added quickly with an apologetic look at James. "I am new to the detective business, after all, and—"

"I understand." A stab of affection jabbed at his heart and he patted her hand, eager for her to continue.

"But he wasn't looking for Alfie." Lucy's voice quickened with excitement. "I remember now. He wasn't looking for a person at all. He was looking for a thing."

James was sure of what she'd say next, and he hung on her every word.

"He kept asking me where 'it' was kept, and I didn't have any idea what he was talking about. I suppose in the excitement of all that happened after, I forgot all about it. Can it be?" Her head tipped, her eyes catching the light, Lucy looked at James in wonder. "Could he have been looking for—"

"The Eye of the Devil." James held on to her hand, bridling his excitement and hers. "I don't know how Alfie got mixed up in this whole thing. My contact here in London was supposed to be a fellow named

Claridon, a cat burglar of some renown who occasionally sells his unique talents to the government. Last I heard from him, he'd stolen the Devil back from O'Connor. He was to meet me in that alley in Whitechapel to return it to me. Just to be certain that both he and I were who we said we were, we were supposed to show each other those Indian stone seals."

"But Claridon never showed. And O'Connor did."

"And Alfie had Claridon's seal." Frustrated, James punched one fist into the mattress. "There's a million ways your father might have gotten involved, I suppose, and at this point, not one of them matters. We've eliminated the impossibilities, my dear Lucy. What does that leave us?"

Lucy's eyes shone with excitement. Turning, she took James's hands in hers. "It leaves us with incontrovertible evidence," she said. "The Eye of the Devil is here. In the house."

James didn't have to answer. Lucy knew his answer from his smile. "It's here? You really think it's here?" She laughed, the sound of it as clear as a church bell on a summer morning. "It would solve one problem, wouldn't it? And then we need only worry about Alfie. Oh, James! This is wonderful! We must start our search immediately." With a small squeal of excitement, she bounded from the bed.

James let her get far enough so that he had a perfect view of her bare back and the delicious curve of her buttocks. He wasn't about to let her get any farther.

He held tight to her hands, tugging her to a stop. Surprised, Lucy turned to him. The muted light hugged her naked body, stroking her with softness. It caressed her breasts and touched the plane of her stomach. It hugged her hips and added to the soft, dark shadow between her legs.

"Oh, no! Not so fast!" James knelt on the bed and his arms went around her. "That damned diamond has been here all these weeks," he said, his mouth finding hers. "It can wait an hour longer!"

# Chapter 18

It was two hours later when Lucy finally pulled on her clothes and headed down the stairs to Alfie's study. She was a little unsteady on her feet and a little light-headed in the aftermath of James's skilled and quite incredible lovemaking. She was a little out of breath from thinking about all they'd shared in the last hours, and more than a little anxious to do it all again.

She paused outside the door, collecting her thoughts, holding her eagerness at bay. She reminded herself that this was just the first of many such nights. She and James had years ahead. Years to get to know each other, to learn each other's needs and desires. Years filled with love and laughter and time enough to explore and taste. Time to savor each magical moment.

Alfie didn't have that kind of time.

A cold claw of fear touched the back of Lucy's neck.

She and James might have all the time in the world, but somehow she knew Alfie did not. Time was running out. For Alfie and for Britain. The Queen's Diamond Jubilee was in two days and if the Eye of the Devil wasn't presented to her at the festivities, the repercussions would rip apart the Empire.

The thoughts crowding her head and weighing heavy on her heart, Lucy pushed open the door to Alfie's snuggery, turned up the gas jets, and looked around. Her shoulders slumped and her stomach pitched.

Two days, she decided, would never be long enough to even begin to sort through the monumental disaster before her.

Alfie's study was in no better shape than when last she'd been in it. She had cleaned up the bits of broken glass and puddles of spilled chemicals that were remnants of the night the house had been burglarized. She'd even screwed up the courage to take a mop to the room. But still, the thought of searching through the place was intimidating.

A fine coating of dust covered everything, from what little of the desk and tabletops showed, to the papers, magazines, books, and other gubbins that inhabited every flat surface and even some that weren't so flat.

"Good God!" James stepped into the room behind Lucy and his face fell. "I didn't have much of a chance to look around last time. I didn't realize—"

"There's no use even trying to organize it." Automatically, Lucy offered an apology. There was a precarious pile of old newspapers stacked on one of the upholstered chairs in front of the desk and without thinking, Lucy began to straighten it. The movement caused a chain reaction. The newspapers slid to the floor. The books beneath them followed. The empty bottle on which they had all been stacked tipped, and the smell of stale beer rose in the air.

Lucy groaned. "I should bring in a shovel and a barrel. That's what I should do. I should send it all away with the dustman," she mumbled. "That would teach him a lesson. Wouldn't Alfie be surprised, then? When he gets back . . . when he comes home . . . if . . ."

Her mutterings wedged against the tears that clogged her voice.

She didn't hear James come up behind her but before she knew it, he wrapped his arms around her waist. He pulled her against him and nuzzled her cheek with his. "*When* he comes home . . ." He emphasized the word, and moving away from her, he gingerly searched through the flotsam and jetsam piled on a nearby table. He pulled a face when his fingers met something sticky.

"When Alfie returns, we'll have him muck out this place himself." He grinned over at her at the same time he wiped his fingers against his shirt. "We'll threaten to do it for him if he refuses."

Buoyed by James's support, Lucy smiled in spite of herself. She joined in the game. "Bit by wretched bit," she added, wiping away the single tear that had escaped down her cheek.

"Piece by hideous piece," he said. With two fingers, he lifted what looked to be an animal pelt from the top of the china cabinet and, with a noticeable shiver, dropped it back where it had come from.

"We'll get rid of all the newspapers first," Lucy said. She glanced from pile to pile, shaking her head. "And then we'll get to work on the magazines."

"He may object," James commented, "but we'll hold firm. The newspapers. The magazines. Then that odorous stuff." His nose wrinkling, he looked at the chemistry paraphernalia heaped on Alfie's desk.

The chemistry equipment. The papers. The baubles. It was enough to discourage even the most enthusiastic investigator.

Lucy's smile faded. So did James's.

"It's a formidable job," she admitted. She looked

all around the room, her confidence ebbing. "And we're not even sure if this is the right place to look." Gingerly, she lifted one corner of the blanket that Alfie had left draped over a chair and jumped back, startled, when a small gray mouse scuttled out from beneath it and scurried down the chair leg and under the desk. She shook her head. "Where shall we begin?"

"At the beginning, I think." James strode to the center of the room and glanced around, as if mentally cordoning off the place, dividing the imposing job of searching it into small, easy to manage sections. "You can look through the desk. It may contain some private papers and until I am a member of the family . . ." He gave her a meaningful look, one that sent heat rushing through her body, before he turned his attention back to the desk.

He leaned over it, estimating the size and shape of each of its drawers. "It doesn't look like a good possibility," he commented. "After all, there are only so many places a statue like the Eye of the Devil can hide, and none of these drawers looks nearly big enough." From his back pocket, he took *The Times* article they'd gotten from Mr. Canaday. He unfolded it and tipped the page so that Lucy might see it better.

"Just a reminder, here's what the bloody thing looks like," he said. "The Hindu goddess Kali, in all her ferocious glory. The entire statue is about two feet high." He held his hand over the desktop in an approximation of the height. "And probably about that wide." He held out his arms, his hands a foot or so apart. "It's not a big thing, but it is bulky and with the weight of the diamond . . ." He stopped to think. "It must be quite heavy. There are only so many places Alfie could hide a thing like that."

"Yes. So many places. And they're all in this room." Before she could talk herself out of it, Lucy got to work. While James sorted through the oddments in the china cabinet, Lucy looked through Alfie's desk.

"This is where I found the stone seal," she said. She pushed the center of a flower pattern inlaid in the mahogany on the top of the desk and a tiny secret drawer popped open on the side. There was nothing in the drawer, of course. Lucy had checked it a dozen times before tonight, but just to be sure, she put her hand in it and felt all around. "Empty." She sat back on her heels.

"Nothing here, either." Across the room, James stood and brushed the knees of his trousers. There was a smudge of dirt across his left cheek and feeling Lucy's eyes on it, he wiped it away with the back of his hand. The front of his shirt was stained with something wet and blue. Ink, perhaps? Or something best left unidentified? Lucy decided not to mention it.

While James looked through the bookshelves, she moved to a table that was set up along the far wall. The Eye of the Devil was obviously not on top of it, but Alfie had an assortment of boxes tucked beneath the table and she went through them, one by one. She found some old photographs and promised herself she'd look them over another time. She noticed a book or two that had gone missing years before, and any number of things that Alfie must have been saving for one of the singular machines he liked to build.

"But no Eye of the Devil." Discouraged, Lucy grumbled and brushed a strand of hair away from her face.

"Of course, it may not be here at all." James was on his hands and knees, his head buried deep in the bookshelf. His voice was muffled and dusty-sounding. He backed out of the uncomfortable position and sneezed before he looked Lucy's way. "Didn't you say that Alfie had a sort of workshop out in the yard? It's just as likely the statue could be there."

"Yes, of course!" It was such a simple solution, Lucy wondered she hadn't thought of it sooner. Heartened, she tossed everything back into the boxes it had come from and tried to get up off the floor. But her knees were stiff. Her back ached. She groped for the window ledge to try to support herself and overreached her mark. Instead, she grabbed on to the oak pedestal where Alfie had enthroned the bust of the Queen he brought home only days before he disappeared. The pedestal rocked and before Lucy's horrified eyes the garish plaster bust toppled to the floor and shattered.

Lucy looked at the mess and her heart sank. The Queen's nose was missing completely. Two of her imposing chins were gone. The bust must have spun as it fell because not only was the front of Her Majesty's face damaged, the back of her head was smashed. Crumbs of gold-painted plaster littered the floor.

"Oh, bother!" Lucy swept away the bits and pieces of plaster scattered all around her with one hand.

"It's a lucky thing the old girl didn't land on your head. You might have been killed!" James leaned across the desk, offering Lucy a hand up.

But Lucy didn't move.

She couldn't.

Her body was frozen in place. As surely as her gaze.

Thinking she'd been hurt, James hurried around to the other side of the desk. "What—?" His words fell dead against the gasp of astonishment that escaped him. He dropped to his knees, his hands resting just above the broken statue. Right where Lucy was staring.

In the dim light of the gas jets that hissed upon the wall, the diamond sparkled like a star in a summer's night sky. It winked at Lucy, red one second, blue the next, its brilliance overpowering, its beauty far surpassing anything she might have imagined.

"Damn!" The single word escaped James along with a sigh of pure wonder. He lifted a piece of the Queen's forehead away and exposed the face of Kali. "There she is," he said, wiping plaster dust from the goddess's horrible face. Carefully, he picked away the rest of the cracked plaster until the entire statue was uncovered.

The Eye of the Devil was about as tall as James said it would be and just about as wide. It was made of what looked like brass and it would have been a perfectly ordinary monstrosity had it not been for the diamond embedded in Kali's headdress.

With both hands, James lifted the statue from the rubble. "It is heavy," he said, weighing it thoughtfully. "And ugly as sin. But the diamond—" He gave a low whistle. "It's no wonder O'Connor's after the thing. It's hypnotic, isn't it? It's splendid!" He laughed. "This little beauty will make a right bonny trophy on Her Majesty's mantelpiece!"

Lucy was hardly listening. Her view was blurred by the tears that glazed her eyes and turned the light that radiated from the diamond into a multicolored kaleidoscope. She ran her hands over the statue. "He really had it! He had it all along! And he was smart enough to buy that bust of the Queen to hide it." As overwhelmed by the statue as she was by the sure knowledge that Alfie had somehow been mixed up in its recovery, she shook her head. "It was here all along, and no one knew it."

"Aye. That's sure enough." As if the walls themselves had eyes, James tucked the statue into the kneehole of the desk. "And we'd best keep it that way."

Puzzled, Lucy glanced his way.

James reached for her hand. His own hands were coated in plaster dust and they felt gritty. "I cannot say for certain, of course, but . . . O'Connor must realize Alfie knows where the statue is. That's why he was here, staying in your house. That's why he sent the burglar to look things over. He was hoping to find it. It's why Alfie's missing, too. I don't think O'Connor's . . ." He paused and glanced at Lucy as if trying to determine if it was wise to say any more. Something in her level gaze must have given him the assurance to continue.

"I don't believe Alfie is dead," James said. "O'Connor is ruthless, but he isn't stupid. As long as Alfie is alive, there's a chance he'll talk. Obviously he hasn't yet, or O'Connor would have the statue. But he doesn't. He doesn't know where the statue is, Lucy, and we've got to make sure it stays that way. If he finds out where the Devil is . . . if he learns we have it . . . he'll have no more reason to keep Alfie alive."

Lucy pressed a fist to her mouth, stifling a sob.

"It's all right to cry. Especially now you have someone you can share your fears with." James pulled her closer, and while Lucy gave in to her worries, he rocked her gently in his arms, calming her tears and her cares.

"We'll find him, Lucy. We'll bring him home. That's not something I'm saying simply to make you feel better. It's a pledge. A promise." He held her far enough away so that she might look into his eyes and see the truth of his words shining there.

"And I don't promise lightly."

"Are you sure this is the best thing to do?" Her face as pale as her white blouse, her words far too blasé to hide the worry that lurked behind them, Lucy watched James put on his coat and reach for his top hat. "Are you certain you'll be safe and—"

"Safe as the Bank of England!" He paused and offered her a grin. "Besides," he told her, "we've been through it all. Last night when we found the statue and again this morning. It's the best thing to do. Trust me." With one finger, he tapped the tip of her nose and offered a smile meant to warm her heart.

It apparently didn't work.

Her brows low over her eyes, her face drawn, Lucy was far too worried to respond to his playfulness. Nor was she convinced.

She clasped her hands at her waist and paced from one end of the parlor to the other, endeavoring as she had been since the night before to find the right argument to make him change his mind.

"How do you know there's no danger?" she asked.

Had it been anyone else, James would have been tempted to offer the truth: Of course there was danger. There was always danger.

Had it been anyone else, he might have snapped out the answer and dared his interrogator to ask if James had courage enough to face whatever waited for him outside the Barnstables' front door. Or he might have laughed and admitted that he welcomed the thrill of danger, especially since he'd been on a sort of forced retirement these weeks, chomping at the bit, though at the time he could not have said why.

But this wasn't just anyone. It was Lucy. And she was worried.

He had to lie.

"No danger." He held up his right hand. "Honest. I've been doing this sort of thing long enough to know. Why, I remember a time in Vienna when—"

A few weeks ago she would have hung on every word. Today, she wasn't about to be distracted. She propped her fists on her hips. "And do you know you won't be followed?"

"Being followed is exactly what I'm hoping for." This much was at least the truth, and James charged into it with all due righteousness. "Don't you see? Someone must be watching the house, looking for the least little sign that we've found the Devil. If I can get the fellow to trail along after me, I won't have to worry that he's mooching around here watching you."

It was a persuasive argument. Or it should have been. But Lucy still did not look certain.

Anxious to reassure her, James went over to the window and nudged aside the curtain. He peeked out. "Look. Come here." He waved, calling her over. "See that fellow over there? The one idling about across the way?"

Lucy followed his gaze. "The costermonger?"

"You'll notice he has a full barrow of fruits and vegetables. At this hour, any costermonger worth his salt would have sold everything off. Besides"—he looked at her out of the corner of his eye, waiting to see her reaction and secretly hoping she'd be so impressed by his intelligence she would stop arguing—"yesterday the same fellow was dressed as a man of the cloth and the day before he was wearing a bobby's uniform."

"Yes, I wondered if you'd noticed." Lucy turned to him. "I didn't want to mention it and worry you, of course, but I—"

"You didn't want to worry me?" James let the corner of the draperies drop back into place. "You knew he was there?"

As if it took all her iron will to keep from pointing out the obvious, Lucy shook her head. "He's beetle-browed and long in the nose. The fellow should know better than to think he can hide behind a disguise." She must have sensed the disappointment James felt at not being able to surprise her. She patted his arm and looked up at him with a smile that was indulgent and therefore should have been annoying, and was completely enchanting instead.

"You see, you are right about one thing," she told him, "we are being watched. And that's all the more reason you should stay put." Before James could react, she snatched his hat out of his hands and tucked it behind her back. "It's far too dangerous."

"I doubt they'd try anything within sight of the Foreign Office." Without missing a word, James reached around her. He was tempted to prolong the contact and enjoy the pleasant way her body fit against his. He didn't. He plucked the hat from her hands, and though it was terribly rude to don it in the house, he settled the hat firmly on his head before she could snatch it away again.

"I might be in danger if I took the statue with me," he admitted, heading for the door. "But even I'm not foolish enough to do that. That's why I'm leaving it here and going to see Sir Digby on my own. As far as they know"—he poked his thumb over his shoulder toward the window—"we haven't found the damned thing yet. Nothing is any different than it has been these past weeks. I'm going out. That's all. Going out as I've done a dozen times before. And you are spending the day at home."

If there was one thing he was learning about Lucy, it was that she couldn't thole defeat. Her shoulders slumped. "Very well." She had followed him to the doorway and she stood on tiptoe to kiss his cheek. "I'll be waiting here for you when you get back."

It wasn't that he didn't believe her. Or that he didn't trust her. But James wanted to be sure. "We don't want to tip our hand, remember, so you won't go off doing any investigating. We've got to keep things calm and quiet so as not to arouse suspicions. And just to be sure—"

"Reporting for duty, sir!"

The parlor door banged open and side by side Harleigh and Farleigh marched into the room. As one, James and Lucy turned to gape at them in wonder.

Though it had been hidden under James's bed, Harleigh—or was it Farleigh?—had somehow managed to get hold of the ancient firearm that James had appropriated from him the night of the burglary. The other Atwater brother was no less resourceful. James had thought his battle sword safe in the darkest recesses of his wardrobe. He'd been wrong. Farleigh—or was he Harleigh?—had it strapped to his waist with a red sash.

Both the Atwater brothers were dressed in tight-fitting but immaculately pressed uniforms, ones that, from the smell of them, had been stored in mothballs for a good many years.

Harleigh and Farleigh each offered James a snappy salute and, at his urging, stood at ease.

"Begging your pardon, sir," the Atwater with the rifle said, "as you didn't specifically call for us—"

"But we thought you might be needing some assistance, sir, and—"

"Thought it might be best if we handled things while you were away, sir—"

"Just in case that blighter across the street—"

"Stop!" Given their heads, the Atwaters obviously would have gone right on babbling. James held out both hands as if to stop the tide of their words.

"What blighter across the street?" he asked, though he was afraid he already knew the answer. "And how do you two know—"

"Doesn't take an Isaac Newton, if you catch my meaning, sir." Farleigh tapped his forehead with one finger. "He's been lolling about out there for days."

"We noticed on our daily reconnoiter."

"And he isn't a pleasant-looking chap, is he, sir?"

"And now you are on your way out, sir, and again, begging your pardon . . ." Harleigh nodded an apology to Lucy. "But we heard you talking, last night and again this morning. Miss Barnstable is worried, sir—"

"And she's not a woman who worries easily."

"And that means there's trouble."

"Which means . . ." The Atwaters snapped to attention.

"You'll be needing some assistance, sir!"

"Yes. Well." James tried to rid his mind of the confusion that seemed to follow along in the Atwaters' wake. "I suppose . . ." He looked from the brothers to Lucy, weighing the possibility of humoring them against the time it would take to talk them out of their scheme.

"I suppose you could keep an eye on things." James knew Lucy well enough to offer a sheepish grin along with the explanation. As if it might help. "You don't mind if they—"

"Stand guard over me? Watch me? Keep me out of trouble?" She threw a look at Harleigh and Farleigh, defying them to deny the charges.

Eager to keep the confrontation from getting out of hand, James took Lucy by the elbow and piloted her over to the far side of the room, out of earshot of the Atwaters. "They aren't going to be guarding you. They are going to be . . ." He didn't have the least idea what the Atwaters were going to be doing. James changed his tack.

"Actually, it might not be a bad idea to have them about creating a stir. If that fellow from across the street comes anywhere near the house—"

"What will they do, talk him to death?"

Lucy hadn't the least intention of being funny, but James laughed. "An excellent plan!" Before Lucy could continue her protest and much to the delight of the Atwaters, he gave her a lingering good-bye kiss and headed for the door. "I'll be back very soon," he promised. "They can't possibly do any damage in that short time."

The only thing left to do was to find Alfie.

James sat back in the cab, thinking through the problem. He had spent the better part of an hour with Sir Digby and, much to the old gentleman's delight, assured him that the statue was safe. He'd arranged to have a coal delivery made to the Barnstable house in the morning, and for the statue to be smuggled out with the colliers when they left.

He'd been very specific with his instructions.

Even after it was safely locked in a vault at the Foreign Office, no one was to let on that the statue was in the hands of the government. If they did, Alfie Barnstable was as good as dead.

If he was still alive at all.

James expelled the thought.

They would find Alfie, he told himself. They had to. For the old fellow's sake.

And for Lucy's.

Unused to the feelings that flooded his body and warmed his heart, but not the least bit willing to ignore them, James let his thoughts drift. He thought about the day he met Lucy, and about last night and all they'd said and done. He thought about the years ahead and wondered at the notion that once he'd thought the future a mystery, and now he could see quite clearly how he would spend it and who he would spend it with.

A smile on his lips, James settled back. His cab turned a corner and ambled onto the street that intersected the Barnstables'. From here, he could see the front of the house. All looked well and quiet, just as he'd left it.

Except for the hansom parked outside the front door.

Every sense suddenly on the alert, every instinct screaming a warning, James tapped on the roof of the cab, signaling the driver to stop. He sat back, taking stock of the situation.

Across the way, the front door opened. For a moment all was confusion. Talking and gesturing, pointing to the waiting cab and back toward the house, Harleigh and Farleigh backed out onto the stoop, trying their damnedest to keep someone from leaving the house. A moment later James saw who they were trying to restrain.

And why.

Her eyes grim, her mouth set, Lucy walked out onto the stoop. The sun had emerged from behind the clouds where it had been hidden all morning, and the afternoon air was warm. Lucy wasn't wear-

ing a coat, but there was no mistake she was on
her way out. She was dressed in the outfit James
recognized as the one she wore only for the most
important social calls: a close-fitting black skirt and
matching jacket, a white blouse and a patterned silk
tie. Her hair was up and she had a straw boater
perched rather high and straight on her head.

With one gloved hand, Lucy politely opened a
pathway between Harleigh and Farleigh and James
saw that she was carrying a parcel.

The package was wrapped in brown paper, but
there was no mistaking its size and shape. It was
about two feet high and nearly a foot wide and from
the way Lucy carried it, it was obviously heavy.

Hoisting it up in her arms, she walked down the
steps and toward the waiting cab and before James
could regain his senses and even think to tell his
driver to follow them, the cab sped away with
Lucy—and the Eye of the Devil—inside it.

# Chapter 19

Lucy's heartbeat pounded to the rhythm of the horse's hooves. No matter how fast the creature went, no matter how nimbly its driver maneuvered it through the city traffic, she couldn't help but think she would be late.

Her fingers as restless as the worries that ran rampant through her mind, she worked over the folded piece of paper in her pocket.

"Shadwell's warehouse in Garford Street." She pulled the note from her pocket and read it aloud to herself, just as she'd read it dozens of times since it was delivered to the house. "With the Eye of the Devil." She was tempted to read no further; the words were already burned in her mind. But she read them again, nonetheless, reminding herself of the urgency. And the peril.

"Refuse, or come later than three o'clock this afternoon, and the old man dies."

Lucy pressed a hand to her heart. Blinking back tears, she set the page aside and looked over the second message that had been delivered with it. The note was in Alfie's handwriting; she would recognize it and his singular manner of fashioning sentences anywhere. As if to prove to her that the message was new and not something written days or even weeks ago, it began not only with the date but with the headlines from this morning's *Telegraph* neatly printed out across the top.

"Mad. Every one of them. Think you have something they call the Eye of the Devil, whatever that may be," Alfie's message stated. "Told the fellow who seems to be in charge that he was wrong, but he's Irish and you know how they are. They are a stubborn race, and this one's no different from the rest. I don't know what he's talking about and I've told him neither do you." These last three words were underlined.

"Won't listen, of course," the note went on. "The Irish never do. Pay him no mind, Lucy my darling. The man's talking crazy. I beg you, stay well away from this business as the man is a bad lot and—"

As if the pen had been pulled from his hand, Alfie's words ended in a blot of ink.

Trying to calm her fears and soothe her mind, fighting to keep herself from checking the watch that hung from a brooch on her lapel, wondering how she would ever make it to Limehouse in time to satisfy O'Connor's demands, Lucy traced the shape of the ink stain with one finger.

Of course, O'Connor wasn't her only problem. When he arrived home, James would be furious to find her gone. She fought back the flutter in her stomach, the one that reminded her that she was shamelessly violating his command that she stay put. She was opening herself up to peril. How O'Connor had learned that they'd found the statue was beyond her. Perhaps he didn't really know they'd found it at all. Perhaps, like a cardplayer, he was calling her bluff.

And she was letting him win.

Simply by obeying O'Connor's summons, she was

letting him know that they had, indeed, found the Eye of the Devil.

James would be very annoyed.

But then, Lucy told herself, he'd been annoyed before.

In the end, he would understand. He would have to.

Lucy clutched the message from Alfie in one hand. "I'm coming, Papa," she whispered. She glanced at the parcel bundled on the seat next to her. "And I promise that somehow, I'm going to bring you home."

SHADWELL AND SONS, LTD. TEA MERCHANTS OF QUALITY.

The sign above the door to the warehouse was old and well worn by the damp that rose from the river at James's back. Carefully, he peered around a stack of barrels piled in front of the warehouse directly across from Shadwell's, watching as Lucy lifted the Eye of the Devil from the pavement where she'd set it when she alighted from her cab.

Limehouse teemed with activity. Sailors and dock-workers strained at their labors. Beggars sat along the pavement side by side with the prostitutes who, too drunk to make their way back to their digs the previous night, had decided simply to sleep it off in the streets. The roadways were packed with drays and wagons, their horses shying at the noise, their drivers yelling to and at each other. Farther up the road, there were three or four prosperous carriages stopped outside a building that looked to be a sailor's mission and was, in reality, an opium den.

Fortunately, it seemed Lucy was too preoccupied to notice the nondescript cab that had followed her from home. Nor did she pay any attention when

James descended from it. She was too absorbed in what she was doing: paying the jarvey, checking the address against a piece of paper she pulled from her pocket, adjusting her jacket and her hat a dozen times over so that James began to wonder if she would ever go inside.

With one heartbeat, James wanted to rush across the road, take Lucy into his arms, and carry her as far away from there as he could. He wanted to shield her from the ugliness of Limehouse and keep her from being entangled in the web of danger and deceit that had the Eye of the Devil as its center.

In the next, he wanted to shake her. He wanted to demand that she tell him what she was doing and why. He wanted to warn her about Shadwell, who he knew to be untrustworthy and ill-tempered on his best days, and about O'Connor for, it seemed, he must surely be deep in this business. He wanted to remind her that O'Connor was ruthless. And dangerous. He was deceitful. And cunning.

But then, it seemed Lucy already knew all that.

She was one of O'Connor's hirelings.

A burst of anger erupted through James, blinding and bitter. But even that wasn't enough to dull the pain where his heart used to be.

Hoping he was wrong—knowing he was not—he watched Lucy knock on the door to the warehouse, and when it opened to her and she went inside, he bolted across the street and around to the back of the building. He'd been to Shadwell's before in his search for the Devil. He knew there was a rickety old stairway that would take him up to the first floor and a doorway there that would allow him access to the catwalk that ran the length of the building.

From there, he could see and not be seen. Hear and not be heard.

From there, he could watch.

He wanted answers, damn it. He wanted to try to make some sense of everything that had happened. He wanted to understand how he'd let himself be deceived by a woman shrewd enough to act the innocent all the while she was part of a sinister plot to undermine the Empire. He wanted to figure out how he'd been taken in by the story of her desperate search for her missing father, and how he'd lost his heart and his soul to a woman who had seemed so brave and so resourceful and so sincere.

A woman who was really a traitor.

"Ah, Miss Barnstable!"

When Lucy walked in, the corpulent man in the finely tailored suit stood up from behind the desk where he'd been seated. Though their proximity to the river made the air inside the warehouse cool and damp, there was a sheen of sweat on the man's forehead and along his top lip. His eyes were small and close set, his lips rather large. Smiling a particularly oily sort of smile, he walked around to the front of the desk, his hand extended.

Lucy didn't take it.

Cradling the parcel in her arms, she glanced around the room. The most singular aspect of the office was that its walls did not go all the way to the ceiling. It did not take Lucy long to see why.

The warehouse was not divided into floors, as any normal structure might be. It was one gigantic expanse under a roof that rose two stories above them, the office like an island partitioned off from the rest of the place.

It was a perfectly ordinary office, from what she could see; fitted out as any reasonably prosperous merchant's office might be. The desk was aged and bulky, as if it had been in the family many years. It sat square upon a rug of some distinction, its colors blazing like jewels in the otherwise drab surroundings. Behind the desk there was a door that obviously led out into the warehouse and across from it, a table that contained a teapot and cups as well as three canisters that were marked DARJEELING, ASSAM, and KEEMUN.

The man still had his hand out when Lucy turned back to him. "You must be Mr. Shadwell," she said. "I haven't come to see you. I've come to see O'Connor."

"O'Connor? Is that the name he's given you?" Shadwell snickered and pulled his hand back to his side where he wiped it against the leg of his trousers. "Not the name he uses 'round these parts," he said.

"I hardly care. No matter what you call the man, I've come to see him. And it is nearly three o'clock." The words were meant to sound flippant. Lucy was very much afraid her anxiety showed instead. She pulled in a breath, steadying herself. "I'd like to be taken to him immediately."

Shadwell was either impressed by her spirit or he was humoring her. She would have liked to think it was the first, but she very much feared it was the second. Smiling his slippery smile, he back-stepped his way to the door behind the desk and stood aside so that Lucy might go first.

"After you, miss," Shadwell said, looking as pleased as if he were leading her straight to her doom. "After you."

From where he was crouched high above Shadwell's office and well into the shadows, James could see from hell to breakfast.

But he couldn't hear a damned thing.

Silently, he berated himself. He should have known better than to think that this perch near the rafters would offer him anything better than a bird's-eye view.

He strained to catch a word or two and heard only the greased syllables of Shadwell's voice and Lucy's muffled replies. And the catwalk groaning beneath his weight.

James settled back and held his breath. Shadwell seemed not to take any stock of the noise. Far below, he led Lucy toward the back door of the office and into the warehouse.

There were windows high up on the walls and with what little light managed to make its way through the dirt that encrusted them, he saw that far across the warehouse, another portion of the building had been partitioned.

The building within a building was thirty feet across and perhaps another twenty deep. It had no windows and only one door that was set directly into the center of the wall closest to James. It also had a roof and James knew exactly what that meant. Once Lucy and Shadwell made their way into the building, not only would he be deaf as to what was going on, he would be blind.

There wasn't a moment to lose.

On his way across the catwalk, he'd seen a ladder hanging some forty feet away. James scampered back the way he'd come. Moving as quickly and silently as he could, he scrambled over to the ladder and started down, praying the ancient thing would hold his weight.

That much of his prayer, at least, was answered.

Poised on the shaky ladder, James reached for the next toehold. He didn't find one. Peering into the darkness below, he saw that the ladder ended well before the floor began.

He had no choice but to jump.

Hoping to use the hum of their conversation to cover any noise he might make, James listened for Shadwell and Lucy to start talking again and when they did, he jumped.

He landed in a puddle of standing water and cursed his luck and his damp trousers legs, but he didn't stop. Keeping to the shadows, he followed Shadwell and Lucy across the warehouse and into the darkness.

The moment the office door closed behind her, Lucy had an uneasy feeling along her shoulders and down her back. She fought the feeling and the worries that turned her blood to ice water, and resisted the nearly overpowering urge to turn and run. She couldn't let Shadwell see her fear, she reminded herself, so she trailed after him through the gloom and each time he stopped to let her catch him up, she held back a little, more comfortable with following after the man than walking beside him.

For a business that advertised itself as a tea merchant of quality, there was a surprising lack of merchandise in Shadwell's warehouse. Nor was there much of anything else.

The building was vast and empty. There were no bales of tea stacked on the floor, no workers bustling to meet orders. It was cool and damp and smelled of mold, and as they crossed the wide expanse, their footsteps fell dead against the rotted wooden floorboards.

Halfway across the building, Shadwell stopped and tipped his head toward a rough structure that had been built along the far side of the place. "He's been looking forward to your coming," Shadwell said, and Lucy didn't have to ask who he was talking about. "Been real anxious to see you and your friend there." He tipped his head again, this time toward the bundle Lucy carried.

Instinctively, Lucy tightened her arms around the package. She was still holding on to it like grim death when Shadwell opened the door to the room and stepped aside to let her in ahead of him.

"After you." He smiled. It was an expression she did not have the courage to meet.

Her eyes straight ahead, her chin as steady as it was likely to get, she stepped into the room. Shadwell closed the door behind her. He stayed outside.

Alone in the darkness, Lucy held tight to her parcel and what was left of her courage. Gradually, her eyes grew more accustomed to the gloom and she looked around. There was little furniture in the place and no chairs. It was just as well. She didn't think she would like to sit down.

The room itself was broken into three smaller compartments. The one in which she stood served as a sort of antechamber to two other rooms, one on her left and another on her right. Both of the doors to those rooms were closed. Directly opposite from where she stood was a table with a single oil lamp burning on it.

"I wondered if you'd come."

At the sound of the voice, Lucy jumped.

Like a phantom, a shape emerged from the shadows. The man stepped between Lucy and the light so that she couldn't see his face, but she knew who it was. She recognized the voice and the Irish accent. "I see you've decided to be sensible."

Lucy wasn't sure she agreed with him, but she wasn't about to let Michael O'Connor know it.

"Where's my father?"

O'Connor made a sound from deep in his throat. "You cut to the chase fast enough, don't you? And here you are asking me questions when all these weeks I've been waiting about that hellhole of a house of yours, hoping for some answers of my own. Where'd you find the Devil?"

Automatically, Lucy hugged the package closer to her chest. "It hardly matters, does it?" she asked him. "What matters is our bargain. The one you mentioned in your message. I can't say I understand why you want this hideous thing, but it's yours—" She fell back a step when he made to take it from her. "After I see my father."

In answer, O'Connor laughed. It was not a pleasant sound, and Lucy was reminded of something James had said about the man a good long time ago.

He had a smile like the silver handles of a casket.

Lucy couldn't see that smile, not with the way he was standing. But she could well imagine it. And now she knew he had a laugh to go with it. One as cold as hell.

"You've got nerves of steel, I'll give you that much," O'Connor said and Lucy shivered when she realized there was a note of admiration in his voice. "Whoever would have thought it of a mousy spinster who did naught but keep her house and tend to that tribe of simpletons she has living with her." He moved a step closer and instinctively Lucy backed away.

"Perhaps after we settle this little affair—" O'Connor paused and she could feel his eyes go back to the parcel. "I like your style. Your panache. And I have to admit, though I was right angry when I first heard about the fellow's stupidity, I have to give you credit for coshing that boy who tried to bring you to me a couple days ago. You're a spunky sort." O'Connor moved another step nearer and Lucy another back. She might have gone right on if she didn't meet with the door.

"Perhaps we can discuss a business arrangement, Miss Barnstable. You and me. You wouldn't be the first woman in my employ." His movement as lazy as his voice, O'Connor reached out a hand to finger the contours of the parcel.

Panic shot through Lucy. It propelled her into motion. She dodged O'Connor and once she was passed him, she flipped around, her back to the flickering light of the oil lamp.

He responded to her sudden movement the way any trained street fighter would. His hand went to his pocket and in an instant he was holding a knife. With a snap of his wrist, he flicked it open. Like liquid fire, the light traced its shape, up from the handle to the well-honed point. Lucy forced her gaze from the knife to O'Connor's face, only to see that his eyes were just as fiery. Just as dangerous.

She stood her ground, her heart pounding against the parcel in her arms. "I'd like to see my father now," she said.

Whatever his intention, O'Connor obviously thought better of it. He eyed her up and down and deciding she posed no threat, he snapped the knife closed and stowed it in his pocket. Still watching her carefully, he led Lucy over to the room on the left side of the structure. He paused and tapped a rhythm on the door.

"Coming!"

Surprisingly, it was a woman's voice Lucy heard respond. Her curiosity piqued nearly as much as her apprehension, she watched as the door snapped

open. A stream of light flooded the dark passageway
and Lucy stared at the woman in the doorway.

Though she knew she'd never seen the woman before, Lucy thought her vaguely familiar. There was
something about her that pricked Lucy's memory,
though she could not have said what it was. Something about her long, thin nose, her height, and her
shape. Something that reminded Lucy of—

"Miss Meerchum!" Lucy's mouth fell open. As if
she'd been punched, her breath shot out of her. Too
astounded to move, she stood riveted to the spot,
gaping at Ardath Meerchum, or at least at the
woman who used to be Ardath Meerchum.

The Ardath Meerchum Lucy knew from the British
Museum was drab and colorless. This woman was
like an oil-painted version of her. Her cheeks were
red. So were her lips. Her green silk dress hugged
curves Ardath Meerchum never had, and exposed a
good deal more of her bosom than poor Ardath
would have ever dreamed of showing to the world.

Lucy's voice was no more steady than her stomach.
It teetered and tossed and her head whirled. "Miss
Meerchum," she said, "what on earth are you
doing here?"

The woman snorted, a distinctly unfeminine
sound, and the eyes that Lucy was used to seeing
behind wire-rimmed spectacles snapped and flashed.
"Fool! You don't actually think I care a fig for you
or your tedious museum, do you?"

Lucy had to fight to keep from hanging her head.
She had thought herself so clever. She had thought
herself such a good detective. And all the while, she
was being watched by Miss Meerchum. Watched and
pumped for information.

And that day they went to *The Times* offices, they
really had been followed. Just as James had said.

Outside of St. Botolph's Church someone really had taken a shot at them. Lucy had no doubt James had been correct about that, too.

It had been Ardath Meerchum.

Her surprise evaporated in the heat of the anger that shot through her. Lucy bowled her way past the ersatz Miss Meerchum and into the room.

The first thing she saw was Alfie.

His beard was longer than when last Lucy had seen him. His skin was paler, and no wonder if he'd spent the time in this grim place. He looked to have lost some weight but it was obvious from the start that his temperament had not changed a bit.

The moment he saw Lucy, Alfie threw down the magazine he'd been reading. He bounded out of his chair so quickly, it overturned. Then he didn't move; he simply stared at her, as a starving man might gape at a banquet.

"Hello, Papa!" Lucy couldn't quite manage to keep the tears out of her eyes or from her voice. Riveted by the sight of him, relieved of her worries at the same time she was outraged at the way he'd been treated, she stared, too, clutching at the parcel as if the tighter she held it, the more control she might have on her emotions.

"I'm so very happy to see you," she managed to say. "How are you?"

"Pink of perfection," Alfie assured her, and she nearly believed him. As at a loss for words as she, he closed the rest of the space between them and took her into a hug that might have been absolutely ferocious if not for the parcel.

Backing away a fraction of an inch, Alfie eyed the package. "I told you to stay home," he whispered, glancing over Lucy's shoulder toward the door. "I told you to keep well away from—"

"Lucky for you, she did come." O'Connor sidled into the room. The woman followed him, slipping into a chair in the corner and watching the proceedings with what could only have been described as supreme boredom.

"I've had about as much of Hy-spy as I am going to take," O'Connor added. "If not for her"—he looked toward Lucy—"you'd be floating in the river."

"Floating, indeed!" Alfie barked out a laugh and loosened his hold on Lucy. He faced O'Connor, his chin quivering with indignation. "As if a petty little thief like you could ever—"

"Put a bung in it, old man!" O'Connor's hands curled into fists and he charged forward, but not before Lucy stepped between him and her father.

O'Connor pulled to a stop and as if they weren't worth the effort, he waved his hands at them. "Bah! You're as aggravating as this old bugger," he told Lucy. "Now give me the damned Devil!" Without waiting another moment, he snatched the parcel out of her hands.

Lucy reached behind her. She caught Alfie's hand in hers and gave it a squeeze of warning.

"You've got what you wanted," she said, moving toward the door and motioning her father to follow. "So if you'll just excuse us—"

"Not so fast." O'Connor went for his knife. He flicked it open and got to work on the twine Lucy had tied around the package.

Lucy didn't wait to see any more. Grabbing Alfie's hand, she pulled him toward the door. Before they ever got there, a shout from O'Connor echoed like thunder through the room.

Lucy looked back only long enough to see him holding the open parcel, his face crimson, his hands crushing the lengths of wire and wads of packing she'd manipulated into the approximate shape and size of the Devil.

"Go!" Lucy screamed to her father. "Run, Papa! Run!" But before he could, O'Connor grabbed a handful of Alfie's shirt. He swung the old man around and pressed his knife to Alfie's neck.

Lucy screamed. The sound overlapped with another noise. The bang of the door crashing open.

His eyes blazing, James burst into the room. With one hand, he shoved Lucy toward the door. With the other hand, he slammed into the erstwhile Miss Meerchum's chair, knocking her head into the wall and toppling the chair over on her.

Lucy had a perfect opportunity to escape.

She didn't take it.

She needed no more than a second to realize that it was impossible for James to keep his eyes on O'Connor and Miss Meerchum at the same time. Lucy moved toward where the woman lay, groaning and insensible. There was a length of cord nearby that O'Connor had cast from the parcel and she snatched it up and quickly tied the woman's hands behind her back. By the time she was done, James had steadied himself and was facing Michael O'Connor.

"You!" O'Connor's voice faltered. His hold on Alfie did not.

"Back from the dead." James smiled. It was a look unlike anything Lucy had ever seen before, a smile that was frosty and ominous, one that promised retribution in full. And not the least mercy.

James took his eyes off O'Connor only long enough to survey the wreckage of Lucy's Devil that was scattered across the floor. He glanced at Alfie to make sure he wasn't hurt. He looked Lucy's way, undoubtedly expecting to see her gone. She wasn't, and as if he was disappointed but not the least bit surprised, he shook his head and turned his attention back to O'Connor.

"I was under your nose the entire time," James said. "Staying in the same house as you."

"You were the one that fool of a coachman failed to kill? Damn and if that ain't odd." O'Connor's laugh rippled the damp air. "You must have nine lives, like a cat. Should have kicked that hard head of yours a few more times back there in that alley in Whitechapel." He yanked Alfie against him, the tip of the knife touching his throat, drawing a drop of blood. "Right about now, though, it don't seem to matter. Your life or his." O'Connor's gaze slid to Alfie. "I'll take whichever I can get."

"Then you'll never get the Devil."

Lucy spoke before she could even think. It wasn't the right thing to say, one look from James told her that much.

It didn't matter.

She had been that close to having Alfie back, and she wasn't going to let the opportunity slip through her fingers again.

"You know we've found it," she told O'Connor. "I suppose I've given that much away by bringing you that thing." She looked toward the parcel. "The real Devil is at home. In Alfie's study. I'll bring it to you. This time, I swear, I'll bring it to you. Only—" She swallowed her tears. "Only, please, you mustn't hurt him."

"He won't." James stepped toward O'Connor. "An exchange," he said. "Me for Mr. Barnstable."

O'Connor did not look convinced.

"She'll tie me," James said with a look at Lucy.

"Before you let the old fellow go. She'll tie my hands and feet. If they don't bring back the Devil—"

"If they don't bring back the Devil in under two hours' time, you're a dead man." As if the words tasted delicious, O'Connor grinned and licked his lips.

James nodded his assent. He stooped and retrieved another length of rope, then handed it to Lucy.

She refused to take it. It was impossible to think that O'Connor would not hear her, but she tried to whisper her words, to have at least that much privacy. "I can't leave you here."

"You have no choice," James whispered back at her. He thrust the rope into her hands. "It's me or Alfie, and I think Alfie's already done his part." He gave her a smile meant to bolster her spirits, and still smiling, he sat in the nearest chair and put his hands behind his back so Lucy could tie them.

It was a singularly distasteful task.

Her fingers trembling and tears staining her cheeks, Lucy followed James's orders. When she was finished with his hands, O'Connor told Lucy to tie his feet.

She knelt to finish the job.

"Lucy."

She looked up from the ropes to find James looking down at her, his expression a curious mixture of remembrance and regret. "Lucy," he whispered, "I love you, and you should know . . ." He glanced toward the wreckage of Lucy's counterfeit Devil. "I'm sorry I didn't trust you."

Lucy couldn't imagine what he was talking about. She didn't care. A thousand questions crowded her mind. Questions about how he knew she was there. And why he'd been so foolish to follow. Questions about why he was trading Alfie's safety for his own and what would happen to him once she and Alfie left.

It was the only question that really mattered, and because of that, Lucy couldn't possibly put it into words. She finished tying James's feet and looked up at him.

"Whatever you're talking about," she said, "it doesn't matter now. All that matters is that we get you out of this terrible place. I—"

"No. Lucy, listen." James leaned nearer, glancing at O'Connor only long enough to gauge their time. "There is something else that matters," he whispered. "You must promise to do one very important thing for me. You mustn't question it or complain."

Lucy sniffed back her tears. "Yes," she said. "Anything. You know I would do anything."

"A sacred promise."

"Yes." O'Connor moved toward them and she turned a frantic look on James, urging him to make his request quickly.

In response, he brushed a kiss to her cheek. "Lucy, my love," he whispered, "you must promise me you won't come back."

# Chapter 20

Alfie brushed most of the detritus from his desk-top onto the floor and plopped himself down plump atop a pile of magazines. Swinging his legs, he sat back and let Lucy scramble by him and over to the bust of Queen Victoria. She removed the statue from its pedestal, picked away the broken pieces of plaster that she and James had fitted in place around the Devil, and lifted the idol from its hiding place.

"You promised him you wouldn't go back."

Lucy looked up from her work to find her father watching her, his fingers combing through his beard.

"Of course I promised," she told him. "What else was I to do? If I didn't promise, he'd be worried about what might happen to me and the statue when I brought it back, and that's the last thing he needs to do." She hoisted the statue into her arms and stood, barely pausing to catch her breath before she headed toward the door. She stopped at the desk only long enough to try to convince Alfie that this wasn't just the best course of action, it was the only one.

"But if I don't go back . . ." Lucy didn't dare speak the words. "You understand, don't you, Papa?"

Alfie didn't answer immediately. For what seemed a very long time, he studied Lucy, as if after all this time away, he wasn't quite sure he knew her any longer. "I heard what you two said to each other."

"Of course you heard." Lucy turned, ready to hurry out and into the cab waiting at the front door. "That's how you knew what I promised."

"It's not what I meant."

At the feel of Alfie's hand on her sleeve, Lucy stopped. She turned to find her father looking thoughtful and far less jubilant than a man should look when he's suddenly found himself free after so many weeks of confinement.

Alfie's voice was as pensive as his look. "I heard what he said to you. And you didn't have to say anything back to him at all. I saw the way you looked at the man. You love him, don't you?"

Lucy couldn't trust her voice. She nodded instead.

"And he feels the same way about you?"

"Yes, Papa. He does." She turned to leave.

This time, Alfie's touch was more insistent. He tugged at her sleeve. "He's a good man?"

Lucy couldn't help but smile. "A very good man."

The way he always did when he was thinking very hard, Alfie tugged at his left ear. He looked from the Devil to Lucy and back again to the statue.

"Well, that's settled it then." Alfie hopped down from the desk. "What do you say, my girl?" he asked, threading his arm through Lucy's. "Let's mount a rescue."

Like a general addressing his troops, Alfie paused at the door of Shadwell's warehouse. He threw back his shoulders and thrust out his chin. "Ready?" he asked.

Lucy wasn't sure.

She might have been ready if her father had listened to her advice. If he had stayed at home where he belonged and far from the danger she knew awaited them inside.

"I'm ready." She lied as smoothly as she moved between Alfie and the door. "You stay here and make sure the cab waits for us. I'll be back in just—"

"Oh, no!" It was surprising how quickly Alfie could move when he had to. He scooted around Lucy and blocked her way to the door. "Are you mad? You don't think I'm going to let you go walking in there alone, do you? Well, let me tell you something, Lucy Barnstable, I—"

"No. Let me tell you something." One arm still hooked around the Devil, Lucy reached for Alfie's hand. She gave it a tentative squeeze, holding her anger and her terrors in check, fighting to make her father see reason. "I need to make sure that James is safe and well. You understand, don't you? Besides, you—"

"No. I won't be better off out here." How Alfie knew exactly what she was going to say was a complete mystery. His bushy eyebrows rose and he stuck out his chin so that his beard stabbed toward her.

Lucy refused to back down. She moved toward the door. "Yes, you will. You've spent enough time in that awful place and you're not going to go in there—"

Lucy's words dissolved in a muffled gasp of surprise. So did whatever Alfie was going to say in response.

A carriage screeched to a stop beside them and Harleigh and Farleigh Atwater jumped down from the driver's box. No sooner had they settled themselves on the pavement when the carriage door snapped open and Miss Foxworthy, Mrs. Slyke, and Mrs. Miller and her son, Jack, got out.

His musket slung over one shoulder, Harleigh

pulled himself up to his full height. "Can't allow
it. Simply can't. Wouldn't be proper sending you in
without reinforcements, if you take my meaning." As
if to emphasize the point, Harleigh sniffed. Ill at ease,
he glanced over his shoulder toward the carriage.

"That's why we followed you," he explained.
"Why we went through all the trouble of
purloining . . . that is to say . . . borrowing this
carriage. Wouldn't have done it if it wasn't an emer-
gency. Had no choice. No choice at all. Desperate
times. Desperate measures. That sort of thing."

"Right you are!" Farleigh agreed. He glanced
toward the others of Lucy's tenants who were gathered behind him and when they voiced their
agreement, he turned a remarkably steely eye on
Lucy. "At your service." He clicked his heels together. "All of us. At your service."

"But I . . . That is, I . . ."

A little dazed and far more moved by the show of
support than she could tell them, Lucy stared at the
people gathered around her.

The Atwaters, she realized, were fairly chomping
at the bit. Eager for action, Harleigh tugged at his ill-
fitting uniform jacket. Anxious for the crusade to
begin, Farleigh fingered the haft of his sword.

Their fervor was contagious; even the ladies were
affected. Though it was clear she couldn't hear a
word of what passed between the others, Miss Foxworthy's eyes were aglow, and her tiny, pinched face
was a high color. Wrapped in an enormous knitted
shawl, she looked more mouselike than ever. She
blinked rapidly and her nose twitched with excitement. Though Lucy did not even dare to think what
she intended to do with it, the old lady had a battered trumpet tied around her neck with what looked
to be the cord of her bathrobe. One hand on the

instrument, she stared at Lucy expectantly, waiting for instructions.

Lucy was too bewildered to give any. She turned to Mrs. Slyke.

If anything, Mrs. Slyke looked more ill-tempered than usual. Her eyes flashing, her ample upper lip curled even more than was customary, she glowered at Lucy, at Alfie, at Miss Foxworthy and the Atwaters, and at life in general. Lucy wondered if she had somehow been forced into being one of the vigilantes or if she was out of sorts simply because she, too, was anxious for action.

There was no mistaking how Jack Miller felt. The boy jumped from foot to foot and it was only his mother's steadying hand that kept him from charging into the warehouse at full speed and in full voice.

In fact, it seemed that Clara Miller was the only one who had retained a shred of common sense and for that, at least, Lucy was thankful.

Mrs. Miller did not look convinced that this was the right course of action. Nor did she look the least bit excited. As if she sensed the danger that pervaded the place like the fog that floated in off the river, she darted a look about and kept one arm firmly around her son's shoulders.

In typical Alfie fashion, Lucy's father ignored Clara Miller's wariness. He noticed only the others' show of support. Alfie rubbed his hands together, his voice as rapturous as the look in his eyes. "Ah!" he beamed. "The Baker Street Irregulars!"

"Baker Street Irregulars?" The warm rush of gratitude that Lucy felt dissolved in a cold wave of reality. She looked around, at the gray shades of evening that were beginning to creep around the edges of the place, and at the bleak facade of Shadwell's warehouse. She stared into the exhilaration that glowed from the faces of her tenants and thought instead of a smile as sleek as coffin handles and of the man who owned it. A man who would stop at nothing to possess the statue she carried in her arms.

Lucy's stomach lurched. "It isn't a game, don't you understand?" She looked from her tenants to Alfie. "How can you pretend it's a game when"—Lucy's voice clogged with tears—"when James's life hangs in the balance?"

Alfie stuffed his hands into his pockets. Mrs. Slyke looked embarrassed. Miss Foxworthy, knowing she'd missed something important, tipped her head toward Lucy and cupped her ear. It was Harleigh who finally spoke, Harleigh who put a hand on Lucy's shoulder.

"We understand," he said, his eyes surprisingly clear, his voice as steady as she had ever heard it. "Obvious the young fellow needs help. And just as obvious he means the world to you. That's why we're here. We're ready. For anything."

"That's right!" Farleigh's mustache quivered. "Just like Goojerat." As if a new thought occurred to him, his eyes sparkled. "I say, Miss Barnstable, have we ever told you about—"

Lucy stopped him, a hand on his arm. She scrambled to say something that would make them see the light of reason. If only she had more time! More time to think. More time to convince them that they were being as foolish as they were foolhardy.

But she didn't have time.

And neither did James.

The thought sank inside her, freezing her through to the bone. Her mind made up, Lucy looked at her boarders. "All right. Have it your way. You want to help. You'll help. You." She looked at Jack and Clara Miller. "I want you to go—"

"Aw!" Jack's face fell. He did his best to twist out

of his mother's grasp. "Crikey, Miss Barnstable, we comed all this way. You can't send us away. It ain't right, and it ain't fair. I can fight!" The boy threw back his slender shoulders.

"I know you can." Lucy stooped so that she was eye to eye with Jack and lowered her voice as if sharing a confidence. "I know you are the bravest of them all, Jack. That is why I am giving you the most dangerous job." She stood and looked at Clara, silently communicating her urgency.

"You must get to the Foreign Office and fetch Sir Digby Talbot," Lucy said. "Don't let them put you off. They will try. They will tell you that you need an appointment or some other such rubbish. Don't listen. Tell them James Dungannon sent you." She emphasized the name. "Make sure Sir Digby knows that James Dungannon sent you. They will have to listen then. And when they do, bring them here." She glanced at Jack. "Can you do it?"

Puffed up with importance, Jack threw back his shoulders. "Yes, ma'am."

"Here!" Lucy pulled a banknote from her pocket and shoved it in Clara's hand. She flagged down a passing cab. "I don't think you want to take the stolen carriage," she told Clara.

Mrs. Miller nodded her understanding and Lucy turned her attention to Mrs. Slyke and Miss Foxworthy. "There must be a back door," she told them, pointing down the alley that ran along the side of the building. "You two go there and wait. Don't do anything. Don't talk to anyone. If anyone tries to leave the building, let them. Especially if it is Mr. Grogan who used to board with us." When it looked as if Mrs. Slyke might start asking questions, Lucy hurried on. "Watch where he goes. That's all you have to do. He'll have this with him." She showed them the idol. "Watch and see what he does with it."

She sent the ladies on their way and turned to the Atwaters. "You two can stay here at the front door," she told them. "I have the same instructions for you. Don't try to stop anyone. Especially Grogan. Watch. And wait. We should be out shortly."

Surprisingly, Alfie didn't say a word, but when Lucy moved toward the warehouse, he fell into step next to her. "We." Sounding infinitely more smug than he had any right to, he held open the door. "That's what you said, my girl. Glad to hear you've come to your senses."

Lucy stepped into the warehouse. "It's not what I meant at all," she said, but when the door closed behind her, she was glad Alfie was at her side.

James wasn't much for prayer. In his experience, prayers weren't nearly as useful as were nerves of steel, a will of iron, and a head that was harder and thicker than both.

Yet when the ropes around his wrists finally slackened enough for him to move his hands, he offered two prayers of thanksgiving: one for the gloom that had covered the fact that he had been assiduously, if furtively, working to release himself. And another for Lucy's rope-tying skills and the uncanny ability she had to make her knots look good enough to satisfy O'Connor when they were, in fact, so poorly tied as to make them ineffectual.

No sooner had he finished the prayer than he revised it. There was a third reason to be thankful: He'd been able to talk Lucy out of coming back.

And a fourth reason, he reminded himself. For once, she'd been sensible enough to listen.

Trying to look as nonchalant as it was possible for

a man to look when he was trussed like a Christmas goose, James sized up the situation and any number of escape plans. Always honest, or at least as honest as he was forced to be, he had to admit that this was one of the most desperate scrapes in which he'd ever found himself. Things weren't looking good.

He had taken care of Shadwell earlier and for that much, at least, he was grateful. Now, he only needed a way to get by Miss Meerchum and Michael O'Connor.

His eyes hooded, his face an impassive mask, James leaned back and surveyed the scene, committing to memory every last little detail of the room. Miss Meerchum was seated at the table idly flipping through a stack of magazines, her face a study in boredom in the light of the single oil lamp that burned nearby. O'Connor was hunched against the wall to her left, marking time with the impatient tap of his knife against the wallboard.

There was not the slightest doubt in James's mind that O'Connor intended to kill him, and he only wondered that he had not done it yet.

O'Connor couldn't possibly think Lucy would actually come back?

The thought pushed every other consideration out of James's mind.

She wouldn't actually do it, he told himself over and over. She couldn't. Even Lucy was not that much of a daredevil.

The thought brought a strange comfort, a kind of warmth that reminded James that no matter what happened to him, he had the consolation of knowing that Lucy was out of harm's way. By now, the statue was with Sir Digby. James had no doubt of that, just as he had no doubt that the chaps at the Foreign Office would try a rescue of sorts. He only hoped they'd be in time and if they were, that he had his ankles loosened from the damned chair.

He'd hate to be shot like a fish in a barrel.

James was still working on the problem when he heard a voice.

"Is anyone there?"

Lucy's voice.

"Hell and damnation!" James didn't care who heard him or what they thought. He swore vigorously. Besides distracting Miss Meerchum and O'Connor from Lucy, it diverted their attention from the fact that his right leg was nearly free, and it helped disguise the sudden anger that flooded him. And the very real fear.

"Lucy, damn it. Turn around right now." James raised his voice so that she might hear him. From the sound of her voice, she was already in the antechamber outside the room where James was prisoner. And that was close enough.

"Get the hell out of here, Lucy! Go!"

Moving like the wind, O'Connor came to attention. He whirled around and silenced James with a blow to the jaw.

James's head snapped back and he tasted blood. His vision blurred, then cleared again.

"Lucy!" James tried again. "Get the hell out—"

This time, O'Connor kicked him square in the stomach.

The air rushed out of James along with his warning. The world reeled and pitched. His chair tipped over at the same time the door opened and Lucy walked into the room.

This time, she hadn't wrapped the Devil.

With his ribs aching and his lungs on fire, James let the thought drift through his head.

This time, Lucy wasn't going to take any chances.

She had brought the idol unwrapped, so that O'Connor would know she wasn't trying to deceive him, and she carried it up in her arms, face out. The diamond sparkled through the gloom. It looked a damned sight like the sparks that exploded through James's head.

Lucy wasn't sure what made her pause inside the doorway. It certainly was not to make an impression, some sort of pompous entrance that might leave O'Connor and Miss Meerchum in awe. If anything, her hesitation made it more likely that they would see the damp spots her hands were leaving on the Eye of the Devil.

She hardly paid Miss Meerchum and O'Connor any mind. She'd heard James cry a warning and as soon as she was inside the door, she looked for him. She found him in a heap on the floor, still tied to the chair.

"We had a bargain, sir." With a brutal look at O'Connor, Lucy charged across the room to James. She set the statue on the table next to the oil lamp and bent to examine him, and when she saw the shallow rise and fall of his chest, she breathed a sigh of relief.

"I told you I would bring the statue," she said, frowning over at O'Connor at the same time she fished a handkerchief from her pocket. Kneeling, she touched the handkerchief to James's chin. She wiped away a trickle of blood and fought back the tears that threatened to betray her concern and the fact that she was appalled and disgusted and very much afraid.

"You promised you would keep him safe," she added. "You told me—"

"Damn it, Lucy," James's voice was labored. His eyes fluttered open. "I told you not to come."

Lucy didn't answer, nor did she hesitate. Her movements fueled by outrage, her fingers swift and sure, she untied James's ankles. Even though she suspected that his hands might already be free, she made a show of unbinding them, just to keep O'Connor off guard, and when she was done, she eased James away from the chair and helped him to sit up.

He was barely conscious. Lucy hooked an arm around his shoulders to keep him from sliding back down to the floor. "You did tell me not to come," she whispered, smoothing a strand of hair from his forehead. "And I did promise. I suppose you must know the truth now. I had no intention of ever keeping my word."

How James managed a smile, she wasn't sure. One corner of his mouth tilted up. "I hope you don't take all your promises so lightly, Miss Barnstable. There is the little matter of our marriage that I've been meaning to discuss with you and—"

"Shut up!"

O'Connor's voice cut through their words and Lucy felt James tense. His own gaze slightly out of focus, he looked into her eyes, urging caution. Lucy turned just in time to see O'Connor level a gun at them.

O'Connor chuckled. "Heartrending. The both of you. But if you'll excuse me . . ." The gun still aimed at them, he crossed the room. "I've got better things to worry about than the two of you mewling at each other. I obviously don't give a damn about our bargain," he said. He stroked the statue, his eyes shining like the diamond in Kali's headdress. "Now if you'll just hold still, we'll get this the hell over with."

"What!" Too outraged to be afraid and far too angry to pay any attention to the fact that James was clawing at her sleeve, trying his damnedest to keep her where she was, Lucy sprang to her feet. "But you promised! You said if I brought you the statue—"

"Didn't I tell you?" O'Connor chuckled. "I'm a terrible liar. Good-bye, Miss Barnstable!"

Lucy waited to hear the report of the gun and to feel of the sting of the bullet. Instead, she felt the floor go out from under her. James grabbed her around the knees and pulled her to the floor at the same time the door burst open and Alfie charged into the room, his greatcoat flapping, his face the picture of fury.

"Oh, no, you don't, you manky bastard! You won't touch my girl!"

The next moments were chaos. Somehow, Lucy managed to crawl over to the table and grab the statue, and though James was still a little unsteady on his feet, he sprang up and went for O'Connor's gun. The strategy might have worked if a single shot in the air didn't bring them all to attention.

"I think we'd better stop now." Her voice as smooth as ice and just as cold, Miss Meerchum lowered a pearl-handled pistol. Alfie stood just to one side of the table, and she stole up behind him and pressed the gun to his temple. It was a small gun and very pretty, a woman's weapon, but Lucy had no doubt it would be serviceable enough if Miss Meerchum decided to use it.

James knew it as well as she did. Grabbing Lucy's hand, he stepped away from O'Connor and Lucy set the Devil back on the table.

Miss Meerchum purred her contentment. "As charming as this has been, I must admit, my dear Miss Barnstable, that I have better ways to occupy my time. This is nearly as tedious as all those days I spent at that dry as dust museum. Nearly as dull

as I found your company." Lucy saw her finger
tighten on the trigger.

"Of course you have better ways to spend your
time! Who can blame you!" The words tumbled out
of Lucy, as desperate-sounding as they felt. She
forced a smile and looked at her father, praying he
would take the meaning of her look and read her
thoughts as he seemed to have done so many times
before. "My father and I are known for passing our
time in more pleasant ways as well. We love to read,
don't we, Papa? Sherlock Holmes. You remember our
favorite story, don't you, Papa? 'A Scandal in
Bohemia'."

Alfie didn't indicate that he understood. He didn't
dare. His eyes straight ahead, he slowly reached
around Miss Meerchum and knocked the oil lamp
from the table.

The lamp crashed to the floor and the oil spattered.
Alfie darted out of the way. Miss Meerchum was not
so quick.

Her green silk skirt caught fire. Startled, Miss
Meerchum dropped her gun. She jumped up and
down and slapped at the flames, but her movements
only made things worse.

The fire skipped up her skirt. It danced to her
shoulders and into her hair. Panic and pain curled
through her, twisting her features into a mask of
agony. With a horrible scream, Miss Meerchum
headed to the door, leaving a trail of fire behind her.

Flames caught the magazines on the table. They
spread over the floor. They devoured the brittle wall-
boards and shot to the ceiling and sparks erupted
into the warehouse. The room filled with black
smoke that caught in Lucy's throat and blinded her.

"Lucy! Get out!" Through the curtain of acrid
smoke, she saw James struggle with O'Connor. She

felt him grab her and hurtle her toward Alfie who was waiting at the door. He held out a hand and called her name.

The smoke swirled around Lucy like a living thing, its hands clutched around her throat. It poured into her lungs.

"James!" She spun around, searching through the darkness for him. Overhead, a beam groaned and cracked and sparks flew down around her head. They singed her cheeks and burned her eyes. "James!" Ashes blocked her sight, mingling with her tears. "James!"

"Here!" For an instant, the curtain of smoke parted and Lucy saw O'Connor on the floor. James came at her and the curtain closed behind him. He pressed a handkerchief over her mouth and wound his arm through hers, tugging her toward the door.

She might have made it if O'Connor hadn't grabbed her.

His hand closed around her ankles like iron fetters. Lucy screamed. She couldn't move.

"James!" Fire licking her boots, Lucy clutched at James's sleeve. For an instant she saw him, his face blackened with soot and smoke, his mouth set in a dangerous line. He went after O'Connor at the same time there was a flurry of movement from the doorway. With the deafening noise of musket shot, Harleigh and Farleigh Atwater rushed into the room. Before she could tell them to find James, they each had her by one arm. They dragged her out of the burning room.

By the time they got into the warehouse, the brittle floorboards had already caught. Flames thrashed up the walls to the high ceiling and overhead, windows shattered from the heat and showered then with bits of glass.

Lucy fought free of the Atwaters. Smoke billowed from the makeshift building, but she paid it no mind. She rushed back inside. The smoke burned her lungs and clouded her vision. She couldn't tell if it was James or O'Connor, but she did see that there was only one person in the room. He was lying unconscious on the floor, and as Lucy watched, a beam from the ceiling above groaned and cracked. It crashed down on the man, crushing him in an avalanche of fire.

"No! James!" Lucy made to dart into the room. She never got that far. Through the heavy screen of smoke, James ran out of the room. The ceiling collapsed behind him. He didn't stop. He didn't slow down. He snatched Lucy's hand and ran as fast as he could from the makeshift building, and when they got back to where the Atwaters waited, they each grabbed one of the old men. Side by side, they ran just ahead of the flames that engulfed the building, heading for the street.

By the time they got there, Alfie was already out on the pavement across the road. His head bowed, his chest heaving, he pulled in mouthful after mouthful of rank Limehouse air, and when Lucy ran across the street and dropped a kiss on his cheek, he coughed and smiled and patted her shoulder.

"Good work, my girl." He winked.

Lucy looked over her shoulder to where James was busy making certain that Harleigh and Farleigh were unharmed and from there to the pandemonium that swirled around her.

Sir Digby was there. He darted back and forth, checking the progress of the fire, directing the efforts of the local fire brigade, issuing orders to a contingency of fellows who were, if their finely tailored clothes were any indication, from the Foreign Office.

Clara Miller and Jack stood nearby. Mrs. Miller looked relieved and Jack looked overwhelmed by the excitement. His face glowed with the reflection of the fire.

Even Miss Foxworthy and Mrs. Slyke were there, and Lucy stared at them in wonder. They were seated shoulder to shoulder on the pavement, square on top of Miss Meerchum, who, in spite of the fact that her gown was half-gone, did not look to be nearly as injured as she did infuriated. She kicked her feet and swore, but the dramatics had no effect whatsoever on her watchdogs. Puffing a wayward curl of hair away from her face, Miss Foxworthy smiled in perfect delight and Mrs. Slyke scowled with consummate displeasure. Neither of them moved an inch.

It was, altogether, an incredible spectacle, and in between accepting the blanket that someone handed to her and throwing it over her shoulders, Lucy did her best to take it all in. The noise was deafening. Fire bells clanged and the fire itself roared as it gutted Shadwell's empty warehouse. Above it all, Lucy heard her name.

"Lucy Barnstable!" James's voice rumbled over the cacophony, and Lucy whirled to find him finished with the Atwaters and ready to turn his attention full on her. He did his best to glare at her, an expression that might have been infinitely more effective if he hadn't grabbed for his left arm and winced at the same time.

Anxious, Lucy darted forward. The look on James's face warned her not to get too near.

His eyes bright against the coating of soot that rimmed his face, his Scottish burr more pronounced than ever, he scowled at her. "Ye promised ye wouldn'a come back," he yelled over the noise.

"I did." Lucy chanced a step nearer.

"And 'A Scandal in Bohemia'?" he asked. "What was that all about?"

"A Holmes story. He starts a fire. In order to save something very precious."

James didn't look impressed. "It was a stupid thing for ye to do."

"It was," she agreed. She took another step.

"Ye could be deid."

"But I'm not." Lucy smiled. She looked down at her boots, covered with dirt, and at her filthy clothes. She wiped the back of one hand over her cheeks and realized, too late, that the only thing she accomplished was to smudge the dirt that was on her face and make her look more bedraggled than ever. The crown of her hat was burned away and she whisked it off her head and sent it flying. She took a few slow steps in James's direction. "I'm not dead," she told him. "And neither are you."

"Ah! Glad to see that you're both well." Sir Digby was hardly the kind of man who cared that he might be interrupting. There were more important considerations. Watching as a section of the warehouse roof caved in and sent the fire brigade leaping back from the building, he stepped between James and Lucy. "My carriage is just down the road." He waved for it. "I'll have my driver take you home. In the morning, we can discuss this whole disastrous affair." As if uncomfortable, he cleared his throat. "Glad to see you made it out all right, old chap," he told James. "But there is the little matter of the Devil . . ." A section of the warehouse wall collapsed and Lucy saw Sir Digby's hopes—and those of the Empire—collapse with it.

Like the smell of smoke that permeated her clothing and her hair, disappointment seeped through her happiness. She pictured the hideous idol deep in the heart of the flames.

James followed her gaze and her thoughts. "I'm afraid we've come up a bit short," he told Sir Digby.

"Indeed." Sir Digby looked glum.

"Indeed not!" Alfie appeared at Sir Digby's side. His face was black with ash and there was a gash on his forehead that someone had already had the sense to stick a plaster on, but he was smiling like the sun. He reached beneath his charred greatcoat, pulled out the statue, and presented it to Sir Digby.

"There you are, sir," Alfie said. "Delivered into your hands and from you, to Her Majesty with my compliments."

His smile as vast as his prestige, Sir Digby accepted the statue. "But how—?"

"How did I come by it in the first place?" Alfie smiled back. "All the fault of that Claridon fellow. He had the thing, you see, though at the time, I didn't know it. He hired me . . ." Alfie pulled back his shoulders. "He hired the Alfred Barnstable Consulting Detective Agency. I was meant to meet with him one night so that I might run a message for him. I imagine that's why you had that handbill Lucy told me about." He turned to James. "I was to deliver Claridon's message to you. Instead I found Claridon nearly dead. He only had time to whisper a warning, and to let me know where that thing was hidden." Alfie indicated the Devil.

"And that there Indian seal was clutched in his hand. I knew it meant something, though I didn't know what. And I knew it was important. I heard someone coming so I grabbed the statue and the seal and got out of there as fast as I could."

"And saved the Empire in the meantime!" Sir

Digby laughed and thumped James on the left shoulder with delight.

James winced.

"You'll have to get that looked at," Sir Digby told him. "Hate to have a lame arm hindering you."

"I assure you, Sir Digby, it won't." James turned to Lucy. "Nothing is going to hinder me from taking care of the things that really matter."

And with Sir Digby looking on, and Alfie beaming his approval, he hooked his right arm around Lucy's shoulders and dragged her against him.

"You took a terrible chance," he told her, smiling down into her eyes. His face was gritty. His eyes were red. He smelled of smoke and Lucy had no doubt that he would taste of ashes.

She couldn't wait to find out.

"Yes." Lucy wrapped her arms around his waist and tipped back her head. "I did. For the first time in my life. But there are some things, I think, for which it is worth taking chances."

# Chapter 21

"Queen's weather. That's what they're calling it." Alfie drew in a deep breath of fine summer air. He glanced at the thousands of people who lined the pavement and crowded the windows of the buildings all around, waiting for the Queen's Jubilee procession to pass. "As fine a day as ever there was," he declared.

"Yes, I'll have to agree with you there." His right arm threaded through Lucy's, his left arm in a sling, James smiled down at her. "A fine day," he agreed.

He might have said more if a great cheer had not gone up from the crowd. The parade began.

For the better part of an hour, Lucy watched in awe. Wave upon wave of brilliantly outfitted soldiers passed them by: superb horsemen in singular-looking slouch hats fastened up at the side and khaki uniforms, foot soldiers and mounted troops, and (much to the dismay of the Atwaters who were watching with them) a contingency of Sikhs. There were representatives from China and the Malays, Cypriots and Rhodesians, Australians and Canadians and New Zealanders.

It was an incredible show of pomp and power and Lucy was as caught up in it as the thousands of others who watched. Next came the dragoons and the Lancers and the rest of the splendid cavalcade. They were followed by Her Majesty's children and her grandchildren and great-grandchildren, all of whom were welcomed enthusiastically by the crowd. And finally a carriage drawn by eight cream-colored horses.

The roar that greeted the sight of it surged up the street and all around Lucy. People waved white handkerchiefs until the entire street seemed a wonderful, moving cloud of silk.

The carriage slowed, and there was a little, quiet old lady dressed all in black. Her mouth drawn tight, she acknowledged her subjects, and when the carriage drew up on a level with the place where James and Lucy were watching, she signaled it to stop. She bent her head, explaining something to the equerry who walked beside the carriage.

The man bowed and smiled. He crossed the road and walked over to James.

"A word, if you please, Mr. Dungannon," the man said.

Lucy's heart skipped a beat. She looked at James in wonder. He neither questioned the man nor hesitated. His arm through Lucy's, his look inviting Alfie along, his head high, he crossed the road to speak to the Queen.

"Ah! Mr. Dungannon." Victoria accepted James's dashing bow and the slightly awkward curtsy Lucy managed to make. "It's good to see you. I understand we owe you our thanks. Again."

"I am always at your service, you know that, ma'am."

"And you." The Queen turned to Alfie. "You have helped us a great deal, Mr. Barnstable, and we will not forget it."

Alfie's mouth opened and closed. He blinked rapidly. At the last moment, he remembered himself and gave Her Majesty the kind of bow of which legends are made, sweeping and graceful, and so elegant, Lucy could not help but be impressed. And completely surprised.

His respects paid, Alfie stepped back, tears of pride shining in his eyes.

The Queen smiled her acknowledgment and turned to Lucy. She had a small, soft face, a grandmother's face, and Lucy could not help but smile in response to the benevolent look in her eyes.

"And you. I understand that without you, we would be deprived of Mr. Dungannon's excellent services. You must promise you will always look after him so."

"That is a promise that will be quite pleasant to keep, Your Majesty." Lucy dropped her another curtsy, this one far more artful than the last.

"Good." The Queen smiled and signaled to her driver to be off again. Before they could get going, she thought of something else. She looked at James. "Everything is arranged," she told him. "The special license is waiting for you at the palace. I am to be invited?" She looked from Lucy to James.

"Of course." James bowed his thanks and the Queen's carriage started up again.

"Special license? Invited?" Happiness bubbled inside Lucy. "Is there something you've forgotten to tell me?"

"Don't say that!" James laughed. "I'm never going to forget anything again. Let's just say I've done some planning." He took Lucy into his arms and kissed her, and overhead a burst of fireworks painted the sky, sparkling like diamond rain.

"You see, it's elementary, my dear detective! You

will marry me, won't you?" James asked. "If you don't, there will be one old lady who will be very sorely disappointed at missing the celebration."

Lucy's kiss was her answer and James's enthusiastic response the only reply she would ever need.

Dear Reader,

Each book is special to its author. Each has its own challenges, and each comes with its own set of discoveries and surprises.

*Devil's Diamond* is no exception.

The idea for the book came to me a very long time ago. I pictured a lady detective, a man with no name. I knew I wanted to set the book in Victorian England because it's my favorite historical time period.

The rest, as they say, is history, and the challenges, discoveries, and surprises began nearly from the start.

I have always been a fan of the Sherlock Holmes stories, and it was certainly a challenge to weave the mystery of the era and its most famous detective into a story that was—first, foremost, and always—a romance.

That's where the discoveries came in. It was wonderful discovering that the words came, if not easier, then at least a little more enjoyably, while I was listening to the lush, romantic strains of Puccini and Verdi. Another discovery: to get to know Lucy and James and all the other people who inhabit the book.

The surprises included a book I unearthed at a local antiquarian bookstore. It's called *Sixty Years a Queen*, and was published soon after Queen Victoria's Diamond Jubilee in 1897. The book includes a complete recounting of the life of the woman who gave her name to an age and, of course, lots of information about the Jubilee, including photographs of the parade, menus from the many galas that followed, and even the music used in the church service.

It's a gem, and so fascinating, I've decided to revisit the festivities. Join me this winter for *Diamond Rain* and meet Ben and Isabel, two lovers with a relationship as incendiary as the fireworks they're providing for the Jubilee.

As with every book, there are people whose help and advice made the writing of *Devil's Diamond* easier. My thanks to Vera Kap, French teacher at Our Lady of the Elms High School in Akron, Ohio, and to Bente Bob, of the Foreign Language Department of the Cleveland Public Library, for their help with translations. And as always, thanks to my family for their continued support.